DEUCE

Vivian
DEUCE
a novel
Zenari

INANNA poetry & fiction

Toronto, Ontario, Canada
www.inanna.ca

We gratefully acknowledge the support of the Canada Council for the
Arts and the Ontario Arts Council for our publishing program. We also
acknowledge the financial support of the Government of Canada.

Cover design: Val Fullard
Cover art: Nina Ezhik / Shutterstock.com

Deuce is a work of fiction. All the characters portrayed in this book
are fictitious and any resemblance to persons living or dead is purely
coincidental.

Library and Archives Canada Cataloguing in Publication

Title: Deuce : a novel / Vivian Zenari.
Names: Zenari, Vivian, 1968- author.
Series: Inanna poetry & fiction series.
Description: Series statement: Inanna poetry & fiction
Identifiers: Canadiana (print) 20220272832 | Canadiana (ebook)
20220272840 | ISBN 9781771338998 (softcover) | ISBN
9781771339018 (HTML) | ISBN 9781771339025 (PDF)
Subjects: LCGFT: Novels.
Classification: LCC PS8649.E5615 D48 2022 | DDC C813/.6—dc23

Printed and bound in Canada

Inanna Publications and Education Inc.
210 Founders College, York University
4700 Keele Street, Toronto, Ontario, Canada M3J 1P3
Telephone: (416) 736-5356 Fax: (416) 736-5765
Email: inanna.publications@inanna.ca   Website: www.inanna.ca

For my teachers

"Who knows but that, on the lower frequencies, I speak for you?"

—Ralph Ellison, *Invisible Man*

CONTENTS

CONTENTS

1

GILDA HAS RIGHT OF WAY

While checking her phone to see if Pete's Facebook page had reappeared, Gilda drove through an intersection and struck a police van.

Gilda tasted blood in her mouth. She had bitten the inside of her cheek. She was gripping the steering wheel and pressing the brake pedal to the floor with her sandalled foot so hard that the car's engine vibrated through her body.

Perhaps she had imagined hitting the van. Her mother, Beth, always said she had an overactive imagination.

She glanced at the rear-view mirror. No. Several metres behind her car sat the police van, motionless. It had spun nearly 180 degrees, and one end of the van's rear bumper hung from its chassis. The word "Forensics," in reverse in her mirror, was stencilled on the side of the van. She looked through her front windshield. The left side of her car's hood had a crinkled ridge on the normally flat horizon. On the black road beyond, silver and red flakes of metal and plastic shimmered like confetti.

The traffic light turned green in her direction.

Gilda did not question what she should do next. She had right of way. She slid her foot from the brake pedal to the accelerator. With a twist of the wheel, she made a hard left and turned back in the direction she had been going before she hit the police van.

She zoomed along the freshly paved road of the new subdivision. Flanking the road on either side were pastures of weeds and low dirt piles. Beyond the pastures stood houses, some of them under construction, some finished, all tall and narrow. For months she had used this route to work to avoid morning traffic, which normally was nonexistent here.

In the rear-view mirror, she saw two people, tiny in the distance but clearly in uniform, get out of the police van.

To her left, a dirt road intersected her paved one. She swerved onto the dirt road and then turned right onto another dirt road past another cluster of homes under construction. The dirt road merged with a paved one that led to the minor highway into St. Albert that she frequently used.

She kept her Civic in sync with the medium traffic for a couple of minutes until she noticed the turnoff to a park ahead on her right. She swung into the turnoff and headed into a parking lot marked with short, thick green posts of pressure-treated wood. She dropped her speed, and, at the right moment, she tapped the gas pedal and drove directly into one of the posts. The car stopped with a jolt and a crunch.

She got out of the car and was pleased to see that she had hit the post in the same spot as she had struck the police van. The ridge at the front of her hood was taller.

A truck pulled off the road and halted beside her. A middle-aged man with a comb-over and a beige bomber jacket leaped out.

"Are you okay?" the man asked.

"Yes. It was my fault. I was looking at my phone on the passenger seat, and I went off the road." She left out the part about driving through an intersection and colliding with a police van.

"Distracted driving." Sympathy dissolved from the man's expression.

"Please don't report me." She pointed at the Civic's crumpled hood. "I already have to tell my boyfriend about our car." The boyfriend part was a lie, but so much had happened in the last twenty-four hours to make the lie a minor negative element among many negative elements. Her dread wasn't fake, at any rate.

The man smiled tightly. "Punishment enough, eh?"

"Yeah."

The man shook his head. He returned to his truck and drove away to join the trucks and cars on the band of grey to St. Albert.

She got back in the car and started it. Her phone lay on the floor in front of the passenger seat. The display had blanked. She picked it up and checked again for the Pete Peterborough page. Not there. On a whim, she searched for a Philippa Peterborough page. There wasn't one. Not that Gilda expected to find one, since her twin's Philippa identity existed before Facebook.

He hadn't answered her texts from the night before or this morning, so she sent a new one: "Facebook deleted?"

Gilda felt numb. But she had to keep driving. She had a meeting.

She arrived at the squat grey-green buildings of Blatchford Business Park and pulled into the lot for Melon Press. She turned off the ignition and noted that she had driven all the way from the park to work with her seatbelt off. Once inside the building, she took a deep breath. The smell of carpet, latex paint and electrical wiring, combined with the cool metallic breeze of air conditioning, the artificiality of it all, soothed her enough for her to remember to greet Neela the administrative assistant with a smile and wave as she walked past the reception desk. The clock above Neela's desk read 8:32. She was two minutes late.

Tom's office was around the corner from reception. Gilda entered the room and eased the door closed. Tom loomed over his big messy teak desk, and Manuka, Gilda's immediate supervisor, perched in one of the two guest chairs. Manuka's head was tilted to the left in a welcoming attitude that Gilda knew Manuka had learned from a management book Tom had bought her.

Gilda dropped into the empty guest chair. "Good morning, Tom. Good morning, Manuka."

"Good morning!" Tom smiled at her as though absolutely nothing untoward had happened to her or to anyone today. "Sorry about the short notice." Manuka had told Gilda about the meeting right before quitting time the day before. "Manuka reminded me that we need to have this talk with you, and it so happens a hole opened up in my schedule at the last minute." He beamed as though something extraordinarily fine was happening.

The upshot was that during the upcoming annual retreat, the afternoon session would focus on the first volume of the company's new book series, *True Crimes of Alberta*, for which Manuka had recently appointed Gilda as project manager, a promotion of sorts though without a pay hike. During the session, staff could offer ideas about changes in procedures for the company overall, and the company would implement those changes for the *True Crimes* series. "That's more efficient than fiddling with an ongoing project." The morning part of the retreat would be a broader, "big picture" idea-building exercise run by a professional facilitator. During the morning, the *True Crimes* series wouldn't get mentioned. "We'll discourage it, in fact! How does that sound, Gilda?"

"Great!"

"Good to hear. I'm looking forward to this, and I hope you are too."

"Yes," Gilda said. "I am."

Tom had to run, he said, because he needed to grab breakfast before heading off to a meeting with the investors. Automatically Gilda and Manuka rose, said goodbye and walked out. Together they angled in an aimless trajectory through the cubicle area of the office.

"I'm sorry to have sprung that on you," Manuka said. "You know how Tom is. He's spontaneous, which is good, but it means that sometimes the rest of the team must be flexible. Should we get a coffee from the break room before we get back to it?"

Gilda heard typing and smelled the bacon from someone's breakfast sandwich. "Um, thanks, but I have a couple of ideas I'm burning to get down on paper. I need to do some brainstorming."

Manuka's eyes lit up at the word "brainstorming." Manuka loved brainstorming. "Fantastic. Have fun!"

Gilda reached her cubicle with relief. The cubicle's grey upholstered dividers blinkered her from the world outside. She plopped down in her overstuffed faux-leather chair and let the foam and hydraulics wheeze for her.

The first book in the *True Crimes* series centred on a man who had been found dead in the trunk of a car in the parking lot of an evangelical mega-church. The book was supposed to uncover new details about the murder but also unveil Alberta's criminal underworld. The author, Ian Auma, a former newspaper journalist, had told Manuka and Tom that his book would be "readable, compelling literary journalism, like Truman Capote's *In Cold Blood*." Gilda wondered about a person who said he could write on par with Truman Capote, but since Tom and Manuka trusted Ian, Gilda couldn't do much except take the promotion. She hadn't expected that her project would be a testing ground for suggestions made at the annual retreat. Everyone at Melon Press could voice their opinions about the project, and people whose ideas were adopted would feel like they had the right to scrutinize her project's day-to-day operations. To know all that and have to deal with so much else. The hit and run. The nurse book. Pete—

She remembered her yogic stress class and took two deep breaths from the diaphragm.

She got up and headed to the cubicle belonging to Jensee, the layout artist for the nurse book. The light from three screens bounced off Jensee's glossy black hair, turning it silver.

Jensee spoke, a purr of low-pitched monotone. "Hey, Gilda, how's it going?"

"Great. I'll be finished the bluelines this morning."

"Awesome."

Jensee's middle monitor displayed the cover of the nurse book, a history of a local nurse's union. The cover was dark pink with light pink swirls around a head-to-waist shot of a sepia-toned, old-timey nurse stretching a cloth bandage in front of her with both hands. The image of the nurse was good, technically speaking. The pink-on-pink background, however, was ghastly. So much for promoting nursing as a gender-neutral profession.

"Any plans for the weekend?" Gilda asked brightly.

"Not so much. My boyfriend's friend invited us to a birthday party." She made a face.

"Then let's make sure you get out of here at a reasonable hour."

Jensee tucked one sheaf of hair out of her eyes. "Gee, thanks."

Gilda wondered how far Jensee was directing her sarcasm. Even under auspicious conditions, Gilda didn't read people well, and this morning she was not experiencing auspicious conditions.

She returned to her cubicle, brought her laptop to life and checked Facebook. Pete's messages to Gilda remained on her page even though Pete's page was gone. Over the last twenty-four hours she had studied all his messages to her, searching for clues. She kept coming back to one message from a few months ago: "Hey, big-brain, have you read any Ralph Ellison?" At the time, she had interpreted the wording of the message as not a real desire for information but rather as a casual and random insult. She recalled other insult questions from Pete over the years: "Hey, brain, if a tree fell on your head in a forest, would you feel it?" during junior high, "One year of university and you're still a virgin, aren't you?" when she was at school to the more recent "Why are you so down on *my* job? Aren't you just a human spellchecker?" As always, she tried to take his questions seriously. She had phoned him, and they had talked about Ralph Ellison's novel *Invisible Man*. Now she wondered if his Facebook account's disappearance was related to the novelty of Pete reading a book.

She started hyperventilating. She slowed her respiration and forced the resentment out of her in thick, slow huffs. She had to keep it together. She needed to finish the bluelines today so that she could focus on Ian Auma and book one of *True Crimes of Alberta*.

At this late stage, she couldn't change much, since so much as one change required going into the file stored with their printer in Manitoba. The trick was to resist any change that the ordinary reader wouldn't discern. An editor's eye, Gilda knew, was not the same as an ordinary person's eye. At bluelines, the editor had to pretend to be both an ordinary reader and a professional who was gifted at noticing details. Today Gilda had to check the index pages. So much could go wrong on the index pages. Yet all she was supposed to do was skim the surface and decide if any errors were also problems. Her inclination was to treat all errors as serious; to be pragmatic, she had to go against her nature. She had to meet her deadline, make sure the union got its pink book, keep Tom and his investors jovial, get Jensee to a birthday party. The Pete problem was too big; it had to wait.

2

WHAT PETE IS DOING WHILE GILDA IS WORKING ON THE NURSE BOOK

Pete was about to leave the professor's apartment when his mother called. She greeted him as "Philippa." Why? He was wearing Pete clothing, so why would she do that?

You dumbass, he told himself. She was on the phone and couldn't see him. He was losing it.

"Don't pick up any beans for Sunday," Beth said. "We have some."

For Sunday lunch, Pete normally brought over the string beans.

"I can't come," he said. "I've got something on."

"That's vague."

"I don't want to bother you with the details."

"You're not bothering me. I'm a details person."

Beth was not actually a details person. Had Gilda told Beth about his recent disconnection from the digital world? Maybe, though Beth didn't understand tech well. "I've got a date," Pete lied.

"I'm thrilled and nervous for you."

"Do you think I've never been on a date before?"

"You've never called them dates."

"And now guess why I don't talk about my personal life."

"Sorry."

"I'm heading out to work, Mom. I gotta go."

"Good luck with the date." Beth ended the phone conversation as she always did: abruptly, with a hang-up click that sounded sharper than any other person's.

Philippa looked down at her body. Black crotch-drop jeans, black T-shirt over the super-flattening sports bra, buttoned up blue-checked cotton shirt that dropped past his ass, black and white sneakers, leather jacket. It was time to get back to Pete. She shut his eyes, opened them and looked down at himself, chest to crotch to toes. Done, more or less. After the end of his hour bus ride, he walked into Tokens as Pete, not Philippa.

#

Behind the long sales counter stood Norvell, expressionless as usual, though he nodded when Pete came in. Their boss Jerry waved on his way into the storeroom behind the counter, moving like a demon to get ready for the store to open.

Pete ambled behind the sales desk. "Hey, Norvell. How's it going?"

"Fine." Norvell paused a quarter of a second, a long time for him, and continued in his usual machine-gun speed of speech. "Did you start *Beowulf* last night?"

"Uh, no." Pete smiled nervously. It was like he was back in school trying to get away with not having done homework. Norvell's crash course in culture was almost like school. Every few days Norvell asked about Pete's progress. Since Pete was housesitting for the professor, he didn't have access to the books in his own apartment. "But I'm reading *The Songlines*." The professor, being a professor, owned a lot of books, and *The Songlines* happened to be both on his shelves and on Norvell's reading list.

"Oh, yeah?" Norvell's voice slowed to that of a normal person, what Pete thought of as Norvell's work mode. "What do you think of it?"

"I like it a lot."

"I thought it was pretty good too." He asked the question he always asked: "Did you learn something new?"

"For sure. I learned about the natives in Australia and about walking versus settling." The Australian girl from Banff bounded into his mind.

"The songline idea is really interesting," Norvell said. "The idea of using songs as maps. A map of sounds, not pictures."

"Right," Pete said. "Like a soundtrack to your life, but . . ." He blinked. That was a stupid thing to say. "Or maybe not."

"That's absolutely what it is." Norvell's rosy cheeks bloomed. "A soundtrack. A trail of sound."

"Whoa." Pete had said something clever but hadn't known it. He liked when that happened. Gilda and their father Ralph always acted like they were the smart ones, but Norvell was proof that people didn't need school to know things. Pete was on his way to being book-smart as well as street-smart, thanks to Norvell. If only Norvell didn't blush so much. He needed to steer Norvell into more intellectual territory and away from emotions like respect or love. "Has Bruce Chatwin written anything else recently?"

"No," Norvell said. "He's dead."

"Too bad," Pete said. "What did he die of?"

"AIDS."

"Huh. He seemed pretty straight to—" Pete stopped talking. He'd forgotten about Norvell's secret boyfriend, who was in the medium security prison in Bowden. "Not that I'm an expert on that kind of thing. It doesn't matter what he died of or how he got it. Or anything."

"You're right," Norvell said. "It doesn't matter."

Pete had nothing against gay people. Norvell must know that. He didn't seem offended. The phone call with Beth had thrown Pete off and almost into the shit. He needed to stay cool.

Pete logged in to the cash register. He didn't like logging in anymore, because that reminded him too much of his pledge to avoid the digital world, but he had resigned himself to using computers at work. It wasn't that he was allergic to computers. He just had principles now.

3

GILDA DREAMS OF POLICE

When Gilda got home from work, her mother wasn't there, to her relief. Likely Beth had gone shopping after her usual evening service at Saint Clare Church. Gilda checked if her collision had been reported on the news or social media anywhere. It had not. A giddy joy rose up, but as soon as she felt it, guilt swept it away. She had, after all, fled the scene of an accident.

If she were not above evading the laws governing car accidents, didn't that mean she suddenly had weaker grounds on which to correct other people's errors? Now, Neela could send a rejection letter without double-checking that she used the correct boilerplate, and Gilda couldn't say anything. Things would spiral down from there. If a title page were printed upside down, the printer could now shrug and leave it. Customers wouldn't complain about reversed title pages or typos. The security company wouldn't call the police when the alarms went off. A police forensics van only made sense in a world in which people tried to determine who broke a rule, never mind which rule was broken.

Gilda called Philippa, who didn't answer, so she left a message: "Again, what's up with Facebook? Call me." Gilda dialed Pete's work and got voice mail. She didn't leave a message, since her call was personal. Two options remained: call her father or talk to Beth when she got home.

Pete loved computers. He had mocked Gilda about her absence from Facebook so viciously that she opened an account once she turned sixteen—she didn't believe in lying about her age. Pete had taken a year of a computing program at the Northern Alberta Institute of Technology before dropping out for reasons which Gilda was unsure of but were probably related to his disinterest in formal education and his summer job after his first year in NAIT to revamp Tokens' website and social media presence. Pete abandoning Facebook conveyed something worrisome. Correction: more worrisome than usual.

Gilda fell asleep on her bed, phone in hand.

#

She dreamed about the police van. In the dream, she crashed into it but instead of driving away, she got out of her car and fled on foot through a swamp. Police officers jumped out of the van and chased her. Three black dogs also leaped out of the van and joined in. She was the one they had been after all along. Gilda realized that she was in the neighbourhood that she had grown up in. She ran past the 7-Eleven and into a back alley. She turned into a little girl. In the dream, she knew had a younger brother, someone who was not Philippa, although she couldn't see him. Gilda ran into a house and found her mother smoking a cigarette at the kitchen table.

"Since when did you start smoking?" Gilda said in a childish voice.

"Since when did you start running from the cops?" Beth replied. "You're supposed to run toward them." Beth was not going to help her evade the police.

#

Awake in her bed, Gilda saw the clock radio glow 3:34.

In her dream-haunted sleepiness, she knew that the police were shockingly relevant to her waking life. If she were caught, she could be charged with leaving the scene of an accident, failure to obey law enforcement, failure to obey traffic signals. She took traffic laws seriously. In elementary school, she had been a school crosswalk student patroller.

Philippa hadn't been a patroller. She thought patrollers were losers. She made her own rules, ignored the judgments of others. What good had all that defiance brought? Pete took four and a half years to finish high school and dropped out of NAIT to work at a game store. Now in his mid-twenties, he didn't seem to have much money. He didn't seem to have a steady or rewarding social life. Dropping out of Facebook at the height of its popularity seemed to be a feeble attempt at sticking it to the man.

Gilda winced at "man." Why? Because of Philippa. Traditional gender designations such as "man" and "woman" had become taboo in some parts of contemporary society, especially among scholars and young people. Gilda had first-hand experience with gender trouble. Indeed, her family would serve as an excellent case study.

4

GAME THEORY

Pete awoke to faint green light from the balcony window and to an awareness, but no concrete details, of the night before. He rolled out of bed, staggered into the bathroom and threw up in the toilet. He eased himself back into bed. He didn't believe in hangover cures. Best to just let the day ride. Luckily, it was Saturday.

At about three o'clock in the afternoon, he forced himself to get up. His stay in the condo ended in a few hours. He had to make himself and the condo presentable for when the professor arrived. Pete made the broth from a ramen package but without the noodles. After he tossed down the broth, he sat in an armchair and watched the rain fall outside the window through the gaps in the plants. Across the window, the professor's plants sprouted from pots, climbed up mesh and wrapped around each other's tendrils. He imagined the plants trying to help with his annoying family. He'd heard that plants could communicate. He didn't know if the species mattered. Not that he knew what species these were. Gilda might know, but she would say, "Why do you want to know?" and Pete would have to make up something to hide the fact that he was living in someone else's place. Pete had learned from his study of games that a defensive position was easier to maintain than an offensive one. If Pete wasn't careful, though, he would push Gilda into Action Mode, and if Gilda were already in Action Mode, as he suspected based on her texts and calls, he might force Gilda into a different mode, something more powerful. Double Action Mode.

Pete couldn't let that happen, not when he was on the verge of fixing things the way he wanted them.

He dozed off.

He woke up, saw the clock and panicked. Now he had only two hours to make the place look and smell like something other than a place where someone had been sleeping off a hangover. He needed a good reference from the professor. With a reference, he could set up another house-sit and thrust his BASE jumping into full throttle. He didn't feel a hundred percent, but he had to get up and clean.

A little after eight, the professor arrived, tanned and smelling of air conditioning. He saw that the plants were healthy and handed over Pete's fee with a promise to act as a reference for any future house-sit. Pete did his best to smile and show gratitude. He had no trouble, because he actually felt gratitude. He didn't have to pretend about that.

5

BETH WONDERS IF PETE COMMITTED SUICIDE

At breakfast, Gilda told Beth about Philippa's missing Facebook page. Beth and Gilda were sitting in the tiny kitchen with their customary grapefruit, cinnamon toast and orange pekoe in the blue and white teacups Beth had found at Goodwill.

"The worst-case scenario," Beth said, "is that he's planning suicide."

The chance that Pete might one day become suicidal had occurred to Gilda. She didn't want her mother to know that, so she reacted with a combination of horror and skepticism. "How could you be so cavalier about that, Mom?"

"It can happen to anyone. Mind you, I talked with him on the phone yesterday."

"He called?"

"I called him to tell him we didn't need string beans. He said he wasn't coming for lunch on Sunday because he had a date."

"He called it a date?"

"You're full of rhetorical questions. Anyway, yes."

Gilda felt a pang. "He's up to something."

"He always seems to be." Beth paused. "We can call him at work right now."

"He doesn't work on weekends."

"Oh, right. I keep forgetting."

Why she forgot, Gilda didn't know. Only with his full-time status had their little family started coming together for Sunday lunch. Maybe her mother was getting old and forgetful.

"I don't know about you," Beth continued, "but I don't feel panic. I spoke to him yesterday."

Gilda felt panic. Rationally she shouldn't, though; she decided to try to let it go, pending further investigation.

Beth went about her Saturday in her usual way—tea with a couple of friends from work, then a visit to the senior's centre for a papier-mâché club meeting. Gilda thought about going into work, but she decided that with the bluelines done, she ought to give herself a break. The break involved her pacing, watching YouTube, watering the garden, and standing in the garage to look at the damaged front end of her car. Her mother may not have noticed the damage because of the way they parked, Gilda on the right side, Beth on the left, so that Beth needed to circumnavigate her long-bodied Oldsmobile to see the Honda Civic's front. At work Gilda had told people that she had hit a post. She might need to flesh out that explanation for Beth.

Gilda went in her room and searched the internet for recent police hit-and-runs and for Pete Peterborough. She found nothing about her hit-and-run, but she found enough about Pete to update Beth when she returned from her Saturday outings.

"He cancelled his Instagram and Twitter accounts."

"I suppose that's suspicious." Beth looked up from the kitchen table where she was sipping tea and browsing through a cookbook. "Do the police get involved when people cancel Facebook? Sometimes Facebook comes up on *CSI*."

Gilda shuddered at the allusion to *CSI*. "Probably not."

"Your dad said that the police waited two weeks after he contacted them before they started to track down me and Philippa that time."

"Why do you have to bring that up right now, Mom?"

"I'll shut up. I'll go light a candle at church and throw some money at a saint." Beth went to church every evening, including weekends.

After supper and while her mother was at Saint Clare's, Gilda inspected Pete's old bedroom. He had slept there a month ago when they had watched the first season of *Breaking Bad* together, and he might have left clues. She couldn't remember the last time she had gone in there, even though her bedroom was next to it. Beth had kept things neat, so any evidence of a *CSI* nature would have been vacuumed and Pledged out of existence. The room contained a single bed, Pete's childhood desk and two white Ikea bookcases crammed with board games. On one of the shelves she found a familiar object. It was a puddle-jumper, a propeller toy that flew a short distance when flung into the air with a twist of its stem. Gilda ran her finger over the smooth white wood of its stem and the curves of its two brown propeller blades. Their father had brought two of them home from Japan during a tour with his quartet. Gilda had a red one, but Philippa had preferred it over the brown one, so she had played with Gilda's until she broke it. Philippa had managed to keep hers intact all these years.

Gilda launched the puddle-jumper. The clattering collision of the toy against the wall, the window and the chest of drawers got on her nerves. She would need a big empty space.

She walked out of Pete's room just as Beth was settling down for her nightly television after church. Beth flipped channels, presumably looking for *CSI* or something similar. "Did you find anything?"

Gilda sat on the arm of the sofa. "Nope."

"What's that you have there?"

"Pete's puddle-jumper."

"Is it a clue?"

"No," Gilda said, "just nostalgia."

"Nostalgia," Beth said. "That's not good." She stopped flipping channels and settled on *CSI*. "What would the police in *CSI* do?"

"Mom, it's a TV show."

"They would look at the person's past, talk to the person's friends. Then they would find the missing person dead in the trunk of a car pushed off a dock. The person who did it would be the one that the show wants you to be suspicious of but pretends to make that person not seem suspicious."

"So I did it," Gilda said.

"No, honey." Beth patted Gilda's hand. "You are too obviously suspicious."

Gilda stood up.

"I've made you mad," Beth said.

"No more than usual."

Certainly, Pete had not committed suicide. Certainly, Gilda had hit a police van and somehow gotten away with it. These certainties, however, were piling up on the stack of certainty in the centre of Gilda's life in a way that made the stack wobble and threaten to tip.

"Where are you going?" Beth asked.

"Outside."

"Why?"

Gilda held up the puddle-jumper. "To play with this."

"Good," Beth said vacantly, eyes on the television. "Play is good."

6

GILDA REMEMBERS HER KNOWLEDGE GAINS

Both formal and informal learning provided comfort and order for Gilda. Nevertheless, Gilda had often felt the hard slap across her ego that notified her that at any time, the learning of new things might open new frontiers of heartache. When she had been a student, the psychic pummellings had come most frequently during difficult exams.

These clobberings sometimes happened outside of school too. One of the first occurred at a friend's backyard birthday party when Gilda was seven years old. She, Philippa and the other little girls spent two hours running through a sprinkler and careening down a homemade Slip 'N Slide. When the party moved inside for cake, she and Philippa changed out of their matching rainbow-striped swimsuits together in the bathroom. As Philippa peeled off her bikini bottom, Gilda glanced at her genitals. Gilda always knew that Philippa's private parts looked different from hers. They were fraternal twins, from different eggs, as Beth had explained. Philippa had her beloved red hair and paper-white skin, while Gilda preferred her own brown hair and cute nose freckles. As thoughts of her superiority warmed her, Gilda remembered a conversation she had overheard at the Hudson's Bay store. Philippa had gone to the toy section while Gilda waited in the checkout line with her mother to buy some pants. Two women in line behind Gilda had been talking about diapers. One woman had said, "I wonder if there's any real difference between the boy swim diapers and girl swim diapers besides the colours."

The other woman had said, "Sure there is. Pee comes out of the underside of the girl, but a boy leaks higher up. They have a penis. That's why boys stand up to pee."

The other woman had said, "I guess you're right."

Gilda knew that Philippa had a penis, but Philippa sat on the toilet to pee just like Gilda did. Wasn't Philippa a girl and not a boy? With a shock she recalled that their father called Philippa "Phil," which was short for "Philippa," but was also a boy's name. The twins from *Rugrats* were named Lil and Phil, and Phil was a boy.

At home after the party, Gilda asked her mother in the kitchen what colour of swim diaper Philippa used to wear. Beth, who was heating tomato sauce on the stove, said, "Pink," but then she peered down at Gilda and scrunched up her nose. "Oh, it's happened," Beth said. She told Gilda to sit on a chair and wait for the sauce to come to a boil. When the sauce came to a boil, she turned down the heat and stood in front of Gilda's chair. Beth told Gilda that Philippa was special. In some ways, she was a girl and in other ways she wasn't. Philippa had a penis, for example.

Gilda said, "But she doesn't stand when she pees. Is that why she used a pink swim diaper?"

Beth said there was no such thing as a boy or girl diaper and that the colour was simply fashion. "Did someone ask you what colour swim diaper Philippa wore?"

"No," Gilda said. "I was just wondering."

That birthday party and those women at The Bay subsequently led Gilda to ruminate further on the differences between her and her sibling. Philippa had been first-born and was the larger of the two. Philippa liked to use her muscle. She could elbow Gilda aside in a rush to the bathroom or car door, and she did. In elementary school, Philippa spoke out of turn, cut into lineups to the bathroom, laughed during serious discussions in class, mimicked the teacher behind his or her back, shouted at Morena because she wouldn't let her use her protractor (Philippa had lost hers and forgotten to steal Gilda's beforehand), goofed off instead of finishing art projects and trucked home a Mother's Day macaroni bottle only a third covered with macaroni. Like a boy. At home, Gilda liked to read and make crafts, while Philippa watched television, cruised the internet and went bike-riding or skateboarding with whomever happened to be outside, including, before that family was evicted, the two dirty-faced boys who lived in the suspected drug den across the street. When Beth found out about the eviction, Gilda made a sound, and for the next two weeks Philippa replayed Gilda's reaction at recess in front of Gilda's friends. "Hey, this is my impression of Gilda": she stuck out her chin, bulged out her eyes, dropped open her mouth and gurgled, "Ugggggggggh." Soon everyone in their grade, even some of the younger students, snickered when they saw Gilda and imitated Philippa's impression in front of her.

The second non-school knowledge-related slap happened when she was nine or ten years old. She and Phil were at her father's house, and Ralph was on the phone by the staircase negotiating with Beth a change in their visitation schedule because of a tour with one of his music groups. Gilda sat on the top of the stairs of her father's new house, while Philippa and Stephen Dorn, the son of Ralph's girlfriend Rachel, were playing in the basement. Gilda sat cross-legged with the good Barbie doll and three Barbie outfits. She pretended that the stairs were a high-rise and the top of the stairs was the penthouse. While Barbie was wondering what to wear for the Oscars ceremony that night, Gilda thought she heard her father in his bedroom say, ". . . when you took Phil to Montreal in a Suburban and left me and Gilda behind."

When her father stomped up the stairs a minute later, she asked him, "Dad, did Mom go to another city with Philippa in a Suburban for a while?"

His face was set in grim wrath. "Why are you snooping?"

"I wasn't. I was playing Barbies."

Ralph harrumphed. "Fine. Yes, your mother lived in Montreal with Phil for a few months when you were a baby."

"But did they live in a Suburban?"

"A Suburban? They took a bus." Ralph suddenly laughed. "Oh. Suburban. No. They lived on a street called Saint-Urbain." His satirical expression faded. "You should ask your mother about the rest. She'd love to tell you."

Gilda did so the following evening, after her father had dropped off Philippa and Gilda.

"You overheard me talking to him on the phone." Beth shut off the television (she was watching *Matlock*) and said, "Yes, I did. What did your father say about it?"

"He said you would love to tell me."

Beth said, "I guess you were going to hear about this sometime."

Her mother's voice sounded sad. Something horrible was going to happen because Gilda liked playing on the stairs and because she was interested in hearing the conversation between her mother and her father, two people who should be living together but weren't, and listening in was the only way she could get a sense of what it might be like to have her parents in the same room together for more than five minutes.

The Suburban story was related to Philippa's genitalia. Philippa's body was a testimony to normal physical variation, Beth said. Philippa, like Gilda, was legally a female. Unlike Gilda, Philippa was chromosomally a male. Philippa had PAIS, partial androgen insensitivity syndrome. In utero Philippa's body had partially ignored its own male hormones. When Philippa was born, her genitals seemed halfway between a male's and a female's: her penis was small, and she had a rudimentary vagina. "Wait, you can look up those words later," Beth said. When they were babies, Beth left Gilda with Ralph and went to Quebec to keep Philippa safe from an operation that was cosmetic and not medically necessary.

Philippa didn't have any surgery, so that was good news, not horrible news. To Gilda, the cosmetic operation put Philippa in the same category as stars with exploding breast implants and facelifts that made eyes unblinkable. Her friend Ashley told her about the cosmetic surgeries she read about in her older sister's magazines.

Beth also confessed that she had never liked leaving Gilda, which was why she insisted on Gilda and Philippa coming to church with her in the evenings.

That enormous knowledge gain helped Gilda understand many other upheavals as the years passed. It explained her and Philippa's disparate puberties. Gilda's fragile head hair became greasy within twenty-four hours of washing it and grew greasier during menstruation. Her hair began to accumulate in new places, and she had to shave her legs and armpits. While Gilda bled, showered and shaved in silent endurance, Philippa seemed untouched. In grade five, Philippa started changing in the locker room dressing stall by herself rather than with Gilda because, she said, Gilda's hairiness was creeping Philippa out. Philippa's breasts were more like the fried-egg yolks of overweight teenage boys than the overturned espresso cups of teenaged girls, so she could hide them under a big shirt. His voice was neither high nor deep. By high school, Pete was five-foot-nine like Beth, but he had friends who were shorter. Pete didn't have Marilyn Monroe hips, so she could wear boy's pants. Her short shaggy hair and absence of makeup completed the image of the boy Pete.

The puberty upheaval explained why Pete went to a different junior high school than Gilda did. Their family moved from the apartment to the bungalow in the summer after elementary school ended. They had to change schools anyway for junior high. Gilda wanted to go to the academic girls' school in the Catholic school system, and at first Philippa said she would go too. But at the last minute, Philippa said she wanted to go to the junior high school closest to the new house. Beth was not inclined to talk Philippa out of anything, so starting in grade seven, Gilda rode a school bus alone for an hour to St. Basil's, and Philippa rode her bike to Highlands Junior High a few blocks from home. At his new school, Pete changed his walk into a cowboyish stagger and upticked his cursing. Because Pete was in-your-face about dicks and pussy, people associated his sexual aggressiveness with masculinity rather than with sluttiness.

Gilda attributed Philippa's behaviour problems to PAIS; later she attributed them to PAIS and puberty. On the first day of junior high school, Philippa told her homeroom teacher, Mr. Episcopo, that "Philippa" was a common male name for Gagauzians, an ethnic minority in Moldova, and his parents had stupidly thought the name would be easier for Canadians to pronounce if spelled halfway phonetically—the real spelling was "Filipä" or something—and for the Christly love of fuck, the teacher should call him Pete. That afternoon, Mrs. Halver, the assistant principal, called Beth at work and asked for a meeting. When Beth arrived home that afternoon, she summoned Pete, who was in the kitchen heating a frozen calzone, to her bedroom for a "talk." Gilda knew about the meeting because she happened to be in the kitchen fetching herself a glass of water. At school the next day, Beth disclosed to Mrs. Halver and Mr. Episcopo that Pete's legal name was Philippa, not Filipä or Pete. The assistant principal was appalled to hear that Pete was, so to speak, a pseudo-hermaphrodite. Beth took advantage of Mrs. Halver's anxiety to convince the school to go along with Philippa's re-identification as a boy. Mrs. Halver was also appalled by the prospect of a genetic male using the girls' locker room. Accordingly, she approved Beth's and Mr. Episcopo's idea that in physical education class, Pete could use the wheelchair-accessible stall in the boys' locker room to shower and change. Gilda learned about the meeting by overhearing Beth's phone call with Ralph. When the call ended, Gilda snuck into her twin's bedroom—Philippa was out with her new friends, Burghie and Granv—and rifled through her backpack. All of the notebooks and school supplies had the name "Pete Peterborough" on them.

She accommodated herself to this knowledge gain easily enough. Their father had always called Philippa "Phil," and when they were with Ralph, Gilda also called him Phil. Within two months, Gilda could switch fairly easily between the three names as context warranted. Days and weekend activities with his junior high friends Burghie and Granv took on the quality of Petemanship. Evenings at home and weekends with Beth and Gilda constituted the realm of Philippa. Weekends with Ralph and his new family remained Phil time. From time to time, Beth had to war against an upstart teacher annoyed by Pete's antiauthoritarianism or against a newly appointed assistant principal who would try to "help" by being "truthful" to Pete, but all Beth would have to do was use the word "Columbine" to render those people mute. Pete could defend himself too. Once, when Gilda questioned his motives, Philippa asked why anyone would be a girl, which was so fucking hard to be, when you could just as easily be a boy.

As Pete, Gilda's sibling came closer to being a Phil, though not close enough to satisfy Ralph. When Pete came home from school, he took off the sports bra and replaced the baggy sweats and long flannel shirts with T-shirts tight enough to reveal the shallow bumps of the breasts Philippa had developed. Sometimes Philippa used a barrette to hold back her bangs while she read Beth's *Glamour* magazines. Beth bought him boys' clothes for the most part, but occasionally she threw in a sparkly pink top.

In high school, the Philippa part of Pete waned. Boys' clothes outnumbered girls' clothes in his student wardrobe. During increasingly briefer periods at home, Gilda's sibling watched television, did computer stuff and studied board games (a new hobby), only rarely with the help of a barrette. When Philippa left the house, and she left the house often, Pete took over.

#

The puddle-jumper flowed out from between Gilda's hands, but once again the toy struck the side of the garage. The clattering of the toy against the vinyl siding reminded Gilda of the sound of her car hitting the police van. She needed more room.

7

PUDDLE-JUMPER

During Sunday's lunch, Gilda and Beth talked local politics, a topic they avoided when Pete was present; he often railroaded political discussions because he didn't pay attention to the news. After she and Beth did the dishes, Gilda went to Melon Press. She tidied her desk and re-organized her file directories. She also test-drove a new route to and from work. The new route took five minutes longer than her old one did, and during weekday rush hour she likely would need fifteen extra minutes, but she didn't mind: avoiding the scene of her crime was more important. An autobody shop was on the new route too.

She returned home in time for supper, which was leftovers from lunch—out of habit, Beth had cooked lunch for three. After supper, Beth settled into the backyard in the white plastic lounger with a Kathy Reichs novel. Gilda retrieved Pete's puddle-jumper from her room.

"Mom," she said once she returned outside, "I'm going for a walk."

"That's new." Beth peered over the top of her book. "You're taking the toy for a walk too?"

"I'm going to test it in a field."

"Hmm!" Beth lifted her book in front of her face. Behind the pages, she said, "You two have fun."

Gilda went out the gate to the front yard and entered the neighbourhood. The sky was early evening blue, the clouds high and sparse. The lilac trees across the street did not have blossoms.

She had missed blossom season. Deciduous trees canopied the side streets enough to conceal much of the blue sky. Other than the lilacs, she didn't know the names of the plants and trees around her, besides the basic categorization of evergreen versus deciduous. She ought to grab a copy of the tree identification guide Melon Press published a few years ago and memorize the tree varieties. She hardly knew the names of the people in the neighbourhood either. Once upon a time she had known some, but those people had moved away or, more frequently, died of old age.

In her aimlessness, she found herself not at a park but at the small strip mall with Paul's Restaurant, the real estate office and the hair salon. The small parking lot had three cars. She crossed the road and stood at the edge of the parking lot. Gilda held the wooden stem of the puddle-jumper between her palms and extended her arms. She remembered Ralph teaching them how to twirl it. He had said it was like rubbing hands together to keep them warm. With a forward flourish, she rolled the stem of the puddle-jumper away from her. The toy flew into the air and fluttered low across the restaurant parking lot. It rode above the top of one car, dipped at the next car and struck the windshield of the third car with the rattle of bones breaking.

She ran to the puddle-jumper, which lay at the foot of the car it had hit. One propeller blade had split and dangled limply from the stem. She saw no marks on the car; in her mind, though, she saw flashing red and blue lights.

That settles it, she thought. Your chances of making it in life are gone. You have beat all your chances down.

A man strode out of the restaurant. He wore a long, waist-high white apron over black clothes, dark brown curly hair, a thin but neatly groomed beard and black thick-framed glasses. Gilda recognized him from somewhere. The hair and eyes and glasses weren't it. It was something else.

The man said, "Hey."

Gilda stared at him hard, on purpose. "Hey."

"What's going on?"

"I was just playing with my puddle-jumper." She held up the broken toy, cradling it in her hands.

"Oh." Suddenly his face flushed red with some unknown emotion. His voice, the flush and the stance jogged her memory.

"You're one of Pete's friends," she said. "Aren't you Burghie?"

The man's face softened. "Gilda."

"You remember me." She looked at the puddle-jumper. "I didn't break anything. Except this."

Burghie took a step forward, lowered his voice. "A customer inside saw something fly through the air, so I had to check it out."

"What did he think it was?"

"A bird, or a frisbee. A grenade."

"A grenade?"

"Some people think this neighbourhood is getting a little rough. You know how it is with older folks."

Burghie told Gilda he had to go back inside the restaurant, but he invited her in. She was going to decline, but she remembered that he was one of Pete's best friends in school.

He tried to hold the restaurant door open for her, but she stopped and waited until he entered first. The lighting and decor were dark: dark wood, dark cork walls, dark orange carpet and upholstery. She noticed two tables of elderly customers, and she wondered which person had imagined seeing a grenade. He pointed her to a booth near the swinging door to the kitchen.

She and Burghie sat across from each other, and he beckoned a woman in a white apron who held a menu under her arm. Burghie asked Gilda, "Are you hungry?"

"No," Gilda said. "I just had supper."

"How about a coffee or tea or something?"

"No thanks."

"Water?"

"Sure, thanks."

Gilda remembered his voice, impassive and gravelly, two characteristics that had never seemed to go together. His seriousness, the nervous dip of his head, reminded Gilda of something else. The night of the Edmonton Folk Music Festival. Burghie had been there.

The server, still standing there, smiled at Gilda. "A glass of water or bottled water?"

"Just a glass," Gilda said. "No ice."

"And how about you, Dallas?" The server's smile expanded.

"I'll have a poutine, Mandy, thanks."

Mandy swivelled on her black heels and headed into the kitchen. Gilda wondered how big her smile could get. Laughter trickled out of the kitchen behind her and the swinging doors.

"How long have you worked here?" Gilda asked Burghie.

"A few months."

"I've never been in this restaurant before. I guess that's why I haven't run into you."

"You still live around here?"

"Still in the same house, with my mom. How about you?"

"I live in Belle Rive now. With my folks."

"Is it always this quiet in here?" Gilda asked.

"Not always."

"Is the food any good?"

"Pretty good," Burghie said. "You can taste some of my poutine when it gets here."

"I'm trying to stay away from that kind of food."

Mandy returned with water for Gilda and poutine for Burghie. When she was gone, Gilda asked, "Does anyone call you Burghie?"

"No," he said. "I'm Dallas now. Well, I always was, except when I was in school. Dallas is my actual name." He looked at the puddle-jumper, which lay in two pieces on the table between them. "What is that?"

"A puddle-jumper. A kid's toy."

"Why were you playing with it in the parking lot?"

"The puddle-jumper needs a lot of room. My plan wasn't that good, obviously."

"I think something good happened," Burghie said. "It was good luck, running into you like that."

"I guess you're right."

"Bad luck for the puddle-jumper, though. I can't say I've seen one before."

"I know where to probably get more," she mumbled.

"Where?"

"At the place where Pete works."

"Where's that?"

"Tokens."

"Is that the store with the huge neon dragon?"

"That's right."

"Cool." He stared at the broken toy. Slowly, he said, "How is he? Pete, I mean."

"I don't know."

"Has something happened?"

Gilda said, "You know about Pete, don't you? Pete and Philippa."

Reluctantly, he nodded. "Does he have a split personality?"

"No. Not really. Maybe."

"I know it's none of my business. I just wanted to know how he's doing, that's all. We were good friends for a while."

She looked at the toy, at Burghie. "He's been acting funny, that's all. Funnier than usual."

"Is it something illegal?"

She grimaced. "I don't know."

"Do you need help? I can give you my cellphone number if you need help."

She shook her head. "Are you in touch with Granv?"

"No. I've lost track of him, unfortunately." He seemed morose.

"Oh. Too bad."

"It is too bad, yes." He added, "What specifically is worrying you about Pete?"

"He's cut himself off from everything online. You know how he was with computers and social networking."

"Yeah, I remember."

Everything she said seemed to be making him gloomier and gloomier. "Well, I don't want to lay all this out on you." She took a gulp of her water and made to leave.

"Did you want to try the poutine?"

She saw the anxiety in his tense mouth. Maybe the food quality bothered him. "No, it's okay," she said. "I better go. It was nice seeing you again, Burghie—I mean Dallas."

Burghie escorted her to the door. "If I see or hear from Pete," he said, "I'll let you know. And please come back and tell me how things are going."

As she headed through the parking lot toward home, she wondered if she had apologized properly for the crashed puddle-jumper. Maybe saying sorry wasn't enough. It rarely sufficed.

8

BURGHIE THE KITCHEN REFUGEE

Burghie was a recent refugee from the Red Velvet Bistro, where he had been a dishwasher for five years. One day in January he arrived to find the doors locked and a notice stating that the store had been shut down by a civil enforcement bailiff. Burghie called his supervisor, who told him, yup, the business had gone under and there was nothing anyone could do about it.

The job had become somewhere to locate himself after his long-time girlfriend, Ivy, broke up with him. He and Ivy had been together for as long as he had been with the Red Velvet Bistro. She had introduced him to the triathlon, and for five years he had lived the life of a triathlete. He went to the gym every morning. When he and Ivy weren't working, they were running or cycling through Edmonton neighbourhoods, even in winter. Their holidays were American triathlon meets. Last year Ivy announced she was thinking of going back to school. "I don't want to leave you," she had said, "and I won't be able to do any triathlons. Is it worth it?" By the time they had their last telephone call, Ivy was counselling Burghie about his future. "You should go back to school too. This triathlon stuff is fun, but it doesn't pay. You can't wash dishes forever." He had known that, but his work schedule had freed him to train. She had decided to go to dental school out of province. She'd grown beyond him, she'd said. With Ivy gone to Toronto forever, Burghie stopped running, swimming or weight training. His love for biking was all that remained of that life.

After the Red Velvet Bistro folded, he had roamed the streets. He sloughed through the snow with his backpack of work clothes slipping from the shoulder of his bulky winter coat, the icy grey wind whipping through the spaces in his hood and freezing the tender skin below the jawline, tipping his lashes with slush that sealed his eyes shut. He trekked like a fur trader or an escapee from a Soviet prison camp. He felt like a political refugee must feel, forced out by wide-ranging circumstances from the place he called home. His unemployment lingered. Since he had not told his parents he was unemployed, he had to pretend to go to work every day. His parents had never asked Burghie to pay rent, though he had paid his triathlon and gym fees. Soon, though, Granddad Burgh began to make snide comments: "What are you doing with all your money now that the girlfriend is gone? You can buy a car instead of going on a bike like a little boy." One day at Sunday supper, Granddad Burgh said Burghie's father should stop letting Burghie borrow the car and make him buy his own. "You have more money. Or do you spend it?" Burghie's father told Granddad to leave Burghie alone. Burghie's mother said nothing, as usual. She had not spoken more than a few words to her father-in-law for as long as Burghie could remember.

After that Sunday supper, he had walked the streets of the neighbourhood of the Red Velvet Bistro for hours at a time. He thought about his high school days and his nonchalance for his future. Often his friends Granv and Pete came to mind. The three buds from Highlands Junior High grew apart once high school began. Granv was in the vocational program, Burghie was in the academic program, and Pete danced expertly between the two programs. None of them were joiners, either, so they didn't see each other in clubs or teams. Burghie and Pete stayed close, but Granv wandered away from them. Granv's mother and father split up, and quickly Granv inherited a new parental figure on his mother's side and several new ones on his father's side to fight against. The last time Burghie saw Granv at school was at the end of lunch break one day in early grade eleven. Granv had stood among a group of other smokers next to the student parking lot. Granv caught Burghie's eye and nodded an acknowledgment before disappearing into the wash of winter-frozen smoke as though he had entered the misty realm of a magical world. A year passed before he saw Granv again, and that was at the 7-Eleven near school. Granv was smoking outside the store. He worked there, he said, but he, his mom and his little brother were moving up north soon. "The money's good, even if the hours are supposed to be a bitch." In local parlance, "up north" meant Fort McMurray, not a place but a state of mind—big money, a small-town feel, one dangerous highway in and out of it.

Burghie said, "I'll miss you."

Granv smiled. "Naw, I'll see you around, homes. I'll come down for my two weeks off or whatever it ends up being and party down."

Burghie had already been missing Granv since grade ten, when their lives, seemingly fused in junior high, began to separate. After Burghie graduated high school, he heard from two acquaintances that Granv had left "up north" for "the coast" (that is, Vancouver) and that he had messed up his life in some vague way. Burghie tried to Google Granv but found nothing. Granv's Facebook was no help. His status, posted months before, just said, "Givin er."

The last time Burghie had seen Pete was at the Folk Festival. He had learned more about Pete then than he had been able to explain.

A couple of days after he allowed himself to think about Granv and Pete, Burghie decided to walk through a different neighbourhood. He walked east of Red Velvet's neighbourhood to one with more car traffic with smaller and older cars and fewer working streetlights. He knew this neighbourhood. He had spent much of his childhood and young adulthood here. The last time he had been there, he had become an adult.

On one of these snowy wanderings through his old neighbourhood, several weeks after he lost his job at the Red Velvet Bistro, he happened on a small commercial shopping square, and he saw a 'help wanted' sign in the window of Paul's Restaurant.

Now, only a few months after being hired at Paul's, the Peter-boroughs had re-entered his life in the person of the young woman whom he had never known well but who had always been in the immediate background. When she exited Paul's, he recognized the rigid, straight-legged gait of the girl who had walked away from him and Pete that evening when she had shadowed them for three blocks to find out where Pete was going instead of staying home to study for finals. Pete and Gilda had fought that night, and when she gave up and left, Pete yelled at her turned back, "And mind your own fucking business!"

She was here again, the grown-up version of the Gilda who had turned resolutely for home, Pete's jeers chasing behind her, her head uplifted in righteousness.

9

PETE GETS A CALL FROM HIS MOM

At ten o'clock Monday morning, Pete picked up the ringing phone at the till. It was Beth.

"Mom, I can't take personal calls during work."

"I couldn't get your cellphone. It keeps saying your mailbox is full. Can't you pay your bills? I hear that if you call your cellphone company and keep them on the phone long enough they'll give you a troublemaker's discount. I heard that from someone at work."

He had to think fast. His mother was on to something, and likely Gilda was the instigator. "Thanks for the advice, Mom, but like I said, I can't take personal calls at work."

"You've never had that problem before. I call all the time."

"It's busy right now." No customers were in the store.

"Let me ask you why you don't have Facebook. Gilda is worried about your Facebook."

Pete imagined Beth on the other end of the line, sitting on her kitchen chair, one stick-leg crossed over the other, leaning forward with her wrinkled elbows on her knees, wearing a pastel-coloured blouse and a pair of her beige cotton pants.

"I just got bored with it, Mom. People can get bored of things, can't they?"

"Sure," Beth said, but her voice sounded unsure.

"Facebook sucks time from doing more productive things. That's why kids can't use it at school. Some businesses won't let their workers use it during company time."

"But you aren't either of those things, are you? How old are you? Twenty?"

"Twenty-three."

"Good Lord!"

"Same age as Gilda."

"Now you're trying to make some kind of joke about me loving your sister more than you."

She was right, but he said, "No."

"You are both evenly neglected."

"Hey, Mom? I've got to go to work now." He had to cut off his mother before she caught wind of anything.

"By the way, how was the date?"

"Fine." What he had really done on Sunday was bar hop on Whyte Avenue. At one pub he found a girl who let him take her to the basement stairs and neck, but at one point she'd said that he was "pretty," and he'd said, "Well, I'm glad someone around here is!" and she'd stomped off.

"Good," Beth said. "I'll let you go, but I'd like to continue this conversation. Could you maybe get the cellphone sorted out? Thanks."

She ended the conversation with that sharp click of the receiver that Pete knew so well. He wondered if she had guessed he was in the process of going off grid. She should know the signs; she had done it herself. Of course, the real problem was Gilda. She had filled his three-message phone inbox, and the texts about Facebook kept coming. He didn't want to explain anything to her. Just because they were twins didn't mean she had any rights to him.

10

GILDA RECRUITS BURGHIE

At quarter after ten in the morning, Gilda called Tokens and asked for Pete. His co-worker Norvell, who had that unusual contralto voice and who spoke too fast, told her Pete was on another line and asked if he could take a message. Gilda waited all day for Pete to call back. He didn't.

Gilda would have to apply her job training to her personal life and design the entire Pete enterprise like a work project. She had come to appreciate the benefits of knowing what to do ahead of time, of loading staff and resources, of having timelines slide to the right or left. She had disliked this lingo at university, but she latched on fiercely once she started at Melon Press.

After supper and while Beth was at church, she walked to Paul's Restaurant, this time without the puddle-jumper, which lay broken on her dresser. Inside the restaurant was a party of two and a party of four. Burghie stood by the party of four with an order pad. He saw her immediately, but he didn't come to her booth until he had entered and exited the kitchen, presumably to place the order.

"Hi, Gilda." He seemed unimpassioned, a state she recognized from their past infrequent interactions, yet she could tell he was pleased to see her.

"I have an idea about how you can help me. Is this a bad time?"

He looked at the two tables of customers. "I have a few minutes." He sat across from her.

"Pete hasn't been returning my calls. Maybe if you called him, he might call you back."

"Okay," he said after a pause. "Do you want me to call him tomorrow?"

"That would be terrific. He starts at ten tomorrow morning."

"What should I say?"

"Say you want to catch up, meet for a beer or something. Or coffee, whatever you prefer." Gilda knew from her project management books that at the beginning of a project, it was important to get buy-in early. Giving team members options facilitated buy-in.

"It'll be weird calling him after so long. But that might make it more likely he'll return my call."

"You're right." Praise helped. "Based on how that goes, we can figure out where to go from there." Emphasize group decision-making. "What do you think?" Solicit opinions.

"I think that's fine."

"I don't want to take you away from work, so I'll go now." Keep meetings short. "Let me know if you need anything, and let me know how it goes."

She thanked Burghie, who nodded in response, and slipped out of Paul's. As she walked home, she reflected on his willingness to please. Apparently he enjoyed helping people. Like any project worth embarking on, this one could be good for everyone.

11

BURGHIE REINTRODUCES HIMSELF TO PETE

Burghie woke up early to make the phone call. Everyone but Granddad Burgh was at work, and Granddad was probably watching a game show in the basement. To be sure, Burghie peeked downstairs, careful not to let Granddad see or hear him, before returning to his bedroom to call Tokens.

A man with a quick voice answered the phone. Burghie asked if he could talk to Pete, and as if Pete were standing right there, Pete came right on the line.

"This is Pete. How can I help you?"

"Hi, Pete. It's Burghie. Dallas Burgh. From school."

After a long pause, Pete said, "Wow. No kidding. It's good to hear from you, man. But a surprise. Death in the family or need to borrow money kind of surprise."

"No, it's nothing like that. I just decided to get in touch with you."

"Is that right. How did you know I worked here?"

Burghie had thought about what to say if Pete asked that question. Burghie had decided that the closer to the truth, the more likely he could avoid future problems. "I ran into your sister at the restaurant I work at."

"Gilda at a restaurant, eh? I wonder what that would be like."

Burghie remembered that Pete had a strange attitude toward Gilda. Just as Burghie used to do when they were younger, he ignored the implied insult. "She told me where you worked, and I decided to call you up."

"Is that a fact."

"I was wondering if you wanted to get together sometime soon for a drink. Just to catch up on things."

"That's a great idea," Pete said after a pause. "The thing is, though, I have a lot going on right now, and I don't know if I can commit to anything."

"That's too bad."

"Maybe I can catch up with you in a little while."

Burghie needed to swing the conversation toward his mission. "What do you have going on?"

"A few things and appointments that I have to get out of the way. Best if we just postponed for a while."

"How long?"

"In few days or so. I'll call you. What's your cell?"

Burghie gave Pete his number. Burghie asked for Pete's number, and Pete said that he was getting a new number because of a stalker. "I'll give it to you when I call you. How's that?"

He didn't know how else to respond to the signal that Pete wanted to end the phone call than to end the phone call. "Okay, sounds good."

Pete said, "Take care, buddy," and hung up.

Burghie called Gilda right away.

"Hi," she said. She sounded gloomy. "What happened?" After he replayed the conversation with Pete, she said, "Well, that's kind of what I expected."

"At least we know where he is."

"Yes." She seemed disappointed.

"I can go visit him at work."

The gloom in her voice lessened. "Visual confirmation would help."

Burghie hung up. He would have to get there, and he didn't want to ride his bike on the freeway. He hunted around the house for his grandfather, and he found him in the garage, cleaning a garden weasel. His cane leaned against the workbench at arm's length. Burghie kept an eye on the cane, a habit he had acquired from childhood when Granddad would threaten to hit Burghie with it if he didn't turn down the television. He didn't remember ever being hit, but the threat had always seemed real.

He took a big breath. "Can I use your car, Granddad?"

Granddad Burgh arched his eyebrows. "Why?"

With his right foot missing too many toes, Granddad Burgh had never driven the car since Burghie could remember. Once in a blue moon, Granddad ordered Burghie to run an errand, for which he used Granddad's car, and as payment, Granddad told Burghie he could borrow the car for himself. "But just once. For one errand." Technically, Granddad owed Burghie a few. He had always suspected Granddad was being insincere and had never asked for the car.

"I want to go to a store and see a friend."

His grandfather raised his eyebrows higher. The thing Granddad Burgh could have said, because he'd said it so often before, was *I didn't know you had any friends*. The response that Burghie didn't give, and never had, was *Wrong again, old man*.

All Granddad Burgh said was "Don't break anything."

His grandfather made a show of digging around in his pocket for the key. He always kept the key in his pocket even though he never drove. He pulled it out and dangled it between his thumb and forefinger. He always did this whenever he asked Burghie to run an errand. He would hold out the key this way, and just as Burghie would reach for the key, Granddad would drop it. Burghie suspected this was his idea of a joke.

Burghie reached for the key, and Granddad Burgh dropped it.

Burghie stooped and picked it up. "I won't be long," he said.

The car was a black 1980 Mercury Grand Marquis. It was a bitch to turn tight corners and to park, but its road travel was buttery smooth, and the journey to Tokens was a pleasure. The neon red and orange dragon on the roof made the store unmistakeable. The Mercury slipped into a parking stall like a dream. When he entered the store, he was impressed by the merchandise—games, action figures, cards, real nerd territory, but the single customer in the store seemed like someone's mother, not a nerd; Pete had never seemed nerdy, to be fair. Another person, a heavy young man with small, intent eyes, stood behind the cashier counter. "How can I help you?" the man said. Burghie recognized the thick voice on the phone from earlier.

"I'm looking for Pete."

"Pete stepped out for an appointment. Was he expecting you?"

"No. I called earlier and talked to him."

"Pete said he would be back after lunch. I can take a message for you."

He gave his name as Dallas Burgh. The name sounded alien. He had been using his legal name for years now, but in the last few days he had become Burghie again.

He returned to the car, texted Gilda to call him and drove home. To avoid any direct confrontation, he slid the car key under Granddad's bedroom door. There was no point in thanking him. "Did you think I did that for you?" was Granddad's typical answer to any polite cashier who had the bad luck of serving him.

Just after six-thirty, while she was still at work, Gilda texted, "How'd it go?" He texted her to say that he had missed Pete on his visit to Tokens but that he'd left a message for Pete to call him. Gilda's reply was "Gr8." He could hear the cynicism in the silent non-word.

When Pete didn't call back that day or the next, he texted Gilda for her brother's cellphone number, which she sent with the words "Good luck."

He called Pete that night. Pete's cellphone was out of service.

Immediately he texted Gilda about the out-of-service number. Her answer came an hour later: "That figures."

He wondered if Pete had switched numbers, as he'd said he'd do.

A mystery on top of a mystery.

When Burghie thought about it more, though, he realized Pete had been hiding from him for a long time.

12

WHEN BURGHIE MET PHILIPPA

The 2009 Edmonton Folk Music Festival was supposed to reconnect them. Burghie and Pete had seen less of each other in the two years after Burghie graduated high school because Pete had done a fourth year so that he could go to NAIT. Burghie had suggested a bar, but Pete said that he could score Folk Festival passes for free from his father, Ralph, who lived in the neighbourhood next to the festival. "He always gives them away. My dad hates folk music. We can do some real catching up and bitching and all that and still be in the middle of a party, like at a bush bash."

They arrived in the early evening and spread their tarps on the top left side of the hill that served as the seating area for the main stage at the bottom of the hill. They gazed down the steep hillside covered in a mosaic of people seated on multicoloured tarps and blankets, felt the thrum of music from the smaller stages hidden inside copses of trees behind the main stage, heard the burr of voices thrilling over music, caught the aroma of meat and fat from the food concessions. They headed down the hill's side aisles to the flats and its beer garden, a blue and white striped tent city surrounded by orange mesh fencing. Pete and Burghie stood in line for a long time to fetch their beers, but Burghie didn't mind. Pete and Burghie hadn't had the chance to chat much on the way to the park since they had ridden their bikes to Gallagher Park through the undulating, winding paths of the river valley.

Burghie said, "I've lived in this city my whole life, and this is my first time here. I wonder why."

"You take it for granted, that's why," Pete said. "My dad told me once that he met a family from Rome, and none of them had been to the Coliseum. They could see it from their kitchen window. To them it was just a building."

"A rundown building too."

"Rundown, you say?"

"The Coliseum is an ancient Roman ruin."

"Huh," Pete said. "Why don't they fix it up?"

"They probably have a bit."

"I guess you can only fix a wreck so much." He laughed. "You and me are wrecks too, eh?"

"What do you mean?"

"We're here to fix up this friendship. Renovate it."

Burghie smiled. "You know it."

"But I think tonight we might 'get ruined.'" He made air quotes with his fingers. "Get it?"

One hour after their arrival, and about half an hour after entering the beer gardens, Burghie asked if they could go back to the hill to hear some music. The beer garden was where Pete wanted to spend most of his time, it turned out. He had high hopes of meeting someone from one of the bands there. "Maybe someone from Broken Social Scene. Is Broken Social Scene here? There's a shitload of girls in that band, right? Like twenty."

"Maybe you'd like to hear their music."

Pete grinned. "Is that why people go to concerts?"

Burghie stayed, and Pete started talking a mile a minute. Quickly Pete revealed his latest obsessions: the board game he was working on and the plight of young people who wanted to smoke cigarettes. "People don't want smokers in their homes. How's a person supposed to be a smoker if they can't do that in their own basements, never mind someone else's? Forget about smoking in bars. That's *done*. You can't even smoke outside a bar anymore." Both Burghie and Pete had quit, which made Burghie wonder why Pete was so outraged. Regarding the board game, Pete said, "It's about conspiracies. You have to figure out which conspiracy theory is not just a conspiracy theory but a real conspiracy."

"Like in Clue. You have to guess who really did it, not who just theoretically did it."

"Hey, that's a good comparison," Pete said. "I could market it as a kind of Clue game, but for older people who want more complex games."

"Like a murder mystery game."

"That's another good comparison. Though murder mystery games are out of fashion. It's more like a German-style strategy game."

"Like Settlers of Catan or something?"

"Yes, but not with tiles. With a board and tokens. No, there are tiles, but you overlay them on the board, which has holes so that you can plug the tiles into the board. Each time you play, the tiles go in different places. You plug in the tiles as you play, and you move around and try to find the real conspiracy. I think I might even call it that: Real Conspiracy."

"Sort of like Clue, then, where at the start, cards get drawn out of the deck and put in an envelope?"

"Clue does that, doesn't it?" Deflated, he pondered the inside of his beer cup. "I think it's time for another one."

Burghie suggested that they go back to the hill and listen to music instead. They picked their way up to their distant spot, but even from there, electric guitars from below throbbed mightily, and a deep voice growled along, punctuated from time to time by a blast of horns and a small choir of backup singers. They couldn't hear to talk to each other. After the band stopped playing, Pete said he would go back to the beer tent and get another one. The new act came and went, and Burghie decided to check on Pete, who wasn't answering his texts. In the beer gardens, he found Pete at a table alone with three beer cups and two empty cooler bottles. Pete looked at Burghie with glassy eyes and slurred softly, "I need to go home."

"Can you get on your bike?"

Pete shifted in his chair. "No."

Burghie knew from previous conversations that Pete had a roommate. "Can your roommate pick us up?"

"No roommate."

"No?"

Pete raised his head, and a shadow, more than just from nausea, ran across his face. "She moved out." He gave a sloppy salute. "She said I'm creepy."

"Is there someone else you can call?"

Pete gingerly pulled his cell from his back pocket. Just as carefully, he held it up to Burghie. "My little black book has lots of people. Lots."

Just as Burghie took the phone out of Pete's hand, Pete slumped down on the table, head on crossed arms, and sighed.

Burghie knew Pete's old password from high school: "U!FUCK2." Luckily for him, Pete hadn't changed it. He opened the contacts and noted unhappily that Pete hadn't added his own street address, a policy of Pete's since Granv told him the story of a turncoat gang member who'd forgotten his cellphone in the back of his kingpin's car and was tracked to his girlfriend's because he'd put her address in his cellphone. He did, though, have a phone number of someone he recognized: Ralph Peterborough—Pete's dad. He remembered that Pete's father lived in Cloverdale, right next to the park.

When he called the number, the man who answered sounded irritated. "Pete? At this time of night?"

He explained the situation. When the voice spoke again, the irritation had increased, but he said, "I'll come get you by the entrance. Look for a black Suburban."

Burghie struggled to get Pete on his feet. A security person saw him, though, and between the two of them, they got Pete to his feet and guided him to the pickup spot. They waited only a minute before a black Suburban cruised by and stopped at a side street in the residential area across from the park. The Suburban's side door popped open, and Burghie and the security person navigated

Pete onto the back bunk. Burghie recognized the driver as Ralph Peterborough because he had the same hair colour and face shape as Pete. Burghie sat in the back bunk with Pete, and after Burghie thanked the security person, the vehicle rolled slowly down the street.

Mr. Peterborough looked back at them from the rear-view mirror.

"He had too much to drink," Burghie said.

Pete groaned into semi-consciousness. "Not the fucking Suburban!" He groaned again and dropped his head back against the seat.

"Are you Phil's friend?" Mr. Peterborough looked much older than the time Burghie had seen him during the dildo incident, his face more chiselled and wrinkled, but he wore what seemed to be the same oversized glasses.

"I'm Burghie. I mean Dallas."

"I remember you. One of Phil's soldiers at arms."

"Phil?"

Mr. Peterborough turned his attention to the road and ignored Burghie's question. He directed the Suburban into a lane of moderate traffic that curved up the hill to the old Forest Heights neighbourhood.

"Where are we going?" Burghie asked.

"To his mother's."

Mr. Peterborough jerked the wheel into the left lane and accelerated the Suburban up the hill. "It's all because of her that Phil gets into these messes. She needs to see what her past decisions have reaped."

Burghie remained silent. He didn't know what Mr. Peterborough was talking about, but he didn't want to get involved. He was still curious, though, who Phil was.

After a couple more minutes of driving, Mr. Peterborough continued. "She wanted to leave Phil the way he was, and this is what happens. Drinking, low self-esteem, confused self-concept."

Burghie said weakly, "You mean Pete, right?"

"What?" Mr. Peterborough said.

"Pete."

"Am I supposed to be calling Philippa Pete now?" Mr. Peterborough said.

"Am I supposed to be calling Pete Philippa?"

He laughed. "You're not much of a best friend, are you?"

After a few more blank seconds, during which Burghie began to gather up the courage to ask again who Phil or Philippa was, Mr. Peterborough said, "God knows I didn't expect to have to manage my offspring at this age." He chuckled cynically. "Look what I have to call him: offspring. Biological offshoot. I can't even call him my son."

Burghie looked down at his friend, passed out now, head back against the seat and chin tipped up to the roof.

Mr. Peterborough continued talking, but in a softer voice. "It can't go on like this. I'm putting a stop to it before this person, call him or her whatever you want, ends up dead on the street or in a drug den."

They drove to Beth's house in a silence broken only by Pete's snores. The car halted in front of the house that Burghie knew so well from the outside but that, he realized, he had rarely entered beyond the front door. Mr. Peterborough dashed out of the truck and rang the front doorbell. Soon appeared on the doorstep Pete's mother and his sister Gilda. He hadn't seen them for a long time, but he knew them. Gilda seemed older, but not in a bad way. She had in her erect body posture and straight shoulders that awareness of responsibility that she had always had, but like her mother, she seemed unhappy. They trotted down the front steps together, and as they approached, Mr. Peterborough gesticulated at them in a savage mime of outrage. The two women approached the Suburban, and Burghie opened the passenger door for them. They peered inside the darkness and saw Pete, who didn't react to their presence.

Mr. Peterborough appeared behind Gilda and her mother. "You take care of him, now," he said, "or her, or whatever."

Pete's mother said, "So now you want to take care of him. Great. About eighteen years too late."

"Mom, Dad," Gilda said, "stop it!"

Burghie slipped out of his seat. He helped Mr. Peterborough walk Pete up the front steps, but he didn't stay any longer. He got out of there as fast as he could. Out the familiar door, the familiar steps, and then on the sidewalk.

It took him two hours to walk home.

The next day, he took a bus to pick up his bike at Gallagher Park. Pete's was still there.

For a few days afterwards, he called Pete, in part to find out how he was and to remind him to pick up his bike, but also because he wanted to know about Philippa. Pete didn't pick up or return his messages. Eventually, Burghie called Beth's home number. He hadn't forgotten it.

When he told her who he was, she said, in a dry voice, "You must be looking for Pete."

"He won't return my messages. Is he okay?"

"He's fine." She paused. "Ralph made a big deal about telling me what he said to you during the ride."

"I didn't understand much of it."

"Of course you did. Pete is Philippa. Philippa is Pete. He is intersex. Of ambiguous sex."

Something sparked Burghie's memory. On the first day of junior high, Pete told their teacher that his legal name was Philippa but that he wanted to be called Pete. Burghie had been impressed by Pete's brazenness. The teacher's lips had twisted in unexpressed sarcasm, but Pete smiled back with an expression of contempt. To Pete, the error had lain in the adult's character, not his own.

"Oh," Burghie said, more to himself than to Beth.

"Good choice of words." She sighed. "I can't make Pete call you back, though his sister has tried to. I'll tell him you called." She paused. "He was doing okay, you know. Don't let his father make you worry about him."

As the days and then weeks and just time passed, Burghie occasionally thought about Pete. During those wanderings through the years of accumulated memory, his path sometimes branched off to the antagonism between his mother and Granddad Burgh. They hated each other, but after Nana Burgh died, Granddad had no one else but his father to do his insulin injections for him. Physical necessity and ego had collided, and the reverberations had never stopped. The reverberations didn't seem to stop for anyone.

13

ACTION MODE

When Pete took the phone from Norvell and found Burghie on the line, he knew he had a problem. Gilda had gotten wind of something, clued in their mother and tracked down people from Pete's past to help her. All those years of Gilda's interference had made Pete smarter: this time he was ready. He guessed that either Gilda or Burghie would show up at Tokens, more likely Gilda, who would want to make him "face the music." That meant he had to lie low for a while.

He told Jerry that his doctor in the strip mall down the street had a last-minute cancellation and could fit him in right now. Jerry, laid-back man that he was, told Pete to take advantage of the opening. "A noon appointment is too rare to pass up."

At quarter to twelve, Pete headed out for his fake appointment. He walked to the sub place three blocks from Tokens, and with a large meatball sub in hand, wandered around the strip malls for a couple of hours. He had lots to think about, but he felt focused. Partly his focus came from his anger, partly from the sugar in his pop, but most of his energy came from *Invisible Man*; he had wisdom, and the wisdom gave him confidence. Gilda's Action-Mode mission would fail, and he would triumph. Ellison's narrator escaped his enemies by hurtling down a coal chute, and from there he'd planned the new chapter of his life. In the same way, Pete was going to transform this seeming failure at keeping a secret into a success.

Philippa had invented the term Action Mode while playing video games as a kid to refer to characters going into a period of super speed or super strength in short bursts to beat a difficult obstacle. Action Mode took up twice as much energy, so it was risky. Gilda's Action Modes were related to interfering with Pete. Gilda saw her interference as "helping."

The first time Gilda entered Action Mode was in grade six. Philippa was walking down the back alley behind the house with her friends Jermana and Wendi when Gilda came screeching toward them on her bike and blocked their way. Gilda said that she was not going to let them pass her, and if they tried, she would go home and tell on them. When Philippa asked what exactly the problem was, Gilda said that she had overheard Philippa on the phone telling Jermana she and Wendi were going to hang out at the 7-Eleven to find out what time the hookers showed up. Philippa hadn't known what to say, because Gilda was right on the money. Gilda stood there, one pink-sneakered foot on a pedal and the other on the gravel, while Jermana and Wendi screamed insults at her. Gilda's eyes twitched at every "Bitch," "Cunt" and "Bushwhacker" that Jermana and Wendi threw at her, but she didn't move. Jermana tried to clock Gilda on the chin, but Gilda swung her bike around with her super speed and dodged Jermana, who tripped on her flip-flops and fell on her face. Philippa had admired Gilda in a way. Philippa admired Gilda even more for agreeing to not tell their mother what happened in exchange for following Gilda home.

After that evening, he knew that Gilda could come out of nowhere and destroy whatever plan, small or large, he had concocted to make life interesting. Gilda didn't interfere often, maybe only three or four times. Because Philippa and Gilda went to different junior and high schools, Gilda didn't have the opportunity. The last time Gilda had fucked him up was the worst time. Pete had schemed to take a girl named Lauren to the grade twelve aftergrad and have sex with her. Once again Gilda overheard a call Pete made, this time to Burghie about a dildo Pete had ordered from the internet on Ralph's credit card, which he stole during one of Ralph's Sunday naps. Pete had been sloppy: his cellphone had died, and he had lost his charger, so he had taken the desperate step of using the home landline. During that call, Gilda had picked up the phone to call Beth. Before he knew it, Pete was handing Gilda the box with the dildo after it arrived from UPS. At the aftergrad, Pete and Burghie stood around the firepit with shitty beer while Lauren sat on the lap of some other dude.

Now, years later, Gilda had entered Action Mode again, helped this time by Burghie himself.

When Pete returned to Tokens, he made sure Gilda's car wasn't parked there. Once inside, Jerry's wife and store co-owner Linda mentioned that someone had come looking for him and had left a message with Norvell. Linda said nothing about the appointment. Like Jerry, she preferred to minimize involvement in her staff's lives unless the staff volunteered that information.

Norvell, on the other hand, had no such policy. He handed Pete the note with Burghie's message and asked how the appointment went. Pete answered that it had been fine. Norvell asked what the appointment was for. Pete managed to think of a good one—he had wanted to ask his doctor if he should get tested for the male breast cancer gene because male breast cancer ran in the family on his father's side. The doctor had said no, Pete reported.

Norvell found the explanation rational. "That was a good thing to check," he said. "There is the case of the drummer for KISS, to give a pop culture example."

Pete pretended to take the note seriously—he read it, folded it in half and put it in his wallet.

During the rest of his shift, he tried to keep his mind on his personal life, a habit that got him through those parts of the job that didn't interest him. One of those jobs was double-checking the action figure inventory, first in the retail area and then in the back. Taking inventory required too much attention to plan anything. Still, he came up with something, thanks again to *Invisible Man*.

After work, he would call Gilda and accuse her of stalking him. Action Mode always ended with a "face the music" phase. During the dildo incident, Gilda inflicted on him a three-way telephone conversation with their father in which Gilda told Ralph about the dildo, Pete admitted to using the credit card number, and Ralph told Pete he was okay with Pete using a dildo on a girl but not on a boy or on himself. This time Pete would turn the tables and make *her* face the music.

While he was in the back room, he had an unexpected bout of the vertigo.

He eased himself to the floor to wait out the spinning. He wondered what had set it off. When he felt stable enough, he scanned the boxes in the action figure section. Goddamn it. A Captain Jack Harkness action figure from *Torchwood*. Pete hadn't noticed it consciously, but he'd noticed it enough to get the vertigo. He pushed the box deep into the shelf to hide it, but by touching the box, the vertigo sped up.

The roots of his problems always came up from Gilda's feet. Thinking about her in Action Mode had upset him and heightened his sensitivity. Maybe he should call her. To do that he needed a cellphone, even though he had planned to cancel his.

No. He'd been planning for weeks. Why delay it? The texts from Gilda would keep coming: requests for information and demands to come clean on "whatever he was up to." He had to take the leap. He had to do what Invisible Man did: retool his life. Dive in.

Thus on the evening of June 5, 2012, as soon as he got home, Pete cancelled his cellphone service.

14

THE VERTIGO

Philippa had been living with the vertigo well before June 5, 2012. The vertigo happened whenever Pete came across someone who didn't seem either male or female. She had been getting the vertigo for as long as she could remember. When Philippa was little, she called it the ring-around-the-rosy. Later, it was the merry-go-round. In junior high, when Pete learned the word, it became the vertigo.

The vertigo felt a bit like the revolving sensation that overcame him when he stood up too quickly after a long lie-down or during a hangover. The vertigo was more than the physical sensation of dizziness, though. It was also a swirling of thoughts, a looping of impressions, ideas and memories. The vertigo was like looking in a mirror and seeing not only his own reflection but also someone else's, like in a horror movie when the heroine looks in the bathroom mirror and sees a masked man behind her with a knife in his gloved fist. In Pete's case, the unexpected intruder was a version of himself or, more accurately, an infinite number of selves, each connected to the other like a string of paper dolls with no beginning and no end coiling round and round her in a blur.

The first time Philippa remembered getting the vertigo was when she was watching a Bugs Bunny cartoon. Bugs needed to escape detection from a bad guy, so he disguised himself as a woman. He put on a wig, a tight dress and big blocky pumps. His lips thickened and reddened, and he grew long, feminine eyelashes. He didn't put on makeup: he produced these changes at will. Philippa didn't tell anyone about it. She hugged her Care Bear, shut her eyes and lay down on the sofa for many minutes until the vertigo went away.

The first time Philippa saw a real trans person was during Christmas when she was ten years old. She and her mother were at a shelter with other church people and handing out mittens and socks. One hour in, Philippa saw someone open the door and peep inside. The person was thin and tall, had long red hair and wore a miniskirt with knee-high, high-heeled boots. The door quickly shut, but not before Philippa noticed that the face of this person was quite masculine. A few weeks after that, Philippa saw a cop show that featured a prostitute who was a police informant. This prostitute was portrayed by a man who dressed in women's clothes, and the cops treated him like a woman; they called him "honey." The prostitute gave the crucial tip that the cops needed to find the criminal. From that time onwards, Pete noticed more cross-dressers on television and had more of the vertigo. He had to quit watching television with Beth, who liked crime dramas. When puberty started, Philippa often experienced the vertigo while showering.

He didn't tell anyone about the vertigo.

Once Philippa started junior high school, the vertigo happened more often and more inconveniently. During grade seven sex ed class, the nurse said that homosexuality was a case in which gender and sexual orientation didn't match up as they did for many people. Men could be sexually attracted to men, women to women, men to both men and women, or women to both women and men. The vertigo came so strongly that Pete couldn't see properly. Faces, desks and whiteboards blurred in multicolour swirls like a kaleidoscope. He stumbled out of the classroom and into the john just in time to throw up. Later he told his teachers and friends that he probably had food poisoning from the mall food court the day before.

In grade eight phys ed class, some boys tried to break into the handicap stall where Pete was showering. With the boys banging on the door and his head spinning, he wrapped a towel around his waist, charged out of the stall and shoved one boy down on the hard, slippery tiles. Whatever Mrs. Halver and Beth said to each other during their meeting the next day exonerated Pete. He also managed to get his social studies test postponed so that the school nurse could give a special lecture about respecting other people's physical privacy.

"Privacy and private parts," Burghie whispered, sniggering, to Pete during the lecture.

"More like a state secret when it comes to me," Pete whispered back. "A secret weapon. Long-range missile."

His sister's puberty was minor league in comparison. One day at supper, Gilda announced that her period had started, and Beth burst out, "Wow, I have to get you to the specialist, Philippa." The specialist said that Philippa's partially descended testicles had a high risk of being cancerous and should be removed. Philippa was not interested: "Two words, Mom: 'genital' and 'surgery.' They don't go together." Ralph had always wanted Phil to get his gonads removed, but he said the time had passed for him to be able to force Phil to do anything. He said, though, he would pay for penile enlargement if Phil wanted it. That offer hit a sore spot for eleven-year-old Philippa, who'd been proud of the growth of her penis recently, from 2.5 centimetres to 3.5 centimetres (stretched). The next day, back at her bedroom at Beth's house, she sat on the edge of her bed, legs crossed, and closed her eyes. Her head spun. One tear squeezed out of one lid. She snapped her eyes open and stared straight into the face of Flea, who stared back, benign and shirtless, from the Red Hot Chili Peppers poster on the wall beside his bed. "I won't let it break," she promised to Flea. By "it," Philippa meant her spirit. Sure, she could take hormones, as her father constantly reminded her. But she didn't need to. Her spirit was going to live on in the spirit of Pete. Pete was rising from the ashes of Philippa, and he would rise until the end of his time on Earth or beyond.

Rising from the ashes, though, was not easy. Anything could set off the vertigo, or his temper. He knew enough to fake a nosebleed and run into the bathroom when his science teacher, Mrs. Murphy, talked about female and male gametes, but he couldn't always predict the vertigo. Once during a lesson on the atom, one kid asked what it was about a positive charge that made it different from a negative charge, and Mrs. Murphy said it didn't matter. The names were random. "We could call the positive charge the negative charge, and vice versa. They're just opposites."

"This fucking sucks!" Pete bellowed as the spinning began. Mrs. Murphy sent Pete to the office, and in no time, he was back at the specialist's office and having to talk about his feelings. He didn't talk about his feelings or the vertigo. Not much longer after that, he and Gilda were in counselling.

His biggest bout of the vertigo struck that time Gilda emailed him about the word "intersex." She was taking a sociology of sex course at university. "People don't use hermaphrodite anymore. A hermaphrodite is a complex organism that is both genders at once."

Philippa had grown up with the word "hermaphrodite" being thrown around by their parents and doctors. He hadn't heard of intersexuality, and he hadn't heard any other use of the word hermaphrodite. "That's not possible," Pete answered.

"Yes, it is. Certain snails can produce sperm or eggs at any one time. Some fish and sea stars will start out one sex and later turn into another. Didn't you learn this in biology class in high school?"

Pete hadn't paid too much attention in biology, and he'd stopped taking it after grade ten. He replied, "No. Does that mean I'm a snail or a fish?"

"No! It's just that the word 'intersex' better represents people who have sex organs that are hard to define in an obvious way. It's the word that's replacing hermaphrodite for PAIS. People don't use 'hermaphrodite' anymore. It's inaccurate and demeaning."

An hour later, she emailed him the full records of some library books in the University of Alberta library catalogue. She said she could sign them out for him.

Pete replied, "As Mr. Spock used to say, fascinating."

Still, he couldn't stop thinking about the books Gilda mentioned.

He waited for a time when he thought Gilda wouldn't be at the university library. During Sunday lunch one day, he found out that Gilda was studying at home during the upcoming Reading Week. During Reading Week, then, he put on his toque and sunglasses and went to the medical library at the University of Alberta campus with the list of books Gilda had emailed him. He sat at a carrel in a dark corner of the library with the books. He opened one book and saw black and white photographs of naked people A swirling spinning rose up. The vertigo. What was up became down, rolled back up to the top of the loop, and plummeted. He shut his eyes and let it ride to help stop the nausea, something that usually worked.

Years ago, a doctor had shown him pictures like these. The people in the photos had a black bar over their eyes or their heads cropped out. He wanted to see their expressions. When Philippa was young, sometimes she was paraded in front of doctors and their students. She had felt like an animal in a cage. Now Pete wanted to see the expressions of the people to see how they might have felt. He found a drawing of different pubic areas of people with different degrees of androgen insensitivity syndrome, ranked from typical male to highly atypical and then to typical female. He identified his own twig and berries on the scale's mid-range. A few pages later appeared the photo of someone whose body was most like his. The eyes were covered with a black rectangle. The hair was straight and medium grey in the book's monochrome world, but this person could have been a redhead like Pete. The label under the photo identified the person as a patient, like a sick person in a hospital. Pete wasn't sick. Sickness was temporary, unless it was lethal, in which case the problem cancelled itself out. Pete had something permanent. What was the word for that kind of sickness? Chronic.

He laughed out loud and long. He couldn't contain himself. The vertigo went away, he laughed so hard. The dweebs at the tables and cubicles around him turned to look at him. He didn't care. It was just so funny. Even funnier was the idea that Gilda might herself have come to the library and looked at the same book.

When he left the library, he tracked down his favourite dealer and scored a sweet stash of chronic. At night, while everyone else was in bed, he smoked his pot while watching Cartoon Network with his headphones plugged into the television. He didn't care if he got caught with the pot: he'd get in shit, but Beth wouldn't kick him out. She never did. It was time he kicked himself out, get his own place so he didn't have to sneak around. It was hard not to laugh, but he managed it. He didn't want to wake up Beth and Gilda. Let them sleep.

15

CRASH COURSE IN HUMAN CULTURE

Pete's love of board games began when he accidentally read a book about balls. He had been sitting at a table in the library waiting for Serena, who, he had found out, sometimes studied in the library during her spare. Sadly, Serena came in with Parveena, who had hated Pete ever since junior high when he'd beaned her during dodge ball. As they walked past, he grabbed a book that someone had left on the table and pretended to read it. The book was called *The Secret History of Balls*. At first Pete thought it was a sex book, and as a bearer of balls of an unusual nature, he was intrigued. It turned out that the book was about spheres used in sports and games. He discovered that he rather liked the idea of knowing about bandy balls, mari balls and ulama balls. No high school jock knew that stuff, he guessed. Pete searched the school library for similar books, found only one, *The Book of Games*, and had to turn to the internet and then, reluctantly, the public library. He read *Automata and Mechanical Toys*, *Spin Again*, *Traditional Wooden Toys: Their History and How to Make Them* and finally *The Game Inventor's Guidebook*.

Pete liked board games' physical variety: the shiny rocks in mancala, the tiny wooden models of coal, nuclear waste and biomass in Power Grid, the little organs in Operation!, the pits in a Chinese checkers board. He bought games with any money he could scrounge. Eventually he used his growing knowledge about games of chance and loaded dice to start a gambling ring outside the stoner doors at school, and with his winnings he bought board games. He came to resent digital gaming's popularity but decided to use it to his advantage. He did grade twelve again to get his average high enough to be accepted to the Northern Alberta Institute of Technology to learn programming. He hated school, but at least NAIT had a student bar he could pretend to study in. For a summer job, he skipped NAIT's job board and called the city's game store, Tokens, and said he could make their dumpy website a whole lot better. The owners had been impressed with his knowledge of board games, and that knowledge had clinched a job for him. He worked part time at Tokens for two months before he dropped out of NAIT to work full time at Tokens as a combination webmaster, social media manager and clerk. To make his commute easier, Pete moved into a two bedroom-suite in northeast Edmonton with a roommate he found on Craigslist.

At first he felt free, but like with school, the working world put him at the mercy of external forces. He had to do errands for Jerry or Linda, explain things to dumb customers, tidy shelves that other people messed up, find things that his bosses or customers asked for, watch Braedyn the suspected shoplifter, call customers about their orders and argue with knobs who wanted to return opened packages (not allowed). He had reached a point where he reconsidered his decision to drop out of NAIT. Then one day Jerry mentioned he had tried to publish his own board games.

Star-struck, Pete asked, "What were they?"

"One was called Inside the Core, about a civilization in the centre of the earth. I got that one published. It didn't sell well, but I was proud of it. The other was called Take the Gummy and Run. It was for younger kids and was about gummy bears. I realized I would have to deal with Disney because they had a cartoon called *Adventures of the Gummi Bears*, so I gave up."

Pete said, "That one sounded good."

"Yeah," Jerry said. "Food, sex, or Tolkien rip-offs are the way to go."

Pete wanted to talk to Jerry about his own game idea, but he worried he would reveal himself too much. Pete wanted to do a game about a secret society of hermaphrodites (or intersex people, the name didn't matter) in Africa that manipulated the Roman Catholic Church *and* the Illuminati. The game would be set in the present but with links to the past.

One day he told Norvell about his board game idea. They were following Braedyn around the store while pretending to do inventory. Pete gushed over the new games pouring into the store and said out loud that it would be a great time to put his own game out there.

"Have you been working on a game?" Norvell asked.

"I've got a pretty good synopsis worked up already."

"Can I see it?"

Pete said, "Sure, why not?"

Braedyn wandered into the centre of the store, arms loose at his side, and sauntered to the exit. He had given up, at least for now.

Pete took the lunch break that Braedyn had delayed, and he forgot about his conversation with Norvell. Norvell didn't forget. After two weeks of Norvell reminding him, Pete finally caved in.

During his lunch break, Norvell read over Pete's synopsis. "What do you think?" Pete asked when Norvell came to the cash counter to relieve him.

"Interesting. It almost seems like Illuminati built over a Chinese checkers board."

"It's more than that."

"A Gestalt," Norvell said, nodding.

"What does that mean?"

"The whole is greater than its parts. It's a German word."

"You know German? I thought you were French."

"I'm not French," Norvell said. "I'm too watered down. Anyway, I've picked up a few German words here and there."

"How does a person learn a few words here and there in a language he doesn't know?"

Norvell studied Pete for a few seconds before he said, "Just by reading."

"Oh." Pete read once in a while. He even owned a few books, his favourite being the history of Parker Brothers, the board game company. But he hadn't learned any foreign words by reading English books.

"I think," Norvell said, "you need a crash course in basic human culture."

"Culture? As in ballet, or as in learning about how people in Ghana live?" He was thinking back to junior high when he had to learn about a different culture of the world every year.

"Even just Western culture." Norvell's voiced slowed. "If you work in a place like this, you need to know a bit of history at least, but even subjects like sociology, psychology and art."

True. Pete had found that out while he was learning about games. He had to figure out where Egypt was, for example. World War I was different from World War II. Australia used to be a British colony.

That night, Pete tried to read as many Wikipedia articles as he could. He started with the entry "Gestalt Psychology." He clicked on one of the hyperlinks in the first paragraph. At one o'clock in the morning, he finished the Wikipedia entry "Impala."

The next day at work, he reported his reading of the night to Norvell.

"Wikipedia isn't great," Norvell said. "It's better at factoids than knowledge."

Ralph used to tell him and Gilda that knowledge was better than facts. The association with his father made him wary. He let the subject drop and went back to breaking coin rolls for the till.

The next day, Norvell presented Pete with a handwritten list of books on a piece of lined paper. "This is just a start, anyway."

The list was long. "Listen, I'm not a fast reader."

"You don't need to be fast. Slow and steady wins the race."

Pete said. "My mom used to say that all the time."

Norvell recommended that Pete begin with *Aesop's Fables*. He added the title to the top of the list.

That night, Pete found *Aesop's Fables* online and read it over the week. He was impressed by how many animals died to help Aesop teach a lesson. Some of the stories were familiar, like "The Tortoise and the Hare" (where the idea of the slow and steady wins the race came from). Some of the fables, though, he couldn't understand. He puzzled over "The Oxen and the Axletrees" and "The Charcoal-Burner and the Fuller." He was embarrassed. He must be completely ignorant not to understand simple animal stories.

He telephoned Gilda and asked her about *Aesop's Fables*. She said that she hadn't read all of them. She didn't know those two fables, so she hung up to read them on the internet.

Less than an hour later, she called him back. "An axletree is the thing that attaches an ox to the cart it's pulling. A fuller cleans wool."

"Wool?"

"Yes. During cloth-making, someone has to take the wool from the sheep and clean it before it's turned into cloth."

"Did you know all that off the top of your head, or did you Google it?"

"I Googled it," Gilda said.

"I could have done that."

"Of course you could have done that."

"Why this 'of course'? You're not so smart. You had to Google it too."

She took a deep breath. She was trying to be patient with him. He hated that. "Why are you reading *Aesop's Fables*?"

"To self-educate myself."

"That's good."

He didn't like that she thought he was doing something good. "'Kay bye, thanks," he said and hung up.

Over the next few days, he finished reading the fables. When he came across words he didn't know, he Googled them instead of calling Gilda. The stories were pretty good, but they were all about talking animals or, in some cases, people like fullers. He wanted to switch to something more difficult and, frankly, more relatable. At work he told Norvell.

"How much more difficult?"

"A lot more."

Norvell suggested *The Fountainhead*. "It's on the list I gave you."

"Is it as long as *Aesop's Fables*?"

"Longer. It's one of the longer books out there."

"I don't know," Pete said. "Maybe I should go with something medium length."

"How about *The Communist Manifesto*? It's short, but it's dense." Pete had heard about communism from a social studies class in junior high. He'd read a few manifestos on Reddit by hackers. They'd been short and crazy. "What do you mean by 'dense'?"

"Tricky in places. But in other places it's pretty easy."

"Tricky and easy? The way I like my girlfriends." When Norvell didn't react, he added, "I'm in."

He found the text on the internet. It was short and in a lot of ways hilarious. He recognized a sentence from it: "The proletarians have nothing to lose but their chains." The next day, Pete asked Jerry for permission to take his lunch break with Norvell, which Jerry gave without a hassle, so on the unused tournament table, they looked at the manifesto on Norvell's tablet. Norvell made sure Pete understood the part about the withering away of the state. Pete thought that was the most hilarious part. "What, it just goes away? What will the politicians think about that? They'd just send in the army, that's what."

"Then maybe it's time you tackle *The Fountainhead* to see what Ayn Rand says about the state."

Pete was anxious about the length of *The Fountainhead*. He wondered aloud if it were a good idea to pit *The Communist Manifesto* and *The Fountainhead* against each other.

Norvell said, "To be fair, you should be comparing *The Fountainhead* with *Das Kapital*." With his fingers he indicated the width of the two books. "In terms of page count, anyway."

"Is there a movie?"

There was a movie for *The Fountainhead*, but not for *Das Kapital*. Norvell lent Pete both the movie and the book of *The Fountainhead*.

Pete started with the book. He was surprised when the first part, called "Peter Keating," started "Howard Roark laughed." He worried about coming down with the vertigo once he read that Roark was naked. He didn't. He liked the description of the cliff as a "frozen explosion of granite." A couple of pages later, his curiosity grew as Roark walked from the lake through the town and everyone who saw him stared at him and resented him. Maybe Roark was an alien or a superhero, or he was the only human in a town infiltrated by aliens or zombies. The tension kept Pete reading to the end of the chapter. But there were no aliens, superheroes or zombies. Briefly Pete wondered if Roark were autistic, and the novel was in the point of view of this autistic person. By the end of the third chapter, Pete realized that Roark was just . . . better, and other people knew it. Everyone else in the book was an ass, so no wonder Roark felt superior.

Pete switched to the movie. Although the black and white was disappointing, the actor who played Roark impressed him. His face was long and thin with the hardness of his father Ralph, but he had a slow smile that showed a sense of humour that the book Roark didn't have. He liked that Roark would rather stick with his principles than go along with what other people said. This quality reminded Pete of his father again, but also of himself.

The Fountainhead movie reminded him of the Parker Brothers book, so he fetched *The Game Makers* by Philip Orbanes from his spare room and flipped to The Principles of George Parker on page ten, his favorite part of the book. George Parker, the most dominant of the brothers, had twelve rules. He said business success depended on having goals and learning from mistakes. He wasn't against rules, but he thought people should take advantage of them. Focus on strengths, and when confronted with a dilemma, figure out which option most likely leads to the greatest payoff versus the possible loss. Be cool, he said, and don't be an asshole when you lose or when you win. He wasn't against betting, but instead thought that you should bet the most when the odds were in your favour. You might have enemies, but, George said, don't give them a chance: jump into action before they do.

Having now read *The Communist Manifesto*, Pete noticed some similarities. *The Communist Manifesto* had more exclamation marks, but both were lists of rules and beliefs. Pete was pretty sure that Parker was a capitalist, so someone that Marx and Engels were complaining about. Roark was someone Marx and Engels would probably criticize too. *The Communist Manifesto* was much shorter than the Parker Brothers book. Pete needed a medium-sized book to warm up with, and then he could try *Das Kapital*.

He read down Norvell's list of books and spotted a title he recognized, *Invisible Man*. Had he seen the movie with Gilda once? He sent Gilda a Facebook message, and like she always did with Facebook, instead of replying on Facebook, she called him. He asked, "It's about a guy who is invisible and kills people, right?"

"It's not *The Invisible Man* by H. G. Wells. That's science fiction. *Invisible Man*, without "the," is about race relations in the US. At least I think so. I haven't read it."

Well, if she hadn't read it, then he would.

The next day at work, Pete asked Norvell what he knew about George Parker's principles. Norvell knew nothing about the Parker Brothers. "I'm not much of a business person."

Norvell, like everyone else, was not the literal book of knowledge. Even Gilda didn't know everything. She was *a* book of *some* knowledge, not *the* book of *all* knowledge. If he worked at it, Pete could get to her level.

16

LIGHT BULBS

The first chapter of *Invisible Man* swept Pete into a new world. The main character and narrator lived in a basement apartment with a thousand light bulbs installed in the ceiling and cascading down the walls. The second chapter inspired in Pete many days' worth of nightmares. The narrator went to an awards ceremony, but he found himself in a boxing ring fighting other boys as entertainment for the rich white men who'd given him the award. In the next chapter, Invisible Man drove around a rich donor to his college in a limo through the countryside, and after listening to the man's bullshit and accidentally showing how Black people lived and felt about white people, the college kicked him out because he'd forced the donor to see the truth, and the truth was embarrassing.

Pete didn't understand everything—it was not an easy book—but he knew why the narrator hid himself at the end: he'd stopped trusting people.

The changes in Invisible Man's living arrangements especially fascinated him. Invisible Man lived in a college dorm, a rooming house in New York, a Harlem apartment paid by the Brotherhood, and finally the basement of a thousand lights. All he'd been through taught Invisible Man how to survive with dignity. In the basement, he lived rent- and utility-free, and he got his revenge on a couple of people who had humiliated him. The way the narrator lived in the basement reminded Pete of those Freemen on the Land. Pete once played pool with one at Dunkers and had got into a hardcore discussion over a pitcher. He'd figured the man was just a junkie squatting in some abandoned warehouse, but Invisible Man was no junkie.

Thinking about Dunkers made Pete realize that he hadn't been to a bar in a while. He'd spent his free nights and weekends reading. The next night, he went out, and he went out again two nights in a row after that. After a disastrous hangover on a weeknight, after which the next day he had to pretend to Jerry that he had food poisoning, he stopped going to bars for a while and read instead.

His life fell into a pattern, then, of reading books, re-reading *Invisible Man*, getting tired of reading books, going to bars and returning to books after a string of bad hangovers.

At this time, he began to think about house-sitting.

17

LAMOUREUX

One day in April, Norvell asked Pete if he could look after his place for a few days. When Pete asked where he was going, Norvell glanced around. "Let's get Slurpees, and I'll tell you." During spring and summer, staff at Tokens took turns getting Slurpees at 7-Eleven for everyone. In a few minutes, they were trudging through the melting snow to buy flavoured melted snow.

After too long a silence between them, Pete said, "So, what's the big mystery?"

Norvell blushed. He was going to the town of Bowden south of the city to visit his secret boyfriend, Jackson, who was in the medium security penitentiary there.

Pete was impressed. "No shit."

Another blush. "My family doesn't know about Jackson. I don't want them to know yet. My Uncle Ted is also my landlord, so I can't ask him to look after the place. I have a dog and a cat. Well, they're his dog and cat." He swallowed some air. "You've been talking about house-sitting, so I thought you might be interested."

Norvell had been paying attention to Pete more than Pete had realized. He'd been thinking about doing some housesitting to imitate his new hero, Invisible Man. He hadn't thought that he'd been talking much out loud.

By then they'd reached the 7-Eleven. They bought four Slurpees, and on the walk back to work, Pete probed a bit. "So, who is this Jackson guy?"

Jackson was a prison pen pal. He'd been convicted for helping a chop shop recycle stolen bicycles. Though Jackson admitted that he knew about his friends' side business, he insisted that he'd had nothing to do with the thefts. Norvell had since made several visits and was thinking of asking Jackson to marry him.

Pete thought Norvell was out of his mind, but he didn't say that. All he said was "Sure."

Norvell blushed. "That's great, thanks." He needed a house-sitter two weekends from now. Pete didn't have a car to get to and from Norvell's place, which was east of the city in a place called Lamoureux, but Norvell would drive Pete there at the end of their Friday shift, and on Sunday night, he would drive Pete home.

In the days after Pete agreed, he weighed the risks and the benefits as Parker's fifth rule said to do. He suspected that Norvell was in love with him, a serious problem. But Norvell could give Pete something he wanted. The internet had recently revealed to him the world of permanent house-sitting. Free, for pay, local, national and international. House-sitting could take him around the world for almost nothing. To apply for a house-sitting gig, Pete needed references. Norvell could be that reference. Nowhere in that plan, though, was the possibility that he would let Norvell seduce him, and a spurned Norvell might give a bad reference.

Another issue was Norvell's reading list. The internet had lots of lists, but he was getting a tutor with this one, and all for free. Doing Norvell a favour might be a fair exchange of value, as Marx and Engels talked about, at least according to *Wikipedia* (he hadn't gotten much past the table of contents in *Das Kapital*). Norvell had volunteered the list, which made the list a sort of gift. He remembered once at Sunday lunch that Beth had talked about gift giving as a way to show gratitude to a person for being part of your life. Gilda had agreed and said something about gift-giving rituals in Polynesia or someplace. Gilda was usually full of shit with her examples, but thinking about it now, he remembered the part about gifts being more than a sign of gratitude. A gift was a pawn in a power struggle. Taking a gift put the receiver in debt to the giver. Because of the list, Norvell had some power over him. Pete needed to get it back, so he had to pay off the debt.

#

Two Friday nights later, Pete got into Norvell's Tercel and headed out of the city. Outside the city limits, the view from the passenger window settled into a pattern of yellow fields patched with snow and cylindrical hay bales, yellow fields spiked with electrical towers that looked like giant space insects, and industrial buildings surrounded by mysterious farm equipment. The highway headed toward a bridge over the North Saskatchewan River, but before the bridge, Norvell swung the car onto a side road. The road twisted left and dipped under the bridge to a rougher road that ran along the river's west bank. Against the setting sun to their right, tall trees lined the riverside. The gaps between the trees were big enough to show the river, dark grey with silver twinkles made by the glow of the city of Fort Saskatchewan on the other side. A road sign and a map of the village announced the entrance to Lamoureux. At the first intersecting road, Norvell turned left. Behind some trees, the road ended at a domed Quonset, an old woodshed and a trailer house.

The inside of the house smelled like the inside of the Tercel: pineapple chicken balls from days gone by. The coffee table, end tables and chairs served as bases for stacks of magazines and books. Upon their arrival, a dog and a cat raised their heads from their pet beds next to the picture window, but both settled back to sleep in short order. All Pete would have to do is look after Dawg and Mittens. Dawg was toothless and had arthritis, and the cat was too old to do much except sleep and stare. Norvell showed his bedroom, where Pete could sleep if he wanted to: "It's a mess, I know." Yes, it was a mess. Norvell gave Pete permission to eat the food in the kitchen cupboards and the fridge and to use Norvell's bike, which was locked inside the Quonset. The grocery store in Fort Saskatchewan was a ten-minute bike ride. The old shed didn't have anything important in it, but its key hung with the Quonset and house key on the key rack by the light switches.

Pete was worried that Norvell would make a big deal out of leaving—he imagined having to hug—but Norvell kept it businesslike: "See you Sunday," he said as he walked out. The fading chuff of his Tercel signalled Norvell's trip south, and Pete's house-sit had begun.

Pete spent the night flipping channels and fell asleep on the flowery sofa. When he woke up in the middle of the night, he didn't bother switching to the bedroom. He didn't know if Norvell was the kind of guy to change bedsheets. In the morning, Dawg woke him up by licking his face. He walked around the house to get a sense of the place. From the kitchen and the bedroom at the front of the house, he could see a chain link fence and a thick patch of trees. From the bathroom window was a view of house #1a, a normal-looking one-level with brown siding. From the family room window, he saw the Quonset, the woodshed and #2's yard of weeping willows, spring grass shaved down like a putting green, and a pasture that curved up until it met a railway. The woodshed looked like it had been there since pioneer days.

He fed the animals and let Dawg out for a pee. Then he filled a carryout mug with Red Rose tea and walked along the side of Lamoureux Drive to see how far the road went. It didn't go far, and it was the only road. Norvell's trailer stood out from the other houses in Lamoureux, which were either mansions of red brick and white pillars or brick bungalows with stained glass in the front doors. Norvell's place seemed to be the only one with no river view. Besides a pickup or working van driving down the road, Pete saw no signs of a living person. Next to the biggest, brickiest house was a church with a belltower and a niche with a statue of Mary in it. Behind the church was a cemetery, the winter's snow lying in clumps between the tombstones. Most of the names were French, but he saw English and Ukrainian names too. Next to many of them were vases stuck in the snow and holding artificial or dead flowers. Some tombstones were from the early 1900s, made of white crumbling marble, but some were newer ones of pink or grey rock. Pete saw one for a man born in 1968 whose tombstone included space for his parents, who hadn't died yet.

He walked back to Norvell's and killed some time snooping through the stacks of games and memorabilia in the living room. Pete recognized a few of them, like *The Wizard of Oz* edition of The Game of Life, as rejects from the discount table at Tokens; Jerry and Linda usually let staff take home unsellable merchandise. Similar stacks were in the bedroom, laundry room and front entrance. Norvell kept his unboxed action figures on the mismatched dressers of his bedroom in random order, so that Iron Man, Robin, A.L.F. and Bender Bending Rodriguez lined up next to one another.

After a lunch of Kraft Dinner, Pete plucked the key to the shed from the key rack, grabbed a can of Kokanee from the fridge and sat outside in a lawn chair by Norvell's driveway. A single oval cloud hung above him. The cloud looked like a hotdog in a hotdog bun. A ball-shrivelling wind came up, and slowly the cloud moved so that it turned into a hamburger. He put the empty can on the gravel of the driveway and creaked out of the lawn chair.

Entering the shed wasn't completely wrong. Norvell had said the shed key hung with the keys for the house and Quonset. He fingered the key in his hand nervously; he was terrible with keys.

He successfully undid the lock and pushed the door open. The wood of the door was dark brown and slick. The colour and touch reminded Pete of the chestnuts that Ralph bought at Christmas and forced Philippa and Gilda to eat: the smoothness, the hardness and the colour. The air inside the shed smelled like chestnuts too, meaty and sickly sweet. Lines of light seeped through cracks between the wooden slats and the ceiling and allowed him to see a naked light bulb with a short pull chain. The bulb, though dusty, threw enough light for Pete to gauge his surroundings. The shed was filled with crates, cardboard boxes, straw brooms, old rakes, a push mower and a pile of lumber heaped halfway up the shed's walls. At the foot of the pile was a stack of small square paving stones that matched the ones in the walkway to the house. On top of the paving stones lay a crinkled paper bag.

The bag looked empty. Maybe it was someone's lunch from a long time ago, from the 1960s, say, when Ralph Ellison was alive, probably when Norvell's uncle was a kid, and he'd hid in the shed to avoid going to school and ate his bagged lunch there. He was being bullied by a pack of field hockey players and hid to avoid being whacked into the hospital with those hooked sticks. Norvell's uncle survived the bullies, graduated high school, got his real estate licence and prospered, while the field hockey players struggled to start a Canadian professional field hockey league.

The wooden floor was uneven and covered with dirt, grass, slivers of wood, one or two dead ants and, Pete decided, not a dingy rag but the wing of a magpie that a dog had dragged into the shed during the war when dogs had nothing to eat because of food shortages and people ate dog food to survive. The dog had eaten the magpie in desperation, but after eating his first magpie, he grew to like the taste, and from then on became famous in Lamoureux for killing magpies. He made the farmers happy, since farmers hated magpies. After clearing the village of magpies, Magpie Hunter swam across the river to Fort Saskatchewan to satisfy his hunger. One day he got too old to swim, and he crawled into the shed to die. There in another corner of the shed lay the dog's corpse. All those years of eating magpies had pickled his body because magpies were full of pesticides. The dog's body looked like a green tarp rolled into a rough ball.

Near the tarp was a red plastic cooler. He went to it and sat down, and though it creaked under his weight, it held. He looked past the paper bag to a hook on the wall, from which hung a short strand of chain with huge links, something that made sense on a ship but not in a shed.

The shed looked like the narrator's basement in *Invisible Man*. Norvell's shed had only one light bulb, of course, but it had the same aura of isolation, a nothingness filled with light that protected an emotional fullness that the hero was trying to hide from the outside world. Pete wondered if, for Ralph Ellison, there had been a shed or a room that let him create a reality which didn't exist but which poured out of his imagination as though it was true.

He stood up and left the shed, locking the door behind him. Outside, the sky had one or two more clouds in it; the hotdog bun cloud had deteriorated into something unrecognizable. The sun had lowered itself in the sky to prepare for evening.

He smoked a joint outside and went in the house. Carefully he replaced the key. For supper he had Chef Boyardee and a Kokanee, followed by three more Kokanee. He watched three superhero movies from Norvell's collection before he fell asleep.

#

The next morning, Pete listened to cars driving along the main road as he ate his Corn Flakes and drank his tea. The noise had woken him. It was Sunday, and the cars likely were headed to the church. After an hour and a half of phone checking, pet feeding and television watching, another stream of road noise confirmed the end of mass. When the traffic died away, Pete took the shed key from the rack and slipped outside.

Instead of yanking on the shed's lonely bulb, he let her eyes get used to the light there was. Once she could see, she sat on the red cooler. Pete hadn't gotten through enough of Norvell's reading plan to know for sure, but he imagined that meditation was much like sitting in a shed in the dark, waiting for the senses to notice things that normally were invisible. She forced herself to breathe slowly from the diaphragm. The phys ed student-teacher in junior high used to start class with five minutes of deep breathing because he thought it opened the mind and prepared the body for physical exertion. Pete hadn't appreciated the exercise at the time: after the fourth day of this, he did something—he couldn't remember what exactly—that led to him and another boy sitting outside the assistant principal's office for a long time. Now Pete thought it possible that deep breathing locked out trivial thoughts and focused the mind on the body and its sensations.

He had to pee, and one toe itched.

He opened his eyes, dug out a joint from his back pocket and lit up. She breathed in the chestnut-sweet air, and breathed it out, and in, and out, until her body seemed to float above the cooler. The pot smoke and the mustiness reminded Pete of church, especially at Easter when the priest swung the incense holder in front of pictures of Jesus' terrible last day on Earth.

The hairs on Philippa's head and arms twitched like the antennae on an insect. The room was dimmer than before. She heard the faint growling of a distant truck, the tweeting of birds, the throbbing of her blood in her ears. Electricity seemed to be flowing through him.

If he stayed in the shed for ten years, he could apply to be its legal owner. That's what he'd read on a Freeman on the Land website. Norvell wouldn't mind, obviously, and Uncle Ted seemed laid-back and might not mind either.

From out of the corner of his eye, the thick chain struck out at him like a snake. Someone told him to run out of the shed, and to keep running. Go, go, go!

She jumped up from the cooler. The snake turned back into a chain and hung limp from its hook. He obeyed the command anyway and ran out of the shed.

Sunlight bathed her. The vision was gone, but the voice was still there, saying, go!

She stomped out her joint. He was used to waiting out the vertigo, and he waited out the voice. He stood in the sun for a long time. The voice stopped. Still he waited. When he began to feel thirsty, Pete went into the house and had a beer.

With the beer, the smell of old microwaved popcorn, and the burble of the television, he phased back into the normal world, for the most part, though he couldn't forget the call to go. She still had one foot in this world and one foot in another.

#

By the time Norvell came home that evening, Pete had shaken off the voice, but he worried it would come back if he did anything to stir up his feelings.

He asked nonchalantly, "How did it go?" Stick to business.

Norvell lowered his suitcase on the floor. "Very well," he said solemnly.

"Can you give me a lift back home or should I call a cab?"

Norvell blinked, said "Sure." Pete had put his packed bag by the door hours ago.

On the drive into Edmonton, Norvell seemed too tired and preoccupied to talk. Pete felt the same, but he decided to stay in character and act talkative. When Pete mentioned his walk to the cemetery, Norvell perked up. He gave a brief history of Lamoureux, the details of which Pete paid little attention to. To himself, he repeated the word "om." He kept his mind as empty as he could.

At home, he passed the night with barely remembered dreams of escape.

18

PETE CALLS IT BASE JUMPING

During the next few days, Pete went through the motions at work. His real work took place in the evening at bars on Whyte Avenue.

On one of those nights, he threw back two Jägermeister shots and had a revelation. The "go, go, go!" voice in the shed reminded him of a war movie or a videogame cutscene of soldiers leaping out of airplanes to parachute into the jungle for a sneak attack on the enemy. To go meant leaving a place of relative safety, like an airplane over a war zone, and obeying a purple-faced sergeant who ordered you to jump to your seeming death so that you can save the world.

Pete wasn't a physical athlete. He was a mental athlete. He had wiliness, like Wile E. Coyote. Pete's wiliness had stopped people from guessing his situation. His ex-roommate, Sita, had guessed something, but she had guessed wrong. The Australian girl found out more than he'd wanted her to know, sure. But basically he knew how to stay undercover.

At the bar, three people shouted at the curling match beamed silently down from a television. The sport that put both mind and body at risk was the extreme sport. Chess players might have to sacrifice pieces, but the extreme athlete was his own pawn. He put himself in danger. He stood on a bridge or cliff and fought the urge to step back from the edge. BASE jumpers didn't have much time to react: they had to wear wingsuits because parachutes worked too slowly. Pete had learned about BASE jumping from the Australian girl in one of those second-storey bars in Banff. She had jumped off a bridge with her brother somewhere in Australia.

Pete ordered another Jägermeister. He dumped it down his throat in imitation of a leaping BASE jumper.

He looked up the word BASE on the phone. It was short for building, antenna, span and earth. It also shared a meaning with "base." To jump from a base was to jump away from a centre point or platform, like the word "base camp" for mountaineers. He imagined himself as a BASE jumper at a base camp on Mount Everest. He bounded off the face of the mountain with a wingsuit, landed somewhere, changed his clothes and ran away with a new identity.

Pete could live in a cabin in the woods like a person in a witness protection program or the Unabomber. Or he could go to Lamoureux and live in Norvell's shed. He could go to Norvell's house on some pretext, steal the key to the shed, make a copy of it and bring it back before Norvell noticed. Hell, he could pick the lock, thanks to the skills he'd learned from Granv.

Pete decided against the shed. Shed living would be like camping, and he didn't like camping. He wanted to live in a penthouse or a beachside mansion. The house-sitting websites had many of those. House-sitting would be perfect. He could avoid the constant surveillance of friends, family or bosses. He could live in the homes of rich people on long vacations, and he could work in peace on his board game.

The word "go" meant not so much to leave a place but to head toward another place.

#

The next day at work, he was hung over enough to ask Linda to fetch him a ginger ale Slurpee during her 7-Eleven run if they had one, and if they didn't, then a can of ginger ale. He also volunteered to do backroom work. In the quiet of the big storage room, among the endless boxes of card-based games and far away from Jack Harkness in the figurine section, he worked around the fuzzy part of his brain and thought with the clear part. If he was going to do a symbolic BASE jump, he should begin with a real one. He could start small and try bungee jumping. He'd met people who had bungee jumped, including the Australian girl. It didn't look that hard: West Edmonton Mall had bungee jumping in the World Water Park.

The next day at work, his mind now fully cleared of drunkenness, Pete asked Norvell what he thought about bungee jumping. Norvell didn't think much of it. "It seems like a lot of effort for very little payoff. Whenever I think of bungee jumping, I think of that guy in Virginia who taped a bunch of cords together and jumped off a bridge without measuring the length of the cords. The cords were too long. Splat."

That night, Pete checked to make sure Norvell's story was true (it was). He stayed on the internet, looking up BASE fan sites and house-sitting websites, until midnight. Not time well spent, but at least he'd avoided the bars. Invisible Man seemed to get out from time to time, but mainly he stayed home. Bars could have been a serious distraction from his lightbulb project, which sounded like a lot of work.

Pete opened his ratty copy of *Invisible Man* to the prologue, the best part, and read: "Please, a definition: A hibernation is a covert preparation for a more overt action."

He'd looked up "overt" a long time ago. It meant "open," the opposite of "covert." Covertness meant being sneaky, mysterious, hidden, like living in a basement rent-free and stealing electricity. If Invisible Man lived today, he would have to steal bandwidth, or else he'd have to give up the internet. Pete didn't think cutting ties to all networks was realistic or possible because of government surveillance through security cameras and loyalty cards. He only wanted to escape dependence. He needed to keep some structure around. He needed a base to jump from.

On the third house-sitting website he checked, he found a person in Edmonton, a professor going on a two-week research trip to Austin, Texas.

The professor responded to Pete's message almost instantly. The next evening, Pete found himself at a Starbucks on Whyte Avenue sitting across from a grey-haired man with a thin neck and sad brown eyes. The professor said he was leaving in a few days. The person he'd originally lined up for the house-sit, a former student, had run off to Toronto to patch things up with his girlfriend. "That'll teach me to trust a student," the professor said. "You're not a student, are you, Pete?"

"Not a chance."

The professor had a lot of plants and needed someone to water them. He asked for two references, but Pete felt optimistic. The prof was desperate.

The next day at work, Pete asked Norvell and Jerry for references. Norvell seemed fine about it, though when Pete mentioned he was getting paid, Norvell felt bad for not paying; Pete said, "Don't forget: I drank a lot of your beer." Jerry said he would give one as long as Pete wasn't thinking of quitting to take up house-sitting as a career. "I've heard that some people are permanent house-sitters," Jerry said. 'It's a cottage industry." He smiled with an eyebrow lift that made Pete think that he was supposed to answer or laugh. "That was a joke," Jerry said. "I'll give you a good reference even though you didn't think my joke was funny."

Later, Norvell explained that Jerry was probably making a joke about pre-industrial labour. "Are you still reading *Das Kapital*?"

"I'm working my way through it." Pete wasn't, but he wanted to keep Norvell happy.

At home that night, Pete pulled up *Das Kapital* and stared at the table of contents. Being a house-sitter didn't make someone totally off grid, but it was different than the way most people lived. The permanent house-sitters of the world didn't buy into normal. If you saw them walking down the street, they might seem run-of-the-mill, but they weren't. They were all revolutionaries. House-sitting was like Invisible Man's hibernation stage, or the lose-your-turn stage in games that good players took advantage of. During the hiatus of a lost turn, Pete sometimes came up with his best strategies. House-sitting was like the free fall of a parachute jump, a pause in time, like a lost turn. All parachuting stages were important: the packing of the chute, the planning of where to jump and when, and the boarding of the airplane. After the free-fall stage came the ripcord-pull stage and then the touchdown phase, when the soldier landed softly in the jungle outside the fortress. The middle phase, where you fell, unprotected from the sky, looked bad. But it was a necessary phase. It was also the most fun. The best part.

\#

Two nights later, the professor called. He'd been hired.

Three nights later, Pete watched the prof shut the door, and he was alone. The condo wasn't much different than his own apartment, though it had more books and much nicer furniture. On one wall in the living room was the Murphy bed where Pete would sleep. As a kid he had always wanted a Murphy bed so that the bed could slam shut on him one day and trap him in the wall for a bit, provided he could get out. The balcony window was supposed to give a view of Whyte Avenue, but the professor had too many plants. Plants crawled and slithered from hanging planters and giant pots and small pots crammed onto two industrial shelving units. A narrow path allowed him to reach the screen door through an archway made by a wide-leaved climbing plant that spanned two shelving units. Other than watering plants, Pete had no other responsibilities. The professor said he could use the desktop computer in the library, a separate room with books and a desk.

Pete looked at the condo keys in his hand. They felt like keys to the world. Symbols, it turned out, weren't just in poems. It was the other way around, probably. Stories had symbols because people had symbols in real life. He would never say that to Gilda. It was always best to keep Gilda out of his loop.

Since he was on Whyte Avenue, and it was Thursday night, he went to Dunkers, his favourite Edmonton bar.

19

GHOSTS

The house-sitting suited him. From the professor's place, the bus ride to Tokens took longer, but Pete was much closer to Dunkers. His house-sitting duties were very light. The water that Pete dripped on the plants once a day didn't seem necessary—the balcony window was permanently steamed. He wondered if the books in the library benefited from the humidity. He knew that Edmonton's dryness frustrated comic-book collectors. The humidity was good for him, anyway; his hair and skin felt softer.

One night at the professor's condo, Pete was sitting in the leather armchair in the library and pushing back his cuticles when he noticed one of Norvell's recommended books on the shelf next to him: *The Songlines* by Bruce Chatwin. He read most of it that evening instead of going to the bar. The book was about Australia's Aborigines. They used to walk about and sing songs that acted like maps to ancient places, like a kind of singing GPS. But it was more than that. The songs were what the Aborigines thought created the world. The song came first, just like when the Bible said, "In the beginning was the word." The other thing Pete liked about *The Songlines* was the idea that the world was divided into the people who walked and the people who stood still. The entire history of people was about the tension between the nomads and the settlers. Chatwin seemed to like the walking people more, though he also thought the walking people were dangerous.

Pete pulled down the Murphy bed and lay on his back. He crossed his naked left foot over his bent right knee and looked at his left big toe. Chatwin said the big toe proved that people were designed to walk. Big toes separated the walking humans from the climbing, skittering apes. It hadn't been the white Australians who had come up with the idea of singing the world into existence. Pete liked the idea that so many white Australians were descended from ex-convicts from a prison colony. And what made them so self-satisfied? The Australian girl had been self-satisfied. During the summer after high school when he lived in Banff at the ski lodge of someone Burghie knew, he met tons of Australian girls. Smiling, blonde and confident, they were expert skiers even though they lived in a hot country. In Banff, Australians worked at the retail outfitters and the bars. They all knew each other and joked about the difference between Aussies and Kiwis. At one of these stores, he met the Australian girl. Not even six hours passed before they were at his place. She almost ripped his pants off before he could get things under control in the way he needed to. He told her, in as nice a way as possible, "Hey, darlin', let me do that." She started laughing and said, "What's the matter, mate, don't you like dominant females?" And she yanked his underwear down. She stared at his junk for two seconds and said, "What's going on here?" before he pushed her away and pulled up his underwear. His push had been strong—she fell backwards and hit her head against the corner of the television stand. She screamed, and he tried to run over to help her, but she held up her hand. "Fuck off!" she said. She stood up on her own, touched her head and saw blood. He wanted to apologize, but he didn't have a chance. She grabbed her purse and ran out without shutting the door behind her. He was sure that she would call the police, but nothing happened. He hid out the rest of the next day in his room. That night, he took the Greyhound back to Edmonton.

Lying in the Murphy bed in the professor's condo, Pete realized that house-sitters, at least the dedicated ones, were nomads. They stayed put for a while, sure, but then they moved on. The Australian girl was probably back in Australia, living in a ranch or whatever they lived in, raising sheep and staying put after a year pretending to be a nomad. He didn't want to pretend.

The next night, Pete went to Dunkers and played pool with strangers. The night after that, he returned to see if a woman he had met the night before was a regular. Apparently not. But he stayed and watched a car race on television with a group of Danish university students who were celebrating the middle of spring term. He went home late and smoked the weed he bought from one of the students.

He was extremely hung over the next morning, to the point where at work Norvell asked him if he was hung over. Pete said no, but Norvell didn't buy it. "I've seen a lot of hangovers in my family, believe me."

"Jerry and Linda haven't said anything," Pete said.

"Let's just say that they know when you are hung over."

"What does that mean?"

"They've mentioned it to me."

Pete had to be careful. Granv's dad had been laid off more than once for coming into work hung over or drunk. Pete did his best to be on the ball the rest of the day. He volunteered to watch Braedyn, who came in at his usual time, so that other people could do their normal work. He fixed Linda a coffee when he went to the staff room to get his tea. Linda thanked him and said nothing about him possibly being hung over.

That night, he felt confident about his decision to go to Dunkers, even though his mouth was still dry and his stomach had no interest in food. Students tended to fill Dunkers on Thursdays, and he liked checking the undergraduates over. At the long tables, he saw the usual Dunkers crowd: old men in lumberjack jackets, faces stubbly and hair uncombed, working-class guys in raggy T-shirts hawing and hacking from years of smoking, and middle-aged women with backcombed hair and flower-printed shirts having a beer with a husband or boyfriend. The bar had university types too, in groups of four or five, wearing torn jeans, cloth loafers and braided wristbands, the girls not wearing anything much different than the boys, though they tended to have longer hair.

Pete sat at the dingy beaverboard bar, drinking from his pint of Traditional, and wondered if he had a chance with two thirty-somethings standing at the other end. They were twirling their hair in their fingers and baring their perfectly straight teeth in short quick laughs.

A man and a woman sat down between Pete and the thirty-somethings. The woman looked like the Australian girl. It couldn't be, he knew; he had met her in Banff years ago. He couldn't look away from the woman, though. She didn't seem to notice. Eventually she and the man moved from the bar and sat at a table nearby. The man's back was to Pete and blocked most of the woman's face. It wasn't just her face that reminded him of the Australian girl. It was the easy swing of her arms as she swept them up and down while she talked and laughed at everything the man said. The loudspeakers playing ZZ Top and Elvis Costello made it hard to hear her. Her accent would be the real test.

When the Costello song ended, he strained to listen to her voice.

The next thing he knew, he was leaning against the wall in the hallway to the bathroom, and a man in a Harley-Davidson T-shirt was talking. "Hey, are you okay?"

Pete shut his eyes. He felt sick.

"I think he's having a stroke," someone said. It was the bartender.

Pete didn't think he was having a stroke. He felt pain only in his lungs. He was gasping and panting because the air wasn't getting into them fast enough. It was like someone had punched him in the stomach. The room was spinning.

Someone said, "Does he have a Medic Alert bracelet?"

"Call an ambulance," someone else said.

Pete could not let anyone put him in an ambulance. He could not let anyone inspect his junk. That wasn't going to happen again.

The bartender said, "Hey, can you hear me?"

Pete heard rumbling in his head. A spinning rumbling. He had to yell to hear himself over it. "I'm okay." His voice sounded like he was talking inside a shower stall.

"Did you have too much to drink?" the man in the Harley-Davidson T-shirt asked.

"I just served him one pint," the bartender said. "He must have come in already toasted."

"I'm fine now." Pete told the bartender what he wanted to hear. "I'll just go home."

The bartender tried to talk him into staying until his dizzy spell went away, but Pete said that he lived nearby and would be okay. The Harley-Davidson man escorted Pete to the door and outside. On the way out, Pete noticed the mystery woman looking at him with a smile. She said something in an accent; at least, she had a funny way of speaking. Then again, everything he heard had a strange echo, as though his head had become a giant canyon that sounds were pouring into.

The night air cuffed Pete's face and revived him. The Harley-Davidson man asked, "You sure you don't need a cab?" The man was probably the bouncer, not a concerned citizen. Bouncers saw a lot of bizarre shit. What would the Harley-Davidson bouncer say if he knew what Pete was dealing with?

As Pete walked to the condo, his sight and hearing returned to normal, but when he reached the professor's building and headed up the elevator, he didn't feel better. In the shiny metal walls of the elevator, her reflection was pale and distorted.

20

GO, GO, GO!

The next two nights, he stayed in. He sat in the professor's leather armchair with a beer and *The Songlines,* reading and re-reading. At the end of the second night, he stood up, went to the professor's computer and installed a Tor browser.

Facebook first. Facebook didn't like people cancelling their accounts. He left a message with Facebook customer service saying he wanted to delete his account entirely. The cellphone was another matter. He couldn't figure out how to cut his cellphone and still keep in touch with Jerry and his landlord Ed. Did Invisible Man cut himself off completely? No. Invisible Man had filled his apartment with electricity. The point was isolation, not deprivation. Not having a phone was deprivation.

What else? Instagram, Twitter, LinkedIn. Delicious. Flickr. Foursquare. Google+. Was Myspace still a thing? Yes—though not for him, not anymore. Tumblr. Reddit. Yelp. 4chan. SA. Yahoo Groups. Craigslist. Kijiji. He doublechecked Pinterest: he'd never sunk that low, thank Christ. Skype. A YouTube channel he started when he was in high school. PayPal. WhatsApp. Snapchat. BBM. BugTraq. He Googled his own name, and from that he found a cloud account as well as three porn sites. Were there only three? He couldn't figure out how to get rid of his Apple ID without calling Apple, so he clipped off all he could from his profile and promised himself to call Apple customer service later. He was sure he had other accounts out there that he'd forgotten about, but there was nothing he could do about that. As for his bank account, Jerry paid him through direct deposit, and since he had way too little money to interest a Swiss bank, he would have to leave it until he thought of a workaround. In the same category was his government ID. He needed email if he wanted to reach anyone who wanted a house-sitter; he would use only his Hotmail.

In the professor's closet, he found a black fedora. With the fedora brim pulled low over his face, he walked to an Irish pub nearby. No one he knew was there, but he flirted with three women from out of town who were impressed with his career as a house-sitter.

21

PHILIPPA AND PETE COEXIST IN BLACKBIRD MYOOZIK

In the early days of living off grid, Pete had to get used to the limitations as well as the freedoms. At work, he had to log in to the till and go online; he needed a job, though, so he tolerated it. The worst was riding the bus to work without a cellphone. He didn't want to overhear any more whining from teenagers or stupid arguments between old women about whether Superstore or Walmart had better shopping carts. He had an old iPod shuffle, but to use it, he had to fetch tracks from an online source. In the past, this source had been an illegal download site registered in Belarus. He couldn't go to that site anymore and stay true to his new self. He didn't need the internet, just like Invisible Man didn't need to belong to any activist group or sign on with electrical companies. He would have to be sneaky.

Fortunately, Pete was living in the apartment of a man who had barely left the nineties and so had a turntable and CD changer. Invisible Man had a turntable in his lightbulb room. Pete could get a portable CD player like the one Ralph had. He could also rip tracks off a CD like in the old days and transfer the files to the iPod. The professor's music tastes were eighties new wave and classical music. Pete needed another source for CDs. Luckily for him, Whyte Avenue had a music store, maybe the last of its kind in Edmonton. Pete had passed it many times while bar hopping. He put on his leather jacket and cowboy boots. Under grey skies and spitting rain, he walked the five blocks to Blackbird Myoozik.

Inside the store, Pete had expected a meat-locker ambiance. Instead, the space was warm: the walls were painted chocolate, and the floor was dark hardwood. Two other people were in the store, not including the solemn thin dude behind the cash counter near the front entrance. Sparkling jazz music played overhead. In the alternative section, he spotted an album by his old obsession, Red Hot Chili Peppers. Past the alternative section was the jazz section, and at the back of the store were blues and classical.

If this was the only place to get CDs without going online, he would have to learn to like blues and jazz. Invisible Man listened to Louis Armstrong's "(What Did I Do To Be So) Black and Blue?" He found two Louis Armstrong CDs.

Pete sneezed, and sneezed again. His upper arms felt itchy. A bearded man in a flannel plaid shirt and jeans was standing in front of him in the classical section. She sneezed again.

The man said, "Bless you."

Philippa snapped back, "What kind of cologne are you wearing?" She had an allergy to some perfumes.

The man grew sad. "I'm not wearing any."

"Are you sure?"

"Yes." The man smiled weakly.

"I'm allergic to perfume." Philippa made her voice sound harsh. "You should be careful with that kind of thing in public. All kinds of people are allergic."

"But I'm not wearing any." He seemed embarrassed, wimpy even.

Philippa felt a surge of power. "What's that smell, then?" He didn't really smell anything.

"I don't know."

"I'm not imagining it, Red. All I got is perfume allergies. I got tested when that fucking Coco Mademoiselle my stepmother gave me nearly killed me."

The man chewed on the bit of hair below his lower lip. "You wear Coco Mademoiselle?"

Philippa had a list of insults she'd been gathering the previous week from her time spent in bars. None of them left her mouth, because she looked down at herself. Leather jacket, leather cowboy boots. Cowboy hat. Black baggy pants with saggy crotch. Open front of jacket revealing a baggy black sweatshirt with the word "Budweiser" in the centre. She was not Philippa. She had come here dressed as Pete.

Pete and Red stared at each other. Finally, Red turned away.

Pete tucked his chin to her chest to hide his face. He strolled up the aisle toward the front of the store and pretended to look at an album rack labelled "Local Artists." For some reason he couldn't see any of the albums properly. He needed air.

He went outside. Around him, the rain fell more heavily. He tried to locate the lumberjack through the front plate glass of the store, but he couldn't see that far into the store. In the reflection on the glass, translucent people walked behind Pete's reflection. One person held an umbrella over her head as she passed.

His reflected face looked like Philippa's. She was dressed as Pete and had behaved in the store in Pete's power-tripping asshole mode. So, then, who was she?

The spinning began, first in her head only, then the world outside her began to spin. She shut her eyes until the vertigo slowed. The world stopped spinning, but somehow the emotions related to the vertigo cut themselves loose from the spinning and hauled themselves inside her head. She wasn't dizzy, so she felt safe walking, but she was still in the vertigo.

Pete was fed up with having to walk home after some kind of disgrace. He didn't feel disgraced about herself but about the way that people treated her. Disgrace: diss-grace. Grace was a religious idea that had something to do with God deciding that he was going to be nice to you even though you didn't deserve it. To diss a grace meant to insult the idea that you were nice or, to get religious about it, to diss the idea that God should be nice to you. What the hell did perfume have to do with whether God should be nice to you?

Who cared if he was allergic to a perfume? So what if he thought the fake lumberjack was wearing Coco Mademoiselle? The fake lumberjack thought it was okay to dress like a lumberjack even though he wasn't one. What the lumberjack was implying was that it was weird for someone dressed a certain way and act a certain way to wear Coco Mademoiselle. The lumberjack had been unfair. Pete didn't like people who were unfair. To teach unfair people a lesson, fair people had to react unfairly to show what it felt like to be on the receiving end of unfairness.

Wherever Pete went, things went sideways like that. Nobody seemed to be on his side. He wished that he knew someone who understood what it was like. He should get out of town and start over. His mother did that once. Gilda had told him, and after that, Beth had admitted it. Beth had taken his baby self away. Maybe it was time to take himself away.

22

PETE SPEAKS TO BETH, GILDA AND RALPH IN ONE NIGHT

For the rest of the week of June 5, 2012, Pete came to work well and good hung over. He made sure to volunteer to go out to 7-Eleven so that he could clear his head, but he couldn't get off cash duty, which he desperately wanted to do. When Jerry asked if he was sick, he said he wasn't. Jerry seemed to believe him, at least to his face, unlike Norvell, who glared at Pete all day. He stayed away from Norvell as much as possible; he didn't want to hear what Norvell had to say. Hearing Norvell talk about his hangover could make Pete do something stupid like confess.

By Friday, he couldn't shake off the hangover from two nights before, never mind the night before. After work, since a drink was as good as a walk to 7-Eleven to clear the head, he bar hopped Whyte Avenue. To pace himself, he drank red-eyes. By the time he headed to his third bar, rain was falling. Pete stood on a street corner and let the wet slap his face until he felt ready to move to the next bar. The third bar wasn't his favourite at the best of times, but it was nearly deserted, which is what he wanted. He sat at a table in the corner with an ale and drank until he felt the urge to telephone Beth.

He went outside to look for a phone booth. Edmontonians promenaded through the light show of city nighttime. The streetlights dropped moony reflections on the black sidewalks, and the red and yellow headlights of the cars slid along the buildings like comets. The storefronts' orange and blue lights washed the sidewalks and roads. Down the street was a British phone booth that bars sometimes put out to create a British atmosphere. The phone booth, red and shiny, enticed him inside. Not that he needed enticement. He had no problem calling Beth. Nothing about Beth intimidated him. Beth could be sneaky—that was where Gilda had gotten it—but provided that Pete was being up front and not trying to be sneaky himself, he got along well with Beth.

The phone booth was fake, so Pete walked until he found a working one.

Beth answered the phone with a bubbly hello. "And how is my Philippa today?"

"Fine."

"And are you out and about? I hear Whyte Avenue."

"Good guess."

"I used to go to Whyte Avenue back in the day. It was a lot rougher then. Still, good times. I'm having as good a time here with Gilda. We're watching a wonderful movie. Have you seen that movie about the man who falls in love with a sex doll?"

"Gilda's pick, right?"

"Yes, but a wonderful one. And what are you doing on Whyte Avenue?"

"The usual."

"Wonderful," Beth said. "Have we had too much to drink, Pete? Is that why we are calling our mother from Whyte Avenue at night?"

Pete didn't like the combination of her cheerfulness and theorizing about the reason for his call. He needed to gain control. "No, Mom, I'm just calling. I said I would."

"That's wonderful," Beth said. "It's a good use of your time. I thought Gilda was the efficiency expert, but you've picked up some of that too. Not from me, of course. That's all your father. I've never been the organized one in the family, God knows. I'm including my family and your father's family here. In any family, I would be the least organized."

"Mom, have *you* been drinking?"

"Oh, sure," she said. "Yesterday was my tenth anniversary at Alberta Health Services, and I got this nice bottle of Prosecco. Have you heard of it? It's wonderful. I had two bottles of it, but I've finished one."

"Is Gilda there, Mom?"

"Gilda had a glass herself. She doesn't know how much I had. And are you alone on a street corner with too much to drink? Gilda is the best person to have around in these situations, but she can't be in two places at once."

A police car or ambulance drove down a nearby cross street, and the siren drowned all other sound. Pete waited for the sound to end.

"Philippa?"

Pete said, "Congrats on the anniversary."

"Thanks, honey." Beth paused to cough off-receiver. "It's been a good ten years. Ten years fly by, you know." Her tone changed. "No regrets, mind you, but you begin to wonder. It flies by, and you think, what have I done? And you know what I've decided?"

"No, Mom, I don't."

"Pay some attention to the flying. Where you're going, and all that. Where you've been is one thing. Where you're going is another."

Pete knew he'd had a few drinks, but his mother seemed to have had much more, which meant he was the adult in the situation. "Sure, Mom. Are you watching the movie with Gilda now?"

She laughed. "Right! I can't miss more of it. Gilda's not one to keep her finger on the pause button."

Pete heard a rustle, and then Gilda was on the phone. "Pete?"

"Is Mom drunk?"

"She's had some. She's not a big drinker, so that wine got to her head. She likes this movie, and she's in a good mood. How about you? Are you drunk?"

"No, why would I be?"

"It's Friday night, and you're outside somewhere on Whyte Avenue, and you called Mom."

"For your information, I called Mom because I said I would. Also, I want to find out what the hell you're doing."

"What am I doing? What are you doing?"

"When I asked you what you were doing, I wasn't just being polite. Why did you track down Burghie and sic him on me?"

"I didn't track down Burghie. I ran into him at the restaurant he works at."

"You don't go to restaurants unless it's for work," Pete said.

"If it makes you feel better, I was in a parking lot in front of a restaurant, not in the restaurant, when I ran into Burghie."

"You never go outside."

"I told Burghie where you worked, and he decided to look you up, I suppose."

"He decided? I doubt it!"

"Why not? You and Burghie were friends for a long time. You live in the same city. It's likely that you or I would run into someone from high school at some point, and that at some point one of those people might want to get in touch again."

"Theoretically."

"Unless of course you are up to something and are getting paranoid about being detected."

"I'm not."

"If not, then why are you calling from a phone booth?"

"That's stupid. There are hardly any phone booths anymore."

"'Hardly any' isn't the same as 'none.' I hear traffic in the background."

"Well, no shit, Sherlock. There are cars in the city. Maybe I have my window open."

Gilda sighed. "What happened to your cellphone?"

"Nothing."

"How are we going to get in touch with you? You aren't on Facebook. Your emails bounce."

"It used to be that people didn't have phones, and they got along all right."

"You are talking to me on the phone, you realize."

"I mean personal phones. I bet that in the olden days every town had one phone and people had to book appointments to use it."

Gilda sighed again. "Are you going to be able to get home? Are you by yourself?"

"There's plenty of people around."

"Maybe you should go home."

"You always know the best thing to do. Even when you do things that are wrong, you do the best things. Getting Burghie to track me down. That was wrong. It was the right thing to do, but it was wrong."

"Should I call a cab for you?"

"I can walk home," Pete said.

"You live too far away."

He had forgotten. He didn't live in the professor's condo anymore. "Yeah, that's right. I live too far away." He tried to say this in as casual a voice as he could.

"What is going on?" Gilda asked.

"Nothing," Pete said. "I'm fine."

He hung up. He looked out across the street and around him to see if anyone had noticed what he had been saying. He couldn't tell. The few people who were outside were walking past him too quickly and without enough attention to hear him. A few had umbrellas. They had thought ahead. He wished he had thought ahead. Not that he wasn't thinking. He hadn't thought of an umbrella, but he had thought of other things. Made other plans. He could make plans as well as Gilda. He was even beating her at it.

His father would appreciate the joke he'd played on Gilda. Ralph was the philosopher in the family. Only Ralph knew that Pete lived inside a cosmic joke.

He called Ralph's cell. When Ralph came on the line, the first thing Pete heard was music in the background, jazz. The word jazz reminded him of what had happened to him at Blackbird Myoozik.

"Hello?" Ralph said.

"It's me, Dad. Phil."

"What's going on?" Ralph asked. "Are you in trouble?"

"Now why would you ask that? Can't I call you for the sake of calling?"

"You never do that." The music swelled in the background. Ralph raised his voice. "Listen, I'm at a reception, and I can't hear you or talk to you for any length of time. Why don't you call me back tomorrow?"

"When?"

"In the afternoon. I have a brunch and a rehearsal after that. I should be reachable by three or so."

Pete felt hungry all of a sudden. "What kind of brunch?"

"A fundraising brunch," Ralph said. "It doesn't matter. How about three o'clock tomorrow?"

"Is Rachel there?"

"Yes, why?"

"I should talk to her too. She's my stepmother and everything."

"Have you been drinking, Phil?"

"No," Pete said. "I'm at a reception too. So there." He hung up.

He left the phone booth and stood in the rain. A siren blared nearby, and lights flashed across the wet streets and wet buildings. Police were always on Whyte. Him standing outside in the rain might seem suspicious to paranoid cops. Maybe someone would think he was a terrorist. He was pleased by the idea. A creator of terror. A terror artist. A maker of mayhem, a supervillain, a cross-gendered Joker. He imitated The Joker's laugh to see if anyone would stop him, but no one did. People cruised by, a handful with umbrellas over their heads, on their way to whatever life had put in front of them. Pete was the jokee, maybe, not the joker. The butt of the joke. The junk of the joke. His jokey junk.

A chill ran from his toes to his chest. He had to get inside. He turned and went to the first door he saw. It was a Starbucks. He went in and stood in the vestibule. Someone wanted to leave, and he had to go right inside to make room. From the tables and couches, eyes swivelled in his direction. Toward the joker with the jokey junk. The eyes returned to their coffees and their coffee-drinking companions. They couldn't look at him. He was too jokey.

He left the Starbucks but bumped into someone who was walking in. The person said "sorry" and kept going, but Pete called after him, "You're damn right you should be sorry!" The person didn't turn. Pete couldn't tell if it was a guy or a woman. Not that it mattered.

Pete waited outside for an hour until the person left, and Pete trailed the person until he stopped at the corner for the pedestrian lights. Too many people were around to start a fight. Pete turned the corner and kept walking. The rain pelted him. He would have to take a taxi to his apartment on the north side. Then he would walk away from that too.

23

PETE SAYS GOODBYE

The next morning, while he lolled in bed from her hangover, Philippa thought about her mother and Montreal. Because of Beth, Philippa had been named after a bed and breakfast owner, and because of Beth, Philippa had spent a part of her early life away from Edmonton and her sister. For Beth to leave one kid behind like that had been extreme. Theirs was an extreme family. BASE jumping was in Pete's genes.

Once he felt able, he shuffled to the computer and searched the house-sitting websites for a gig in Montreal. He found one quickly: a person named François needed someone to look after a dog and two cats in a one-bedroom condo apartment for three months. Pete registered with the website and got more details. This François wanted two references from previous house-sitting clients. Pete had that, so he emailed François. He made himself a tea and noodle-less ramen, and he went back to bed.

Later that day, the condo owner responded and asked for the references. Pete said he needed to contact his second reference, who was out of town. That was a lie; Pete wasn't sure the drunk was out of his voice, and he didn't want to phone the professor that way. He could talk to Norvell Monday at work.

If Pete left the city, he left his job. If he left the job, he left his income. Ergo, he needed a job in Montreal. He hadn't completed his computer training, but he could whip up a website, so he could make money freelancing. The question, though, was whether he could do that in Montreal. He had taken French in junior high, but he was nowhere close to being fluent. He imagined a niche market: people who were bad at English but good at French and who needed an English version of their websites. He knew that the hockey and football players in Montreal, never mind their coaches, didn't always know French. So many were American or Swedish these days. He fell asleep while thinking of who else might move to Montreal and need an English website.

He awoke Sunday morning and went to the scuzzy restaurant down the street. He ordered their lousy hash browns and eggs and used the house phone to call the professor and ask for a reference. Lucky for Pete, the professor wasn't a churchgoer and was home. The professor was happy to give Pete the reference and, as he said, help Pete start an adventure in life. When Pete hung up, he thought about calling his mother to say he wasn't coming for Sunday lunch, but he figured that they knew that he wouldn't be over. Anyway, they could neither confirm nor deny it, since he didn't have a cellphone.

By the time he jettisoned himself out of bed Monday morning, François had emailed back. Pete had saved François from the humiliation of getting his mom to look after his place. "You know the way mothers are," François wrote.

Pete knew, all right. He was going to experience a lot more of the way mothers were in the next week. He would have to be out of Edmonton in six days. He had to tell Jerry and his landlord that he was leaving, but he dreaded telling his mother the most.

At work, he eventually found Jerry and Linda together in the staff room. He told them he was thinking of doing some travelling and wanted to quit for a while to go to Montreal. "A leave of absence, like."

Jerry was enthusiastic. "A young man like you should go have adventures. I backpacked around Europe, but I know people who did a cross-Canada tour."

Linda also seemed enthusiastic, though her reasons were more sinister: "You should do that before you get married and have kids. After that it's impossible."

Pete offered to help Tokens with their website updates from long distance, and Linda and Jerry seemed satisfied with that arrangement. They agreed to pay him a retainer once a month for website maintenance. He then explained when this was all happening.

"You're leaving on Sunday?" Linda finally said to break the silence.

Pete explained the situation: he found someone in Montreal who was desperate to get someone to look after his place for three months, and now that Pete had found it, he felt bad about not going through with it.

Jerry said, "I wish we had more notice."

"I thought you said I would still be able to work for you."

"Yes, but—" Jerry looked at Linda. "A change in position isn't covered by the labour laws, is it?"

"There are laws for changes in position, yes." Linda continued meditatively, "I suppose, though, that this is temporary—three months, you said?"

"Three months in Montreal, yeah." Pete had already decided that the three months would end with him finding another house-sit, maybe somewhere in Europe or, better yet, in Fiji. He decided not to say anything about that until he had a sense of how his employers would feel about him being away at all.

Linda said, "The girls are out of school for the summer. Soon they could take shifts on the weekdays."

Jerry chewed the inside of his cheek. "We should sit down just you and me, Linda, and talk about this."

While his bosses were in conference in the staff room, Pete asked Norvell for a house-sit reference. "I'm going to Montreal for a while."

Norvell blinked, blushed. "You're moving?"

"Not permanently. Just for a couple months."

"A vacation?"

"Not really. I'll be working there."

"Where?"

Where indeed? Norvell had touched a sore point. Pete mumbled, "Oh, you know, web stuff, like what I do for Jerry."

"But you're coming back."

Norvell sounded so doubtful that Pete wondered if he'd blabbed his long-term plans to Norvell like he'd blabbed about wanting to house-sit. Pete felt sorry for Norvell. Not that he had any romantic feelings for Norvell, but he had feelings; it was hard not to have feelings for someone who was probably in love with you and who had helped you launch a new life. "I'm coming back."

Norvell perked up a bit. "Sure, I'll give you a good reference."

Later that day, Jerry and Linda called Pete into the staff room. This opportunity was fantastic for Pete, Jerry said. Pete would come back a more fulfilled person. Besides, Jerry said, their girls could get some experience working longer shifts, and the work would keep them out of trouble. From the look Linda and Jerry gave each other, Pete guessed that their oldest daughter Una was getting out of control. The website was his to do.

After Pete got home, he jogged to the gas station down the street and called his landlord to give his notice. Pete had two months on his lease, and he didn't care if he lost money for those two months. He would pay the rent but clear out as much of his stuff as he could. Whatever Ed did with the empty space was his business. Ed was surprised to get a phone call (Pete normally texted), but once Pete explained that Ed wouldn't be losing any money, Ed said it was fine as long as Pete put all of that in writing in hard copy. In an hour, Pete ran home and printed out a letter, and he popped the letter in the landlord mailbox in the lobby.

Pete had to take some game-related stuff with him: the mock-up of his board game as well as a few games to use for reference. Some things he wanted with him for sentimental value: the Rook card game (one of George Parker's first successful games), the Parker Brothers book, and the little magnetic checkers and chess travel game that he and Gilda used to play with in the back of their mother's fuchsia Ford Taurus station wagon on road trips. Everything else, he decided, he would offer to Norvell.

The next day he asked Norvell to look after his game collection. Pete didn't need to say anything like "You owe me one, Norvell" like he expected. Norvell immediately agreed. "It would be an honour." Somehow he already knew that Pete had gotten their bosses' okay to leave for a while. Norvell called it a sabbatical.

"Isn't that a satanic party or something?" Pete asked.

"You must mean a witch's sabbath."

"Witch's sabbath? Never heard of it."

"A sabbatical is a long break from work."

"Oh."

At six o'clock, Pete joined Norvell in the parking lot. Norvell suggested they eat some takeout, and Pete talked Norvell into getting drive-thru at McDonald's. "My treat." They ate in the car while driving to Pete's; on the way, Pete made Norvell stop at a pawnshop to buy two extra suitcases. At Pete's apartment, Norvell stood guard outside while Pete went in and out with armfuls of boxes. The car filled up before Pete's apartment could be emptied. Norvell said, "We're going to need a bigger boat." He had to explain the reference to Pete.

The next day, Norvell arrived at work in a rusting cube van. It was his Uncle Ted's old work van for the HVAC company that Ted operated at another of his properties. After work, they returned to Pete's apartment and stuffed the cube van with the rest of the boxes. Along with the games were a few house things he didn't want to leave behind. Before Norvell left for home, Pete suggested a place for his stuff: that old shed he'd seen but had definitely never been inside of.

At closing on Friday, he said goodbye to his bosses and Norvell. His bosses were easy: a handshake for Jerry, a hug for Linda. Norvell was tougher. "You're still doing the reading, right?" Norvell asked.

Pete thought he saw a tear fill the lower lids of Norvell's eyes. That had to stop. Gruffly, Pete said, "Don't sell my stuff."

"I won't." The tears dried up. "The games are in the house, and the furniture is safe in the Quonset."

The word Quonset disappointed him; he'd hoped his things were in the shed. All he could do was shake Norvell's big mitt. Poor Norvell shook a little. Pete was glad that he could be gone from Norvell's sight and give Norvell time to get over him.

Pete had planned to call his mother after work, but by the time he got home, he was too tired. Instead he called at nine the next night and after some fortification from the bar side of a nearby pizza place. He used the restaurant's house phone to call Beth.

"Mom, I have some news."

In the background, he could hear gunshots, rising voices and a crescendo of music. Beth was watching one of the *CSI*s. "Is that a fact?" Beth asked.

"I'm moving to Montreal."

"Did you say 'moving' or 'going'?"

"Moving."

"Now why would you do something like that?"

"I need a change of pace."

"What was it about the current pace that was causing you problems? Too slow or too fast?"

"Too slow."

The television noise de-crescendoed to nothing. She likely had turned down the volume. "Why Montreal?"

"Lots of interesting things are going on in Montreal."

"I thought the economy was a little depressed over there."

"It has a lot of culture."

"Culture?" Beth paused before she continued. "So now you're interested in culture."

"Museums, nightlife, that kind of thing."

"You're going for the museums?"

"I'm leaving Sunday morning."

Pete heard a background drone of voices and throbbing music: a commercial was on. Beth said, "This Sunday morning?"

"Hey, Mom, I have to take a whizz real bad, and I want to talk to Gilda, so could you get her on the phone?"

"Uh, sure." Pete heard some rustling on the other side of the phone; she had covered the mouthpiece of her phone with her hand. After a minute, Gilda's voice faded in. "What's going on, Pete? Mom's upset."

"I'm leaving town."

"Why?"

"Because."

"Where are you going?"

"Montreal."

"Montreal? Are you serious?"

"I am. I'm leaving Sunday morning."

"Tomorrow morning?"

"Yeah. I've got my ticket."

"Is this some kind of stupid joke, Pete?"

"No."

"I knew you were up to something."

"Okay, gotta go," Pete said. "Goodbye, Gil."

"Don't you dare hang up on me—"

When Pete reached his soon-to-be ex-apartment, he regretted having gotten rid of all the chairs and having drunk all the booze. All he could do was prop himself against the wall and stare at the only thing left, the sheet-less and blanket-less futon that would serve as his bed and that he would have to leave behind. He hoped Ed didn't mind.

Unlike the narrator's room in *Invisible Man*, his empty apartment had just a few light bulbs. Pete turned off the last one, the one in the kitchen. That was better.

#

Everything in Montreal had something foreign about it. The airport was a nightmare of nearly recognizable advertisements and absolutely unreadable ones. He heard a few words of English from two people by the taxi stand, but mostly he heard French. The taxi driver was familiar enough in type—a Middle Eastern man who spoke acceptable English—but the DJ on his radio spoke French between French songs. The streetlights were slimmer, the roads were rougher and the billboards advertised brands Pete had never heard of. Outside the taxi, some of the houses had green-grey roofs with high peaks like the roof of the Hotel Macdonald in Edmonton. The security buzzer to François's building on Lalonde Avenue in Montreal had a thinner sound than the buzzers Pete had heard in Edmonton apartments. This buzzer sounded more nasal. Alien. The steps in the staircase to the third floor creaked differently, and the air in the stairwell was humid. When François opened the door, Pete received another dose of foreignness. The owner of the house-sit had shiny black eyes, a short beard and short messed-up hair like a European model. His English was heavily accented, though Pete could understand him.

François had moved his personal items to his mother's house, where he would stay for a few days before heading to Vancouver to work at his company's branch office. Pete had use of an outfitted galley kitchen, the bathroom and the bedroom, where the bed was stripped bare, with folded fresh sheets on top. He said Pete could use the computer in the bedroom if he wanted to, though the network was slow. He gave Pete the contact information for the building manager and directed Pete to two pages of handwritten instructions on the kitchen table. Most of the instructions related to pet care. François introduced the pets—a tabby, a calico and a black-and-tan chihuahua, who looked up politely from their three identical brown pet beds at the base of the balcony window. Pete asked, "Can you write the names down for me?" The written names didn't help much: Minouche, Nigella and Popo. Pete couldn't imagine ever saying the names out loud.

François leaned over his pets, stroked them gently, one by one, and murmured to them in French. Then, in what seemed like no time at all, Pete was alone.

With the apartment key safely in his back pocket, he did a tour of his new quarters. In the living room, a flat-screen television was mounted above a gas fireplace flanked by two large windows that gave a clear view of the brown and grey roofs of the walk-ups and the broccoli tufts of the tall trees planted between the buildings. The round, brown coffee table in front of the fireplace had nothing on or under it. A papasan chair with dark pink cushions faced the coffee table and shelving unit, and a brown sofa with more pink cushions faced the fireplace and the television. The parquet hardwood floor was bare but shiny with fresh varnish. The chihuahua snoring and the traffic burring from outside were the only sounds.

Above the sofa was a large square painting of a woman's head on a yellow background. The woman had dark brown hair in an updo, and the updo was splattered with yellow paint as though the background had dripped onto it. The woman's eyes were hidden by long straight bangs, so what dominated the face was the woman's thin nose, high cheekbones and scarlet-lipped open mouth. Her open mouth was a big toothless abyss. She seemed to be yelling out of the canvas. Pete even looked behind him to see what the woman was yelling at, but all he saw were the white Ikea dining table and chairs.

Pete looked again. He wondered if in fact the woman was a woman.

A wave of vertigo slammed into Pete. He stumbled onto the sofa and shut his eyes. He opened and closed his eyes three times, but the spinning did not stop.

Okay, I get it, Pete thought. He'd gotten out of Edmonton easy. The easy part was over. Tomorrow he had to call Philip, the person he was named after, at his B&B, the place that, according to Gilda, Beth and even Ralph, he had spent part of his early life.

The dizziness weakened to become not so much a rotation but a vibration.

He didn't know Philip's last name, and he didn't know the name of the B&B. He knew what street it was on, though. Over the years, he had managed to lump together the name of the truck model his father had favoured for transporting musical instruments and children and the name of the neighbourhood where his mother had taken him all those years ago. Suburban, and Saint-Urbain.

24

NORVELL THINKS ABOUT PETE WHILE HELPING A CUSTOMER BUY DICE

The woman wanted to buy some dice for her friend as a birthday present. Norvell came out from around the counter and took her to the tower of dice. The tower was a four-sided stand of Norvell's height. Clear plastic bins were arrayed around it from knee height to its summit, and the dice in the bins were organized by size and number of sides.

"Do you know what kind of dice you want to buy?" Norvell asked.

"Not really."

Newbies tended to be attracted to the jewel-toned, translucent cube dice. The regular white and black cubes bored them, and the non-cubes scared them. Some people didn't understand why dice could have four sides, eight sides, twelve sides and twenty sides. They didn't consider those shapes to be dice.

"Should I buy one of each?" the woman asked.

"That depends on what games your friend plays."

Pete's knowledge of dice far exceeded his own. Pete knew about platonic solids and their suitability as dice.

"I don't know that it matters," she said.

Norvell had taken it upon himself to be a mentor to Pete about history, philosophy and literature, yet in many ways Pete was more in tune with the world than Norvell could ever be. He was more book learned than street learned. Street learning was more valuable. That was why his mentor role hadn't extended into anything more personal. Norvell didn't know much about friendship or what went beyond friendship.

"Why are there so many?" she murmured. Since she didn't make eye contact, Norvell understood that she was talking to herself. She didn't intend for Norvell to answer. He wondered if he needed to help her anymore. He had to unlock the bins for her. Maybe he should go back to the counter and grab the key.

Norvell wanted to gain control of his life. He thought that he had done this by moving out and by getting into a romantic relationship. He understood that he had managed to combine the desire for independence and for a relationship by having a boyfriend who was incarcerated. Norvell had defined "control" in a literal sense. Guards, alarms and barbed wire patrolled his relationship.

"Some games required special dice," Norvell said.

"Hmm." She twisted a bit of hair around her finger.

He had no idea what Jackson did outside the visitor room. In that sense, Jackson had control over Norvell. What Jackson did in prison was closed to him. Once Jackson had mentioned offhandedly that he'd "done things" with fellow prisoners. Frankly Norvell had expected that, but he didn't know if Jackson had been willing or not. Not all sexual activity in prison was coerced. The acts may even had been instigated by Jackson himself. Norvell remembered him joking about the "greetings" new arrivals got. He had made air quotes around the word "greetings." That had been the first time Norvell had a good look at Jackson's hands. He liked them, those short fingers, the colour contrast between the top of his index fingers and the fleshy undersides of their tips.

"Do the colours matter?" she asked.

"It depends on the game."

Norvell knew that he was sexually attracted to Pete. He had never had sex with anyone (not including himself). When he thought about sex nowadays, he thought not of Jackson but of Pete. Now Pete was gone.

"I like the crystal ones," she said. "Maybe I should get a rainbow of colours. What is that again? ROY G. BIV?"

"That's a cool idea. Keep in mind, though, that some games need specific kinds of dice. There are games that need four-sided dice, or twelve-sided dice."

"Oh, I know that." The woman laughed. "I just need to decide what I should get him. It's almost a joke gift."

He knew homosexuality was socially accepted in many circles, but in his family circle, it was not. In fandom circles, some groups accepted homosexuality while others did not. The fandom circles that only included men revealed an implied or unconscious homosexual desire. Nevertheless, he had seen enough online comments of "fag!" or "that's gay" that echoed his experiences being taunted in high school with "fag" to realize that the default in society generally was anti-homosexual.

"I see," Norvell said.

Pete seemed hypermasculine. He talked about going to bars and dating women. In other ways, though, Pete seemed more gender neutral. A macho man would not work in a game store. Pete seemed to help his mother cook Sunday suppers, and he dressed in a fairly gender-neutral way.

"Do you have gift receipts?" she asked.

Norvell said, "We keep a gift registry of sorts, so that if your friend wants to return them we can look him up in our records. We can't take back opened boxes, though."

"Oh."

All a person had to do was spend some time reading about the medieval European church to see that the sexual anxiety people had today was a remnant of the church's unwillingness to acknowledge the kinds of sexuality that in the past people used to accept. What had ruined things was Manichaeism, fear of sexually transmitted diseases and the need to constrain female sexuality so as to maintain men's political and economic dominance.

"It seems like you need some time to decide." Norvell had learned that phrase by watching Pete deal with customers. "If you want,

I can show you some packaged dice sets we have at the front of the store. Just come get me when you're ready, and I'll show you. And if you have any other questions, please stop me or any other staff member, and we'll be happy to help you out." These phrases Norvell had also learned from Pete.

"Great, thanks!"

Norvell returned to the front counter. No one else was in the building except for Jerry, who was working in the back. Soon Linda or Una would come in for the noon rush. Pete would not come in. Pete, with his swagger, his intellectual ineptness, his reliance on verbal barbs to conceal his naiveté, his tendency to interrupt a perfectly good argument with inane objections, his habit of mixing two similar Slurpee flavours in his cup so that whatever subtle differences may have existed were erased by the mixture, his custom of describing, in excruciating detail, his bar adventures from the night before. Pete was gone.

25

TWO PORTRAITS OF LONELINESS

Norvell Batty

For as long as he could remember, his eyes were slits in a round ruddy face. His neck disappeared into his domed shoulders, and his arms plumped out of short sleeves like smokies. His hands, usually curled into anxious fists, were dimpled above the knuckles by excess fat.

His school grades lingered around the low average side, and since he feared the kind of mockery he received from his sporty, macho uncles, he didn't talk much to teachers or classmates, so he had no way to make an impression. In grade ten, he joined the wrestling club at the urging of his older brother, Vince. Unlike Vince, Norvell showed little promise. He gained weight but didn't grow sleek. He stopped coming to practices and was withdrawn from the roster by mid-season. Vince had wanted to get him out of his shell, and when that failed, Vince shrugged off the failure as part of Norvell's essence. His parents made no demands. They insisted only that their youngest finish high school, something they had never done; he graduated a year after his brother, so the accolades went to Vince. Norvell socialized almost exclusively at the food tables at cousins' birthday parties and family picnics. When he grew older, he found more satisfaction interacting with people on *World of Warcraft* forums. After graduation, he tumbled into a part-time job at the donair shop owned by his aunt's new boyfriend, Ted. Although grateful for the money, Norvell saw his own face every second day in the mirrored front entry of the donair place, and he couldn't deny to himself that he was sad.

One day on a free Saturday, he walked to Tokens and watched a World of Warcraft card game tournament. He instantly liked the people, including the owner, Jerry, though he didn't say so at first. He didn't talk to anyone that day. He returned, however, and sooner than he expected, he began speaking to people there. Eventually he joined Tokens's WoW club. He spent many hours with like-minded people in the game room; at Tokens he talked more than all his years at home and school combined.

One night he found himself running the game room's till when an employee didn't show up. "Do you mind keeping an eye on things?" Jerry had asked Norvell.

That day Norvell realized he had some basic competencies. He could handle cash well. While he was handing back cash for jujubes, a customer stopped by and asked for help finding Killer Bunnies. Norvell knew where to look, since he had browsed the shelves many times during breaks between rounds. After his third stint as game-room cashier, Jerry asked if Norvell would like a part-time job in the main retail space.

Norvell was good at his job. When customers asked him a question, he had the sensitivity to know when to give advice and when to let them think. One quiet night he read the box notes for a board game called The Castles of Burgundy, and he didn't understand the history behind the game. For the sake of his profession, as he considered it to be, he took non-credit courses at the University of Alberta's Faculty of Extension ("Gnosticism and the Occult" and "Great Works of Western Literature") with the few hundred dollars he had inherited from his grandmother's estate. When his money ran out, he asked to work full time at Tokens, and Jerry agreed. Norvell realized that Jerry liked him, which was something new—to be liked rather than loved grudgingly. With a full-time job, Norvell expressed interest in the rental house in Lamoureux that Uncle Ted had hinted could be his. Soon he was living there and tending his uncle's pets. His parents sold their house that year to become snowbirds, and with his brother living in Surrey, he spent a lot of time family free, except for his visits to Jackson. All told, his life was a humble package.

At least until he met Pete. Pete epitomized the extroverted rabble-rouser that the Batty family admired but had failed to produce. Pete was hardly a mover and shaker, but his family's background (government worker, professional musician) gave Pete better odds than the Battys, as retail clerks and semi-skilled labourers, had.

Norvell loved Pete.

Gilda Peterborough

Halfway through elementary school, Philippa rejected Gilda. When Philippa decided to attend a different junior high school, Gilda knew the break was formal and probably permanent. When Philippa became Pete, the separation between the twins widened into a canyon.

At ten years old, Gilda decided that she couldn't tell anyone about her and her family, so she shut the door on the world except for the small crack that she sometimes called hope but usually called the pragmatism of daily life.

This pragmatism derived from her understanding of adulthood. From her mother, she adopted the belief that she had to do something useful—"productive," her mother said. She chose a career with no connection to musicianship or medical services. She knew what she liked—reading—so she poked about for a way to apply her likes to her livelihood. She found a publishing program at MacEwan University College. For part-time work, she proofread for a medical journal and took the late shift at the *Edmonton Journal* as a casual nighttime proofreader. She joined the Editors' Association of Canada. She dressed in dark blue and grey in public, including in class, and she did her best to seem friendly in a business-casual way. Against the odds that her more cynical professors offered, a year after graduation, the sleep-deprived and emotionally solitary

Gilda landed a job at Melon Press as a receptionist and then as an editorial assistant.

One night after work, hope peered through the crack in the nearly closed door. To celebrate the end of harrowing two-volume conference proceedings about doctor-assisted suicide, the project staff spent the night in an Irish pub. There Gilda played darts with the warehouse guys, drank beer with Manuka, dished gossip with Jensee and shouted at the hockey game on the televisions above the bar.

Hope and pragmatism dovetailed that night. On other nights, she sat in her cubicle struggling to winch a project upwards at her end so that the production could slip back on schedule. On those nights, Gilda rubbed eyes scalded with screen fatigue and long-suppressed tears and wished that the light from that crack in the door would gleam again, touch her lightly, like a priest brushing ashes on her forehead, and make her a believer again.

26

GILDA FINDS BURGHIE IN THE NEIGHBOURHOOD

The day after Pete left town, Gilda came home late from work. She microwaved the leftover curried peas and chicken breasts that her mother had put on a plate in the refrigerator, poured herself a mug of still-warm tea from the teapot by the sink and joined Beth in the basement.

Beth was watching CBC News in the near dark. "I found out a few things today," she said without preamble.

"Like what?" Gilda winced at the snip in her voice, but she didn't have the energy to apologize. She had worn herself out at work staving off anxiety so that she could be productive. The anxiety had put up a fight. In the too-frequent unproductive stretches of time, Gilda had thought about Pete's phone call on Saturday and about all that Gilda and Beth had not said to each other after Pete hung up.

"I called your father after church today to see if he's heard from Philippa."

Gilda couldn't remember the last time that Beth had willingly talked to Ralph. Once she and Philippa turned eighteen, all that visiting Ralph stuff, Beth had said, was up to them. On that eighteenth birthday, Beth had invited Ralph to a birthday dinner at The Keg, and after he turned her down, Beth had never again called Ralph, at least to Gilda's knowledge. "And?"

"The last time Philippa spoke to your father was the same night that she called us from Whyte Avenue. You thought she seemed a little drunk."

Beth had been a little drunk, too, but Gilda decided not to mention that. "What did Phil tell Dad that time?"

"Your father said Philippa tried to pick a fight with him. More likely Ralph tried to pick a fight with Philippa."

"For sure."

"When I said that I thought that your father had tried to pick a fight, me and your father got into a fight. The useful part of our conversation ended."

Gilda appreciated her mother's willingness to deal with Ralph so that Gilda didn't have to. Now that line of inquiry was exhausted. "What should we do?" she asked.

"She's been gone only one day. Maybe she'll get in touch with someone in the next few days."

"What if he doesn't?"

"I don't know." Beth put down her teacup and switched off the television. "By the way, what happened to your car?"

Gilda hadn't expected to have to answer that question today, but she had been preparing herself for the eventuality. "I hit something."

"Obviously, but what did you hit?"

"A post."

"You must have hit it pretty hard."

"I did."

"Not whiplash hard, I hope."

"No."

"When did this happen?"

"A while ago. Mom, I've been pretty preoccupied these days, what with Pete and this big meeting I have coming up."

Beth touched Gilda's arm in commiseration. "I've smashed a few headlights in my day. Lucky for you it's summer, not winter."

"I'll get it fixed before daylight time ends."

"What is this meeting you mentioned?"

Gilda had told Beth about it more than once, but the details seemed not to stick in Beth's mind. "The annual retreat on Friday is going to focus on my new project. You know, the crime series."

"Oh, right." Beth had the air of not having remembered. "Presentations are tough. I don't have to give them, but when one of the counsellors has to do one, I have to walk on eggshells around them."

That reminded Gilda of something she had to do. She had to tell Burghie. She hadn't told Beth about Burghie, so she couldn't be explicit about why she had to go to her bedroom now. "I should go to bed, Mom. I'm worn out."

"Okay, dear," Beth said. "I'm staying up."

Gilda went into her room and texted Burghie. She waited fifteen minutes before remembering that likely he was working and unable to answer his phone. She wanted to get this over with. She must be efficient. Face-to-face meetings were more efficient; she had read that. Besides, it was like she was firing Burghie. Doing that face-to-face was more humane. Not that she had ever fired anyone before.

When she left her bedroom, her mother was still sitting in front of the television, where two men in a darkened lab leaned over a stainless-steel counter and examined a piece of fabric in a clear plastic tray.

"Mom," Gilda said, "I'm going for a walk."

"A walk?"

"I need to clear my head."

Beth looked speculatively at Gilda. "Walks can do that, yes."

In Paul's Restaurant, two tables were occupied, and Burghie, who was standing like a soldier by the cashier counter when she walked in, brought out a pot of her requested tea with no delay.

"I have an update," Gilda said after Burghie eased himself into the bench opposite hers in the booth. "Pete's gone to Montreal."

Wheels in his brain seemed to whirl and then click. "When?"

"Sunday. He didn't say when he was coming back. He told us the day before he left."

Burghie leaned back, rubbed his cheek and chin as though it helped him to think.

Gilda said, "I don't suppose he got in touch with you."

Burghie shook his head. "Did he call you with a cellphone?"

The quiet turning of gears in Burghie's head had manufactured a good question. "No," Gilda said. "From a public phone somewhere."

"I didn't know there were such things anymore."

"Well, there are."

Burghie winced. Gilda's voice must have had a bit of a chip in it.

"Sorry," she said. "It's just that this is so stressful. Work is stressing me out too. I have a big meeting at work this week."

At the word "sorry," Burghie's edginess diminished. He had always seemed mellow because of his deadpan face, but she suspected that his placid demeanour hid a roil of emotions. His approach to surprise and disorder probably explained why as a teen he had been able to ride Pete's emotional turbulence. Burghie would be an excellent bureaucrat. He would be the barometer, the canary in a mineshaft. If Burghie started balking, management would have to fix things immediately rather than stall and wait for the crisis to blow over.

"Is there anything I can do?" he asked.

"I came here to say that I don't know if there is anything more you can do." Gilda smiled in a way she hoped didn't seem insincere. "I appreciate what you've done so far. But now that he's out of the city . . . "

Burghie nodded. "If you can think of anything that you need help with, I'm here."

"I appreciate that, Burghie."

Gilda made to get up. Burghie said, "Do you want something to eat or to drink? More tea?"

"No, I better go. It's getting late for me, and I'm sure you have things to do."

Burghie stood when Gilda did and followed her to the entrance. "See you," he said.

Gilda reached out her hand. Burghie stared at his hand for a second, then took hers. His hand was much larger than hers.

On the walk home, she took the same route she had taken the first time she walked home from the restaurant. She had been cradling the pieces of the puddle-jumper in her hands then; tonight she could pay attention to the houses she was walking past, to the darkening sky and the leaves that fluttered on their branches, the colours of the flowers in the hanging baskets and the sprays of daylilies planted against the tiny square bungalows manicured by the elderly people that populated the neighbourhood. She felt badly about interrupting Burghie's life to keep her sibling under control. Now Montreal would have to deal with Pete, at least until Gilda could figure out how to get him home, and at least until she had any energy for it. She had her own problems. She couldn't say that to Beth, though. She would have to be calm, cool and collected, like Burghie.

#

The next evening, Gilda was putting the last of the supper dishes away when Beth walked into the kitchen from the direction of the front door. Normally Beth returned from church through the back door.

"Guess who I found on the way home? One of Pete's old school friends."

"What?"

"Come here. Out front."

Gilda dried her hands on the dish towel and untied her apron. She followed Beth into the front sitting room and outside. In front of the house, in the gutter of the road, was Burghie, who straddled a road bike. He wore the black clothes and white apron of his uniform at Paul's.

"Do you remember Dallas?" Beth asked.

"Burghie." She tried to give as much weight as she could to the word without betraying any specific emotion for her mother to clue in to, but with enough emotion and volume for Burghie to understand that she was much surprised to see him in front of her house.

"Burghie! I remember that name," Beth said. "Dallas was a blank to me, I have to admit. Burghie. Burghie on a bike even more so. Why is that?"

"I used to ride my bike here." Burghie rocked on his bike slowly as he spoke. His face was impassive. The impassivity and the rocking Gilda remembered from a long sequence of mornings, Burghie oscillating on his bike in front of the house while Pete wrangled himself out the door.

Gilda said, "What brings you to the neighbourhood, Burghie?"

He didn't answer soon enough for Beth's taste, so she answered for him. "He says he works in the neighbourhood, and he decided to visit his old haunts. He works at Paul's Restaurant. You know that one?"

"Yes, I know that one," Gilda said.

Burghie lowered his head and stared at the edge of the curb.

"I told him I hoped he wasn't looking for Pete," Beth said, "because Pete just left town. He up and moved to Montreal. I don't suppose he got in touch with you beforehand, Burghie. You used to spend quite a bit of time together, and he may have contacted you. I hear that's what Mormons do before they can become full-fledged Mormons. They have to call all the people they committed sins against and apologize."

Burghie lifted his head part way through Beth's speech as though seeing her would help him understand her point. When Beth stopped talking, his eyes darted at Gilda, as though waiting for her to intervene. Gilda didn't intervene. She wanted him to feel uncomfortable.

"Yes," Burghie said finally. "I was looking for Pete."

"That's too bad," Beth said.

"Pete hasn't lived here for a while," Gilda said. "I thought you knew that, Burghie."

"Maybe I did once," Burghie said. "I guess I forgot."

"If I remember, Burghie knows quite a bit about cars," Beth said to Gilda. "Maybe he can help you with your car problem."

Burghie looked up at Gilda with interest shielded partially behind embarrassment. "What kind of problem?"

Gilda looked at him steadily. "A busted headlight and front end."

"How did you get it?"

"It doesn't matter."

Beth said to Burghie, "Am I right about you and cars? I have a vague memory of you and another friend working on a car together."

Burghie tilted his head. "I don't remember that. I'm pretty good with bikes, but not cars."

"I could have sworn," Beth said.

Burghie thought some more. "My grandfather is pretty good with cars. Or maybe you're thinking of Granv."

"Granv! That's a name I remember too. Whatever happened to Granv?"

"I don't know. He moved out of town."

"Too bad." She half-turned toward Gilda while she spoke to Burghie. "I think Gilda is cheaping out. Maybe she doesn't want to get her insurance involved."

"Mom!"

"I don't know how else to explain why you're driving around with a broken headlight. That's not like you."

"I told you why, Mom."

Beth returned her focus to Burghie. "Maybe your grandfather can help."

Burghie shuffled on his bike. The bell on his bike pinged. "My grandfather isn't the best person to go to," he said. "He's kind of grumpy."

"Mom, when I have the time I'll take it in."

"Why don't you come in for a tea, Burghie?" Beth said. "Or do you drink coffee?"

"Thanks for the invitation, Mrs. Peterborough." Burghie smiled nervously, tipped his head down before looking up again. "I should head to work now. My break is almost over."

"It's Ms. Conrad. It's good to hear that restaurants are giving their staff breaks. I've read in the papers about some restaurants not doing that."

"I'm fine, Ms. Conrad." Burghie put a foot on the bike pedal as though to push off. "But I should go."

"If you're ever in the neighbourhood and you have the time, come on over. It's nice to see Pete and Gilda's old friends again."

Beth stayed outside to watch Burghie pedal away, but Gilda went immediately into the house and back into the kitchen.

"Isn't that strange," Beth said upon entering the kitchen, "to see one of Pete's friends at a time like this? It's karma or something. Isn't that what people say? Karma?"

"That's not really karma." Gilda grabbed a drying towel and a pot. "Karma is something different."

"Too bad about his grandfather." Beth picked up another drying towel. "I wonder if he has family problems. Sometimes these intergenerational households have a lot of tension."

Gilda thought, Mom, you work in health services as an administrative assistant, you aren't an actual counsellor. Out loud, she said, "I can finish the dishes myself, Mom. You go ahead and watch TV. I think I saw a commercial about a new episode of *CSI* on tonight."

"Well, that can't be. It's the middle of summer. Everything is in reruns."

"I can do the dishes myself, Mom."

Beth shrugged. "Sure, then. I'll see you downstairs."

Gilda finished drying and putting away the dishes while experiencing a grumpy mood herself. Burghie. She picked up her phone and began to text him but stopped. He was back at work and probably wouldn't answer her text anyway.

She went downstairs and watched an old *Cops* episode with her mother until she couldn't stand being there.

"I'm going for a walk, Mom."

"Again?"

"It's nice out."

"Maybe you're getting addicted to it. That's good. It's much better than going to the gym in the morning like you do. The sunshine gives Vitamin D."

Addiction was not the word that Gilda had for it, she thought, as she walked to Paul's Restaurant. Necessity was more like it. Necessity was taking her away from other things. She could have taken her car to a mechanic with all the time she was spending going to and from Paul's. This Burghie and Pete situation was swallowing her life.

Mandy fetched Burghie out of the kitchen for her, and he sat in the booth with Gilda.

"I'm not sure what that was," Gilda said. "What was that?"

"Just like I told your mom. I was on break, and I decided to ride around the old neighbourhood."

"Do you always ride your bike to work?"

Burghie nodded.

"Well, if I ever need to get my bike fixed, I know where to go," Gilda said.

He smiled mischievously. "Do you need your bike fixed?"

"No!"

His humorousness fled under the pressure of her firm negative, but he didn't become docile. "You're the one who came back into my life, not the other way around."

"Come into your life. That sounds melodramatic."

"Sorry." His head dip indicated submissiveness, but Burghie didn't stay quiet. He spoke, slowly, as though piecing together what he was saying. "Maybe it's good to return to the past. Sometimes life needs more continuity. It was weird for me to get a job in this neighbourhood, I know. And it's weirder to see you again. To hear Pete's voice on the phone. But it's a good weird. Seeing you again, hearing Pete, seeing your mom, reminded me that the past isn't ever gone. It goes on whether you know it or not, in that direction you stopped looking in. Then one day you look in that direction again, and there it is."

"Burghie," Gilda said. "You're a philosopher."

He smiled, a weary one, but weary with a sense of release behind it. "I'm not just a pretty face."

Gilda laughed, and Burghie asked, "You aren't mad at me, are you?"

"I was just surprised to see you. I hadn't told my mom about you, and I didn't want to spring our little stratagem on her. I'm sorry I pretended that I hadn't seen you for a while."

"No, I get it," Burghie said. "Your mom seems cool and everything, but sometimes you have to be careful around your family."

"She's hardly cool."

"I think she is." Burghie's expression darkened. "Better than what I have to deal with at my place."

"Your grumpy grandfather."

"Yeah."

"Why are we still living with our parents, Burghie?"

"Comfort. And economics."

"It's not so comfortable."

Burghie said, "It's perceived comfort. The economics, though, are real, at least for me."

"Well," Gilda said, "if Pete ever moves back here, maybe you and him can be roomies."

"Maybe all three of us," Burghie said.

"That would be something. Me and Pete living together."

"You did when you were kids."

"But Pete took pains to make sure he went to a different school than I did. Then he moved out. Now he's really moved out."

"Do you think he left to get away from you?" The eyes behind Burghie's glasses were impassive. Maybe to him the question was innocent, but it wasn't innocent to Gilda.

She said, "I don't know why he left."

"Look," he said after a pause. "I have to get back to work, but you can drop in whenever you want, or text me, if you need anything."

"If by some miracle Pete reaches out to you, I'd appreciate it if you told me, even if he tells you not to tell me."

As she walked home, she congratulated herself for not laying Burghie off, as it were. He had useful Pete experience. Pete and Burghie had been co-conspirators in many plots, including the notorious dildo escapade, and she suspected there were many more escapades that she didn't know about. Burghie seemed more mature now too. That didn't mean she shouldn't check up on him and remind him of his responsibilities. He was on her team, and team members needed to be policed.

27

BURGHIE MORE OR LESS PROCLAIMS HIS UNDYING LOVE FOR GILDA

The evening before the annual meeting, Gilda was standing in the middle of her bedroom with her eyes closed, practising her yogic breathing, when her phone pinged.

It was a text from Burghie. "Can we meet at Pauls 2nite 930."

She had been standing like that, door shut, for an hour, in an attempt to exorcise the day's events. At work, Manuka had circulated the meeting agenda, and the only item listed for the afternoon was "Case Study: True Crimes of Alberta." Two days earlier, Ian Auma had emailed Gilda to the effect that his book was proceeding as he'd hoped: "crazy and fun and unexpected." She didn't like the first or last of those words, so she dreaded having to bring that email up with the entire company. They would be primed for critical analysis by that point in the meeting. On top of her work mess was the chaos of Pete, especially now that she knew he had moved to Montreal for mysterious reasons. Burghie's text piled on stimulation that she didn't need. What could she do, though? He was on her team, and loyalty to the team was everything.

Gilda sat on her bed and responded to Burghie's text. "Y?"

"Got 2 tel u somtin."

She tried and failed to continue her breathing exercises. Instead, she went on YouTube and watched baby bat rescue videos for about an hour until it was time to leave.

Gilda left her bedroom to see her mother in the television room ironing a white blouse and watching *Blue Bloods*. Gilda said, "I have to go, Mom."

"Is something wrong? It's not Pete, is it?"

"No. It's just a friend. He wants to go out for coffee."

"A friend?"

"Yes, Mom, I have friends." Gilda half-faked the mild outrage of hurt feelings.

"That's nice," Beth said. "If you need to drive, you can take my car."

"We're just going to Paul's Restaurant. I'll walk."

"Paul's? Why does that place keep popping up now? Is it trendy? It's been there forever, and I haven't been."

"I can give you a review of their tea, but that's about it."

Gilda felt Beth's eyes on her back until she reached the stairs. On the way out the back door, she heard the squeal of wheels and a gunshot.

A summer sunset had tinted the sky by the time she reached the restaurant. The parking lot had only two cars in it. Next to the phone booth in the corner of the parking lot, Burghie waited astride his bike. He wore his work clothes, including his long white apron, which was tucked between his legs.

"Can you ride with that apron on?"

"Yeah. I have to wash the apron tonight anyway." His face was more mobile than usual. He seemed shifty-eyed, and for the most part, Burghie was a steady-gaze person.

"What did you need to tell me? Is it about Pete?"

"No." Burghie squeezed both handbrakes on his bike, and the brakes whimpered. "No."

"What then?" Gilda didn't want to be here. She wanted to be home, looking over her prep notes about the *True Crimes* series, or meditating, or flipping channels while her mother ironed in the background. She'd even prefer sitting on the sofa next to Pete while he pontificated on what he knew about the world, which wasn't much, fumbling gamely over the things he didn't know while she corrected him or batted away his insults.

"I wanted you to know," Burghie said, "that this thing with Pete has been good." He stopped. "I don't mean that Pete disappearing is good," he continued. "I mean that it's been good to get back in touch."

He rocked back and forth on his bicycle seat. Something squeaked. The frame was too small for him: he should be struggling to touch the ground with his toes, but he sat atop it with his feet flat on the ground. It was probably the same bike he rode to their house in the morning to meet Pete on the way to junior high school. Sometimes she had watched from the bathroom window as Pete and Burghie left together, Pete on foot and Burghie on his bike in the gutter beside him.

He said, "It's been good seeing you again."

"Maybe that's why I find you easy to work with. We've known each other a long time."

"Almost ten years."

"This thing with Pete is tough, and I'm grateful for your help."

"Yeah," Burghie said faintly. He strengthened his voice. "We know where he is, though."

"I'm not sure what to do. It's a free country, and he's an adult, but I don't want to lose touch with him. I still think I can do some good, you know? I need to change the way he feels somehow. I don't think it's right that he pretends we don't exist."

"Totally." Burghie licked his lips. "Everything you said just now is exactly how I feel."

"That's great. Being on the same page is really helpful."

"I'm glad you know we're on the same page."

"I've developed a sixth sense about that kind of thing. It comes from having a job where everything has a deadline and everyone is always running late. I've learned to notice when people are working at cross purposes."

"That's good." Burghie lifted one foot off the ground to its pedal, as if he were about to cycle off, but slowly he returned his foot to the ground. "As long as you think I'm helping you."

"Helping me? You mean Pete. And you. He's your friend."

"I lost touch with him."

"Pete is an expert at losing touch. It's that macho thing he puts on to protect himself. I actually think that it's because you got in touch with him that he decided to leave."

"Oh."

"He saw his past chasing him down, and he didn't want to deal with it."

"We all do that, though," Burghie said softly. "Not deal with things. Protect ourselves."

Gilda shivered and looked up at the sky. She had walked out of the house without a sweater, and the hairs on her arms were arching themselves. The late evening chill warned that the seemingly never-ending summer day was coming to an end.

"You're cold," he said.

"That's what happens at night." She smiled to reassure Burghie that she was fine: he seemed nervous. "I better get home now. It's late. I have that meeting tomorrow."

"The retreat."

"Exactly. Time for me to retreat too."

"Do you want me to walk you home?"

"No, it's just a few blocks, and it's still daylight, basically."

"It's no problem. I'd like to."

"You have a much longer way to go than I do."

"Okay," Burghie said. "Well, then. I'll let you go."

Slowly he turned his bicycle around and pedalled away. He had pulled the long apron up so that it bunched at his waist, but one loose flap of white material waved forlornly at her as he rode away.

When Gilda was a block from home, she tried to remember why she had gone to meet Burghie in the first place. He had texted her. He had something to tell her. What was it?

Only later, while she was flipping channels alone before going to bed, her mother having already gone upstairs, did Gilda realize what Burghie had been trying to tell her.

She left the television on a show with two moody young people in a dark room glowering at each other amid the rising sound of a mournful cello. Vampires, probably. She went to the bathroom to brush her teeth, and by the time she came back into the television room, the vampires were kissing.

28

MELON PRESS'S ANNUAL RETREAT

The annual retreat took place in a conference room at the Marriott Hotel in the south end of the city; Tom had insisted on this spot, Manuka had reported, because he wanted to remove the staff from their geographical comfort zone. Tobil, the art and production manager, had a different explanation: Tom wanted to use the word "retreat" without having to spend the money on a real retreat, which should take place in a quiet natural setting over a weekend, not in an aging hotel off the main highway during normal working hours. Normally Gilda liked the austerity of conference rooms, the hollow echoes against the open ceilings, the air dry and metallic, as though some heavy-duty astringent had been applied to all surfaces. As soon as she walked into the hotel's conference room, however, she felt uncomfortable. In part she was reacting to the conversation with Burghie the night before. Maybe, after yesterday, the air took on a metaphorical value, represented the aridity of her social life and the implications of that aridity regarding Burghie and her inability to reciprocate Burghie's feelings for her.

The other problem was the room's layout. She had attended a few conferences in her life, so she was unfazed by the room being too big for the number of people and by the overstuffed buffet table covered in glasses, cups, thermoses, pitchers, muffins, mini-Danishes and fruit platters. What surprised her was the café-style decor. In the centre of the room were four round tables covered in red and white checkered tablecloths. Draped over each tablecloth was a giant sheet of white paper. Centred on the paper were a box of coloured felt markers, a pad of sticky notes and a vase with red and white carnations. As well, the room contained a stranger, an astonishingly handsome young blond man in a navy-blue knit cardigan and slim-fitting black pants. He looked like a male model from the Hudson's Bay flyers that came with the newspaper. He and Manuka stood together at a podium in front of the tables.

Gilda had time to fix herself a tea at the buffet table before Manuka's voice hissed then boomed over the loudspeakers for everyone to take a seat. Gilda chose the table farthest from the podium. Joining her at her table were Tobil, Neela and Jensee, who trotted after her from the buffet table with a minty tea. Greedily, Jensee fingered the table's pad of sticky notes.

As soon as the four tables were filled, Manuka introduced the handsome stranger as Dodge Chino, a facilitator from Rogers Ainsling and Associates. Manuka stood aside, and Dodge centred himself in front of the microphone. "Tom asked me to do an exercise with you. He'll be here after the break." Dodge had a draggy California accent that added glamour to the instructions he subsequently gave. The staff were to discuss the "catalytic" question written in green felt marker in the centre of each table's paper runner: "How can Melon Press become the best mid-sized publisher in the province?" The question was broad to allow stakeholders (as he called his audience) to generate their own ideas, and they had to encourage each other to contribute. People could talk, but people could also write ideas on the paper. "Remember," Dodge drawled, "listening is another form of contribution." They had half an hour.

"Half an hour?" Tobil grumbled. "That's a long time."

Jensee placed a piece of paper on her knee. She scribbled a note without looking down and slid the slip into Gilda's lap. In wide, fat lowercase letters, the note read, "Dodge Chino is hot." Gilda crumpled the note and stuffed it into her pant pocket so that it wouldn't accidentally appear on the table.

For half an hour, the people at Gilda's table turned the question round, argued, scribbled on sticky notes and doodled with coloured markers on the giant white paper. If Pete were here, he would laugh at the sight of adults writing with markers. Gilda liked it, though. It freed her mind from the vicious little martinet of a superego that interfered with Gilda whenever she tried to plan or write something. "That was terrible," the superego would say. "You have got to be kidding. Are you sure you have that right?" The superego was the part of her that made Gilda proofread her text messages. She was grateful for that aspect of her personality with respect to her job, which called for an attention to detail that most people couldn't tolerate. Her reputation probably led to the table choosing Gilda to arrange the sticky notes on the giant piece of paper in the way that she found most effective.

When Dodge called time, each person had to move to a different table, where they would do the same exercise with a new group of people. "The goal here," Dodge said with his Santa Monica smile, "is to connect ideas from your last table with ideas generated at the new table."

At her second table, Gilda sat with Cheyenne the ordering and shipping person, Ivan "Turbo" Anderson the head of marketing and public relations, and Laney the marketing assistant, all of whom took the exercise much more seriously than Gilda's first table had. At this table, Gilda's idea to "make a formal policy and procedure manual to preserve corporate memory" wasn't pushed aside in favour of Jensee's "get health-club membership discounts."

After another half hour, each person had to return to their first table, "seed" the table with ideas from the second table and summarize one key idea from the resulting conversation on a sticky note. From the second table Gilda had come away with the idea that change was unavoidable, and the task of a business was to steer itself toward the most beneficial changes, rather than steer away from changes that might harm it. Gilda's summative sticky note reiterated the corporate memory idea, but with the additional idea of adaptive corporate intelligence systems. Tobil's and Neela's notes both had a variant of the idea of wanting fewer non-productive meetings. Jensee's sticky note, "I bet Turbo is banging Laney," appeared in Gilda's lap. Gilda put Jensee's note in her pocket.

Dodge then dragged away ("reaped" was his word) each table's giant paper, sticky notes and all, and the staff engulfed the buffet table for a coffee break. While everyone else foraged, Dodge and Manuka mounted the papers on the wall for everyone to look at. People were supposed to walk around with their little paper plates of fingerling Danishes and strawberry slices and look at what people had written on the papers. Many people, including Gilda, did the walkabout. During the break, Tom waltzed in with a waggle of fingers in greeting and a grin. "How's it going?" he said to everyone he passed on the way to the podium.

Tom's arrival signalled the end of the break. Dodge announced "a café of the whole," whereby every person at every table, out loud, stated to the entire room the one main idea they had gotten from the meeting so far. Manuka scribbled down each idea using another stack of sticky notes, these ones pink instead of yellow. Gilda's main idea was "people seem genuinely interested in making Melon Press a great place to work." Jensee said, "People want to get out of doing actual work." Neela said, "People want to communicate better," and Tobil said, "There are deep divisions within the company."

During the buffet lunch, Gilda couldn't eat. She walked around and appraised the swirls and scribbles on the papers on the wall. She had fun guessing who had suggested what: Tobil likely suggested "switch from Microsoft to Apple." Jensee's fingerprints were all over "better toilet paper in the woman's bathroom." Gilda had heard Turbo say many times "focus on a core clientele" and "conceptual corporate memory should derive from an adaptive corporate intelligence system." Gilda had suggested "hire an extra person in the editorial department" and "automate workflow." Her stomach tumbled and twisted.

The second half was the "Case Study Session: *True Crimes of Alberta*." A small rectangular table had appeared in front of the podium. Tom, Manuka and Dodge sat at it, facing the four tables of staff. Gilda gravitated to the same table as Jensee, Tobil and Neela. On the staff tables, someone had put agendas in front of each seat. This time, everyone was supposed to think about changes or fixes ("or even current positive processes that should be carried over," Dodge said) as they could or should be applied to the *True Crimes of Alberta* series. Jensee passed Gilda a note: "We can handle them."

Tom took over the podium. The first agenda item was "The Big Picture." As he often did, he reiterated that marketing was a continuous process and should begin "instantly upon idea conception." Next Turbo stood from his table and summarized the marketing plan. The books were supposed to appear in drug stores and chain stores that didn't ordinarily carry books. The target market was older people with attachments to the province, general mystery and crime story fans, and visiting tourists from "back home" who wanted to know more about the place where their sons and nieces had moved for work.

"How many readers does that make, then, roughly?" Tobil asked from Gilda's table.

"We don't have hard numbers," Manuka said.

Tom said, "We think, though, that the market will be similar to the market for the *Made in Alberta* cookbook."

A gasp rose up from the staff tables. The *Made in Alberta* cookbook had been an idea intended to rival the *Company's Coming* cookbook series created by a local self-publishing company that had become successful across the country and then across the continent (which was more important). Melon Press's cookbook was not as successful as the *Company's Coming* series, as Melon Press had only one book and *Company's Coming* had dozens, but their cookbook had done very well, even in other parts of the country. Nevertheless, Gilda's world view was at odds with management's. She thought that marketing came at the end of the process, rather than the beginning. She didn't say that, of course.

"We could put the name of the cookbook on the covers," Tom said. "From the creators of the *Made in Alberta* cookbook!"

Dodge had listened quietly, but he finally broke in. "It sounds like we are ready to brainstorm about the marketing of this product. Is that what everyone wants to do?"

Gilda fretted over the meeting's marginalization of Dodge. She had counted on Dodge to keep the discussion on a tidy trajectory. But now Tom was out there saying whatever came to the top of his pointy head, and Manuka was going along with it. It was criminal what Tom and Manuka were doing to Dodge. That passive aggression was typical Tom, though, popping in whenever he felt like it to shit on things. She wondered if Dodge was being set up to shield Tom's ego from any flack against his ramblings during the meeting. Tom could do what he wanted, in the end. Melon Press wasn't a non-profit organization or a government-run institution. Tom had things personally at stake. Of course, no one cared about Ian Auma, the author at the heart of the project. Everyone else pretended to care about the book, but Gilda was the only one working to make sure Ian didn't flake out and drag the whole thing down.

Manuka said, "Gilda, would you like to explain the current production status of the *True Crimes* series?"

Gilda would not like to, but she had to.

"The *True Crimes of Alberta* series will be produced one book at a time at a rate of one a year. The writer of the first book, Ian Auma, is researching the book, and he will submit his manuscript by the end of the year. The book will then go into production and be ready for print by early next year."

"So, no one here has seen the book yet," Xavier the systems administrator said from the table next to her.

"That's right," Gilda said.

"That's why we've chosen this project as a prototype," Manuka said. "We can adjust processes before the processes begin rather than during them."

"But the project has started," Tobil said. "We have a writer, and he is writing."

"Yes?" Manuka voiced the question mark because she was trying to show Tobil that she didn't approve of where he was going.

Cheyenne jumped in. "Then the *project* has started." She looked at Gilda across the red and white tablecloths that separated them. "Right?"

"Yes," Gilda said. "But not by much. It's more like that writer has started. He is a contractor and not staff."

"So," Cheyenne said, "the project *has* started."

"No one has claimed otherwise," Manuka said drily. "The writing part is not something we tend to capture anyway. We don't write the book in-house."

"Ian has a contract, though," Cheyenne said. "That's in our contract database, right?"

Gilda's frustration must have been obvious, because Tom said with a laugh, "Be careful, Cheyenne, because from the look on Gilda's face, you may be the subject of the next book in the series."

It was hard to hide one's opinions forever. Thoughts could unconsciously affect actions, even something as simple as a facial spasm or the way one interacted with others on topics unrelated to the crime. Gilda had learned to read her ineffable sibling, for example. For some time, though, Pete had hidden many things from her.

Dimly, Gilda heard Manuka say, "But that isn't part of the project per se."

"I think we're getting off track here," Dodge said.

Beth had engaged in criminal activities when she took Philippa to Montreal. She had been hiding, or trying to hide, from the legal system. Beth had been found out, despite her efforts. Of course, Beth may have wanted to be found. Maybe her plan had been to get caught and to come home to Gilda in Edmonton. If she hadn't been caught, Beth could still be living in Montreal, or God knows where else, and be a missing person.

"The plan," Dodge said, "was to brainstorm about the current process, consider alternatives to the current process, then attempt to forward engineer these alternatives to implement a future process. I think we should stick to this plan."

And the thing with Burghie. She should have sensed that he had a crush on her. He'd probably had it since they were teenagers. She had missed his signals. Even after he'd come right out and said so, an hour had passed before the truth sank in. If everyone missed the signals, nothing would get done. Society depended on the interpretation of codes, clues and cues. Without detectives, lawyers and judges, wrongdoings would go unsolved and unpunished. In that law-enforcement-free world, criminals would have to confess in writing immediately upon breaking a law for them ever to be charged and convicted.

Tom said, "Yes, most definitely."

She had crashed into the police forensics van, and she hadn't got caught. She had gotten away with a crime like so many people before have with unprosecuted misconduct . . . such as the terrible mental torture that families and societies exercise on others yet never get punished for. Gilda had to do something before things got out of hand.

"I thought we *were* brainstorming," Cheyenne said.

Gilda was a project manager. She should be hands-on. She had to go to Montreal.

The meeting continued around her. Tobil, Cheyenne and Xavier argued about the implications of starting the project log before or after the author submitted the first draft. From there, discussions swung to disastrous projects from the past and the numerous beefs that had festered within the staff's collective unconscious. Tom halted the meeting fifteen minutes early ("Let's start the weekend early!"), and, set free, Gilda went home to continue brooding.

29

GILDA ABANDONS BETH

On Sunday, Gilda sat in the kitchen, a bowl of raw green beans in front of her, and told Beth she was going to Montreal to find Pete. "I suppose," Beth said finally, "it's a kind of poetic justice. I never did like poetry much. I suppose your love of poetry is a reaction to that. A poetic justice."

"I didn't know you didn't like poetry," Gilda said.

"There's a lot you don't know about me." Beth reached into the bowl and pulled out a handful of beans. "That's only natural. Children aren't supposed to understand their parents." Meditatively, she began to trim the ends of the beans. "You should find Philip McDonald, the owner of the bed and breakfast and who Philippa is named after." Beth said that she had last been in touch with Philip on Facebook. "A few months ago, I liked their new recipe for scones."

"Why didn't I know you kept in touch with this guy?"

"I didn't think you would be interested."

Gilda grabbed her own handful of beans from the bowl. She snapped off the ends quickly and loudly, and she piled them on a paper napkin. She had bought the beans at Superstore. The beans in their garden were still vestigial, pale nubs protruding from the centre of wilted flowers. She had taken up gardening to help Beth, who was getting slower and stiffer, her legs and fingers thinning as her flesh evaporated to reveal the outlines of her arthritic, osteoporotic bones.

"Then again," Beth said, "Philippa may not really be in Montreal."

Gilda had thought of that possibility, though she hadn't mentioned it to Beth. So much, again, for having to coddle her mother. "If that's true, there's nothing I can do besides going to the police."

"We could hire a private investigator."

Gilda was surprised at her mother's suggestion. Bolstered by Beth's openness, she asked, "Did Dad hire a private investigator when you went to Montreal with Philippa?"

"Not that I know." Beth grew thoughtful. "He hated that TV show *The Rockford Files.*" She stood up, left the room and came back with a scrap of paper with Philip's email address on it. "Might as well try Philip. I don't know if Philippa knows his name, but she might."

Gilda went to her bedroom and composed an email to philip@lalobelie.com. "I'm Gilda Peterborough, daughter of Beth Conrad, your friend from Edmonton. My sibling Pete is in Montreal, and I wonder if he has got in touch with you." After she sent the email, she returned to the kitchen, where Beth had started cooking. They spoke little as they ate their meal—beans and pork cutlets—and did the dishes together. They separated for a time, Gilda with her novel, her mother in front of the television, but in the evening Gilda joined Beth on the sofa for *CSI*. The episode involved a juror found dead in a sealed deliberation house with eleven other jurors. In an unrelated subplot, a woman admitted to knowing more about the death of her sister years earlier than she had revealed at the time of the murder. Nasty stuff.

The next day at work, Gilda avoided any discussion of the annual retreat. When Jensee brought it up, Gilda coolly responded that it had gone as well as could be expected, a cynical enough answer to satisfy Jensee, though the accompanying glare she gave to Jensee, and reused later for Tobil and Neela, staved off further opinionizing. For the rest of the day, she aimed her obsessive, analytical weapons inward at private, personal targets: her sibling, her parents, Burghie. Inside that fog of battle, she slipped out of her corporate self-identity more than a good employee should; she made sure she stayed away from the staff room and other opportunities for co-worker socializing.

Later that evening, Philip's response to Gilda's email arrived. The gushy opening, the "so nice to hear from the famous Gilda," the exclamation points! In any event, the answer was no: no news of Philippa. Of course, Philip was still glad to have Gilda visit him if she decided to come to Montreal. He hoped her mother would come too! It had been a long time! Smiley.

Reporting this all to her mother, Gilda made sure to leave out Philip's invitation to Beth.

Beth asked, "I bet he invited me to come there. He always invites me."

Gilda didn't want her mother following her to Montreal. She wanted this to be more poetically just than it could be if her mother tagged along. She wasn't sure how to put it.

She didn't have to, for Beth said, "Don't worry. I'm not going anywhere."

Fortunately, Gilda had already booked a few days off at the beginning of August. She asked Manuka if she could take the last bit of July off too: she had extra vacation time. Gilda counted on Manuka feeling sorry for her, and indeed Manuka's eyes widened and her mouth softened when she said, "Of course." That night, Gilda went on a discount travel site and bought a plane ticket and a modest hotel room for a two-week stay.

The next task Gilda needed to do was talk to Burghie. She hadn't communicated with him face-to-face since the night she realized that he was infatuated with her. He had since sent her a few messages asking about Pete, but Gilda had replied with versions of "Still nothing to report. I hope you are doing well." She knew that it was wrong to leave Burghie hanging long term. She didn't want to abandon him. She would keep him informed.

Accordingly, she walked over to Paul's the next evening. No customers were in the restaurant, so Burghie immediately took

Gilda to their regular booth. She turned down his offer of tea and told him she was going to Montreal.

He seemed unsurprised. "Are you going by yourself?"

"Yes." Gilda kept her voice neutral. "I had time booked off work anyway. I'm going in two weeks."

He offered to help Gilda from Edmonton. "I can see if that guy Norvell is in contact with him."

"You want to spy on Norvell? That's fine, but the person I need spying on is my mother."

Eyes askance, he said, "I'm not sure how." After a moment, he added, "I could walk over there before work. Or call her."

He was proposing to do a great deal, and she couldn't shunt his offer aside, despite her misgivings. "How ever you want to do it. That would be great." She changed her mind about tea. She had asked him a favour, and since he was doing it, she owed him a bit of emotional closeness, even if only a morsel.

They didn't talk while she drank her tea and he ate his fries. Mostly they stared at their own hands. Once her teacup was empty, Gilda left. The heartbreak in Burghie's eyes was too much. She had planned to shake his hand, but touching him would have been the worst thing possible.

In the days preceding her departure, Gilda kept her dealings with her mother similarly dispassionate. Beth tried to push her ancient travel hair dryer on Gilda; she didn't need one. Beth tried to talk Gilda into having Beth drive her to the airport; Gilda said she would take a taxi. Beth suggested a visit to Tokens might be useful; Gilda thought quite the opposite, since Beth's idea was to coerce, in some vague way, whoever worked there to reveal all they knew. "Somebody knows something," Beth told her. Gilda doubted it.

At Melon Press, Ian Auma maintained radio silence, and the enthusiasms of the annual retreat abated. People stopped quizzing her about her car's headlight, as though the headlight was supposed to be that way now. On the last day of work before Gilda's vacation, Jensee made a show of putting a stack of sticky notes on her desk.

Manuka told Gilda of a poutine store her friend said was good. "But I forget the name. The Marquise?"

"I'll Google it," Gilda said.

She kept in contact with Burghie in the shallowest way possible. Two nights before she left, she went to Paul's and had another tea with him. They said little to each other.

"That toy you brought that first time," he said at one point. "What did you call it?"

"A puddle-jumper."

"Were you able to fix it?"

"Nope," she said.

They said nothing for a while.

"Is going there a good idea?" he asked.

"Sure."

She left with another of her small hand waves, a gesture she was sure she had adopted from him. In response, he ducked his head in a half-nod and stood, straightening his apron as though getting ready to go back to work.

#

Forty-eight hours later, Gilda sat in the window seat of an airplane flying eastward in the early evening over the Canadian Shield, and she found herself, despite her best intentions, thinking, "How does that feel, Mother?"

30

BETH IN FLIGHT

Things were quiet at the health services branch in Northgate Mall. The waiting area had no children or babies, and the four adult clients, all waiting for booked appointments, made no fuss. They fiddled with their phones. Cellphones were a marvellous invention that way.

Beth sat at her station behind the welcome counter, hands on her knees. In this freedom of silence, she imagined Gilda's airplane soaring over her head eastward.

As a child, Gilda had always been the seeker in hide-and-go seek. Philippa and Beth would hide in closets, behind the chest of drawers in the children's shared bedroom and, one time that Beth knew of, Philippa had crammed herself into the dryer. She had scolded Philippa about that one, but Philippa had said, "I kept the door open a crack, Mommy, so it's okay. And I won!"

That time, yes. Beth hoped that her children would win. She didn't know if that were possible. She could dream, though. Because of their harmlessness, dreams were underrated.

#

When she returned home from work, she fed her cats, Entry and Exit, and sat at the kitchen table with a crossword puzzle. She ate an early supper of leftover pork cutlets. Just before seven o'clock, Beth left for church at Saint Clare's, where she kneeled at the pew for half an hour, ignoring the service as usual, and thought about her current day and about days past. Normally after church she watched television with Gilda, telephoned Philippa or read a book before going to bed. What she would do this night she didn't know. Even though their weekday evenings did not intersect except at dinner time (and not even then sometimes), she and Gilda tended to watch the news together. On weekends Beth sometimes had Saturday afternoon coffee with her work friends Darlene and Edith. Once in a while she attended a matinee concert, usually the world music ones—she loved drums, fifes and unusual string instruments. She was a member of a paper crafts group at the seniors' recreation centre and did much of her casual socializing there. Her ambition was to make a china cabinet of papier-mâché. On weekends she and Gilda did housework, went clothing shopping if Beth didn't have any other obligations and, at night, watched a movie at home or at the theatre. Beth didn't see as much of Philippa, though sometimes they talked on the phone, and occasionally Philippa came over on weekends for a movie night. Philippa made the popcorn. Most Sunday afternoons, the three of them dined in her little kitchen for lunch. They talked about what they were cooking, buying, eating or cleaning, about the cats, about what other people they knew or saw on television cooked, bought, ate or cleaned, and about other people's pets. Sometimes Philippa talked about games and Gilda about publishing. Church scandals entertained all of them, especially those related to upper clergy. They avoided talking about things they disagreed on, a short but explosive list: peanut bans at schools; the people Philippa met at bars; things Philippa did at bars and the frequency with which she did them; and Gilda's opinions about what Philippa did. No one ever brought up Beth's two trips to Montreal or Philippa's intersexuality.

Even with her children gone, Beth could still pretend to tell God about her predicaments. She still had that.

31

BETH'S TRIPS TO MONTREAL, AS TOLD IN CHURCH

Ralph had thought it a duty to take Beth to Montreal. He had studied music there years ago, before he met Beth. Montreal was Canada's cultural heart. History began there, returned there, was filtered of its impurities and was sent back out again.

Beth was interested in the sights in the literal sense, the visual appeal, not the history behind the appeal. She wanted to gawk at the sharp arches of Notre Dame Cathedral, the drunken exhibitionist partiers parading down Saint Catherine Street on Saturday night, the gravy pouring from a platter of French fries and cheese curds. She wanted to stay in a big chain hotel in the centre of tourist action. Ralph, however, won the coin toss. A coin toss often mediated their decision-making, since Beth and Ralph were a highly incompatible couple, and they knew it.

He booked a bed and breakfast in Mile End, the old Jewish neighbourhood where writer Mordecai Richler had grown up. Beth didn't know who Mordecai Richler was, so Ralph sat her in front of the television to watch *The Apprenticeship of Duddy Kravitz*. Ralph considered the film to be a watershed of Canadian film history. "Watershed" was Ralph's word, not Beth's. For the word "watershed," she imagined a homely backyard shed, such as the battered green-and-white aluminum one in their backyard, but with a giant waterspout sticking out of the side and from which water constantly flowed and drowned her beans and petunias. She watched the movie nevertheless. Beth thought Richard Dreyfuss was much cuter in that movie than he was in *Jaws*, but she couldn't get over Dreyfuss's hideous cackle.

La Lobélie Bed and Breakfast in Mile End consisted of two adjacent units in a three-storey, row-house complex on the neighbourhood's main street, rue Saint-Urbain. The building was reddish-brown brick with black trim around the doors and windows, and it was fronted by a tiny courtyard fenced with black wrought iron. Ivy and pink lobelia streamed out of the pots and onto the front steps, so that Beth and Ralph had to walk over the trails of pink and green to get inside; the tender little flowers trembled as she and Ralph lifted their sandalled feet up and over them.

The entrance hall presented four ways of escaping it besides the front door: an open threshold on the left to the guest parlour—labelled as such in a petit point sign in a gilded frame—an open door ahead to the kitchen, a shut door on the right of the kitchen and labelled "private" in petit point, and a staircase beside the private door. Beth wondered if the owners had broken building codes to construct the entrance hall and if they habitually broke other kinds of codes. The kitchen was completely white and so had an air of cleanliness. Otherwise, the house smelled like the rug that Beth had slept on one summer when she ran away from home and lived with her motorcycle-riding boyfriend. The floors were covered with wide planks of worn hardwood, rather like the floors in her granny's farmhouse in Vermilion, and like an old farmhouse, the walls had old green wallpaper of white flowers on thin sepia vines, spotted here and there with water stains. All the trims—baseboards, handrails, closet doors, regular doors—were dark brown with an organic haze of lighter brown on them.

Their handsome host Philip and the dependable-looking sub-host Murray emerged from the kitchen, greeted them kindly and toured them through the lamp- and sofa-stuffed guest parlour and the adjoining guest dining room. They returned to the entrance, and Murray helped them and their luggage up one flight of stairs to the short hallway to their room.

The room smelled of humid apples and candy hearts.

"'Shabby chic,' I think they call it," she said to Ralph after Murray left them.

Beth liked the bedspread of heavy white chenille with white yarn-like tassels along the edges. At regular intervals across the chenille were crocheted flowers of various sizes, some green, some pink, some blue, some yellow. On the first Saturday afternoon of their trip, Beth lay alone on the bed while Ralph scoured the neighbourhood for someone who knew Mordecai Richler personally. She had made Ralph go alone because she was tired and because she thought he was on a wild goose chase. She stretched out on the bed on her side and fingered the soft flowers on the bedspread in a way that reminded her of doing the rosary back when she was in her elementary school's rosary club. Using the bedspread flowers, she began to do a rosary of her own invention: Holy Mary, mother of blue flowers, pray for us sinners. Holy Mary, mother of green flowers, pray for us sinners.

After several minutes, she heard a knock at the door. Because of her chanting, she had hypnotized herself into believing she was nine and living in her childhood home, so she answered in the way she used to answer the calls of Granny Kate, who had been deaf and forced everyone she lived with to speak with unnecessary loudness. "Come in!" Beth screamed.

One of the B&B owners eased the door open. "Uh, are you okay?" It was Philip, the handsome one.

"Could you hear me?" Beth said.

"Yes."

"I'm sorry."

"I was spooked. You sounded like my grandmother just before she slipped off to the crazy place in her head."

"Do I look like a grandmother?"

Philip's eyes widened. "No, no."

Beth felt embarrassed. Why had she said that to the poor man? She invited Philip into her room.

Philip became her other favourite thing about the house. He had blue eyes and fawn-coloured curly hair, much like Richard Dreyfuss's hair in *The Apprenticeship of Duddy Kravitz*. He taught cultural studies at a college in town. He specialized in the history of the antivivisectionist movement in Victorian England. Murray was a furniture builder who had always dreamed of owning a bed and breakfast.

"So, you're living Murray's dream?" Beth asked.

"It's okay to help someone you love to live a dream, you know."

In response, Beth revealed to Philip the nature of her marriage. Philip listened to the confession steadily, breaking only once to fetch a bottle of Prosecco and two champagne flutes.

"People say that artists are spontaneous," Beth said. "But he has a script that he makes his musicians follow."

"He has a score," Philip said. "That's normal."

"Okay. But Ralph is like that with everything."

"When you have a group of people working together, it's good to have a plan."

"Sometimes life doesn't give you a plan. Sometimes there is a plan, but it's boring or doesn't work or doesn't account for what other people want or need. Then you're supposed to change it. Adapt."

Beth had much more to say about Ralph. After Beth told the unfortunate story of the wool sweater and the milk carton, Philip stopped her.

"Maybe you should get a divorce," he said.

"Bad timing. It turns out that I'm pregnant."

Philip congratulated her, apologized for bringing alcohol into the room and backed off on that point when Beth said she wanted to toast to her unborn child. She said she would name the baby Philip.

The next morning, Philip served a breakfast of fresh fruit and homemade hummus garnished with kale. "We're out of sparkling white for the mimosas," Philip said as he stood before them in his Victorian manservant outfit. "I make a pretty good Shirley Temple."

Beth hadn't yet told Ralph about her pregnancy. A few days before their vacation, her doctor's receptionist called her at work to confirm the test results. She began to take maternity vitamins, but stealthily. She didn't think Ralph would be happy: he had been excited about the trip, reading a guidebook and two Mordecai Richler novels simultaneously, rhapsodizing about bagels and bragging that he knew what a person could buy at a dépanneur. The vacation went as planned by Ralph: walking tours narrated by him, two nice dinners at two nice restaurants, three visits to three different museums, plus a gratuitous trip to a dépanneur. For Beth's sake they toured Notre Dame Cathedral. Ralph had never been impressed by Canada's version of the Parisian cathedral—he considered the substitution of European marble with Quebecois wood "a bit provincial"—but Beth's fingertips glided in silky pleasure over dark brown railings polished by the hands of centuries of people before her. On their last Saturday night, they walked Saint Catherine Street, which was anticlimactic. She had envisioned a giant outdoor nightclub or the riots after a Stanley Cup final. "I saw lots of drunkenness," Ralph said after they returned to their hotel room. "You must not have been paying attention." Likely his senses had been sharpened by another failed afternoon of hunting for acquaintances of Mordecai Richler. She had been distracted too.

#

Early the next year, Ralph and Beth Peterborough had their first child in Edmonton. The child ended up being children: twins. When Beth found out she was pregnant with twins, Ralph announced he wanted two children of matching sex. He liked the symmetry. He also favoured rhyming or alliterating names. Not that she thought they had control over the issue, but Beth thought having a boy and a girl would be "getting it over with." Ralph commented, "But our situation is different, isn't it, Beth?" He was forty-nine and Beth was forty-four. They had stopped thinking about pregnancy five years earlier. As soon as the doctor had confirmed that she was having twins, Ralph ran off and got a vasectomy.

"I don't know what the big rush was," she said to the wincing Ralph when she picked him up at the urologist's clinic. "I can't get pregnant while I'm pregnant."

Between gritted teeth, he muttered, "I had to do it some time."

Their children were two girls. Delighted, he wanted to name them Gilda and Gloria. Beth argued that she should choose the name for one of them. A few coin tosses later, and the fraternal twins were named Gilda and Philippa. Gilda was a brunette with pale skin (her mother's colouring), while Philippa was a redhead with the inexplicable olive cast of the Peterboroughs.

A month later, Beth was not surprised to learn that one of her children was both male and female. An endocrinologist made the official confirmation, though Beth had guessed right way that Philippa's lower body could not be explained easily. Philippa had a small penis (or a large clitoris), and her testicular sac was divided in half and flabby as though it were empty. An ultrasound revealed that Philippa had a vagina, but it was small. She also had male gonads embedded in her lower abdomen. Philippa had partial androgen insensitivity syndrome. That is, the baby was chromosomally a male, but because the fetal body had not responded properly to its androgens, the child was born with genitalia that seemed halfway male, halfway female. A growing team of doctors recommended that Philippa get genital surgery to look more like a female, as they thought that genital ambiguity could be psychologically damaging to the child and to the child's parents. Beth thought surgery on a newborn was cruel. Ralph was against that particular surgery too. He took the chromosomal XY as a definitive marker of Philippa's gender; he wanted Philippa to have surgery, all right, but the kind that made her look more like a boy. Beth thought Philippa should decide what to do when she was older.

Ralph did some research, and Beth, looking over his shoulder, read along, but her conclusion was not the same as his. "The baby's

DNA indicates male," Ralph said. "That's all there is to it. We can't change the DNA, but we can make the body fit that DNA better."

At that moment, the furrow that lay between Beth and Ralph widened into a ravine. The word "we" did it for her. "We" assumed unity between her and Ralph, but in practice "we" was the word monarchs used to indicate that their decrees represented both the will of the people and the will of God. In one stroke, Beth became alienated from Ralph and she stopped believing in God.

Beth felt so strongly against any surgery at all that in mid-October, two days after she and Ralph had another fight about surgery, she loaded herself and baby Philippa onto a Greyhound bus to Sault Ste. Marie. In Sault Ste. Marie, she bought a ticket to Montreal.

Eventually she stood in the foyer of the bed and breakfast, unannounced, with two overstuffed diaper bags at her feet, Philippa sleeping in her arms. Beth felt safe. A year earlier, the bed and breakfast had been Beth's refuge from her life in Edmonton. To her, the girls had been created, if not conceived, in this building.

Philip was touched that Beth had decided to spend her first girls-only vacation there. Only after two weeks had passed did Beth, spurred by Murray's question about how long she was planning to stay, admit that she had taken Philippa from home without letting anyone know where they were.

Murray's coffee thermos froze over the guest breakfast table in mid-pour. "That's technically kidnapping, isn't it?" he asked.

"I'm also guilty of child abandonment. I had to leave Gilda behind."

"Who's Gilda?"

"My other daughter. I had twins."

Murray put down the thermos. "Philip! Come out here right now!"

"I know." Beth sniffled tears despite herself. "I am a mess. My life is a mess. But I'm not going to let Ralph mess up this baby's life before it's barely started."

Without asking if Murray or the newly arrived Philip wanted to see, Beth unsnapped Philippa's onesie and revealed the sweetly pink yet problematic genitalia. "I cannot let Ralph bully me into getting surgery for this baby."

Philip had remembered some of Beth's stories from the year before: the milk and sweater story in particular was stored in his long-term memory. He brushed Beth's arm, looked down in Beth's lap at the baby bundled in a blue sleeper and pink hat and blanket. He said to Murray, "Can we keep them?"

"They aren't a litter of kittens," Murray said. "We'll be breaking some kind of law, I'm sure."

"My heart is breaking," Philip said. "Can't they stay at least one more night?"

Murray shuddered, nodded and pushed himself away from the table and out of the dining room. Philip took Beth and Philippa to the private sitting room, and he brought her a pot of mint-ginger tea and the scones served at two-thirty for those who checked off the "tea" option on registration. Beth hadn't.

"I need to get some strength," Beth said. "I'll go back eventually."

"Murray's unhappy," Philip said, "and I can't let that go on forever. But you can stay a little while."

Murray moved Beth and Philippa to the attic-style third-floor guest room on the left half of La Lobélie. Beth offered to act as a housekeeper for the B&B, and in no time, she was doing laundry, mopping floors and dusting the bric-a-brac around the house. She schlepped the baby along slung on her back while she cleaned rooms and installed Philippa in the guest high chair while she prepped food and washed dishes. Murray become reliant on her too; in less than a month's time, Beth's shortbread appeared on the plate of goodies in the common room in the evening. Whenever paying guests stayed, however, Murray complained to Philip about the fake guests upstairs.

At night, Beth often looked out the window of her room and studied the falling leaves and, later, the falling snow of backyard Montreal. Philippa, a light and infrequent sleeper, kept Beth up at night. Beth paced, baby in her arms, her thumb stroking the bottom of the baby's naked foot, him sweaty and trembling from interminable shimmying sobs. Sometimes Beth imagined that she was holding Gilda, not Philippa, and would pretend that Gilda's feet were different from Philippa's, wider and longer. Her pacing made the ceiling below her creak, and Murray worried about bad customer reviews. She said she could pretend to be the house ghost if that would help. "I could be the Ghost of Christmas Past." December was approaching, and she might be spending her first Christmas as a mother without both children. The sobs from the attic didn't always come from Philippa.

She expected Ralph to track them down eventually, which he did in early December. Beth had been careful about not leaving a paper trail: she had paid cash all the way to Montreal, withdrawing money from an old RRSP she had established as a young woman soon after she moved to Edmonton, yet she understood that her planning couldn't account for everything and everyone. The Montreal police received a tip, the Edmonton police detective said over the phone the night he called the B&B.

Beth stalled her legally imposed return by creating goodwill: she told Detective Hoydal about Ralph's plan for the surgery. She said that she didn't want the doctors to interfere with God's plan. Beth didn't believe that any God had any plan, but her statement won her a week of abeyance in Montreal. The abeyance came to an end, though, after Detective Hoydal hinted that they would soon arrest her and throw Philip and Murray in with the bargain.

Two months after they left Edmonton, Philippa and Beth were escorted to the Montreal airport by two police constables. She and the baby were met at Edmonton International Airport by Ralph, a police constable and a social worker. Beth had expected to be led away in handcuffs, but that didn't happen. Instead, the police constable asked if she and the baby were all right. The constable and the social worker didn't show much interest in Ralph—Beth guessed that Ralph had dissatisfied them in some way. The constable asked if she was okay to go home with Ralph. Of course she wanted to go home, she said. Ralph nodded curtly.

They went home, Ralph in the police cruiser, Beth and Philippa in the social worker's car, to find Gilda, a new tooth decorating her solemn smile, cradled in the arms of a teenaged babysitter.

The next day, Beth was ordered to report to the police station, where she was formally charged and fingerprinted, and, to her surprise, released. Soon afterwards, the charges of parental abduction were dropped because of a low probability of conviction and the complainant's disinterest in prosecution.

Ralph's disinterest presaged the brisk degeneration of their marital bond. Christmas Eve dinner was a wordless affair over a meal Ralph ordered from a local caterer. Even Philippa was strangely silent. On Christmas morning, Ralph helped Beth help the children unwrap presents. She gave Ralph four pairs of dress socks and a Tafelmuzik CD. "I have that one already," he said. He gave her two *Company's Coming* cookbooks. He then left for his office to prepare for a January tour. When he came back from the tour, Ralph said that if she didn't want Philippa to have any surgery at all, he didn't want to be married to her. Beth and Ralph started divorce proceedings.

Eventually Ralph married Rachel, the administrative assistant of the arts management group one of his orchestras had hired. Beth later found work for the Alberta government's health services department, and she let Irene the teenaged babysitter mind the kids when Ralph didn't have them and when the kids weren't in school. The awkwardness of her arrest had complicated her friendship with Philip. Murray was barely civil over the phone. Email and then Facebook made their relationship possible, and Beth was forever grateful for computers in that regard. She couldn't do much more than the shallow connection that Facebook afforded. Her children took too much of her energy and patience. Little Gilda, thin of shank and face, often ran into a corner and cried for no apparent reason. Hyperactive Philippa treated all commands she received from her mother and father as suggestions. She obeyed better when the command was colourful. "Put the plate back on the table" didn't work, but what did was "If that plate ends up on the floor in a million pieces, Philippa, you are going to gain an intimate knowledge of the time-out chair."

As the twins got older, they went through some rough terrain. One evening, Beth came home from one of her earliest unaccompanied trips to Saint Clare's to find a hole in the wall from Gilda's foot, a shattered glass cabinet from the television's remote control that Pete had thrown at Gilda but had missed, and a deep cut in Pete's wrist from him reaching into the cabinet to remove the remote control and conceal the evidence. Beth arranged for her children to get counselling. After a couple of individual sessions with separate counsellors, Pete and Gilda started Thursday joint sessions, but Pete stopped coming home from school on time on Thursdays. Pete attended one solo session; after three missed appointments, Pete's counsellor gave up. Gilda kept going until final exam time, when she stopped, and she never restarted them. "I'm good, Mom." Beth was not convinced, but she went along.

The counsellors gave Beth a joint oral report after one month's time. According to his counsellor Carl, Pete didn't know what Gilda's problem was. She always tried to interfere with his life, and when he protested, she flipped out. She was obsessed with school and thought Pete should be too. But like everyone else on the planet knew, school was useless. Did that famous painter Leonardo DiCaprio go to university to learn how to paint and design flying machines? Not likely. "No one said he became a genius by sitting in a classroom and taking notes." No, Leonardo did it all on his own. When the counsellor attempted to address Pete's "disorder of sexual development," Pete was unimpressed. "I'm doing terrific." According to Gilda's counsellor, meanwhile, Gilda thought Pete's defiance of his mother about counselling, his cruelty to his twin and his tendency toward criminality all derived from Pete's intersexuality. No one understood all that Gilda did on her family's behalf, and "no one" included Beth. Gilda didn't usually agree with her father, but Ralph had one thing right: Pete was headed toward dangerous shoals. "Philippa and me used to play Barbies," Gilda said, "then one day in grade six, she pulled off their heads. That's a cry for help!"

The reports didn't help Beth come up with a way to deal with her children beyond acknowledging their sibling rivalry. Pete had a high-spiritedness, aggression and pride that Ralph must have had at the same age and helped propel him off the farm and into the music program at McGill. Pete didn't have a musical bone in his body, couldn't draw worth anything and had no talent for sports, but he had Ralph's spirit, and that spirit had nowhere to go. Pete's genitals had nothing to do with it; she had to figure out where to put her spirit, that was all, and until that time, everyone had to move out of the way. Gilda's complaints about Pete had to do with his bad behaviour; the girl seemed happy enough otherwise.

The counsellors said that the children might be reacting to the hostility between the parents. They also wondered about Beth's flight from Edmonton and if that was a continuing trauma either parent had brought up. Beth admitted that she told Gilda about Montreal outright after Gilda had overheard a phone conversation between Beth and Ralph. As for Pete, Beth didn't know how he had found out, but when she had walked in on the remote-control fight, Pete had blurted out, "I know all about that Montreal thing, by the way, Mom." Beth suspected that the fight had something to do with Pete finding out about the Montreal stage of his life. Gilda's version of the fight didn't mention any confrontation about Montreal: she had said the fight was about control of the television. Pete would only say that Gilda's version was mostly correct but with a spin that, he said, "only Gilda could put on it."

"Still, children sense things," Gilda's counsellor, Aman, said. "Younger children who are taken from one parent by another parent don't understand exactly what's happening, but they put the pieces together in a way that makes sense to them at their level of development. For some of these children, their period away from home seems to be like a brilliant game of hide-and-seek or pretend."

That was what games were, weren't they, a set of rules people obeyed for a short time. When the game was over, you went back to the normal rules of life. When hide-and-seek ended, you didn't assume your friend was hiding from you because you didn't see them. You said, "Oh, Jack is in the bathroom," or "Jill went home half an hour ago." Marriage and divorce were like that too. Divorce was when the rules reverted to what they were before marriage, or more accurately, divorce was when the game changed to a new one, from hide-and-seek to tag. You're it one weekend, he's it the other weekend. No, not tag. More like king of the castle. Or Simon says.

Am I going to keep listing names of games? Beth thought. Too bad she hadn't paid more attention to the board games Pete used to talk about. She could have listed them too to help kill time.

#

With a waft of chicken soup smell, the two old nuns in the pew in front of Beth hobbled into the centre aisle. The priest and the deacon bustled around the chancel and apse, putting things away. Mass was over.

They had rough spots, but all families had them. Real trouble was different from a rough spot. Real trouble was rare.

32

ALEATORY

On the way out of the metro station, Pete reached into his back pocket for the address to La Tortue Flambée, and though the slip of paper was there, his apartment key wasn't. He patted himself down. No key. He'd probably lost it on the train when he checked for the paper for the umpteenth time. He jogged back to the station. The middle-aged woman in the service booth there said in clear English that he could call the lost and found, but he should know that no one would call back for two days.

According to the wristwatch he'd taken to wearing since he went off grid, he arrived at the restaurant forty-five minutes late. The outside's mottled brick walls and neon green turtle above the door was matched on the inside by mottled brick walls and a hostess with a neon green shirt above her short black skirt. "Hey, can I use your phone?" Pete asked the hostess. He spent five minutes in the coatroom on the house phone with the transit lost and found line, the phone number provided by the hostess, who, like the phone line, had an English option. He left a message but couldn't give a contact phone number because he hadn't memorized the landline number of his flat.

When he asked the hostess if Philip McDonald had already arrived, he was surprised that she took him to a table with someone still sitting there, since Pete was plenty late. Philip was middle-aged with short curly hair and a sharp chin under a thin face. A fondue pot of liquid bubbled in front of him with the smell of pepper and onions. Pete explained that he had lost his apartment key and had been trying to find it.

Philip asked, "Can you talk to the building manager?"

If he stood outside his apartment's front doors, Pete said, he probably could see the building manager's phone number on a sign by the mailboxes. He couldn't read the sign, it being in French, but he guessed that no one else would put their phone number in the lobby of an apartment building. "That's how it works in Edmonton, anyway."

"Here too," Philip said. "The building manager may not be around this time of night. If you want, you can stay at the B&B tonight, and tomorrow I can drive you to your building."

"If it's no trouble."

"We're kind of set up for that," Philip said, "so no trouble."

"How much?"

Philip said, "I'm not asking you to pay anything. I'm helping you out. You're the son of a family friend."

"I am?"

All through this, Philip had seemed calm and nonjudgmental, but he sounded surprised at Pete's question. "Yes, of course."

They settled in front of their hot pot with a plate of yam chunks. Philip asked why Pete was in Montreal. Pete made sure to answer the question in a way that drew attention away from his past and toward his future. "There's a whole big world out there. I don't have anything tying me down, so why not take advantage of it? Quebec is like being in a foreign country, so why not do that instead of having to get a passport or figure out how to get foreign currency?" He was antsy about finding work in Montreal. Did Philip always know French or did he have to learn it at school? What businesses might want an English-only web programmer and game store retail clerk? Was Quebec going to separate or what? Did Philip know of any board game publishers in Montreal?

Philip could only answer the French question: he was an anglophone, but he had gone to a French school until university. Too quickly for Pete, Philip moved on. "And how is your mother?"

"Still single and not looking, which is good, because it was already weird to have my dad dating and then marry someone, and having my mother doing the same thing would be super freaky."

"My parents are divorced too, so I empathize."

Another plate of food arrived, this time breaded cheese and bundles of seaweed stuffed with something mysterious. After they worked on this plate of food, Philip returned to the subject of games.

"I used Grand Theft Auto in one of my courses on violence."

"I don't do those games much. I'm a board game person."

"There does seem to be a resurgence of board games. I noticed recently all the versions of Monopoly. It's fascinating how the rules are being revised to appeal to contemporary life, with debit cards, for example. Board games are used in product tie-ins. Disney Monopoly, Batman Monopoly. A board game franchise for film franchises. A doubling—"

"Monopoly is a terrible game! Who wants to play a game that takes seven hours and that eliminates players? It's basically a game of chance too."

Philip nodded politely. He ate for a bit, and then he asked, "Do you know if there are any games related to animal experimentation?"

"I haven't heard of one, but there probably is. There's a game about everything. Why, are you experimenting on animals?"

"No, no. I teach cultural studies. I've done research on the Victorian antivivisectionist movement and—"

"The whatzit?"

"The antivivisectionist movement in the nineteenth century. Antivivisection means the same as anti-animal experimentation."

"Oh, you're an animal rights person. I guess that's why there's no meat here, hey."

"I'm a vegetarian, yes. But if you want to order meat, please do."

Pete didn't, since he didn't know who would be paying. Philip then seemed to think that Pete was interested in vegetarianism, so he talked about Montreal's vegan and vegetarian restaurants and organic food stores.

"Does that mean you don't eat poutine?" Pete asked.

"There are non-animal-based gravies," Philip said. "For vegans there are substitutes for cheese."

Philip seemed to know more about food than games, so they talked about good places to eat around town. The food at their restaurant ended up not being bad, especially the dumplings and a cheesy breaded thing, though he'd love a chunk of steak. He hoped that the B&B wasn't vegetarian. Philip paid for the meals.

In the passenger seat of Philip's Kia Sportage, Pete admitted to himself that the man impressed him. Philip was like Gilda when it came to being a know-it-all, but when Philip talked about things, he talked about them like a normal person. He didn't throw in factoids to show off, like Gilda did, but as part of the conversation. Philip tossed out little bits of information that seemed practical rather than preachy, such as how good the metro was for travel and how much easier it was to buy alcohol here. Pete lost track of time in a good way.

Eventually the car entered a dark alley and pulled up behind a brick building. Philip led Pete through a door into a plain but sweet-smelling kitchen. Standing in the kitchen was an unhappy looking old man.

"Murray, this is Pete." Philip gestured to each person in turn. "Pete locked himself out of his apartment. I said he could stay overnight. I'll drive him to his apartment first thing tomorrow."

Murray nodded, but his face tensed up.

"I'll set him up in the spare room," Philip said. "You go back to what you were doing."

Murray nodded again, and he walked out. The thud of his heels on the wooden floor ended at an invisible set of stairs, which Murray took as heavily as an elephant would.

Philip sighed. "Well, let's get you set up."

"I can go."

"No," Philip said. "It's fine."

Up two flights of stairs was a landing with two doors. One was open to a bathroom with a clawfoot tub. The other door led to a bedroom, which was long and narrow and painted white like the kitchen. The top of the walls and the slanted ceiling were decorated with ivy patterns, and the old-fashioned quilt on the single bed had matching ivy patterns. A big window let in golden light from streetlights outside. Philip said the television worked and had cable, though he admitted that many of the channels were in French. Philip invited Pete to come down and get something to eat or drink, but Pete said that he wasn't hungry. He was a bit hungry, but he didn't want to seem desperate, and the expression on Murray's face made Pete want to stay upstairs. He told Philip he hadn't adjusted to the time change and needed to get some sleep. "How about a drink?" Pete asked, half-joking, but Philip took the joke seriously, or at least half of the joke, because he left and came back with a tray with a tall glass and a pitcher of water.

He went to bed, and a knock at the door woke him. The old-fashioned alarm clock on the bedside table said 7:40. He struggled out of bed and opened the door.

"Are you ready?" Philip said. "I have to go, but you can have something to eat."

Pete had no memory of agreeing to an early morning wake-up call, but he didn't argue. The smell of baking and grease was too strong. Down the stairs, Philip led Pete into a room labelled "Guest Dining Room" and probably the equivalent in French. By the long wood table, Murray stood at attention, dressed in an old-fashioned suit and a white chef's apron, holding a carafe of coffee. Philip told Pete to sit at the table, and Murray stood to one side like a butler. Breakfast was back bacon and eggs, toast and maple butter, and the best coffee he'd ever had. While Murray stood, Philip sat at the table and Pete threw questions at him.

"I stayed here when I was a baby," Pete said.

"Yes, you stayed in the room you're in now."

"No way! Was that the same bed I slept in with my mother?"

"No," Philip said. "You had a crib next to the bed."

"You were not a quiet baby, either," Murray said, the first words he said to Pete that morning.

Philip said, "Babies tend to be noisy."

"You remember me?" Pete said to Murray.

"Yes."

"Do I look the same?"

"You were smaller."

Philip glanced at Murray but said to Pete, "Well, if you're done, we can head out. Let me get my car keys." He slipped out of the dining room, and Pete was left alone in the dining room with Murray.

Murray put down the carafe, left the dining room and after a minute returned with a business card with the words Le Gîte La Lobélie B&B surrounded by little purple flowers. Murray flipped over the card and put it on the table in front of Pete. On the back of the card was written the word "Yasir" and a phone number.

"You probably don't want to hang out with old guys while you're here." Murray tapped the number. "You should call this person. He'll be able to show you around town better than Philip or I can." He pushed the card toward Pete. "Here, put it in your pocket now so you don't lose it."

Pete had to obey that command. After all, losing things had led him to the bed and breakfast in the first place.

A few seconds after Pete put the card in his wallet, Philip rushed into the dining room. "Okay, let's go."

After saying goodbye to Murray, they went. The drive to the apartment was mostly silent, but Pete probed a bit. "Is Murray mad at me?"

"I don't think he's mad," Philip said. "Just surprised."

"I think he's mad."

"He wasn't expecting you, that's all. He'll be fine."

Pete knew what it was like living with an angry person. Gilda and her Action Modes probably were driven by her being mad at him. He'd been able to escape her by living his own life, but that wouldn't be easy for Murray and Philip to do, since they worked in the same place. Moving out had helped him neutralize Gilda. Anyway, she was in Edmonton, so she couldn't be a problem. Probably.

"Listen," Pete said. "If anyone from Edmonton tries to get a hold of me, would you mind not saying anything?"

Philip kept his head straight ahead on the road but flicked his eyes in Pete's direction. "Anyone from Edmonton?"

"My family, I mean."

"Don't they know you're here?"

"Yeah, but still."

"You don't want them to know you contacted me?"

At the hurt in Philip's voice, Pete rushed out his answer. "No, it's not you. It's just that I don't want them bugging me all the time. My sister especially."

Philip made a sound that sounded like he would go along with this plan, but Pete wasn't sure.

"Please?"

Philip said, "Okay."

He dropped Pete off in front of François's apartment after Pete promised to contact him again. Pete got the name of the building manager by peering through the glass of the front doors. He had no cellphone, of course, so he used the smelly phone booth two blocks away. The condo manager knew English, thank God, and he promised to come by the apartment with a locksmith.

As Pete waited for the manager and the locksmith, he came to terms with the fact that life without technology was a pain in the ass. A key was a kind of technology too, of course. He wondered if his hero in *Invisible Man* would find it funny that he couldn't handle a simple tool like a key. Invisible Man had been a "thinker-tinker" (Pete had to look up "tinker" on the web) and installed thousands of lights in his apartment without the power company knowing. Invisible Man would have been a good programmer if computers had been invented then. A lot of things were different between then and now. If only Pete knew more than he did about things. If only he could figure everything out right away. If only things didn't seem based on luck, good or bad.

After a long wait, Jean the building manager and the locksmith showed up. Jean was angry, but like Murray, and so many other people in the world, pretended not to be. The locksmith only spoke French, and the manager spoke perfect English. Pete said to put the locksmith's invoice in François Uni's name, "for legal and language reasons." The invoice was in French.

Once he got into his apartment with his new key, Pete went to the remaining unopened suitcase and removed from it the plastic bags and boxes of dice, cards and books. He laid them out on the dining table. Standing and waiting outside doing nothing had given him the urge to work on his board game, Exandorwai.

#

The next afternoon, Philip called Pete on François's landline to see how he was doing.

"Fine." Pete had been sitting in the living room, staring at the television and pretending to watch a French-language *Storage Wars*. He was forcing himself to stay away from the desktop computer in the bedroom that François said Pete could use. He told Philip that watching television should help him learn the language of his new city, but Philip said that getting out into the city would be a better way. "Get the touristy things out of the way: Saint Catherine Street, Notre Dame Cathedral and Old Montreal. They're worth it, but they're the tip of the iceberg."

That night, Pete took the metro to Saint Catherine Street. He walked up and down the street, impressed by the throngs, which reminded him of Banff on a long weekend. Eventually he went into a pub with the hilarious name of The Cock n' Bull. He had a few pints and watched baseball on the bar television. He chatted up a group of three gorgeous women, and he left the bar with a glow.

The next afternoon, Philip called again. "Murray thinks my ideas are for old people. Do you like dancing?"

Pete was hung over and didn't feel like dancing, but he knew Montreal was famous for its nightlife. With enough beer in him, he had been known to stagger along with a pretty girl to Katy Perry or Pink. Philip recommended a place that Murray had suggested, the Club, or, as it was officially called, Le Club.

That night he put on his going-out clothes and took a taxi to Le Club. It was not the kind of place Pete was used to going to in Edmonton. The cover charge almost blew his alcohol budget. Inside, Le Club seemed like a classy mall running on emergency power. It had three levels, each visible to the other because of the central open shaft with glass and metal railings to keep drunk people from falling from floors three and two onto one. Pillars bathed in white light propped up the level; other than the downlights over the long L-shaped bar, Le Club had no other illumination. The clubbers shed their own light with their phones and the glowsticks around their wrists and necks. The music rumbled in heavy bass and searing melodies of synthesized repetition. The songs were wordless or barely recognizable as words—sometimes the words were in French, Pete suspected. The air had the metallic coldness of air conditioning but also seemed to have been infused with lemon gin. From time to time, he sneezed as though his perfume allergy were acting up. He rarely found himself in places where people wore high-end perfumes, which meant the quality of patron here was higher than he was used to. He was shocked at the price when he bought a beer. He was also shocked to see that the person who served the beer to him seemed to be a man dressed as a woman.

Somehow the server knew to speak English. "Here you go, honey!" She stopped and looked at him up and down.

"What's the matter?" Pete yelled back over the music.

"Nothing, darling." The server's pink glowing collar marked the nod. The server made to move away, but Pete leaned forward.

"What's with this?" Pete imitated the scanning.

"You're cute," the server said, "but you should work harder at getting uptown."

Pete wanted to get angry, but the server smiled, squeezed Pete's arm and moved on so that all Pete could do was glare at the server's back until her glowing collar was swallowed by the shadowy shapes of the dancers and drinkers. He felt the vertigo coming up and decided to station himself before it really hit.

For an hour, Pete leaned against the railing on the second level and stared down at the dance floor with the lone bottle of beer in his hand. He was fascinated by his reaction to the flashing lights, silhouettes of men kissing men, women necking with women. The vertigo flowed in and out of him so much that Pete was getting a buzz. After a while all he could see were dim blurred streaks of white, pink, orange and yellow. When he finished nursing his beer, he decided that he couldn't stay any longer. He groped his way through the near dark to the winding staircase down to the main floor and pushed his way through the crowd to the exit. He stood outside the club, waited for the dizziness to end and took a taxi home.

Back in his apartment, he poured himself a finger of vodka from François's kitchen stash and lay on the floor. The two cats slunk over from wherever they'd been and sprawled by his head. He stared up at the picture of the red-lipped woman. What was he doing in this place far from home? His mother had taken him to this city when he was a baby. That had been his reason for coming here rather than any other city needing a house-sitter for hire. Now he wondered if he had taken himself too seriously. Who cared if he had been here as a baby? He'd been at his mother's mercy, so from his perspective being in Montreal had been a random event, nothing he'd chosen. He had been a pawn. Was he still a pawn? Not if he'd chosen to come here. He wasn't a pawn anymore. He had never fully controlled his life in childhood. His folks could have raised him as a boy, got him surgeries that changed his life. The server at Le Club was influenced by her own parents too, and so had the seemingly straight men there, laughing with their buds and their female friends. Who knows why those people had gone there? Maybe it was for some reason other than getting wasted at a club on a weeknight. Some childhood drama might have pushed them there.

He pulled himself onto the sofa and dozed off. He woke up after a dream featuring a glass cube. Night had fallen completely then. The room was dark, the face of the red-lipped woman a shadow. He went into his bedroom, properly undressed and enjoyed a normal hard sleep.

The next morning, he made tea and did web maintenance for Tokens. Both tasks took him one hour. He spent the rest of the day looking at English-language job postings in Montreal, eating the blueberry muffins he bought at a store down the street, watching YouTube videos of people playing Settlers of Catan, and lying on the floor to look at the painting and think.

By four-thirty, he was ready to follow through on his thinking. He went to the second-hand store five blocks away and bought some club clothes. On the way home, he stopped at a place called Pharmaprix, basically a Shoppers Drug Mart, and bought a six-pack of a local beer with a picture of a devil. He also bought razor blades, cheap hoop earrings and a tube of red lipstick.

He returned to Le Club, but this time he went as Philippa. With his usual cowboy boots, he wore a knee-length red leather skirt and a sparkly black top. She arrived earlier than Pete had the night before. It was not as busy, but it was not empty. Philippa ordered the same beer that he'd ordered the night before. This time a woman took some interest in her, smiling at her blouse and pointing at her skirt, but Philippa didn't go to her or let her approach.

Philippa found who she was looking for: the server who had given her that up-and-down look. The server smiled, handed her one of the mystery shot glasses that she was carrying on her tray and motioned for Philippa to knock the shot back. Philippa did so, and she loved the sharp burn. She felt a little light-headed, but it was nothing she couldn't handle. Her earlobes throbbed. Inserting the earrings had not been pleasant: it had been ages since she'd worn earrings other than the two tiny black studs Pete wore sometimes to keep the holes in his earlobes open.

"Are you okay?" The server put a hand on Philippa's arm. The server's thinly plucked eyebrows lifted. "Hey," she said into

Philippa's ear. "I know you. You're the country boy who was in here last night."

The last time someone had put Philippa and Pete together was the lumberjack in the music store. That time, and all the other times like it, he'd felt like he was supposed to feel ashamed; he did feel ashamed. Here, he didn't feel shame; shame was out of place where a song's jagged melody boomed in his ears and the base shook his bones, where three men stood in front of him, their arms wrapped around each other's waists.

Philippa let herself smile. "Good eye!"

The server gave a thumbs-up.

33

PETE MEETS MURRAY'S FRIENDS

The day after, Pete wasn't sure if going to the club had been a good idea. Whenever he thought of his two hours in the club in women's clothing, the world whirled in front of his eyes. He didn't know why he'd done what he'd done, and thinking about why made the spinning worse. Once the vertigo stopped, he left his apartment to stock up on ramen noodles. Otherwise he flipped channels and worked pokily on his board game. He lost track of time. Suddenly one night, Montrealers were celebrating Saint Jean Baptiste Day, which seemed to be their version of Canada Day. Most stores were closed, and he had a hard time finding a spot in the bar down the street. It felt like someone else's party. He went home and stayed there. The weekend ended with no sign of the upcoming week being any different.

In a burst of loneliness, he picked up the business card that Murray had given him and called the number scrawled on the back. After a stream of French, Pete heard "leave a message." He said, "This is Pete Peterborough. Murray gave me your number. He said you could show me around town. I'm from out west. Call back if you want, here's my number."

The next day, a person named Garen called. The name on the back of the business card was Yasir, but Garen said talking to him was like talking to Yasir. "We're roommates, we hang out together, we're inseparable." Garen had that chirpy voice of people who on rainy days see the sun shining through the clouds, not the clouds that covered it.

"Do you know Murray too?" Pete asked.

Garen's voice changed, like the rain and wind had kicked up and he was having a hard time seeing blue. "I know Murray."

Pete wanted to trade stories with this person about Murray. To butter up Garen, he used the telephone skills he'd learned at Tokens. "Great! Can I leave Yasir a message?"

Instantly Garen perked up. "No problem, I can take a message."

Later that night, just before Pete was about to go out and get drunk, Yasir himself called. Speaking English with a slight non-French accent, he invited Pete to a place called Café Le Feu for drinks with some friends. Yasir asked where Pete lived, and Pete gave his street address. "The Village," Yasir said. "Great, that's walking distance." Pete took a taxi over because he didn't trust his sense of direction.

Café Le Feu smelled of Middle Eastern spices and bread. Black and white photographs of burning buildings decorated the cork walls. Everyone was talking, and Pete heard more English than French. Slouchy servers in black clothes drifted around in the near dark between round tables. Pete wore his leather jacket and black jeans, which made him look like the servers, but a middle-aged man spotted him anyway and waved him over to his table. The man wore a bright blue shirt and a black and white scarf, as Yasir had said on the phone that he would wear.

Yasir shook hands and introduced himself and the other people at the table. One was Garen, dark-haired like Yasir but also dark-skinned, bearded, mustached, taller and younger. The third person seemed to be a man who was dressed effeminately. He was clean shaven, with long dark hair held back with a red elastic band, eyeliner (it seemed) and (perhaps) false eyelashes. He wore a flowered print shirt, wide-legged red pants and red TOMS shoes.

"I'm Sarry, as in 'Garry' but with an S, not like 'sari' the Indian clothing, though I have nothing against saris, I think they're beautiful." Sarry spoke with a strong French accent, but his English was clear. His hands were large and well-manicured, and his handshake was so firm that the black cocktail ring on his thumb pinched the fleshy band between Pete's thumb and index finger. Pete's head spun a bit, halfway, really, as if unsure what to do.

A waiter approached the table, but before Pete opened his mouth, Sarry said, "Today's theme is 'Russia.'" Sarry pointed at the three drinks on the table. "Everyone is having a drink with a Russian theme. Garen and Yasir are having Black Russians, and I'm having a White Russian."

Pete didn't like the taste of coffee in his alcohol. "How about anything with vodka in it? Vodka is Russian, isn't it?"

"Oh, that's too easy!" Sarry said.

"What if I ordered a brand of vodka with the word 'Russian' on the bottle, like Russian Standard?"

Sarry said, "You aren't any fun, are you?"

Him not fun? On what planet except theirs? These were the kinds of people he avoided when he was at bars, talky, smart and smart-alecky people. He went to bars where people like this never went.

When the server returned, Pete asked what kind of Russian drinks he could get.

"Ask Bart to surprise him," Sarry said to the server.

Pete decided that, them being out of his league, he might as well see what the rules in this league were. "Yeah, surprise me."

The drink, when it came, was translucent white with an olive pinioned to the edge of the martini glass rim by a tiny paper umbrella. A curl of orange peel sat at the bottom of the glass.

"This one's called Russian Bodybuilder," the server said. "Bart's creation."

Sarry applauded. "I'm jealous. How does it taste like, Pete? I want a full review."

The drink was pepper vodka and gin, plus the olive and the orange peel. Pete could taste each ingredient distinctly. It was pretty awful. "He made this right off the top of his head, I'm guessing."

"Not everything can be a winner, I guess," Garen said.

Pete thought about leaving. Before he could, Sarry leaned over and patted Pete's arm. "So, you're a friend of Murray's, is that right?"

"He's more like a friend of a friend of my mother's."

Yasir said, "He's new in town and Murray thought we could show him around."

"How do you know Murray?" Pete asked Yasir.

"Murray and I go way back."

Sarry said, "They were in the club scene together."

"He was exiting when I was entering," Yasir added.

A shadow of a frown passed over Garen's expression.

Sarry said, "Double entendre, anyone?"

Pete didn't know what "double entendre" meant, and even though he didn't say anything, Sarry laughed as though he could read Pete's mind and thought Pete was funny. "That means 'dirty joke.'"

Yasir said, "Murray and I were dating back when Murray was a carpenter in the facilities department at McGill and I was an undergraduate."

"A May-December thing," Sarry said.

"We still keep in touch," Yasir said.

"And Garen is jealous," Sarry said.

Garen muttered. "It's awkward, that's all."

For the rest of the night, Pete did his best to avoid saying anything important about himself. The others talked about their jobs and mutual friends and enemies he didn't know. Murray's name didn't come up again. In the meantime, Pete finished the Russian Bodybuilder and ordered a vodka on ice, then another vodka on ice.

When Pete ordered a beer, Garen said, "Are you planning to make this an all-nighter? Yasir and I have to go to work tomorrow."

"I'm good." Pete tried to be nonchalant. "I have to go home right away too. This is the last for me too."

The beer was supposed to clear the vodka and gin haze in his head, but the next stretch of time was hazy. He remembered standing up. Later, he found himself being held at the elbow by Sarry as all four walked out of Café Le Feu. Later, he was being walked home only by Sarry.

Then Sarry and Pete were climbing the stairs to François's apartment.

"Show me you can open your door," Sarry said. "Then I'll leave."

He was smart about drunk people, Pete gave him that. He opened the door and said, "Thanks."

"Pas de problème," Sarry said. "See you again, okay?"

Once inside, the quiet made Pete very aware that he was alone. He slumped onto the sofa.

He spotted something written in pen on the back of his hand: Sarry's phone number. The vertigo, Pete's old friend, came to visit then.

34

GUILDA DIES

A few days later, Yasir called and invited Pete to a celebration of life at his home. Pete didn't know what a celebration of life was. It sounded suspiciously like a funeral.

"It's kind of that. It's for someone famous in Montreal who just died. Guilda. A local celebrity."

"Gilda?"

"He was a famous drag queen in Montreal. We thought it would be a good excuse for a party. Come!"

Pete had never met anyone else named Gilda. He knew about an old movie called *Gilda*; his mother suspected that his father had that film in mind when he picked the name, though Ralph denied it. Pete had never seen the film, since he hated black and white movies. As much as he might have wished for her death sometimes, the idea of a dead sister didn't automatically fill him with happiness. Still, going to a funeral in honour of someone with the same name as his sister was too much of a coincidence to skip out on. He wasn't doing much anyway. He hadn't been able to drum up work, so he'd spent his days walking up and down the streets, going to a local bar and pretending to watch sports until he was just sober enough to make his way home. He also wanted to know about a Gilda who was a "he."

Yasir and Garen lived up a hill past Pete's apartment in a neighbourhood that verged on being crappy but kept it together enough to remind Pete of his childhood Edmonton neighbourhood. On the door of their second-floor flat hung a framed glossy photo of a person who looked like Marilyn Monroe but who Pete had to assume was the Montreal version of Gilda. His own Gilda was dark-haired, never wore makeup and probably had never worn a low-cut sequined dress.

When he got inside, Yasir came to him through the crowd of strangers and thumped Pete lightly on the back before slipping a black band around Pete's bicep. The music and the heat in the small sitting room stood out the most. The heat he blamed on the crowd and the walk up the hill and the two flights of stairs. The music was operatic singing with a pop-music backbeat like from *The Phantom of the Opera*, the only musical he'd been to, one of a long line of bizarre Christmas presents Jerry and Linda had given to their employees. At this memory of his past life, Pete's stomach knotted.

Sarry materialized at his side, and the knot in Pete's stomach floated to his head and sent the room rocking side to side. Along with a black armband, Sarry wore a huge black floppy hat with a short veil that stopped above his eyes, a pink satin sleeveless dress with pink platform sandals and a pearl choker. "Hi, there! Remember me?"

Pete wanted to say, "How could I forget?" but before he could, Sarry put his hand on Pete's arm and said, "Garen makes a great gin martini. Do you like gin? I saw Guilda order a gin martini at a restaurant once, so I told Garen to make gin martinis at all his parties."

Sarry led Pete by the elbow, an act Pete appreciated because of the vertigo, to the kitchen where Garen, dressed in black pants and a black shirt, shook a silver shaker and poured out a silver liquid into martini glasses. Sarry picked a full glass off the counter and plopped the drink into Pete's hand. He took a sip. Pete hated gin, but it was alcoholic. He took another sip, and the vertigo began to ease off.

"Good, hey?" Sarry said.

Before Pete could say one way or another, a tall, loud woman reached out her arms and gave Sarry a bear hug. French words poured enthusiastically out of her mouth. With Sarry safely in the woman's arms, Pete slunk off, holding his glass in front of him like a dead animal.

He squeezed through the crowd into the corner of the room next to a large-screen television that was playing a psychedelic movie. On the screen, a woman stood in a windy field and ripped up her flouncy dress with a pair of scissors. For no reason the scene jumped to a campfire by a river. The sound was off, or else the noise of the twenty-five or so people and the operatic music drowned the movie soundtrack out. Two other people were looking at the screen, a man and a woman wearing armbands but otherwise dressed like office workers on casual Friday. They had big smiles on their faces, and each held a can of Molson Canadian.

"Where did you get the beer?" Pete asked.

"In the fridge," the man said.

The woman looked at Pete's drink and said, "Though a Garen martini is better."

Pete said, "I'm not a martini guy."

"We could switch," the woman said.

Pete liked the idea of switching drinks with a young normal-looking woman at a house party. He wondered what the man might think of it; both people wore wedding bands. She held out the drink, and the man with her grinned, so Pete switched drinks with her. He took a swig of the beer: that felt a lot better.

"Mmm," the woman said. "I feel like I'm in a James Bond movie when I'm here!"

The man and woman, Andrew and Violet, were married. Violet knew Garen from church, loved his parties, and came whenever she and Andrew could get babysitting. "Twins," she said. "Not every teenager on the block is willing to look after twin toddlers."

"I'm a twin too," Pete said.

Andrew and Violet wanted to know what it was like having a twin. The topic had bored him long ago, but this couple was so nice that he didn't want to ruin it by saying what he really felt, that there was no such thing as twin ESP, that he didn't have much in common with his twin. Instead he said it was great growing up because he always had a playmate. In reality he had stopped playing sincerely with Gilda by the time they were nine.

Andrew said, "I was an only child myself. The idea that I had to look for playmates for my child, like my mother had to do for me, filled me with dread."

"Now we have other kinds of dread," Violet said.

Andrew said, "The dread of cleaning up after two kids eating spaghetti in high chairs."

Pete smiled goofily. He asked if he could get anyone a drink, and he went to the kitchen to grab two Canadians from the fridge. Garen, still making martinis, said he noticed Pete talking to his friends Andrew and Violet. "They're nice, aren't they?" Pete agreed. "Does Violet want another martini?" Pete said yes. While he made the martini, Garen said he lived in Alberta one summer as a tree planter. Some people Pete used to hang out with in bars in Edmonton were tree planters. Garen had been good enough to be promoted to supervisor but had quit after two months. "I love the outdoors, but after a few weeks I found out that I need civilization mixed in with it. I need buildings, with walls, not tents. I need restaurants."

He returned to Andrew and Violet with the martini and the beer. Pete stayed quite late at Garen and Yasir's party, talking mostly to the church people but not exclusively. From time to time, Sarry sailed by and offered to fetch another martini, which Pete turned down, though Violet took one. "I'll check again in half an hour to see if you've changed your mind," Sarry said every time Pete said no. He became tipsy, no doubt, but he was soberer than he had been at a gathering with alcohol in a long time. He didn't remember all the things he said, because he'd talked a lot, but he remembered clearly that Andrew mentioned a chance to maintain the website that his boss's son had set up for his machine shop six months ago but hadn't kept up.

Just after one in the morning, when Pete announced to Yasir that he was going to leave, Sarry popped in and asked if he could share a taxi. "I walked here, but there is no way I'm walking downhill in these shoes." Pete didn't have the cash flow to say no to Sarry.

In the taxi, Sarry took off his hat, leaned back in the seat and said he would never wear so high a heel at a party again. "It seemed like a good idea at the time," he said. "In the end I like wearing sneakers." He sighed. "I should have been moving today. My landlord is going to be pissed. Well, it was for a good cause. Someone like Guilda doesn't come around every day. He brought so many people in Montreal together, you know?"

Pete didn't know. Sarry chatted gaily during the short drive. "It's great that Garen and Yasir have stopped pretending they're just roommates. I wonder if those church people know what they're getting when Garen volunteers at their church's movie nights. Mind you, Garen seems religious, so maybe it doesn't matter to them. I don't even know what church exactly it is that Garen goes to. Garen's parents are Jamaican. Aren't Jamaicans Seventh Day Adventist? Garen gets a bit of a Jamaican accent when he's on the phone with one of them. You should hear it."

Pete's stop was first. Sarry waved goodbye from the parting taxi with the accompanying shout, "Happy Canada Day!"

Not until he got out of bed in the morning with a headache and stumbled through the muggy, sickly sweet air to the dépanneur for a lousy coffee did it click that it was the first of July, Canada Day, as Sarry had said. Pete had spent part of a month in Montreal.

On the streets in his neighbourhood, an unusual number of U-Haul vans and pickup trucks were parked in front of buildings with people moving things in and out of them. Pete passed one apartment that had household items piled on the sidewalk: potted plants, a chest of drawers, a stack of kitchen chairs, a metal tub full of cooking pots, a basket full of doodads. He used to have the urge to move. That urge was gone, at least for now.

35

PETE'S SOCIAL LIFE UNFOLDS

A week after the Guilda party, Sarry called. Pete hadn't remembered giving Sarry his phone number. Sarry explained that he had asked Yasir for it: "Yasir said you were looking to find some friends, so he thought it was okay."

Pete was irritated. He had just negotiated his first website project through his contact with Violet and Andrew at Yasir and Garen's party, and he was trying to figure out which layout would be better than the lousy one it already had.

"I need help moving," Sarry said. Everyone he knew had helped someone else move July first and didn't want to do it again. One friend who said she would come wasn't reliable, and he would be shocked if she showed. "Everyone moves on July first here, and I was supposed to move that day too, but my landlord gave me a break because I'm just moving into a new suite in the same building, and no one is going into mine, but still, now would be a great day for me to move, so could you help?"

The phone number that Sarry had scribbled on Pete's hand had been a sneaky way to recruit a free mover. Pete had to swing into a help-a-buddy-out mode instead of beat-a-guy-off-with-a-stick mode. Sarry didn't live that far away, and the move seemed easy since all the furniture shuffling would happen inside one building.

"Sure," Pete said. "When?"

"Now?"

Armed with the address and directions, an hour later Pete reached the front door of a ragged concrete apartment walk-up, ridged and grey. Sarry greeted Pete through the tinny intercom with a chipper "Great, entrez!"

Sarry's apartment was on the main floor, and the door was open when Pete reached it. In the apartment, boxes littered the floor, as Pete had expected, but some of the room seemed perfectly tidy. Still lying dormant were an Ikea futon sofa, pillows artfully placed along its back, a glass coffee table with a candelabra and a glass cabinet full of tiny crystal animals. Some of the boxes on the floor were still open.

"You aren't finished packing."

"Yes, I am," Sarry said huffily. He put his hands on his hips. When he did this, he drew attention to his extraordinary outfit: a low-hipped pair of blue tights, red socks and a cropped tank-top. "More or less. I need help with the heavy stuff, you know."

Sarry was a cheerleader type of mover, full of high fives and whoops when they reached a milestone or carried out a risky move, like taking the chandelier upstairs by putting it on top of the glass coffee table. Despite his thin body and girly clothing, Sarry had no trouble holding up his end of a sofa, and he easily carried a full box of books on top of an end table. While he worked, he talked about the people in the building. The person whose apartment he was moving into had inherited a miniature poodle in a will, and the building didn't allow pets. Omar's new poodle had been fortuitous for Sarry: she had wanted to move off the main floor since Leon moved in two years ago. "He keeps calling me a tranny," Sarry said. "I told him most people don't like being called tranny, but he keeps saying it. I told him, 'Don't you know what neighbourhood you're living in, Leon? You're going to get a mob of angry queers and trans people breaking down your door one night if you're not careful.'" The new Sarry apartment had a good view of a clutch of trees near the decrepit parking lot behind the building. The previous resident had tidied up nicely before leaving, which Sarry said was "so totally typical. Omar is such a sweet guy."

The bed was a mattress and box spring that Sarry lay directly on the floor. "I don't know why, but I like having it on the floor," Sarry said while they heaved the box spring up the two flights of stairs.

"Mattress frames are easy to get hold of," Pete said.

"Maybe I'm just cheap." Sarry laughed. "Do you think?"

"Probably," Pete said.

Sarry laughed again. Once upstairs in the new bedroom, he insisted on leaving his clothing in their boxes. "My landlord said he was going to paint, so there's no point."

"If he's going to paint, he's still going to have to get around all the furniture." The bedroom was small, and they barely had room to manoeuvre the mattress in and lean it against a wall.

"I know, right?" Sarry said. "I wished he had painted it already."

"He could paint the bedroom first. We can put the chest of drawers and mattress in the living room for now, and you can move it into the bedroom after this room's painted."

"But you're here now," Sarry said.

"I can come back." Pete's deadpan answer didn't reflect the regret he felt immediately after speaking.

Sarry squeezed Pete's hand. "Oh my God, that would be so great!"

Whatever had been in the new bedroom Pete and Sarry re-moved into the living room so that the landlord could paint the bedroom more easily. The living room was larger and fit all the boxes and furniture, which, Pete noticed, didn't really take up much space. Sarry didn't have a lot of stuff. Pete said yes when Sarry said he would pay Pete with a beer at Café Le Feu that night. Pete walked home, his hamstrings and shoulders sore from lifting, wondering why he got himself involved with this airhead and with whom he was still going to be involved for some time, it looked like, at least until Sarry's landlord decided to paint the walls. Pete had spent two hours moving.

Not long after Pete returned home, Philip called.

"I just wanted to see how everything is going with you. How was Le Club?"

"It was interesting," Pete said in as neutral a way as possible.

"I'm glad it was at least that. Moving to a different city can be lonely. I know I was lonely when I moved from Sherbrooke to Montreal."

Pete didn't know where Sherbrooke was, although he had heard the word. He knew there was a pretty good liquor store in Edmonton called Sherbrooke. Maybe Sherbrooke was in Alberta?

"No, Sherbrooke, Quebec."

"Is 'Sherbrooke' a French word?"

"No, an English word. Don't forget that Britain took over Quebec in the eighteenth century." Philip changed the topic in that way teachers did to skip over someone's dumb answer to a question. "I thought you might like to meet someone from your neck of the woods who lives here now." She was a woman who worked in IT for Philip's department. She had moved from Peace River two years ago.

"Peace River is like a two-hour drive north of Edmonton," Pete said.

"Oh." He continued, as though the difference between Peace River and Edmonton wasn't clear to him and he didn't understand Pete's point. "Yelena said she would be happy to show you around. She knows what it's like to move to a new city."

Pete had never had any luck with anyone he'd met who was from Peace River, but he didn't say so. To cover up his lack of interest in this Peace River person, he told Philip about his meetings with Murray's friends.

"How did you run into Murray's friends?" Philip asked.

"Murray gave me the phone number for one of them. Yasir."

"Oh?"

In his head, Pete said, "Oops," but he couldn't act as though he'd noticed the sudden ice in Philip's voice. "They were all right people, I guess," he said nonchalantly. "That one guy Sarry was a bit out there."

"Ah, Sarry." Philip's mood lightened. "I like Sarry. Sarry was a bit of a celebrity once upon a time. She used to do the weather on the local news, but she was fired when she announced on air that she was going to start transitioning."

"Transitioning?"

"Presenting herself as a woman instead of a man."

"Like, get a sex change?"

"So to speak," Philip said.

Sarry did that on TV? "Wow." That took guts.

"Wow indeed." After a pause, Philip asked, "Did Murray say why he gave you Yasir's phone number?"

"He just said that Yasir might be able to show me around town."

"I see. Well." Philip said he would call again soon with an invitation for supper, once he coordinated with Murray, that is.

Pete clicked off the phone. He remembered that Murray had waited until Philip had left the room before giving him Yasir's number. Pete disliked Murray even more now. Not that it was any business of his, but why would Murray give Pete a phone number without telling Philip?

Pete walked to the kitchen table and picked up a plastic bag of playing cards he had started modifying for his game. Murray's deceptiveness struck Pete as something he could work into his game.

#

At Café Le Feu that evening, Sarry said that Pete's willingness to help him move was a sign that Pete considered Sarry a friend. "And friends don't let friends down. So, I called my landlord Wiley, and he's going to paint my apartment tomorrow during the day. The next day you can move my bed back into the bedroom, and you can wipe your hands of me and my move forever if you want."

Sitting with Sarry was the unreliable friend, Zora, a brunette who worked at the organic food store nearby. She had shown up at Sarry's place many hours late. The three of them spent their hour together listening to Zora explain the benefits of vegetarianism. She was more of a talker than even Sarry was, so when Pete returned home, the buzz in his ears was not from the screwdriver Zora ordered for him but from the constant drill of her voice.

The next day, Philip picked Pete up and took him to supper. They went to a Thai restaurant instead of staying at the B&B, Philip explained, because he had lost track of time and hadn't had time to cook. Pete thought that story was probably bullshit. Philip didn't say anything about Murray or what Murray might have been engineering behind Philip's back. Instead, Philip tried to talk Pete into going back to school, maybe getting a bachelor of science degree in computers. Pete had no interest in going back to school, but he let Philip think that he was open to it, since once again Philip picked up the tab. Philip also recommended that Pete join a club of some kind, a "board game fanciers club," and he attempted a brainstorming session about job searching that made Pete think of his father. Pete liked the attention, but he didn't take Philip's attempts at career planning seriously. He had just received a formal contract from Andrew, and he was feeling optimistic about his prospects.

On Wednesday night, Pete went to Sarry's apartment to move the bedroom furniture into the bedroom, whose new pale grey paint reminded Pete of pigeon feathers. Sarry had bought a metal bedframe, which Pete had to help put together. "You talked me into it," Sarry said. "I can't live like that anymore, like a—what do you call them?—a hobo."

The day after the move, Garen invited Pete to play a friendly soccer game. When Pete asked where, Garen said they played above the Village. When Pete asked where the Village was, Garen said, "Don't you live in the Village?"

"I live in downtown Montreal."

"The Gay Village in Montreal. The gay neighbourhood. You know."

Pete didn't know. Garen asked for Pete's address. "That's close to it, yeah," Garen said. "Use Avenue Papineau. Cars can't go up in that direction, so if you're driving you need the next street over."

Pete didn't want to walk, so he took a taxi. As he watched his neighbourhood whoosh past him from the passenger window, he wondered what was so gay about his neighbourhood. He didn't see it.

The soccer game ended up being not too bad of a time. Pete was officially a substitute, and he didn't substitute for anyone. All Pete had to do was sit in a lawn chair and drink hard lemonade out of a Gatorade bottle from someone's beer cooler. Sarry was there, and he didn't play or drink; he gossiped with the other players on the team. Yasir and Garen took the game more seriously than Pete thought was worth it. The opposing side wore tie-dye T-shirts and pink shorts, and they kicked Yasir's team's asses.

Yasir, Garen, Pete and Sarry walked home together; Montrealers had a funny idea of what was walking distance. Although Yasir and Garen lived in a different neighbourhood, they took up the invitation to see Sarry's new apartment. Pete noticed here and there men walking very close to other men, but other than that, it didn't seem gay. As for the apartment, Sarry had fixed it up, and Pete noticed a painting that now hung in the kitchen. It was of one half of a face, the eye drawn with a thick black line, the iris blue-black, its eyebrow arched impatiently. A tip of a lip appeared at the bottom edge of the frame so that it seemed that the impatient person was smiling.

"Where did you get that painting?" Pete asked.

Sarry thwacked his chest. "From right here."

"You mean—"

"I painted it, yup."

When Pete got home, he looked at the painting above his sofa. In the corner was the signature Sargon Umra.

The next afternoon, Yasir called to invite him to Café Le Feu for Friday games night. After careful consideration, Pete grabbed the travel checker and chess game he had brought from Edmonton. He associated the travel game with being in small spaces on road trips, in the back seat of a station wagon or in a one-room motel room in the Okanagan on a hot day. At Café Le Feu, only Sarry wanted to play checkers or chess. "It's kind of antisocial, isn't it," Garen said, "since only two can play." Sarry admitted that he didn't know how to play chess but was willing to learn. "I'm a—how do you say?—a quick student." Instead they played Masterpiece, a simple game but better than the other choices at Le Feu. Pete lost badly, but he had enough to drink to know that it didn't matter.

The rhythm of a new life set in. During the day he worked on his current jobs or looked for new contracts. He played soccer on Thursdays and spent Fridays at Café Le Feu at game nights. Saturday nights he went to The Club or someplace similar with Sarry, Zora, Yasir, Garen and their friends. He never mentioned that he had been there before, but he found out the name of the cross-dressing server, Sharl, who didn't seem to recognize him in Pete's new club clothes, as selected by Zora and Sarry. Some days Pete felt lonely, but Sarry would knock him out of his funk by doing or saying something ridiculous. Pete worked on his board game too. He was making good progress.

36

SHOW ME YOUR WORLD

Sarry called Pete early one evening and insisted that Pete let Sarry see his board game. The night before at Le Feu, Sarry had probed Pete about the details. "I have never met someone who made board games. Video games, yeah: there's too many of those people. But a board game, with dice and everything?"

When Sarry arrived, once again Pete was impressed by Sarry's physical transformation from meeting to meeting. She wore knee-length black pants with bright red cuffs and black and white sneakers. On top she wore a black sleeveless T-shirt with a red and pink scarf that looped over her neck two or three times into a wide, loose collar. In each earlobe, she had two studs made of a black gemstone.

Pete waved toward his game mock-up, set up as usual on the kitchen table. Sarry peered over the table, hands on hips. "What do you have here?"

"I'm using pieces from existing games so I can test my game before actually trying to make my own board."

Sarry pointed at the Chinese checkers board. "I recognize that."

"I borrowed it from Dom at Le Feu."

"Do you talk to Dom a lot about your games?"

"No, but he heard me talk to Yasir or someone about needing a Chinese checkers board, I guess, and he had it ready for me when I went there next time."

"I see." Sarry added quietly, "Is that all he gave you?"

"What?"

"Nothing."

He had heard what Sarry had said, but it didn't make sense. Sarry had a bad habit of muttering things.

Sarry studied the deck of Illuminati cards. "What is this?"

"Illuminati. It's a game."

"I've heard of the Illuminati. They control the world, pull the strings of big business and government. People used to talk about the Illuminati at a place I used to work, but not serious."

"What kind of work was that?"

"A TV station."

"You worked in TV?"

Sarry smiled. "For better or worse. I'm glad I did it, but I was also glad to leave. Well, I had to."

"How come?"

"I quit. On the air."

"Oh, yeah. I remember hearing something about that."

"People in Edmonton were talking about it?"

"Oh, I don't know about that." Pete had never been a watcher or reader of news. "Philip McDonald said something to me about it."

"Philip! I like Philip. You and Philip were talking about me?"

"I can't remember why you came up, to be honest."

"Do you and Philip like to gossip?"

"No."

"But you were!" He smiled teasingly. "You like gossip, hey? I like gossip too." He tapped Pete's forearm. "I didn't think you were the type."

"Okay, fine," Pete said. "I like to gossip. Do you want me to talk about the game or what?"

"Sure!" Sarry said. "The game, the game. I am here for the game! I like playing games!" She brought her fingertips down lightly on the table top. "Chinese checkers are from Dom the hot waiter at Café Le Feu. And the Illuminati? Where do they come from?"

"They're mine. I brought them with me from Edmonton."

"What do the cards do in the game?"

"In the original game, that's all there is. You have a set of cards in your hand and you lay them down in patterns."

"Like in dominos, or what?"

"Kind of. Do you play dominos?"

"I used to watch people play dominos in the old folks home I volunteered at in high school." She paused. "How do you lay down the cards?"

"You're trying to get points. You can't lie them down in any particular order, either. It depends on the class of cards you have and which card you are using during a round."

"Like suits?" Sarry asked.

"Sort of, yeah, but more complicated."

"Kind of like bridge?"

"You play bridge?"

"Not much anymore. I learned to play because of the old folks home." Sarry said after a pause, "Are you allowed to do that? Combine two board games other people have made? There's copyright and patents, no?"

"Eventually I need to hire an artist to design my own cards and board. I'll have to find a manufacturerer for them and the other game pieces. There are game pieces that I can buy, kind of this generic kit that someone made up and sells. I have to go on the internet to get the kit, though."

"Oh, right, you have an anti-internet thing. That's a problem, no, when you are working on websites?"

"As long as the internet is only for work, then it's okay."

"It must be hard to avoid going on the internet for other things."

Pete remembered something that Gilda liked to say. "I look at it as an opportunity."

Sarry laughed. "That's a good one. An opportunity. I like that. So maybe you need someone to order the pieces for you? I can do that for you. That's not illegal, is it, in this no-internet religion of yours?"

"No," Pete said. "And it's not a religion."

"It's not, hey? Are you sure?"

"Yes." He knew what religions were. He used to go to church with his mother and sister every day.

Sarry twisted her pursing lips into a smile. "I'm pretty good at graphic arts and drawing. Maybe I could help you? Do sketches for you, mock-ups."

"If you have the time. I couldn't pay you or anything."

Sarry waved the suggestion of pay away. "My pleasure, believe me. This could be fun. I'd have to think about what an Illuminati looks like."

"It's not an Illuminati game, though. I have my own things."

"What things?"

"I invented something that is more powerful than the Illuminati."

"Well, it's about time someone did. Those Illuminati seem like assholes. What does your game have?"

"They're like the controllers of everything. I call them the Exandorwai." He said the last word slowly. He wasn't sure that he had ever said the word out loud before in anyone's presence but his.

"Exandorwai? What is that?"

"The controllers of everything."

"Like gods?"

"No, not gods. They're people but a special kind of people."

"A race?"

"Not exactly. It's hard to explain."

"Bien sûr," Sarry said. "Special people are hard to explain. Do you try to explain these Exandorwai in your game?"

"Yeah. That's it. I try to explain them."

From the intensity of Sarry's expression, Pete sensed that he had to be careful. He was on the brink of discussing the game with someone else. A total stranger, though? No. A collaborator, a potential partner. The Parker Brothers had entered a partnership when they began their expansion of the family business into a multinational one. It was a moment of decision. A tipping point.

"Is it hard?" Sarry asked quietly. "If it's too hard to explain, maybe you could write it down."

"It's written down. I have a plan."

"If you have a written plan, then you are on your way. If you want me to do the mock-ups, I could use the plan to help me design what you want. It's up to you, of course, what you want. It's your project."

Sarry seemed to appreciate this was Pete's scheme, and no one else's. Norvell had been blunter with his advice. Sarry's style was softer. It was much better than his father's "you're an idiot" style, or his mother's easy acceptance of everything, or Gilda's pretend rationality and fake fairness while she snuck around and interfered. This was something else coming from Sarry. Businesslike.

"I know it's hard to plan something new," Sarry said. "It was hard for me to explain what I had decided to do." She gestured to her body with a flourish. "To become this."

Pete didn't know what this all had to do with board games. Nothing. But Sarry wanted to talk, so fine. "I bet."

"I didn't want to, at first. Then I had to. Maybe it would have been better if I had been more, I don't know, *attentive*. Cautious. But maybe doing it like I did, in front of the camera, in front of everyone was more . . . efficient." Sarry spoke calmly, like the people Pete ran into who were office workers and managers, the Kurtzweills, his teachers, explaining how to operate a photocopier or how to fill an order with one game company versus the other game company, how to add JavaScript versus how to add HTML. Maybe this was the way George Parker explained to his staff how to package games to keep the size of the boxes small.

"Impersonal," Pete said. "Just telling it the way it is."

"Right. Just the facts. Like telling the weather. Maybe that's why I decided to out myself on air. You can have theories and make models and create computer simulations about the weather, and that works, but you can't do that for people. People are too different from each other. Unpredictable. All you can do is come up with yours, and if other people don't like it, that's their problem." After a silence, Sarry said, "Do you have anything else to show me?"

"No. I can email the plan if you want."

"I want. And speaking of want, I'm hungry. What are you doing now? Or do you want to grab a drink or something at Le Feu?"

Pete was famished, and he could eat at Café Le Feu better than he could at home. It would be like a business meeting. Of course, he wouldn't necessarily choose Sarry for the final product—he'd have to see how good Sarry was—but he was on his way to something concrete. He should find someone a little less high-maintenance to be part of his business venture. Still, Sarry was enthusiastic. She liked to keep it light, too, which Pete appreciated. In the end, she was fun and smart. It was a risk, but he could see the benefits of working with Sarry.

Just before Pete was about to steer Sarry out the door, she said, "Hey! That's my painting!"

She walked into the living room and stared up at the red-lipped woman.

"I saw the signature and thought as much," Pete said.

"*Lady of the Eighties,*" Sarry said. "We meet again. Who did you say owns this apartment?"

"François something."

"I don't know a Something," Sarry said. "I sold the Lady when I closed up my studio. It was like a garage sale. Do you like her?"

"She grabs your attention."

"You should have seen her in person."

"That's a real person?"

"Yeah. I'm not sure I should tell you." She smiled. "Maybe one day."

On their walk to Le Feu, Sarry asked Pete about his life in Edmonton. Pete told Sarry that he had a twin sister, his parents were divorced, his father was a conductor and musician, and his mother worked for the health department.

At Café Le Feu they ran into some friends of Zora, and they talked about something else other than Pete. All during the evening, Pete kept looking at Sarry's expressions. When Sarry smiled at Pete, Pete liked it.

#

Three days later, Pete and Sarry were the only two in their group to show up at an agreed-upon meeting at Le Club. Pete wanted to go home rather than stay. He'd been at Le Club too many times. He refused to dance, so the place bored him. "I'm more into bars and pubs, like back in Edmonton."

"Let's do that!" Sarry slapped her hand on the wall in the lineup outside the Club. "Show me your world!"

Sarry had to tell Pete where to find Pete's world in Montreal. "A pub," said Pete, "with music, but not with dance music. If there's dancing, it's just in a little square in the centre of the room. Everyone else sits at tables, drinks beer and drink specials, hangs around the bar and hits on each other. Then stumble home drunk before the cops come out."

From Le Club, Sarry escorted Pete through Centre-Ville to an Irish pub on Cathcart. It was filled with college students and people who finished college ten years ago. The lighting was gloomy, the music was Top 40, and the patrons packed themselves against the big bar and at the stand-up tables around the measly square of parquet that served as a dance floor. After an hour or so, Sarry got tired of Pete's pub jokes and dragged Pete out for some food. As they walked, Sarry wanted to know what Pete used to do after the pub. Pete said, "Marco's Donair," and Sarry remembered that four blocks away was a good shawarma place. They ploughed through the crowd of tipsy partiers that were migrating from one drinking establishment to another. The dark, noisy interior of the shawarma place was as full of people as the streets were, but they found a free table in a corner. Pete didn't know if a donair was the same as a shawarma.

Sarry said, "It's all the same stuff, trust me. I ate ethnically when I was growing up." They shared a plate of fries. "Say 'frites,' at least," Sarry said. "Use at least one French word a day." Sarry had offered to help Pete learn French. "I'm not pure laine, but not many people in Montreal are, let's face it."

"What's pure laine?"

"Someone who goes French all the way back to the years of Louis the Fourteenth."

"That's a long time ago, right?"

"Almost in the Jesus era."

After they finished their shawarmas, they returned outdoors to sidewalks so crammed with people that Pete didn't realize that they were being tailed until it was too late. Two hunched shapes swept around them and in front, and suddenly they were surrounded in the mouth of an alleyway by six men in ball caps and boots.

"You fags looking for some action?" one man said.

"Merde," Sarry muttered.

Pete faked a move to the left, raised his right hand and slid his left hand slowly into his pocket as though he had a knife in there, a feint he had used in various bars in his past to good effect.

"Take it easy, assfucker," another man said. His face was pulled open with a wide sneering smile. "Let's do this man to pretend man."

Pete counted two shots to his head and one to his gut before a squadron of defenders swarmed in. They frightened the attackers off by their numbers, not by throwing punches, though one person ran after the hoodlums with his cellphone out as though filming their escape. Pete and Sarry brushed off people's insistence on calling the police or ambulance. "We're okay," Sarry said to a white-faced girl. "Just make sure those shits become YouTube stars."

The crowd, though not completely satisfied, streamed around them back to normal. Pete and Sarry checked each other's wounds.

"You've got a cut on your lip," Pete said.

"You have a big swelling on your eye that I think is going to turn into a shiner tout de suite." Sarry smiled weakly, then her eyes shifted around her. "We should go before some other frat boys get the scent of blood, sweat and queers."

Sarry called a taxi from her phone and then insisted that they go back into the shawarma place to clean up so that they didn't scare off the cabbie. They went in, ignored the stares, Pete in the men's bathroom, Sarry in the women's.

When they met up again outside, Sarry said she wanted to go home and "deep-clean" herself to wash away the ugliness of the last hours. "You know, though, everything until that last part of the night was fantastic."

On the ride to her apartment, Sarry said, "I recognized two of them from the restaurant. They were staring. I ignored my instincts."

"You could tell?"

She nodded. "This hasn't ever happened to you before, has it?"

"No." More than once Pete had been jumped in an alley, and he'd jumped people in an alley, but he had never tried to beat up people because they were gay. In one or two fights in his past, people had called him a fag, but he took that as just one in a long line of insults people used before a bar fight. He was sure he'd used that word himself.

"Well," Sarry said, "welcome to my world."

"How often does this kind of thing happen?"

"Too often," Sarry said. "It's better in the Village."

When the taxi stopped at Sarry's apartment, Sarry squeezed Pete's hand, said, "I'll call you tomorrow," and Pete was in the car alone. The taxi drove down Saint Catherine Street through the Village. People were walking alone, in groups, and in couples. Men holding men's hands, women holding women's hands. He and Sarry hadn't been holding hands, but something had made those fuckers think he was gay. Maybe it was the way Sarry looked. Pete looked down at his clothes. Or the way he looked.

When he got home, he lay on the floor in front of *Lady of the Eighties*. He looked up at the blank, dark ceiling. Tonight he'd had a giant spotlight shining on him, at least as far as those gay-bashers had been concerned. He understood why the narrator of *Invisible Man* had hidden in a basement filled with light. Whether Invisible Man liked it or not, bright lights had been shining on him all the time. In his basement, he took control of the light, made it his own, so that he could see himself as he saw himself.

#

Pete knew his Edmonton family would have been shocked to know that, days later, he and Sarry were walking along Amherst Street to look at antique stores. Pete had recovered enough from the attack for him to agree to have Sarry show him more of her world. The Pink Balls, or *Les Boulles roses* as Sarry called them, floated above them, strung like Christmas lights across Amherst between its buildings. Most everyone was looking upwards, though a few, Pete noticed, were mushing forward onto whatever destination they were travelling toward. He supposed that, like the Coliseum in Rome, the locals simply had gotten used to them.

"I don't know about that," Sarry said. "It's pretty hard to ignore. Some people are just pretending to ignore it, to look cool or non-touristy."

"Probably not what the inventor had in mind," Pete said.

"Who knows? Anyway, you can't control people. Artists know that. When you create something, your creation can get reinvented."

Their first antique store was a large dim room crammed with dark wooden armoires, dining tables and chairs, hutches, cabinets, tiny desks with big mirrors and matching tiny chairs. On top of the furniture were ceramic bowls, teacups, plates, brooches, earrings sitting on doilies and metal trays, ceramic figurines of birds, horses and dogs, pincushions stuck with fancy dress pins.

Pete asked, "How do you know what's good and what's not good?"

"You learn, just like you learn everything else."

Pete wandered past silver tea services, hats with veils, rings, glass animals in locked glass cabinets, floor lamps with crocheted shades. Eight hundred dollars for a painting of a dog with a dead duck in its mouth, nine hundred dollars for a man in a green suit standing next to a tree.

"Do you buy stuff from these places?" Pete asked.

"Sometimes." Sarry picked up a white bumpy candy dish, looked underneath it and put it down. "You know that little table by my television? I bought it at a shop on Amherst."

"I bet my mom would love it here."

"Maybe she can come here and visit you," Sarry said.

Beth probably liked the brick and rock of the Old City and the old churches like the big one in Mount Royal where the tour buses went. She must have liked it: she'd liked the city so much that she brought him here when he was a baby. As he looked at a turquoise pendant hanging from the neck of a mannequin, he wondered if she had come to Amherst one day with him in her arms and taken him to this exact store.

As they left the store, he asked Sarry, "How old do you think that last store was?

"I don't know. Some of these places have been here forever, but forever for me is like the 2000s." She looked up. "*Les Boulles roses* were just put up last year. Who knows how long they will stay?"

Sarry liked to answer a question with another question. If Pete wasn't careful, one day he and Sarry might go on and on trading question for question until doomsday.

They went into three more antique stores, then Pete reminded Sarry that he had a meeting at Le Feu with a prospective client. On their way to Le Feu, Sarry asked Pete what he thought of the antique stores.

"They were okay."

Sarry laughed, touched Pete's arm. "Ah, well, too bad. Maybe it will grow on you?"

When they got to Café Le Feu, Yasir and the prospective client were not there yet. Dom materialized at their table with their usual, a rum and Coke for Pete and cranberry and vodka for Sarry. Dom lingered to find out what they had been doing, but Sarry shooed him away. "Vraiment, Dom, give us some space."

After Dom stalked away, Sarry said, "But you like it here, Le Feu? We come here a lot, but not too much, right?"

Pete had to admit that he liked the café.

"Some people think the Village is getting commercialized." Sarry stirred her drink with the barber-pole stir sticks that came with every cocktail. "There are too many tourists, some say, it's turned into a gay-themed Disneyland. But I don't care if I live in Disneyland. In our Disneyland, nous deux wouldn't get jumped in the street by homophobes looking to boost their cred with the KKK."

The thing was, Pete had known people over the years who might have kicked a gay man in the head given a chance. He wasn't sure how close he had come to being one of those people.

"Earth to Petey!" Sarry reached across the table and gave Pete's arm a squeeze. "Come back to me, doll."

Pete wasn't sure about many things now.

37

GILDA IN MONTREAL

Gilda arrived in Montreal too late in the evening to do anything but sit on the edge of her bed and stare sleepily out her hotel window. The hotel was down the street from an old Hudson's Bay Company store on Saint Catherine, and it overlooked a small city park where the shadows of pedestrians flitted under streetlights and the illuminated façades of shopfronts. In the hotel room's window, she could also see, somehow behind the view of the outdoors, the reflection of the dull hotel furniture and her wan face.

The time change played havoc with her scheduling. She woke up later in the morning than she had wanted to. From the lobby restaurant, she bought take-away tea and a muffin and sat outside in the park on a bench. The shadows of last night had become solid human figures making their way along the sidewalks, and the park was now home to half a dozen jewellery vendors. On the street corner by The Bay, people watched a busking guitarist while they waited for the light to turn green. Teenaged boys in Nikes and reversed ball caps stalked past in groups of three speaking loudly in a language she couldn't identify. Young women with pink shopping bags laughed and skittered across the pavement on their tall, thick-heeled sandals. The thrump of dubstep blared from an open car window in the flow of car traffic.

Though she knew it was futile, she tried to find Pete in the crowd. As the morning progressed, the individual motes in the streams of people and cars changed, and the guitarist busker was replaced by a busker with a bongo, but the streams themselves remained, and Pete was not within them. Gilda was part of the stream, even though she sat on a bench rather than lugged a knapsack or swung a shopping bag, or dodged between two cars on a bicycle. The motes in the stream had their places to go, roles to fulfill. Two magnificently clothed women hastened past her with adamantine fashion-model faces, as though the whole world was their runway. Gilda looked at her blue cotton pants and white sneakers from Winners.

Glumly she stuffed the rest of her muffin into her mouth. She should phone Philip's bed and breakfast. Once she took this step, she could not go back and undo it. It was like starting a new file in her project management software. Once she created a start point, people with the right view access could see how her project was doing. She couldn't speed away from the point of contact, unknown and unnoticed.

She returned to her hotel room and called the B&B. The answering machine put a hole in the space of time she had set out to fill. She didn't want to go out into the city until she heard back from Philip. When she thought of Montreal, she imagined it as a city of hockey riots, spontaneous street parties, and loudly gesticulating fashionable men and women walking in and out of crowded designer clothing stores. A caricature, she knew. Nevertheless, she feared missing a call. Some streetside visual stimulation, a gothic church or pastrami sandwich shop, might distract her, and she didn't want to find herself stuck somewhere that was so loud she couldn't hear Philip talk. Thus, she waited in her room, flipped channels, played a game on her phone, looked out the window.

Three hours later, her cellphone rang, and a cheery voice said, "Hello, this is Philip McDonald from Le Gîte La Lobélie B&B. I'm returning your call!"

"It's Gilda Peterborough from Edmonton. Beth's daughter. I'm in Montreal."

In the pause before his reply, the stream of life shifted.

38

REVERSE SHOT

Philip dialed the number left on voice mail thinking it was a potential customer. Now he had to face the reality of his own duplicity. Weeks earlier, he had lied to this person now on the phone about not having heard from Pete. He had typed his response to Gilda's questions on Facebook with confidence, based on the principle that it was not his place to interfere with Pete's decision to be secretive with his family about his whereabouts. As a gay man, he had learned to appreciate the importance of privacy and of secrecy within families. Now he was no longer sure if he had done the right thing. He had not too long ago learned that Murray had given Yasir's number to Pete. He decided not to talk to Murray about the phone number. He would pretend that this handing out of numbers was no big deal. He had to pretend too, therefore, that lying to Gilda was also no big deal.

"Of course!" Recovering. "You contacted me on Facebook or email."

"Facebook."

"And now you are here in Montreal?"

"Yes," she said. "I'm looking for my sibling. I decided to come to Montreal to look for him."

"Sibling" was an odd word to use. It threw him off. "Did you say you were coming here?"

"I can't remember. I don't think so."

"Do you want to stay in my B&B?"

"Did I suggest I was? No, I wasn't planning to. I didn't think of it, honestly. I'm staying someplace else."

"Oh, that's no problem, of course," he said. "It's not like there is only one place to stay in Montreal."

"That's true." The woman laughed awkwardly, and Philip felt guilty about making her feel uncomfortable. "What I called about," she continued, "is that I wanted you to know that my mother sends her best regards."

"That's sweet. Please let her know the same."

"Maybe we can meet for coffee."

"Sure!"

"And if Philippa happens to contact you, I'd appreciate it if you could let me know."

Philip had been under the impression that as an adult, the sibling was called Pete, and that Pete identified as male. "I'm sorry," he said carefully, "but did you say Philippa?"

"Yes," she said. "Sometimes she goes by different names, though."

"Oh."

Gilda said, "You know about Philippa, right?"

"What about Philippa?"

"He's intersex."

Philip paused. "Yes."

"Sometimes he goes by the name Pete."

Her voice reminded him of the students who came to his office, pale-faced, asking for a higher mark because they needed to get their grade-point average up for a scholarship. The voice of a proud person about to break down. This time, though, he wasn't a professor who had to abide by academic rules and statistically required failing grades. He didn't need to treat information like a sacred commodity. He didn't want to break a promise to Pete, but he didn't want lies to pile up on lies. "Yes, Pete. Pete has contacted me, yes."

"He has? When?"

"I can't remember exactly. Not that long ago."

"That's good news," Gilda said. "What is he doing?"

"He seems fine. He has a job, and he's made some friends."

"Do you happen to have his contact information?"

"Yes."

"Can I have it?"

Here he had to consider his position. It was too awkward to even give a name to this position. Was it wrong to give contact information to people without seeking permission first? Usually. Was this a special circumstance, though? Yes. How special, though, it couldn't be easily determined. How to deal with this? Be a professor.

"I'm not sure how to respond to that question. I'm not saying he's keeping himself away from people, but at the same time, a phone number is personal information, and unless I have his permission, I'm not comfortable giving it to you. I'm not saying I won't ever give you the information. I need time to think about it. I can take your phone number, though, and get back to you?"

Professors were so-called because they professed. As a professor, Philip avowed a set of knowledges associated with a discipline and thus enunciated himself into a knowledge community. Part of the knowledge community to which he professed to belong took privacy seriously, as a human right of self-identification. He must profess a belief in the sacrosanct nature of self-identity as determined by the subject for itself, especially in a post-post-Enlightenment age where the private and the public are always intertwined, not for the benefit of the person, but in fulfillment of public panopticonization, the rigorization of the disciplinarity of the

Gilda was talking, and he had missed some of it. "If I haven't heard from you in two days," she was saying, "I'll call you. I'm just jumpy about him, that's all."

"I'll call you tomorrow no matter what. How's that?"

"Okay," Gilda said.

The call over, Philip stared into the mirror above the phone desk. In the reflection, he saw not only his perturbed face but the image of Murray, who stood in the kitchen holding an empty loaf pan in each hand and looked in Philip's direction.

"Who was that?" Murray asked.

"That was Pete's sister."

"His sister?"

Philip turned from the mirror. "Yup."

"What does she want?"

"She tracked Pete down to Montreal and wants to know if I've seen him."

"Oh." Murray commenced moving his loaf pans from the drawer by the oven to the top of the counter in preparation for the next morning's banana bread.

"I said," Philip said, answering an unasked question, "I would ask Pete if I could give her his phone number."

The loaf pans clanked against each other. "Fair enough," Murray said.

Philip walked past Murray to the refrigerator and checked the supply of old bananas—they had enough. "Do you think?"

"You could have given her the number too." Murray reached for the cupboard beside him and took down the jar of brown sugar.

Philip rested his hip against the counter. "Would that have been ethical, though?"

"There's no law against it."

"Is that the standard I'm following?" Philip murmured back.

"You're overthinking things. Asking Pete if you can give Gilda his number is the other option. It's a fair option, like I said."

Philip noticed that he was pressing his hip too hard against the counter's edge. "I do overthink sometimes. The academic's disease." That had been Murray's term, and now he and Philip used it as though it were part of their couple's vocabulary, shared between them with no claims made for its origin.

Philip moved away from the counter and the sore hip. He slipped his arms around Murray's waist. "I should just call Pete right now, ask him, and then call her right back."

Murray relaxed into Philip's embrace but kept on pulling things out of the cupboards. "Sure, hon. Or not. It's getting late."

Gently Murray extricated himself so that he could fish the measuring cups out of the baking drawer. "Why don't you get to bed?" Murray said. "I'll be right there." He opened the jar of brown sugar. Murray was busy getting ready for tomorrow's big bake, and here Philip was, burying him with his intellectual woes. How patient Murray was with him.

In bed, Murray asked if Gilda had called collect. Murray didn't like it when guests called collect on their house phone.

"No, she's in Montreal," Philip said.

"She lives in Montreal?"

"No, Edmonton. She came to Montreal to find Pete."

With a rustle of sheets, Murray rolled over on his left side, his back to Philip, in his preferred sleeping position. "That's some serious family shit."

Philip shut his eyes in a wave of sudden, pleasant drowsiness. Not everything was set to normal, but the day was ending well, all things considered.

39

DEFINITION

Pete had finished doing work for Andrew's company, and he hadn't received any material yet from Yasir's friend, who had, during lunch at Le Feu, promised to send some files. Someone in the universe heard his desperation, and its spokesperson turned out to be Sarry. "Hey," she said over the phone that morning, "we need some help with a webpage over here pronto. I told my office manager I knew someone who could do it. You, that is."

Pete didn't have anything going on, so after lunch he walked down to Sarry's office. LGBTQ Youth Alliance was in the heart of the Gay Village in a two-storey brick building. Sarry worked as a publicity person and youth counsellor there. The office manager, Gordon, a stocky man with a chin beard and all-brown clothing, wanted to integrate the Alliance's newsletters directly into the website rather than as PDF files listed in reverse chronological order in a corner of the site. He'd just gone to a seminar for non-profit organizations, and he'd decided to implement one thing from the seminar out of principle. Offhandedly Pete mentioned that the emailed newsletter could be turned into a blog or a newsfeed. Both Sarry and Gordon seemed taken with the idea. Still, Gordon seemed to want something more from Pete. Gordon asked, "How do you know Sarry?"

Pete had to think. It seemed like he had always known Sarry. "We met through a friend of a friend about a month ago."

Sarry said, "He's kind of new in town. From Alberta."

"Do you have experience working with LGBTQ organizations?"

"No, but I have nothing against them." He winced when Gordon raised his eyebrows.

Gordon didn't stop the interview right there, thankfully. "Well, if you can send me a proposal, a project timeline and your salary expectations as soon as possible, I can look things over and get in touch with you."

Pete shivered. He remembered taking a course on business proposals at NAIT: or had he registered for it but dropped out of it? "Proposal? No sweat."

Sarry walked Pete out to the office lobby with a big smile. "I think that went well, don't you?" She tapped Pete on the chest. "Get that proposal in, though. Gordon is all business. It'll take more than your looks to impress him."

Pete went home and in a couple of hours emailed a description of what he was doing, a salary that amounted to what he remembered getting paid by Jerry plus 10% since he lived in Montreal and he thought he ought to. When he heard nothing from Gordon that afternoon, he called Sarry in the evening to find out what his status was.

Sarry didn't know yet. "Gordon isn't a fast mover."

"Does Gordon only hire gay people?"

"Interesting question. You sure can't be a homophobe and last long around here, that's for sure. Everyone I know who works here or does stuff for us is queer."

"What do you mean by queer?"

"Don't you know?"

"Not exactly," Pete said. "What is the definition?"

"Well," Sarry said, "think about all the people you've been hanging out with here in Montreal. What would you say they have in common?"

Of course Pete knew what they had in common. They were guys who liked other guys, girls who liked other girls.

"Sure," Sarry said. "Then there's me. I am a type of woman."

"Okay."

"Okay? It's more than okay. I'm taking hormones, but even if I weren't, I would still be a woman. I want to get surgery so that I don't have a penis and testicles and have a vagina and clitoris instead. But even without that vagina and clitoris, I am still a type of woman." She paused. "And I am turned on by men."

"So, you're straight?" Pete asked.

"I'm queer."

Pete and Sarry had been attacked on the street outside the shawarma place because those asswipes thought that he and Sarry were gay. Sarry had been wearing run-of-the mill clothing. Pete thought he was dressed like a guy. How was that queer?

Sarry said, "If I got naked I'd mostly look like a guy, though now I have two little breasts and my hips are rounded and my face is rounded."

Pete couldn't answer. He shouldn't. No, he could. "So do I."

"So do you what?"

"That's what I have. Two little breasts. And a penis."

"What are you saying? You're taking hormones?"

"No."

"You're intersex."

No one had ever asked him that question. No, it wasn't a question. It was a statement. Only his sister and doctors ever used that word. He wasn't sure he'd ever heard his mother say that word. "Yeah."

"I'm right?"

"Yeah."

"Vraiment."

Pete understood that French word. It meant "really." He felt a thrill, the kind that usually preceded the onset of vertigo.

Sarry said, "You identify as a male, right? Pete, not Petra."

The vertigo didn't come. "I do. Now."

"Not always, though? Maybe you were raised as a girl at first and then you changed to a boy?"

"How do you know so much about this?"

226

"I've learned a few things from working here, and from friends. I knew a girl once who was that. She had two X chromosomes and a Y chromosome."

"I don't have that," Pete said. "It's something else for me. Partial AIS."

"Wow, that's kind of rare, hey?"

"I don't know."

"Special."

"Great, I'm special. That's just another way of saying I'm a joke."

"A joke?" Sarry angrily muttered something in French. "Has anyone told you were a joke?"

"I'm telling you that I'm a joke."

Sarry said a few words in French and continued in English. "Now I'm pissed off. You call yourself a joke. You, the guy who is a creator of games."

"What do you mean?"

"Maybe you aren't like most people, but so what? You do your own thing, you make your own model. Make your own game. Make your own rules."

"Oh, I get it," Pete said sarcastically. "Life is a game. The game of life. Have you ever played The Game of Life? It's shitty. You have a blue person and a pink person and that's it. You land on squares based on the spin of a wheel."

"I know that game. If it's shitty, then don't fucking play it. Don't do what other people do. Make your own game."

Pete's throat had constricted. He hadn't ever told anyone about his junk. All the people who knew seemed to have known without him telling them. He had just told his first person, and he was being told he was being an idiot about it.

Sarry asked, "Are you mad?"

"No."

"All I'm saying is that lots of queer people live different, and I think you qualify as queer."

The room spun. Pete pretended it wasn't. "I don't need help."

"Of course not," Sarry said. "But don't be so hard on yourself."

"I'm not hard on myself."

"Good. It's just I was surprised when you called yourself a joke." She took a deep breath, let it out. "I'm flattered that you told me about yourself. It's hard, I know. And it's, you know, an honour." Her voice grew quieter. "I mean it when I say you're special."

The way Sarry said special, with a fillip of a French accent, made the word sound different than Pete had ever heard that word said before. A nicer way.

Pete broke off the conversation then. He said he needed to get back to work and would call Gordon the next day.

He sat down on the floor, waited for the spinning to stop. When it did, he went to bed. One of the cats joined him on the bed and purred him to sleep.

The next morning, he called Gordon.

Gordon said that Pete was the "best person to do it," as long as his references were good, of course.

That night, Sarry called. She was very excited. "Gordon's hiring you. We're going to be seeing even more of each other," Sarry ended.

"I'll do most of the work from home."

"But you'll have to come by once in a while."

"Sure."

"And how does that make you feel?"

"Fine," Pete said.

"That's nice to hear. Can I come over?"

Pete hesitated. She wanted to work now? "I was thinking of starting tomorrow or something."

After a pause, Sarry continued. "It's not a big deal. No, that makes sense. Are you going to Café Le Feu later?"

"I hadn't thought of it."

"Are you sure you aren't mad at me?" Sarry said in a small voice.

"I'm sure."

She sighed. "Great. So, you're coming?"

He had to eat, so he said he was. After Sarry hung up, Pete wondered if there was some strange office politics going on that he would have to deal with. Pete wasn't thrilled with politics. But he was hungry, so Le Feu made sense, and he needed work, so working for this alliance also made sense. He didn't mind being around Sarry more if Sarry was just going to be Sarry the friend and not Sarry the co-worker. In that way, Sarry was less like Norvell. Good old Norvell. Norvell was not a work-friend. Norvell was more like a teacher or advisor. Sarry was a friend first, a co-worker second.

Pete let his gaze wander to the painting above the futon. The red lips, the eyes. Sarry's signature in the bottom right corner.

He went to the chest of drawers where he kept all the clothes he'd bought in Montreal. He put the clothes on. They were the club clothes he had worn the second time he went to Le Club, the knee-length red leather skirt, the sparkling black top. He hadn't worn them since. He gazed at herself in the full-length mirror at the back of the bathroom door.

"Hey, Philippa." The room held itself still for him. "How's it going?"

He replaced the Philippa clothing with old Edmonton Pete clothing before he went to Café Le Feu.

40

FIRST MEETINGS

Gilda had said that there was no point going back to Tokens, but all Beth could think about at work the day after Gilda's departure was Tokens. By her afternoon tea break, she convinced herself that going to a store after work was harmless, even if it was a store she wanted to go to only because Pete used to work there.

After supper and church, Beth drove to Tokens. Once inside, she was gobsmacked by her nostalgia for her home when Pete lived there. The store had shelves and stands, tables and bins covered with games and action figures, tables and glass cabinets stacked with boxes with exotic names and invented places. Two people circled a tower of different kinds of dice like a totem pole. Four or five people browsed the aisles. A card game was going on in a sunny wing of the store, and an adult with the half-bored look of a dutiful parent watched from a smaller table nearby. Who would have thought that parents nowadays would encourage their children to play cards? Beth's mother said that in Winnipeg during the Depression, children playing cards was considered the beginning of the long fall down to smoking and finally to joining gangs or labour unions, groups treated interchangeably by Beth's mother. Beth approached the cashier counter, behind which stood a large young man with small eyes buried under protruding brows and thick cheeks. He said, "Can I help you?"

"You very well might. I'm trying to find out something about my child, who works here."

"A child?" the young man said. "Works here?"

"No, he's an adult, but he is my child. Pete Peterborough."

"Oh." The young man's face turned fuchsia. "Yes, Pete used to work here."

"Used to?"

"Didn't you know he stopped working here?"

"I thought as much," Beth said. "Now I am wondering if you know anything about why he quit or where he's gone."

His eyes crinkled in apology. "All I know is that he took a leave of absence. He didn't quit or anything. That is, he's coming back."

"How interesting. Do you know when he is coming back?"

"I don't know, ma'am," the young man said. "I can get my boss. He would know more."

"Oh, pardon me. I thought you were the boss."

The young man blushed. "I just work here."

"Though you have been informative," Beth said. "Maybe Pete has mentioned your name to me?"

"I don't know." Blush. "But I'm Norvell."

"That rings a bell."

Again he blushed. "I'll get my boss Jerry."

The conversation with Jerry proved less interesting than her conversation with Norvell. Jerry said that Pete had taken an indefinite leave of absence, though he was still being paid to update the website. Jerry wasn't obliged to take Pete back as an employee, though he was inclined to do so, since he liked Pete and Pete was a good employee. "Is there any trouble?"

"Pete has lost touch with the family, that's all. I'm beating the bushes."

"From what I can tell, he seems fine." He took her phone number and said he would call her the next time Pete contacted him. "This may not be kosher, but I have kids too. I know what it must feel like."

Beth walked slowly toward the store's exit, thinking not much about what Jerry said but rather about this Norvell, whom she suspected might know unofficially things that Jerry knew only officially. The blushing raised her suspicions. She glanced over her shoulder, and sure enough, Norvell was looking at her, though he was quick enough to look down when she noticed him. She turned in time to avoid colliding with a shiny-eyed teenager carrying a stack of small, brightly coloured boxes with drawings of angry cartoon rabbits on them. Beth remembered seeing something similar lying around her basement. Another upsurge of nostalgia tripped her stomach up. She had to do something about that nostalgia.

#

At church that night, as with every night, she kneeled and shut her eyes and didn't even wait for the priest to start the service. The meeting with Norvell had stirred up in her memories of her first meeting with her ex-husband. Ralph and Beth met in June 1969 at a party at the Red Cross House, a two-storey house rented by a revolving complement of nursing students: in April the graduating class moved out, and in September a replacement set of first-year students moved in. The nurses' house happened to be painted white, and one day, as neighbourhood rumour had it, someone planted an empty metal garbage can in the front yard flower bed and painted a big red cross on it. Subsequent summer parties at Red Cross House saw the garbage can filled with ice and beer, a nude male mannequin with a red bowtie, and, at Hallowe'en, an articulated skeleton wearing a pirate hat and eyepatch. On the summer evening that Beth walked up to the house to meet her destiny, a shirtless man with a top hat was standing in the garbage can and a woman was trying to talk him into getting out.

Inside, the dimly lit common room wriggled with sweaty, bare-armed and -legged twenty-year-olds stomping to the nurses' LP collection, thumpy rhythms and cracked-voice tenors belting their souls over twanging guitars and tinny snare drums and cymbals. Beth recognized a few faces but knew no one. At the drinks table in a corner of the room, Beth and Ralph reached out for the same bottle of root beer. She allowed him to take the bottle, then he grandly poured out her drink first into an empty beer stein.

"I guess we aren't getting drunk tonight," Ralph said.

Beth came from a family of alcoholics and had never felt comfortable with social drinking, never mind the type where you sat alone at home at the kitchen table in the dark with a bottle of rye. "I drink from time to time, just not all the time and not all at once."

"I know what you mean," he said. "I don't understand how people can get zonked like that all the time."

The word "zonked" charmed her. "We're kind of out of place here," she said. In the centre of the common room, handclaps and Hammond organs choreographed the vamping of a trio of women in nurse uniforms and go-go boots, surrounded by eager, bearded men who threw their arms in the air in time with stomping feet.

"Then why are we here?" Ralph asked.

They went outside for a walk together through the leafy summer evening. They learned that they lived in the same neighbourhood, and both had been at the Red Cross House before, though for two different parties. "It's the opposite of a coincidence," Beth said.

This opposite of a coincidence should have been an ill portent, but it wasn't strong enough for two country people lonely in the big city. Beth hadn't wanted much out of life: a nice house with a dog and a cat, three kids, and a half-decent job doing something that gave her economic access to restaurants, clothes and the occasional vacation in February to a place warmed by sun and sand. Her job in a typing pool for the provincial government contented her. Ralph had more precise ambitions. He'd come to Edmonton after studying viola and choral conducting at McGill University. He served as the director of a choral group in town and another choral group that travelled across the country, and recently he'd formed a string quartet with three friends from the Alberta College Conservatory of Music, where he taught viola. He was curly-haired, tall and thin-shouldered and kept his hands in his pant pockets like the humble farm boys she knew back home, but his sensitive milky blue eyes burned in his pale freckled face with a passion for music and for making a name for himself. This vague prairie city was on the verge of an oil boom and needed someone to shape it. Ralph thought he was that someone. He told her that he liked her small pretty face, her quick smile with the sardonic twist, a small-town upbringing much like his own. He liked her willingness to try new things. She was his muse.

Beth first saw his string quartet perform at the back of the downtown farmer's market. She listened to the quartet with her hands loose at her sides and swayed with the vibrations—not of the music, which she didn't much like, but of the vociferous crowds oozing through the broad aisles between banks of produce, perogy, jam and pickle vendors. Over the passing months she accumulated mason jars and lined the windowsills with them in her bachelor apartment and later her married basement suite. Soon Ralph's quartet shifted to the wedding and fundraising circuit. Their major break was at a fundraiser called the Sahara Opera Nights at the Sahara Restaurant. Soon after that, Ralph joined the city's opera symphony, co-founded and sat on the boards of the Alberta Music Conference and the Alberta Choral Federation, participated in a music festival broadcast on CBC Radio and adjudicated string competitions, all while continuing to teach viola and direct two choirs. Ralph travelled with his quartet, eventually adding guest solo performance stints on the viola in Canada, the United States and Japan. On top of this he did his master's degree so that he could cement his teaching position at Alberta College. He tended to work evenings and study during the day. Beth found herself separated from Ralph more than she would have liked. When he had time, he took her to dinner, art galleries and art-house movies, most of those going over her head, but she liked to eat the carob bars sold in the snack bar at the Princess Theatre. They took classes in canoeing, ballroom dance and Chinese cookery, and they drank espresso at the three good cafés in the city with Ralph's musician friends, who were nice. In February they went on vacations with sun and sand. Ralph could be a bore, but Beth believed that he meant well; because of those improving visits she went out a lot more than the envious women she worked with in the typing pool and later the health department. When he wasn't around, Beth had her work friends, the friends of her youth having dropped away once Ralph appeared on the scene, and she began to attend evening services at Saint Clare Church as driver and escort for her elderly widowed great-aunt Fenna, who had been moved into a nursing home nearby. Since Beth and Ralph didn't have children (try as they might), they didn't have many extraordinary expenses, their mortgage not being that large. Their clashes seemed insubstantial compared to the problems of her friends, Ralph's sisters back in Lloydminster or her cattle-farming brother Samuel back in Crossfield. Since his ambitions did not touch on her world, he had nothing to complain about, and the same was true of her. Her companionship and power as muse were all he needed from her.

Until one found oneself pregnant and wondered how childrearing would function between incompatible parents. In that situation, the owner of a B&B gets an earful, then, doesn't he? Philip came from a different world than either her or Ralph. He knew about diverse kinds of lives and lifestyles, and about bad relationships, having had some, and now that he was in a good relationship, he could articulate what the difference was. That week, for the first time in a long time, someone listened to her. She listened too. She found herself walking among old cathedrals, lively, French-speaking cosmopolitans mixed in with earthier Québécois who had moved into the city from their childhood farms, and she realized that her life wasn't all that she had hoped for. She had pretended to like it because she didn't know of any alternative. That was what Montreal was for her: a locus for an imaginatively constructed ambition that was vague yet filled with potential, something that she had always wanted yet had been unable to articulate because of her narrow upbringing.

The listening drew her back to Montreal. She wasn't merely a work-in-progress for Ralph to shepherd through final rehearsals, or a muse that smiled mysteriously in the wings. She would take her child, the ambiguously sexed infant, into that uncertain yet untrammelled world Montreal represented. Philippa was going to live au naturel, with no fig leaves hiding her inscrutable unmentionables or her unformed yet sensuous personhood. Reality—the law, as well as her guilt at leaving Gilda, since she had always thought of the move as temporary!—retaliated eventually, and she found herself back in Edmonton. Yet she could never return to the self that had walked into the Red Cross House that sultry summer, looking for a life partner and a co-owner of a home.

Had life after divorce gone the way she wanted? Not exactly. Did she hope for something better? Vaguely. She knelt at a pew every night and asked God for guidance. Being nonexistent, God had nothing to say. She longed, nevertheless, for a little voice from somewhere to tell her what she should head toward.

41

TÊTE-À-TÊTE

Gilda spent the rest of her second day in Montreal in anguish. She wanted the phone close by even when charging, so she lay on the bed with her left arm hanging over the edge so that the charger cord could reach the plug in. She left her hotel room twice: once to get something to eat and once in the early evening, when, grown sick of her arm falling asleep and her resentment against Pete having built to a climax, she meandered outdoors as though she were a real tourist. She scanned the pedestrians on the sidewalks and passengers on buses and cars, her hand on her phone in her back pocket. The distant throb of pop music piqued her curiosity, so she followed the sound and the crowds and found herself in the middle of a fashion festival. For several blocks, the streets were closed to car traffic, and modelling runways, lit by stage lights, floated like illuminated barges among a sea of upturned eager faces. Thin women strutted on the long narrow stages in time to crashing bass and eerie electronic melodies. The people who surged around the stages openly ogled the models, whose expressions remained bland under the silvering wash of light on them as though completely bored by the spectacle. Strangely, the clothing on display in the islands of light and sound did not defy logic as did the high fashion runways she saw in glossy magazines. No oversized hats and floor-sweeping veils, no spaceman themes, no improbable layering of fur on silk on feather. The fashion gave off a more prosaic air, businesslike, as though street fashion festivals and other such displays of human flesh and fleshly ornamentation provided a base level of glamour that the city served up like power and water.

The music pounded her head hard, and she returned to her hotel room with a headache. She fell asleep quickly as though wrung out by the effort to spot Pete, but she slept unsoundly. She dreamed of striding models, bone-shaking vibrations, flashing lights.

The next morning, Gilda followed the same routine of her first day in the city, with a skimpy breakfast and a seat on a park bench next to the street vendors, watching the crowds. In the afternoon, she was back in her room, plugging her phone into the socket, when Philip, sounding downbeat, called to say that Pete had not contacted him.

She said, "Do you know where he goes, where he hangs out?"

"You seem distraught."

He seemed distraught himself; she wondered how she had sounded to him. "I came here to find Pete, and I'm facing a dead end. I need to find another trail to chase."

After a pause, Philip said, "Why don't you come by? I can tell you what I know."

She walked to La Lobélie because the more she walked the streets the more likely, despite how unlikely it was, she might see Pete. As she approached rue Saint-Urbain, the midsize towers and bumper-to-bumper traffic motored through to wider boulevards past newly refurbished two-storey buildings. Once she set foot on the street, the architectural style changed to four-storey concrete office buildings with glass fronts and parking lots and then to low commercial buildings and converted warehouses whose red brick fronts came right up to the dry, treeless sidewalk. Rapidly the warehouses gave way to row houses, three storeys of red and brown brick multi-unit buildings with slender black or white metal stairs leading up to top-floor units and down to the main-floor units. Breaking the continuity of the row houses were garage-style commercial blocks one storey tall, sometimes a hair salon, other times a corner store, a graphic design store or pottery manufacturer. Between the buildings and up from the sidewalk, tall, scraggly-barked trees of maple and ash twisted out from the cemented soil and shaded what lay beneath. Suddenly a giant pink church loomed up from an empty parking lot ringed with multicoloured pennants high above. Just as suddenly it contracted behind the row houses as she passed, as though it had been a mirage.

Beyond more row houses, then, and finally she came to the beflowered entrance of a row house with a tiny sign announcing Le Gîte La Lobélie. Inside its small courtyard, she took the same steps to the door that her mother and father had walked up all those years ago. Shortly after she rang the bell, the door opened to her mother's old confidante and her sibling's namesake.

Philip sported brown curly hair, with some salt and pepper, and the tightened skin of a man about to collapse into wrinkles any day now, but his smile, genuine, warmed him to her immediately. He wanted to hug her, she could tell, but she wasn't much of a hugger; she hoped her thrust-out palm, however inflexibly held, denoted the positive intentions of her visit.

After he shook her hand, he led her through a door to the guest parlour, labelled as such by a gilt-framed sign stitched in petit point. The dim light through heavy brown drapes, the floral wallpaper, the floral ticking throw pillows, the framed needlepoint landscapes, the curlicued furniture, the tasselled floor lamps, the scent of lavender, the doilies! He served her orange pekoe tea and a plate of currant scones.

Seated across from her in his matching horsehair armchair, he said, "It's funny. I called Pete and the phone went to voice mail. The person who spoke in the recording was someone named François. I thought, wrong number? But Murray reminded me that was probably the owner of the apartment Pete is renting. Somehow I'd forgotten."

"Murray," Gilda said, seeking clarification.

"My partner. He's busy baking for tomorrow morning. Our last guest ate a lot. Otherwise he would be the one serving tea. Serving is his area of expertise."

Philip seemed very nervous to the point of incoherence. She decided her best bet was to pick up on the last word he spoke and have him react to that. "What is your area of expertise?"

"Cultural studies. I actually used to study gender identity, so I know something about the historical contexts of it." He coughed a little. "I spent quite a number of years doing research on cross-dressers, for example."

As if on cue, both she and Philip lifted their cups and saucers.

"Oh?" Gilda sipped her tea.

Philip swallowed a big mouthful and winced, she speculated, at the heat.

"I recommend a book by Bullough and Bullough, if you want to know more. But basically, in the Western world at least, female-to-male cross-dressers are treated better because they increase in status by their crossing, while male-to-female cross-dressers lose status. Male status is higher, as we all know. Heterosexual male status is the highest, I should say."

She felt like she was in a fourth-year seminar at university but in a world where the professor invited everyone to his apartment. This meeting with Philip was the closest she had come to fulfilling her undergraduate fantasy of intellectual life. In this case, however, she was the only person in the seminar. She alone had to respond to the excited instructor with nods and tilts of the head. Like in all seminars, she was genuinely interested in the subject. Unlike most seminars, the subject was directly related to her life at that moment: her sibling, Pete. No, this experience was more like a detective visiting a suspect than like a student gaining wisdom from a professor. For example, why was he talking about cross-dressers?

To indicate that she had some knowledge of the subject, she responded, "I thought that when people say 'male,' they imply heterosexuality."

"By 'people' you mean . . . ?" Philip looked discomfited. Gilda remembered that when she used to make statements in seminars,

240

the professors often adopted that look. Her enthusiasm got away from her at times, and she had made a mistake.

"Oh, sorry," she said. "I mean society. I mean the hegemony. Because obviously some men are not heterosexual."

"Yes." He seemed relieved at her amendment. "The other thing," he continued haltingly, "is that people are within society, but they also are within their own experiences. It's not enough to consider what society tells individuals to do. Individuals have specific experiences too, and sociology can't account for that well. There is psychology and sociology at work, and sociology doesn't trump psychology necessarily."

"So sometimes people are attuned to what society says they should do or be, and sometimes they're not."

"Exactly. Members of groups that suffer discrimination are particularly vulnerable. The social messages against them are strong and omnipresent. It's hard for people in those groups to see themselves as other than belonging to the discriminated group. Their identity is often heavily influenced by social discourse, to the exclusion of their personal discourse."

As he had been talking, Gilda picked up one of the scones and nibbled on it. She finished it, so it was time she gave her lecturer a rest. "I see. Pete is struggling to negotiate the contours of his own life, but because generally he goes along with society, he seems successful at it."

At the word "Pete," Philip gave a start. Maybe he was thinking of himself when he was explaining. He recovered, though. "When I saw him as a baby, he was Philippa. Your mother dressed him like a girl. Now he doesn't dress like a girl as far as I know. I'm curious what he did when he was old enough to dress himself."

"He started dressing like a boy in junior high. Over the top. He wore those super baggy pants. He wore baseball caps, high-tops, the works. At least when he left the house. At home, he sometimes wore feminine clothes. Or at least more feminine." She thought about what she tended to wear. "It's not like women wear crinolines anymore."

"Maybe he has taken a 'third way' approach," he said. "Mind you, Western society has come to favour androgyny. Unisex dressing is a norm nowadays."

"Unisex." Gilda glanced, surreptitiously, she hoped, at her own clothing. "That's true. As long as Pete stays away from the fringe groups that don't agree with unisex dressing, Pete doesn't have to do a lot to fit in, at least on the surface. But Pete has something extra to deal with that cross-dressers don't necessarily have to."

Philip nodded. "He's intersex." She must have shown surprise, for he added, "Your mother told me. To explain why she came to Montreal." Philip became glum for some reason. "I'm not a physiologist. I can't speak to the genetic and hormonal part of things."

Maybe he regretted not knowing everything about everything: some profs were like that. "You know the word intersex at least," Gilda said. "My dad still uses hermaphrodite."

"Intersexuality is more clinical, but there's something kind of interesting about the word hermaphrodite. It's, what, a combination of Hermes and Aphrodite."

"I checked into that once," Gilda said with derision. "All that mythology and all the baggage that comes with it."

"Maybe it's not fair to throw the myth out altogether. People have used myths to help them understand the world. The Greeks," he added slowly, "had some things to teach us. Maybe I should look into the Hermaphroditus myth. I know someone in classics who does work on gender."

He trailed off, and his face acquired a pinched look. In speaking about Pete in this detached academic way, Philip was no doubt also filtering his theories through his own life.

"Gosh," Philip said finally. "I've been talking a lot, haven't I?"

"No." She thought the opposite; but here was an opening for her. "Do you know where Pete spends his time?"

He stared hard at her, measuring something. "I don't feel comfortable revealing what I know about him. It was his decision not to tell you. For me, it's a question of keeping confidences."

"Was that information you gave about cross-dressing and"—a word popped into her head, and she tried it—"gender-blending all you wanted to tell me?"

"That was some of what I wanted to tell you."

He seemed irritated by her question. She had intended to irritate him, and it had worked. *She* was irritated. She decided to annoy him even more.

"You called me and invited me here because you said you would tell me what you knew. And you haven't." She allowed the indignation to seep in. "He's my family."

Philip's handsome, open, sensitive face now had a cringe frozen into it. He was a person who had taken some blows in life, she bet. He had taken them, and he was able to take more and give some back, but not without knowing what he was doing. "I wanted you to know that he's doing okay, and that I am in contact with him, and that I understand some of his situation."

She couldn't win that easily. She was way outside Philip's circle, whereas Pete, she was quite sure now, was well within it. How well within it, and why he considered Pete to be within it, Gilda didn't know. She didn't think she would find out, either, at least not this day.

She shuffled her purse up from the floor to her lap. "Could you tell him that his sister is in town?" she asked. "I give you my permission to tell him."

That was a cheap shot, and he acknowledged it without backing down. "Yes, I'll tell him."

He led her to the front door, and after a short wave to him, she headed back to her hotel along Saint-Urbain. En route, she didn't think about cultural theory or duty or who deserves to feel obliged to whom, but instead wondered about why Philip worked in a bed and breakfast. Maybe he gave a seminar to everyone who stayed there, free of charge, finagled it into his view of himself as an educator. She had done something like that herself. She had taken advantage of a happenstance and enrolled Burghie into her project.

243

He was a human resource she had recruited and applied to her project workflow. She had repurposed a figure from her childhood for an adult role, lifted him out of the backstory right into the rising action and, she hoped, to a climax and a satisfying denouement. Philip might be doing something similar, but maybe academics were used to playing games like that.

She didn't see Pete on her way home; she looked. In her hotel room, she lay on top of her bed and dozed off with his face in her mind.

She awoke to the sound of email reaching her phone. Burghie had emailed her asking her how she was doing and if she had found anything.

"I'm all right," she typed. "Nothing so far." That had to change. "I'll look 'til I find him."

42

SECOND ENCOUNTER

All weekend Beth thought about Norvell. On Monday, during her morning break at work, she called Tokens. Norvell answered the phone.

"It's Pete's mother. I was dusting Pete's room, and I was thinking about what I could do with all the stuff he's left behind."

Norvell's dull voice grew slower and sharper with wariness. "What kind of stuff?"

"Oh, you know, toys, gizmos, books, comics, cards, signed photographs."

His voice slowed further. "Did he say he wanted me to have these things?"

"No, but instead of giving them all to the Sally Ann, I thought that since you worked at the same place he did that you would be interested. It would be a shame to give all this to someone who didn't appreciate it."

"Are you looking to sell it?"

"No, no," Beth said. "A giveaway."

More caution entered Norvell's voice. "You don't think Pete is going to want these things anymore?"

"The stuff he wanted he took when he first moved out. Does that make sense?"

"Makes sense."

Norvell's echoing of her words seemed to come from politeness rather than real trust. She didn't care: she marched forward with her plan anyway. She asked if he wanted to drive by one day very soon and look at Pete's collections. "Do you have a truck?"

Norvell didn't, but, after a pause, he said that he could come over and look at the collectibles (his word).

The next evening, then, he appeared in her front entrance. Bathed in the evening light of summer, his pink face was cleaner and clearer than it had seemed under Tokens' fluorescents, and his eyes were less squinty. He smelled like hot bread and grease, as though he had waited in a fast food place between closing time at Tokens and their eight o'clock appointment.

"The days are getting darker now, aren't they?" Beth said as she led Norvell down the hallway to the room that used to be Pete's.

"Yes," Norvell replied. His socked feet swished heavily on the Berber carpet. "They have been ever since the summer solstice."

"That was back in June, right?"

"June twentieth, or June twenty-first, depending on where you live."

The peculiar precision of his answer hinted at a quality she could use to get Norvell's confidence. "Do you celebrate the summer solstice?" she asked. They had stopped at the closed door of Pete's old bedroom.

"No, not me," Norvell said. "I find pagan religions fascinating, and I know quite a bit about them, but I don't go so far as to actually participate."

"You're a student of religion, but not a follower of one."

"Exactly." Some life came into his dull voice. "The older polytheistic religions are as good a foundation for spirituality as any other religious sect out there."

"You don't say."

"Some people consider paganism to be primitive, but that may be because they don't understand it. There are all kinds of belief systems that people group under the word paganism. People just put them under one umbrella."

Norvell looked at her expectantly for a response, but her knowledge of the subject had been exhausted at the point where she had said "religion."

The room was as Pete had left it, except neater because Beth looked after it now. The single bed with its red- and blue-striped comforter and the highboy were bare. On the rickety shelving unit Beth had salvaged, from God knew where, board games, action figures (still in their packages), stuffies and DVDs advertised Philippa's post-adolescent obsessions. Six big open boxes lay on the floor around the bed. Earlier she had pulled them out and opened them for Norvell's benefit.

"Go ahead and poke around," Beth said.

Hesitantly at first, but with increasing interest, he rummaged. Unconsciously, she supposed, he narrated his exploration, excitement gradually sharpening that bleak voice.

"Comics. *Batman, Justice League*—hmm—*Transmetropolitan*—Spider-Man, *Detective Comics. Amethyst*—hmm. Magazines. *Fangoria.*" He put his hands inside another box and rifled through it more carefully. "Movie magazines. *Fantastic Films.* Manga. *Lone Wolf and Cub. Pokémon.*" As he continued rifling through boxes, his one-word sentences came more infrequently. From the boxes, he moved to the shelves and skimmed them in silence.

"What do you think?" Beth said.

"So far there's a few things of tangible financial value," he said, "if not of personal interest to me."

"Sometimes it's the collector, not the collection, that makes it interesting," Beth said. "It can be like doing a tea-leaf reading."

"Fortune-telling has been discredited by a wide variety of people and institutions. I know what you're saying, though. People's possessions can be psychologically revealing."

"What do Pete's collections say about him, I wonder? It's harder for me to judge since I'm his mother. You, though . . . "

Norvell blushed. "I know him, so I'm not exactly objective."

"Don't you think that there's something about a person that is mysterious only until you look at the boxes they have hidden in their attics or closets?"

"I don't know." Norvell became shy suddenly. "Is it okay if I look at some more boxes?"

"Of course."

He was a hard nut to crack. She needed patience to get at the meat inside his shell. She hung back while he lifted items out of the boxes and inspected them, games, books, packages.

"What do you like to collect?" Beth asked.

"I don't know if you'd know any of the things I collect."

"Try me."

"*Space: 1999.* The movie *Dune.* Tog'l. Roger Moore James Bond. *A.L.F.*"

Beth had heard of Roger Moore and James Bond. "Does Pete have any of that?"

"Not that I've seen."

"Is Pete more of a mainstream person, then?"

Norvell looked up. "I wouldn't say that."

"No?"

"He's just into different things. Look at these games." He pointed to the shelves. "Not everyone has those games. There's no Clue or Monopoly there. But he has Rook, he has—wow, yeah, he told me about that—The London Game, RukShuk, Go, mancala."

"Do you want those?"

"Sure. Isn't he coming back?"

"I don't know. You seem to know more about him than I do."

Norvell looked down, then around, as though searching for an exit.

"If I'm being rude, say so," Beth said. "I'm not famous for politeness."

"I—"

"I'll go make some tea, some for you too, if you want. Come out to the kitchen when you're ready. The kitchen is at the other end of the hallway."

Beth waited at the kitchen table and drank her peppermint tea in a white mug. Another white mug waited for Norvell. By tradition people served tea in teacups. She always used teacups. Norvell was a big guy, though, and petite bone-thin china with flowers wouldn't work in his big mitts. Tea could pack a wallop no matter what kind of container it was served in. That Lapsang souchong tea she tried once was like hot tar scraped off a new road patch.

A few heavy footfalls on carpet, and Norvell materialized into the kitchen and stood in front of the table awkwardly.

"I'll take it all."

"Really?"

"When Pete comes back, I'll give it all back. I'll store it all together so that they don't get mixed up with my other collectibles. I'll keep his collection together."

"That's a great idea," Beth said. "Are you going to take some things right away? No, wait, have some tea."

"As long as it's not caffeinated tea."

"It's herbal—peppermint."

He sat and drank the tea. In his meaty hand, a teacup would have looked ridiculous. She chitchatted with him, and through the chitchat found out that he had been working at Tokens for almost two years and that he lived alone in a trailer home owned by his uncle in a place she surprisingly had never heard of called Lamoureux outside the edge city of Fort Saskatchewan.

She said, "Pete worked at Tokens longer than you have."

He agreed. "We used to never see each other, but once we both went full time, we had overlapping shifts."

"You probably spent more time with him than I have since he moved out."

He blushed and clammed up.

"There's more in the basement," Beth said.

"More?"

"Finish your tea and we'll go down."

In the basement, the games were in the boiler room, the storage room and the room that was supposed to be a craft room but had become another storage room. The open shelving unit in the television room held a handful of his old games: Milles Bornes, Trouble, Scruples.

Norvell wouldn't let her carry any boxes outside. He toted one big box of action figures to his nineties-era two-door Tercel. The car was filled with fast food bags, books, a suitcase, and a gym bag. He could fit no other boxes.

"I have an Oldsmobile," Beth said. "I can bring some another day."

"Are you sure?"

"Positive. Don't worry. I'll call you to make arrangements."

Once Norvell's beater gargled off, she parked herself at the kitchen table with her tea and allowed herself to conclude that poor old Norvell was lovesick.

43

COALESCENCE

The next morning Gilda woke, showered and descended to the streets. Cars, bicycles, taxis and people whirred past on Saint Catherine Street. The humidity made her body itch with sweat, but she forced her attention to remain pinned to yesterday's events. Philip was right that Pete was a cultural object as much as a person. The redhead without the freckles who had shared a bedroom with Gilda until they were twelve, who had shared a womb with her, who had shared the same set of potential genetic material, was not just a sibling but an archetype for the gender divisiveness that society had struggled with for centuries. The struggle manifested in him, and all that their family had gone through was related to it. A horn honked. She veered off to a side street to escape some of the city noise.

She rested on a bench at the end of a hot dusty street named after a vaguely familiar Quebec politician. In sitting, she was doing something of cultural significance. The stone building across the street with its gaudy red and yellow sign that said Chez Costa; that too was of cultural significance. The vaguely familiar Quebec politician might seem more significant than Pete, insofar as that man's portrait likely hung in a marbled, high-ceilinged government building somewhere, but notwithstanding their relative triviality, from the moment that she and Pete had coalesced around their respective stem cells in the straw-coloured fluid of their uterine sacs, they had been swimming in a cultural ether. Part of that ether flowed through these streets, even though much of it flowed from a different subculture than Edmonton's, this province of French-surnamed politicians and French-language shopfronts. Being in Montreal, she was participating in the same cultural framework that Pete now circulated through.

The heat of the bench seeped up her rear into her hips and torso, her arms and fingers, shoulders and neck, until the warmth exuded from the crown of her skull. She wiped a drop of sweat from her forehead. The humidity here. Above her head, the invisible fluid of social discourse streamed. It erupted up out of her body but also cascaded down on her from above, those invisible signs and symbols of the discourse of provincial politics, personal politics, social politics. The through-thoughts of centuries arced around her bench on the politician's street and above the towers of this island in the St. Lawrence River, careening atoms, an electron storm, currents of words that propagated the beliefs and knowledge that had blazoned Beth in her own mother's womb, originating from the past of the world's belief systems. Alongside the verbal were the biological discourses, the concatenation of genes, the materiel of physical heritage that streamed through her and Pete and all their living relatives and would flow into future ones. In the middle of this stream of consciousness and physiology she sat, Gilda.

A grey car edged past her in traffic. A man in a brown coat chauffeured a younger man in a tank-top, both unsmiling in their front seats. The car and its occupants were mingling with her, the matrix of atoms that made up the smell of gasoline from the exhaust, the dust that flew off the tires. The fact that the men were not smiling reminded her of all in life that was worth not smiling about. She looked down at her feet, at the thick toes trying to spring from the black-strapped sandals. Her thick, itchy toes reminded her of her loneliness, of her mother's loneliness, the dullness of the nurse book, the triviality of Ian Auma's book project and the smallness of her life.

Yet her life was not small, not if she thought about Pete/Philippa as an expression of the cultural mystique of the man-woman, the not-sexed one and thus the all-sexed one. Gilda was a female child, the unloved child of history, who, to be loved, had to fight like a soldier and unwoman herself to do it. Since she and Pete sprang nearly simultaneously from the same loins, both physical and cultural, didn't that mean that if he was part of a mystique, she was too?

Far beyond her bench on a busier cross street, a troika of women strode with smiles, blissful toreadors entering the ring and self-assured about their victories. Women singly moved from street corner to street corner in flat Roman sandals, in wedged heels, jogging shoes and flip-flops, going about their business in the dust pillars and slanting light of late morning, unescorted. Chez Costa's plate glass window revealed a woman standing behind a cashier counter, selling, and another woman in front of her, buying. The clerk at her hotel was a woman, the servers at the hotel restaurant were women. Her mother, a woman, worked and paid for her own home and expenses. Her immediate boss was a woman. Yet Manuka's boss was a man, likely the person who ran the hotel and owned it was a man; the mayor of this city, the mayor of her home city, the head of the university she attended, were men. God was a man, said the church her mother went to daily, and his child was a man. Not a man-woman, a sexless one, but someone who in paintings of his gruesome public death had to wear a loincloth, but, unlike his sainted mother, could be bare-breasted, like the two bronzed and shirtless men who were walking past Gilda.

She rose from the bench and walked. Scant minutes later, she arrived at a small park that sprang up from between two high-rises. A metal metro station sign styled in art deco fronted the park. Lime-coloured grass and grey benches surrounded a square white fountain with a low rushing spray at its centre. She wanted to sit alone but had to make do with a bench on which sat a young man who studied his cellphone. She usually felt tempted by her cellphone's promise of raw information to feed her, but she had enough energy inside without it.

253

Montreal was her hometown. It was the epicentre, the dot in the map that connoted "start here." When she was young, her mother had left her with her father and taken Philippa here, the realm of her sibling's namesake, while Gilda remained in the city into which she had burst from the womb via a nurse's blue-sheathed arms, after which she'd been put aside in a plastic crib to wait for her twin to be born. Abided. For most of her life, she had considered herself the leader of the two in the sense that she did everything first—crawled—spoke—walked. When high school ended and they were out in the world, even though Pete got a job first and moved out first, Gilda had believed that Philippa had been first in the sense of premature, not primary or precocious, but of too early, too raw. Gilda captured the laurels because she planned earlier, acted quicker, gathered her energies way in advance of the push forward into adulthood. By staying with her mother in her childhood home rather than moving out, Gilda had demonstrated her maturity, her awareness of the necessity to look after an aging parent long before Pete had a clue that anyone needed looking after, including himself.

In truth, Pete had early on commandeered the centrepiece of the table of their shared life. He left his birthplace when he was merely months old. Most people waited until they graduated high school to do that. He showed an early awareness of the significance of this city to him and with that awareness, conscious or not, had acknowledged the reality of Montreal's nurturing germ. Beth had not taken Philippa to Montreal; Philippa had taken Beth to Montreal. No—he and Gilda had been in Montreal when they were fetuses. Had Philippa taken Gilda there? Yes, why not say that? He has been here three times, Gilda only two. For this visit, she had planned so hard. She doubted Pete put in the same effort. Maybe it paid to be screwed up: you leapt and started, not waited and brooded. Pete, unaware of the hard work it took to be first, was way ahead of her.

She recommenced her journey through the city, past the fountain and down a street that darkened suddenly in the shadows of a stand of skyscrapers. A tunnel of air swept a piece of paper into her path and made her dance to one side, just as a white plastic bag tumbled in a gust of dry wind at cross purposes to the paper and made her dance to the other side of the sidewalk. No one else walked in this shadowed block. It was colder here. The past threw its cold shoulder onto the future of this historic city. These tall buildings had armoured themselves against incursions of humanity by their brushed steel and tinted glass.

She passed onto a sunnier street with more traffic. Gilda's body warmed with the yellow light and the still air and blue sky. The skyscrapers gave way to sandstone and iron grilles on windows. Taxis crawled, looking for fares. A woman in open-toed pumps clipped past, and a man with a laptop case and a plastic takeout bag spoke joyfully into his headset to someone he loved. She should stop and let her feet cool, give them a chance to get their second wind. No benches were available here, however, just no-parking signs, garbage cans, a mailbox and an anachronistic phone booth.

The shadow of the past and the light of the present. Ahead she saw a sward of grass in a tiny park with a path worn across one corner of the grass. She remembered reading about paths in the city, how city planners tried to control people's movements, but people wouldn't let the city do that. Citizens found shortcuts across half-empty parking lots or across lawns, gave themselves permission to avoid the concrete walkway and stamp an impromptu dirt footpath alongside it. The sanctions of a city did not stop people from choosing the route they needed, committees and city planners be damned. That, Michel de Certeau said, was how people proved that hegemony had weaknesses that people could exploit, and did exploit. The city's hand, extended in the hopes of sealing a deal that people couldn't refuse, was sometimes not grasped. People dropped their arms to their sides, and away they went down the muddy thoroughfare they'd tramped in the rose garden because it was the quickest way home. Pete/Philippa/Phil had circumvented the hegemonic discourse this way, started a new ribbon of talk from his/her singularly wayward feet.

Under Gilda's feet the inner soles slipped against her sweat and the skin burned a little, but the feet had to walk more before she could get to the hotel. She was thinking about calling her mother in Edmonton to talk it out. She might call Burghie to discover where in the river of discourse he stood. She would not be able to find all the answers today, but the significance lay not in the general discourse but the specific one, her own little patch of dirt in her Voltairean garden.

Her next monumental, figurative step was to call Philip and ask to stay at his B&B.

She went into her room and, before doing anything else, bandaged her bloody feet. Should she wash them first? All those years in church made her think of Jesus washing the feet of his apostles. Washing of feet was a washing away of sin. Jesus hadn't needed his feet washed. The Christian Messiah lacked original sin. Thus did a conflict arise between Judaism and Christianity. Perhaps Pete understood the conflict better than Gilda had. Despite his weak knowledge of history, Pete, like her, probably had a well-developed sense of the relationship between fate and original sin from all those years of sitting in church in the evenings with their mother. Pete had gone back to his Eden of Montreal. He hadn't been banished. Pete hadn't done anything wrong. But even if a wrong had been committed years ago, under circumstances not completely clear to him, Pete was imprinted by those wrongs and maybe carried a shard of self-blame within him.

Perhaps Pete expected something to redound to him if he returned to Edmonton, though she scarcely knew what he might be expecting. Maybe it wasn't anything specific. Maybe he was playing a waiting game for something that would never come, like the clowns in *Waiting for Godot*. Or maybe Gilda was the one who was waiting. Maybe there was only one clown in her story, and the real Pete felt forever offstage and existent only in the mind of the solitary, delusional clown-author. The play was a single hander called *Waiting for Nobody*. Not a nice play to be in.

Gilda took out her phone and called. She tempered her voice on the phone to sound like her work voice.

Philip wasn't fooled. "You can come in after four o'clock tomorrow, August first." His voice pitched toward more caution. "It's a smaller room, up on the top. A single bed only."

"That's what I'm used to."

"Then I'd be glad to have you."

The next day, Philip took her and her luggage up the creaky and steep stairs to the topmost floor into a vestibule that smelled of walnut oil and old wood. The bedroom itself smelled of cinnamon and lavender. The ceiling slanted down sharply on both long sides of the room, with a bed tucked under one slant and a low cabinet supporting a modest flatscreen television under the other. Her mother and Philippa's old room, Philip said.

44

JAM

In the middle of the hot dry Edmonton traffic, a fender-bender blocked the single remaining operational northbound lane along a road whose other lane had been closed because of pavement refinishing. Every minute the car ahead of Beth advanced one metre and stopped. She rolled down her window, inhaled sulphur from the pavement refinishing and from the hatred steaming out of her fellow commuters.

Traffic moved forward one metre and stopped.

Beth imagined telling Norvell about the time she and Ralph argued in the parking lot about Montreal. Eight years had passed since their Montreal vacation. Ralph and Beth exchanged physical custody of the children in the parking lot behind her apartment building, where she had been living since they'd sold the house after the divorce. Cold wind blew abrasive snow in the dark and jammed white flakes into Ralph's long gingery lashes. The children found a shrunken snowman someone had built near the commercial garbage bin. Under the flickering amber streetlight above the back alley, Gilda and Philippa tried to pile snow on the snowman's head with their little blue ski mittens, but the snow, sticky yesterday, had dried with the temperatures that had sunk with the snowstorm's arrival at suppertime. Their fistfuls of sawdust snow kept slipping off the snowman's head and dispersing in the wind.

Ralph and Beth had their argument beside Ralph's Suburban.

"It would have been nice if you'd come on time," Beth said. "They have school tomorrow."

"Traffic was slow. It's storming out, if you haven't noticed."

"You're late even in good weather."

"That's not true."

She had to hand it to him: a series of "that's not true"s usually killed her desire for argument. Tonight, though, for whatever reason, she decided to take a perilous conversational road. "Aren't those Suburbans supposed to handle snowy roads? Isn't that the point of them?"

Ralph smiled thinly. "There are many points to the Suburban."

Gilda shrieked. She was brushing a cloud of snow from her hat and shoulders. It seemed that Philippa had thrown some snow at her, either by accident or by design. After the protest yell, Gilda recovered. She continued, with Philippa, to pile snow on the snowman. Their backs to the adults, their matching indigo jackets bent and rose in unison as the children stooped down and stood with snow piles in their mittened hands.

Ralph said, "I think Phil's coat is too small."

She knew Philippa's coat was too small, but Beth was waiting for the late winter sales. She wanted to buy coats for the children that were two sizes too large so that they would fit the following winter. "Why don't you buy her a new coat, then, if you think it's too small?"

"Because I give you money for those things, that's why. As far as I'm concerned, I've already paid for a new coat."

"Coats can cost a lot of money. I was waiting for a sale."

"I know how much coats cost."

"No, you don't. When's the last time you bought coats for the kids?"

"I have so bought coats."

"Maybe back when they were still in their car seats."

"Who do you think was buying clothes for Gilda when you were in Montreal with Phil?"

That was the first time in a long time that Ralph had brought up Beth's visit to Montreal. They had fought often about Montreal during the custody hearings, but not since then.

Wind whipped ice into her face. "You didn't buy clothes."

"That's what you think. Gilda outgrew two sizes in that time. Or didn't you notice that she was bigger when you got back?"

"Of course I noticed," Beth told Norvell, who, she imagined, was sitting next to her in the empty passenger seat of her car. "She wasn't a lot bigger, though." Gilda had been born first, but she was the smaller, and she grew more slowly than Philippa. The night she came back, Beth put the two babies side by side on her bed for the first time in months, and the size difference broke her heart. They had the same chins, the same little snapdragon ears, the same mopey eyes, even though the eye colours had changed since the twins had been separated, no longer dark grey but brown for Gilda and blue for Philippa. Gilda's brown eyes seemed bigger, but they weren't. She was thinner, that was all. Gilda had not thrived.

The memory of the size difference made Beth bark out to Ralph, "Not that you seemed in a big hurry to find out how big Philippa had gotten. When did you bother to track us down? After the Christmas concert season was over?"

"It takes time to hunt down a schemer." His eyes drifted to the children still working away on the snowman and shifted to the Suburban before fixing on Beth. "You left a note saying you and Phil were safe. You called your brother to say you were taking Phil on a trip. You paid cash for everything. You laid over in Sault St. Marie before buying a ticket to Montreal. You moved to a different province to hamper any law enforcement investigation."

"You went on tour in October and didn't make a big effort to find us until you got back."

"I certainly got used to not having you around."

"See? You admit it."

He said, "I shouldn't have married you."

"No kids, then, either."

"Having kids with you has been *great*."

The cruelty of that sarcasm halted Beth's reply.

Ralph continued, "Tell me again who was the one who ran off and left her infant daughter behind?"

"I thought of her every day."

"Thought of. Coming from you, that doesn't count for much. Your thoughts are like cotton candy. They look pretty, but they are mostly air and bad for a kid's health."

The children's voices had stopped. They had their backs to the snowman and looked at their parents.

"Norvell," Beth said to the imaginary young man from the game store, "when I got the kids inside, Pete asked me if Dad had asked me to buy cotton candy for them. He asked why I had said no. 'I love cotton candy, Mommy,' he said. 'Why didn't you do what Daddy said?' He didn't talk to me for two days."

A one-metre gap opened up between her car and the car ahead.

"Gilda didn't say anything," Beth said to Norvell. "I knew she'd heard. I think she heard and understood more than Pete did."

The gap in front of Beth widened more. Someone honked. She touched her foot to the car's accelerator.

What Beth wasn't ready to tell her imaginary Norvell about, though, was Ralph's diatribe from their most recent phone conversation. He'd shouted, "Now the chickens have come home to roost. It's your problem now." She didn't want to tell anyone about that yet. Nor the other thing he'd said, about Murray.

Her car moved forward.

45

THE TALENTED MR. BURGH

Burghie decided to go to Montreal the day after Gilda sent him her first email from there. Two days after he had sent her an email asking how things were going, she had replied, writing that she had nothing to report but adding, "I'll look until I find him." The indefiniteness of her plan dismayed him. Maybe she felt isolated and her mind was whipping around like a bike's back wheel after a bad fall. If she had someone like him with her to talk to, she might see the error of her plan. Just because Pete lived there didn't mean Gilda had to live there. He replied that he was sure she would find him soon. He kept to himself the thought that Gilda might never find Pete.

On the way to work the next day, he passed the side street that led to the Peterborough house, and his handlebars twitched toward the street like a divining rod.

When he arrived home from work, he checked the discount travel websites. He booked a plane ticket and a hotel room for Montreal between August 6th and 10th at a Holiday Inn. He wondered what he thought he could accomplish in four days; then he wondered what he was trying to accomplish. He suffered from the same lack of reason that had taken Gilda to Quebec. What was love, though, he thought as he pulled out his suitcase from under his bed, but irrationality?

The next day at work he told Paul about his planned vacation. Paul threw his hands in the air. "And what am I going to do in the meantime?"

"I know that Rusty wants more hours."

"Rusty is a bus boy," Paul said. "He's not server material, that kid."

"Can't I take a vacation?"

"You think this is like a school where teachers have two months off in summer?"

"I'll be gone a total of four days."

"Four days? Oh!" Paul hadn't taken more than two days off work since Burghie started working there. "Four days is great. That's all a person needs."

Burghie didn't consider this to be a real vacation. His imaginary grown-up vacation involved him sitting on the edge of a cliff on a coastal bike tour and watching the white Mediterranean surf whip against grey medieval stone. Vacations implied leisure for one's own sake, of finding oneself. Instead, he was trying to find someone else. Two people, actually.

Booking a flight and hotel and getting time off work were the easy things. One of the two hard things related to his promise to Gilda to check on her mother. The next day, after the supper rush and after church, as Gilda had instructed, he called Ms. Conrad.

"You haven't gone to Montreal like everyone else," she said.

Burghie gulped. "No, not yet."

"Not yet?"

He said carefully, "I thought I should tell you that I am going. In a week or so."

"Has something happened over there?"

"Not that I know of. I just thought I would go. I have some vacation time, and after she talked about going there, I checked it out, and it seems like a great place for a vacation."

Ms. Conrad said, "I went to Montreal for vacation once. It was so eventful I'll never go on vacation again. Funny how that trip has become so inspirational to young people in Edmonton."

"I didn't have anything to do with Gilda going to Montreal."

"I didn't say it was anyone's idea but hers. I'm just saying that things may develop over there that will have long-lasting consequences. That's what happened to me." She paused. "Are you calling me for advice?"

"No."

"No one calls me for advice. Maybe that's for the best. I don't believe in advice. Did Gilda tell you to check up on me?"

Gilda had used the word "spy." At the time he'd thought she meant "make sure she is doing okay." Based on this conversation so far, he realized that Gilda had used the word "spy" on purpose. As in "see what she's up to."

"Are you still there?" she asked.

"Yes," Burghie said. "I think she felt bad about leaving you by yourself."

"You think that's the reason?"

"I don't know what her reason is. All I have is a theory."

"It's a nicer theory than what I came up with. Paranoia. Power tripping."

"Maybe it's those reasons too," he said. "Combined with kindness."

She laughed. "Could be. Okay. Go to Montreal, find Gilda, and find Pete too. Don't forget to take some time out for yourself. Notre Dame is worth seeing." She hung up with an abnormally loud click.

The conversation unsettled him for the rest of the day, but when he compared it to what it could have been and what he thought would happen when he went home, he felt grateful. As he rode from work to home, his dread grew with the falling darkness. The drivers seemed more careless, the pedestrians at the intersections more sinister in their too-dark clothing and jerky movements.

At home, he found his parents in the television room and told them.

His father said, "Why not wait until winter and go to Cuba?"

His mother nodded. "It's cheap, it's warm."

They had gone to Cuba two years ago and had loved it. Burghie could have gone along but didn't, not being fond of dictatorships.

During their vacation, Burghie had been responsible for cooking meals, but Granddad, already in a snit because he thought Burghie's mother was giving his son's money to communists, refused to eat Burghie's food. The meals piled up in the refrigerator, uneaten, to serve as Burghie's early lunches or silent dinners alone in his room on his days off work. His grandfather stayed in his bedroom watching game shows and, based on the contents of the kitchen garbage, eating canned sardines.

"The ticket is probably expensive," Burghie's father said.

It was, but Burghie said it wasn't. He soothed his parents by normalizing the trip. He told them he was going to Montreal to hike through the countryside, visit the Six Flags there and shop for clothes. Secretly he hoped that he would get to do all that too.

"Don't you have anyone to go with?" his mother said. "You'll be lonely."

"I'll be fine."

He went to bed without seeing Granddad Burgh. As he fell asleep in his room, he created a fantasy of the Montreal vacation: a countryside ramble with Gilda and Pete, with a big walking stick and a feathered cap. He didn't know anything about the terrain, so he imagined the Alps.

The next morning, he received a second email from Gilda. She thanked him and said she wished she had a bike to help her get around Montreal. Burghie re-read the email to find clues in it about her feelings for him and how his arrival in Montreal, if he decided to announce it, might affect her. He decided not to tell her.

When he went to the garage to get his bike out for work, his grandfather was there. Granddad Burgh often spent time in the garage, though usually he stayed away when Burghie was leaving or arriving. He was hunched over the workbench, sorting through a box of screws and dropping them into labelled baby-food jars. His cane lay lengthwise across the top of the workbench.

Without looking up, Granddad Burgh said, "Your father says you're going on vacation."

"Yeah, I am."

"To Kway-beck."

"Uh-huh."

He dropped a screw in a jar with a rattle. "That's a strange place to go on vacation."

Burghie tapped on the garage door opener next to the workbench. As the pulleys noisily began hauling up the big white steel door, Burghie whispered, "No, it's not." Granddad didn't hear to react. When Burghie came home from work late that evening, Granddad Burgh was still in the garage with the screws. Granddad Burgh began talking as though no time had passed between early that day and now. "Expensive, going out east. You got money to go to Kway-beck, you got money to get your own car." He dropped a screw into a jar, and the sound was like a ticking clock or water dripping from a faucet.

Once Burghie stood in the back hallway, the man-door closed behind him, he answered: "No, it's fucking not."

#

Burghie first watched *The Talented Mr. Ripley* during his Philip Seymour Hoffman phase after high school. Unlike Ripley, Burghie wasn't going to Europe on someone else's dime to bring somebody's wayward son home. He was sending himself, and only across a continent, and he was following a girl who was searching for a wayward son, or maybe a daughter. A twin, anyway.

Fuck. He'd forgotten. At the end of *The Talented Mr. Ripley*, Ripley killed his lover. But it was too late: Burghie was stuffed into the aisle seat of a 737. He was on a flight to Kway-beck.

46

LATCHING ON

After she hung up with Dallas Burgh, Beth remained at the kitchen table. She bobbed her teabag in the transparent plastic travel mug labelled "Team" that she had received one year from her workplace Secret Santa. Her gaze travelled out the kitchen window to her neighbour's apple tree. Was that an apple or a yellow leaf? An apple, surely. She searched the back-alley trees for other yellow leaves that testified to the beginning of the end of summer. Normally Beth didn't condone that kind of pessimism, but she felt weak. She may have fruited Philippa and Gilda, and she may have, in small ways, nourished friendships and acquaintanceships and done her job well, but her role in the world remained small. The cosmic layout of life didn't depend on her weedy existence. How much of the universe's soil had any awareness of Beth? Her impact was a drop in the bucket, the tip of one trivial twig on a low branch.

"Oh, stuff," Beth said.

A magpie croaked in the yard. Outside the window was the apple tree, with its yellow leaf or apple.

She had to keep herself busy this evening. She could do housework—and after some sweeping and vacuuming, she could go for a walk or drive to the mall, stroll there for an hour until it closed. Normally, if Gilda weren't at the office, they prepared a meal together and ate it, did dishes, watched a television show or sometimes part of a movie. Once in a while Philippa came over. On the basement sofa Beth sat between the children, not simply out of the old habit of preventing fights but also so both twins brushed against her at the same time. Because Gilda lived with her, always had, except for that brief period in her infancy, working Gilda into her life had not taken much effort. Philippa was more work. Beth had been an old parent, and wisdom had taught her that at some point the warm, wet bundle of cries would grow mature enough to soothe and entertain itself and, yes, even fix its own suppers. Childish dependency was a relatively brief stage in a person's life. The child grew to be an adult and fledged, and the elder in the house became merely a satellite of the greater community, someone's neighbour or old friend, or at least you hoped to achieve even that minimum. Of her role as parent Beth had as evidence a fifties-style kitchen table for four and two abandoned bedrooms.

A robin's syrupy song trailed in from the kitchen window, replacing the caw of the magpie, which seemed to have flown off. With the song of the robin, something softened in Beth. She once had a bachelor great-uncle, really the bachelor great-uncle of a cousin by marriage, a man named Victor, who attended all the big family parties. He fit right there with the adults, drinking, joking and playing cards, but he was the only grown-up who played baseball with the kids in the field next to the schoolyard in Devon where her mother's sister lived. The boys and the girls loved to be around him because of his youthfulness, his antiauthoritarianism, his hostility to talk about mortgages and the proper mixture of weed and feed for crops. He proved that being an adult could be all right, that adults could chose not to be stodgy.

Beth could become a favourite aunt to a person. Even an aunt to someone who was not a blood relative. Victor hadn't interacted with Beth necessarily (she had no memory of even speaking to him), but she could improve on his model, as it were.

Who could that non-niece or nephew be?

That was easy: Norvell. She could latch on to him.

#

That night, while she was staring sleepless at the wall by her bed, the phone rang. She recognized the area code as belonging to Quebec, so instead of treating it as a telemarketing call, she had to pick it up.

A man, neither Pete nor Philippa, began speaking in French, but a few words in he switched to English. She understood the English part: ". . . left in Café Le Feu yesterday."

"Sorry?"

"Pardon me. I'm calling because I found something here at Café Le Feu yesterday, and this phone number was on the object."

"What object?"

"I would prefer, for security, if you told me if you have left something in the café, and then identified it."

"That's funny. You're calling me out of the blue late at night, and I'm supposed to be a security threat?"

The man gave a nervous laugh. "Oh, yes, I see."

"Are you a telemarketer?"

"No, no. I work for Café Le Feu. I am calling about a lost object someone left here."

She had to confess that she was not in Quebec but that her children were.

"Your . . . children were at Café Le Feu?" He sounded disappointed.

"They are adults."

"Oh, yes?" The man seemed more hopeful. "Not you?"

"I'm in Alberta. I haven't been to Quebec in twenty years."

"Alberta! I had no idea, Madame, I'm truly sorry. Maybe I have the wrong number?"

Beth had the man repeat the number, and it was indeed hers. He said, "I thought maybe it was a new area code. New area codes are happening all the time."

"I get that. Maybe you can tell me what object you found."

"A checkers game with a chess game too."

"Now let me think." She found it helpful at times to speak out loud when she was trying to fix a problem, and since the man on the phone was handy, she took advantage. If it was a game, it had to be Pete's. "Yes, that's one of my children's games. What should I do now?"

Café Le Feu said, "You can tell them. Or you can tell me their number in Montreal and I can call them."

Beth was struck again by the mirroring qualities in this mysterious man from Quebec. Beth often thought of her children as "them," as a unit. Still, she didn't want to give Monsieur Café Le Feu anyone's phone number. Instead, she said, she would call one of said children and have her call Café Le Feu herself. Beth asked who her child should ask for. He identified himself as Dom and gave her the phone number for his café.

When Dom Café Le Feu disconnected, she debated whether she should call Montreal and Gilda at the same ungodly hour that Café Le Feu had called her. As she weighed the pros and cons, sleep came to her.

The next morning after breakfast, she called Gilda.

"This is the break I was looking for, Mom." Gilda hung up immediately to call the café's number. After five minutes, Gilda called back. The number belonged to a Montreal restaurant, which was open, Gilda said, from seven o'clock in the morning to midnight.

"Dom Café Le Feu called me after the café was closed," Beth said. "Don't you think that's strange?"

"Maybe he'd just found it."

"He said they found the game yesterday."

"I don't know, Mom. Anyway, I'll go to the café tonight and get the game. Maybe Pete will be there, or someone who knows him might be."

After Gilda hung up, Beth thought what kind of life she might have going forward if, by the time she got home from work, all the mysteries of her life were solved through the intervention of Dom Café Le Feu or Dallas Burgh.

47

THE MACGUFFIN

When Gilda saw the Café Le Feu sign, the words from the song "Que Será, Será" slipped into her head. That song, so oddly placed in Hitchcock's film about an innocent man wrongly accused, reminded her of the absurdity of this visit to the café, this trip to Montreal and all associated memories. No matter how sweetly Doris Day had sung, the song affirmed human powerlessness against fate. Hitchcock could be cruel.

The burbling voices in the restaurant's dining room dropped in volume when she entered, but the volume quickly rebounded to its original decibels. This was a place people went to be seen and to see, and her presence had made only a short-lived impression. The café's decor combined fine dining with bohemian ad-hoc-ism: white tablecloths on tables of non-uniform size, worn wooden floors, cork walls, and exposed timbers and pipes in the ceiling. The air was thick with the smell of fresh bread and oranges. The wall art consisted of a series of sketches of men and women in bikinis and briefs with thick neon lines accentuating crotches, bra-straps and nipples.

A man in black pants, brocade vest and white shirt greeted her in French with the gallantry of a content servant. Gilda fumbled through the script she had practised on the walk to the café. "J'ai reçu un message au sujet d'un jeu."

The host responded smoothly in English. "What kind of game?"

"A chess game. Dom called my house. I'm here to pick it up."

"Ah, yes. Wait, please." He smiled fleetingly before he disappeared into the restaurant. As she waited, she reassessed the decor. The wall art was mildly obscene—in one bikini sketch, the man and woman had their limbs intertwined and they shared nipples, two dots between them instead of four. The sketches lifted a middle finger to the corporatization of restaurants. The customers did the same. Were those two men sitting by themselves in the tiny table by the kitchen entrance in matching fezzes, or was it two women, or a man and a woman?

The server reappeared. "This is it?"

He held the travel-sized magnetic chess and checkers set that she and Philippa used to bring on trips: to Jasper, Kelowna and the Tyrrell Museum and, once, across the border to Coeur d'Alene. For hours, it seemed, they played checkers and chess in the back seat of the fuchsia Ford Taurus station wagon when they weren't playing hangman or Game Boy, reading, sleeping or fighting. She took the game and pried the leatherette case open. All the pieces seemed to be there, including Philippa's makeshift replacement for a lost bishop, a circular black magnet with a crude B drawn with a correction-fluid pen. Printed on the edge of the board in Beth's no-nonsense hand was the area code and phone number, which was still her and her mother's landline number. Pete had brought the game to Montreal like a juju, a reminder of Edmonton or an emblem for the idea of travel itself.

"Thank you," Gilda said.

"You are most welcome." The server asked, "Are you with the person who brought the game here?"

"Yes. It's my relative."

"Pete is your relative?"

"You know him. Is your name Dom?"

"Yes!"

"Does he often come here?"

"Yes, lately," Dom the server said. "He comes sometimes with friends of his."

The word "friends" surprised her, but she continued. "When does he come?"

"For lunch or supper, sometimes after. Do you live in Montreal?"

"No, I'm visiting."

"Will I see you come in again? We have a good brunch."

"I'm staying at a bed and breakfast, so that's not necessary."

"You can maybe come here for supper." Maybe he was the owner operator, or a relative of the owner or the operator.

"I might do that." Time for her shields of privacy to drop. "Thank you for this. Goodbye."

In her room at La Lobélie, she opened the lid and studied the familiar white and black chessboard and the magnetic red, black and white discs of her childhood holidays. Using a fingernail, she flipped over a red disc to reveal a white side. She overturned a black disc. Underneath was a tiny white image of a rook on a black background. Checkers used the red and black sides, and chess used the white and black sides, which had the symbols for the chess piece, except for the pawns, which were blank. She lifted the board out of its tray and turned it over. That side had a red and black board with more discs clinging to it. The white queen and black rook lay among plain discs. Which game did Pete play with his friends, chess or checkers? She returned the board to its tray and its case, closed the case and put the game on the bedside table.

She wanted to talk to someone. She emailed Burghie.

"Things are okay," she typed. "I'm staying at a B&B. I walk a lot. I wish I had a bike."

After using the bathroom and changing into her nightgown, she crawled under the bed covers. She had regained the family checker set, but more importantly she had gained insight into the Pete of Montreal. Maybe she should have stayed at the café longer to see if Pete showed up. But he may never have appeared. What did that person Dom know about Pete? Was the checkerboard a trap of some kind set by Pete to lure her, and had she taken the bait? No, not bait: a MacGuffin. Alfred Hitchcock used the term to explain a narrative device. A MacGuffin is an object of interest that makes characters scamper about and interact with each other and thus create a story. The MacGuffin has no value otherwise. In *The Maltese Falcon*, the MacGuffin was the statue of the falcon that everyone was trying to get their hands on. Everyone thought it was worth a fortune. Even Sam Spade wanted the falcon because it was a clue to the mystery of his partner's death. The falcon ended up being a fake: worthless. In Hitchcock's oeuvre, *The Man Who Knew Too Much* was a film whose title encapsulated the function of the MacGuffin. The main character, played by James Stewart, witnesses someone's death. The doctor has no idea who the man was or who killed him, but simply by being nearby, he and his family, including the singing Doris Day, are endangered. The plot involves the ways in which the doctor extricates himself from plans other people are making for him. His role in the plot derives from chance.

Chance had put the checkerboard in Gilda's possession. An unseen roll of dice had gone her way. Or against it. She didn't know which yet.

48

THERE ARE DIFFERENT WAYS OF BEING

Around lunchtime one day, Sarry called Pete and asked if he had ever been to Île-Sainte-Hélène.

"I don't know what that is."

"Yesterday you said you hadn't seen much of Montreal yet. I'll take you there for a picnic. Nothing is happening right now, yes? Because Gordon hasn't sent you the PDF files."

Sarry had been a co-worker of Pete's for several days and knew what was going on even with Pete's work life. Pete had no reason to say no.

"Bon! It's a picnic date at Île-Sainte-Hélène. And wear a skirt. It's the best for a picnic on a day like today." During their previous night's phone call, Pete had mentioned he was wearing barrettes at home to keep his growing bangs out of his eyes. Sarry had been thrilled and insisted that Pete go out one day dressed in his girl clothes.

He didn't feel brave enough to wear a skirt, but Sarry was wearing one when they met at the metro station. It was a full, long skirt with flowers on a white background that matched her flowing white blouse. An old-fashioned picnic basket hung from the crook of her bent arm. They rode to the old Expo grounds on Île-Sainte-Hélène. After a long walk through crowds that thinned as they moved away from La Ronde amusement park, they crossed a road and reached the banks of the St. Lawrence River. They went down an incline behind some trees and sat on the shore of the river surrounded by flowers and tall grass. On the opposite shore, the city of Montreal shimmered in the summer haze. Behind them and above the treetops arced the metal and glass spiderweb of the Biosphere's geodesic dome. Their private beach was surprisingly quiet, considering how close they were to La Ronde. The steamy heat made Pete glad he wore shorts. Sarry lay on her back, her arms behind her head. One of Sarry's feet touched Philippa's bare knee, still tender from his recent attempt at shaving his legs. Something made Pete decide against moving his knee from Sarry's foot: the heat, the hum of insects or maybe the lapping of the water drained his will.

Sarry talked about her tough negotiation for a day off for the Civic Holiday on the upcoming Monday. "Ridiculous. Nothing is happening at work."

Her voice faded, so Pete was sure Sarry had fallen asleep. The picnic basket lay next to her. Pete reached over to see what was in it.

"Do you like it here?" Sarry was not asleep.

"Yeah."

"I know, right?" Sarry unclasped her hands and stretched languidly from fingertips to toes. In stretching, she had to move her foot away from Pete's thigh. After the stretch, she pushed herself into a sitting position. "You almost would think we're in the country, but we're not. It reminds me of my grandparents' farm in L'Acadie."

"All grandparents come from the farm, don't they?" Pete said.

"Not yours?"

"Of course. Alberta is one giant farm with a big oil rig in the middle."

"Hah!" Sarry slapped Pete's knee lightly. "So, you have been to that giant farm?"

"Not really. I've been to bush bashes at acreages. I went to a farm for a school field trip when I was in grade one. I remember this black and white calf grabbed the bottom of my coat and tried to eat it."

"That's so cute." Sarry's laugh rang like a bell.

"I loved that coat. It was a red hoodie with a front zipper."

"You're funny." Sarry shimmied closer to Pete. Her head was two feet away but everything about her felt closer than that.

"What are we doing?" Pete asked.

"What do you want to do?"

"I don't know." He looked at the picnic basket. "You called this a date."

"That's okay, right?"

"It's a picnic, basically, right? There's food in the basket."

"Bread, cheese, wine, a red and white tablecloth. Romantic, huh?"

Pete felt shy. "It's just that I haven't done this before."

"This?"

"You know." Pete stopped. "With a real picnic basket, and with a—" He couldn't say "man" even though that was what he wanted to say.

Sarry smiled. "With a dot-dot-dot." She sat up straighter. "For me it's less complicated than it is for you, maybe."

"Probably."

"But you should be able to understand a little from your experiences. Some days you wear high heels and makeup like a girl."

"Yeah." He had told Sarry about his second visit to Le Club.

"Well, I'm not like that. I used to dress with a navy-blue suit when I was Sargon the weatherman on TV. Then one day I decided not to dress like that ever again. I want to do more than dress like Sarry, though. I want to be Sarry in all ways. I don't want to switch constantly back and forth from Sargon to Sarry. I did one switch."

"Is there something wrong with moving back and forth?"

"Of course not." Sarry looked down at her hand, which lay near a patch of clover. A bee buzzed around a purple flower. "Bees are interesting. The males don't do much. Most are female, did you know that? They do all the jobs in the hive: get pollen, make cells, make honey. They are also the guards. They can turn any egg into a female by their food. They make a queen with special food too." She touched one of Pete's hands with her fingertips. Her nails were painted black. "People aren't like bees. They have more technologies. Not just computers and smart phones. I mean ideas. With our technologies we can match and unmatch our bodies to our ideas."

"That's a lot of work, changing minds. What if you aren't sure yourself?"

Sarry said, "If you know what you feel, and if you know what to do about it, then you do it. If you don't know what you want to do, if you need more time to decide, then take the time. You take all the time you need. You decide." Her voice dropped. "You do what you want to do today."

The bee rocketed away from the patch of clover.

Sarry moved her hand and clasped it with the other in her lap. "We can eat our picnic. Do you want to do that? I saw you trying to peek inside."

Out of the picnic basket they pulled the red and white-checked tablecloth, put out the plates and the cutlery, sliced the French loaf and arranged on a plate three different cheeses, including Monterey Jack, the only cheese Pete liked, except mozzarella on pizza. To drink was Perrier water for Sarry and a can of pilsner for Pete. There was also a small wine bottle. Pete turned up his nose at the smell from the opened bottle, and Sarry said, "It's not wine."

"What is it?"

"Barleywine. It's a kind of beer. Bart at Le Feu told me about it. He said it was the beer-lover's wine."

Sarry poured out a finger into a wine glass for Pete. The barleywine was sweet, thick and a bit fizzy. Pete said, "It doesn't taste like wine."

"What does it taste like?"

"Like sweet apple cider mixed with something else." He paused. "Sloe gin."

"What?"

"Nothing. Like brandy."

"Do you like it?"

"Yeah, I do."

Sarry took the bottle away, and Pete let Sarry pull him toward her. She put her hand on his leg, then she slipped it under the waist band and down. Her other hand slipped under his oversized T-shirt. Sarry's hand didn't flinch when it found Pete's micropenis.

The world dissolved into the smell of grass and river water and the touch of Sarry's lips against his neck under the hot sun. The world spun round and round as though Pete were on a merry-go-round, only now Sarry spun with him. The honeycomb crescent of the Biosphere blended with the green treetops with waving leaves, the blue river, the clover, the brown earth.

49

BETH AND RALPH'S CHILDREN

At work that morning, Beth checked her personal email and saw a message Gilda had sent the day before. In it, Gilda said she had moved from her hotel to Philip's B&B. That little bugger. She hadn't mentioned a thing about it on the phone this morning. The revelation made Beth more resolved to take action herself.

On her first work break, Beth called Tokens. As she'd hoped, Norvell answered.

"Do you still want those other games I showed you?"

Hesitantly, Norvell replied, "Sure."

"Then why don't I come by your place tonight?"

He explained that he didn't finish work until late, and his place was tricky to find.

"I'll drive to Tokens and we'll caravan from there." She went on to do a sterling job of explaining how this late-evening drive was not at all an inconvenience. She had learned the skill of aggressive passive self-denial from her Aunt Eunice, who in her elder years could ask Beth to drive her somewhere while at the same time be shocked that Beth would go out of the way to help her.

As soon as she arrived home from work, Beth began carrying Pete's possessions to her car, box by box. She made a careful list of everything in case Pete came home and wanted everything back. On a piece of lined legal paper, she wrote the name and manufacturer of each game, action figure, magazine and card set before putting it in her car. She was amazed at how much Philippa had accumulated. At a certain stage of life, Pete bought games with his own money, and after his mid-teens, his birthday and Christmas gifts tended to be games. Ralph bought him games because he thought they were a masculine enterprise. Once even Beth sent Gilda to Toys R Us to buy Pete a game as a gift. Beth couldn't remember what game Gilda had bought.

Beth didn't have time to eat supper. For the first time in a long time, she also skipped church. Her car filled, Beth drove to Tokens and waited in the parking lot. Norvell exited the building's front doors and locked them, and when he stepped away from the building, he seemed surprised to see Beth had shown up. She rolled down the window and shouted merrily at him to lead the way.

Few drivers at that hour were much interested in Lamoureux: only their two cars took the highway turnoff to an underpass and around to a riverside road. The two-lane road snaked along the wide silvery slickness of the North Saskatchewan River in the sherbet glow of Fort Saskatchewan on the opposite bank. After only a minute on the riverside road, Norvell turned left onto a long gravel driveway that ended at a collection of buildings around a Quonset. Beth pulled in beside his hatchback in front of a house trailer. Under the radiance of the sodium light atop a pole next to the driveway, Norvell and Beth carried boxes from the Oldsmobile into the house. The house reminded her of everyone's house in the seventies with its love of dark brown, dark green and burnt orange. She could see the carpet—orange shag—under the cramped and rickety furniture. There was a hint of litter box underneath the dominant odour of bacon and microwaved popcorn. A white-muzzled dog and a chubby cat watched warily from their shared post on the seat of the orange-and-brown armchair in front of the huge television. The stacks of board games she and Norvell brought inside unfortunately contributed to the heaps of games already piled on and around the furniture.

"Thank you very much for these," Norvell said when they had carried the last box in. "That was very kind of you."

Someone had taught this sad young man some manners, and that gave Beth hope for some casual yet constructive conversation.

"Funny, I've lived in this part of the world my whole life," she said, "and I've never heard of Lamoureux."

"Few people have. It's part of Sturgeon County, not Edmonton. I didn't know about it until my uncle told me. I rent this place from him."

"Oh, so your uncle owns this."

Norvell nodded. "He subsidizes my rent because I look after his dog and cat. My aunt is allergic. He had family in Lamoureux back in frontier days. The Lamoureux brothers ran a ferry across the river to Fort Saskatchewan for many years. Historically it's flooded a lot here. Lots of people have built big new houses. Not what I would do. But the land here is worth a lot. One day I'm sure Uncle Ted will sell this. I hope that won't happen for a while."

"Especially now I've given you all these extra things to move."

He shrugged. "Most of the furniture here is Uncle Ted's."

"When you moved from home the first time, did you leave your things behind thinking one day you'd take them eventually?"

Norvell coughed. "Oh, I don't know. My mom and dad started living out of a motorhome when they retired. They go to the US in the winter and set up camp somewhere in Medicine Hat for the summer. I doubt they kept anything of mine."

Beth wondered if the itinerant family was a place of contention in his ragged heart. "Do you have any mementos from childhood here?"

"Not much. I wasn't much of a buyer until after I moved out." He paused. "Do you have more stuff at your place you want to give me?"

He possibly had guessed at something on her mind. "This doesn't include the basement stuff, no."

His cellphone rang out from his back pocket. The ringtone was Norvell's own recorded voice yelling "pick it up, pick it up."

"Go ahead and take the call." Her magnanimity was a direct result of her appreciation for Norvell's manners and unusual garrulousness, outside of her curiosity over who could be calling this obviously dispossessed and distressed creature.

Norvell's eyes darted to Beth. He clicked on the call after Beth beamed encouragement and guilelessness and turned away slightly to fake a concern for his privacy.

"Hey, Jackson, can I call you back?" His voice was sweet. "Oh, someone is here to drop off some things. No. That's not it. It's just a—No, I'm not."

Beth saw the agitation in his eyes, but she kept on smiling and emoted a bit of Aunt Eunice's empty-eyed, fiendish hopefulness.

"No," Norvell said. "A co-worker's mother just dropped off some stuff that belonged to her son and she didn't need anymore. No. I'm not kidding!"

He stopped talking. After a few seconds, he lowered the phone. Norvell was shaking a little as he put the phone into his pocket.

She asked, "I hope I didn't cause any trouble."

"No, no trouble."

The dullness and quickness of his voice made it impossible for Beth to get a sense of his emotions. She let it go, though she promised herself to keep that phone call in mind for the future.

"I have more boxes," she said. "They couldn't all fit in the car."

He agreed to take them, adding that he could use his uncle's cube van to pick them up at her place. She didn't want that: she needed to bring the games to his home so that she could learn how to get his confidence. "It's just one more car trip. Don't worry your uncle about it." To cap off her plan, she asked for his phone number so that she could call him tomorrow to set up a drop-off time. "I need to check my schedule." In truth, he was number one on her priority list, but he couldn't know that. She didn't want to intimidate him.

\#

The next morning at work, Beth received a phone call from Jerry. He and Pete had exchanged emails about updating Tokens' website. "I asked how he was doing, and he said he was doing well. He said he has a few contracts, so he seems to be making money. It's kind of strange, though. He mentioned that he didn't have a cellphone.

You know how people that age treat their cellphones, like part of their body."

Beth didn't think she could convince Jerry that Pete had become a Luddite, so she lowballed it. "Maybe attitudes about cellphones are changing. A new youth revolution."

"My kids aren't going through any revolution, I can tell you that."

"Do you have Pete's email address? His old one doesn't work."

"I'll ask him if it's okay if I give it to you."

"Please do," she said.

Later, after she washed her paltry dishes and placed them in the drying rack, and instead of going to church or watching television downstairs, Beth sat with her tea, the lights off, in the dark privacy of her kitchen. With Gilda and Philippa in Montreal, the only living things Beth had to attend to were Entry and Exit, and at this time of day they skulked in the basement until her bedtime, when they emerged and sprawled on her bed, waiting for cheek rubs. Probably the cats were child substitutes. When the kids were school aged, they disappeared in the evenings to do their own thing, somewhat like cats.

She remembered one time that Ralph had brought Philippa and Gilda home at the end of his weekend, and Philippa and Gilda had fled somewhere in the house, Beth didn't know where, which had left Beth alone with Ralph to bicker.

"I know what it's like, having to fight for yourself," Ralph had said that time. "Do you think I had it easy convincing my family that I could be a musician?"

Their fights rarely included raised voices. Even when they had still been married, no neighbour had ever called the police, no co-worker had looked askance at her in the coatroom in the morning after a snippy word or a bruise revealed an inside battle, a domestic situation. After the marriage ended, their pattern of communication didn't change.

"Who has an easy time?" Beth had retorted. "No one. But it's common sense that a child who gets support from their parents does better in life than the child who doesn't."

Ralph had snorted at the words "common sense."

The heart of the argument had derived from eleven-year-old Gilda tattling to Ralph that Philippa had been telling her schoolmates that the best way to have sex with a girl was to get her drunk. Philippa had also begun wearing baseball shirts from heavy-metal bands like Kreator and had talked about getting a mohawk. During that recently completed weekend with his children, Ralph had seen Phil weave a sewing pin into the tough skin on the side of her index finger near the nailbed to increase, as Philippa had said, her tolerance for pain.

"She was just bored," Beth had said. "Sitting around with your old man watching a bad hockey team—the Toronto Maple Leafs, for God's sake—would drive any kid to do something like that."

Ralph had said, "See, you take things too lightly."

"No, I don't."

"The problem is that taking things too lightly is a sign of lightness in the head."

"No, it isn't."

"You don't grasp the big picture, so you try to slough it off as nonsense or eccentricity."

To Norvell—to whom, she realized, she was pretending to tell this story—Beth said inside her head, "He always considered me uneducated because I had a business administration diploma. After he got his master's degree, he was insufferable."

Ralph had continued, that night years ago, "Nothing you've done has made life easy for these kids. Being children in a divorce is bad enough. But to let Phil go on like this."

"There's nothing wrong with Philippa. And the divorce was your idea."

"Who buys Phil those shirts? Not me."

"Philippa saved up her allowance money for that shirt. Anyway, it's harmless. Remember when people used to walk around with Grateful Dead shirts and wear bandanas? Same thing."

"It's going to get worse, believe me. He is hitting puberty, and sooner or later he is going to realize that he is physically different from other kids his age. The last thing a teenager wants is to be different. I was a pretty normal kid, relatively, and I had a hard time."

To Norvell, Beth commented, "Ralph wasn't normal. He was a freckled redhead and he squinted because his father thought eyeglasses made nearsightedness worse. Ralph was pompous, too, which made it worse. He was teased at school and had no friends. I didn't say any of this that night. That would have been like shooting fish in a barrel. He would have denied it, anyway, even though he was the one who told me."

Beth wished Norvell would say something, but he kept silent. He tended to nod patiently with compassion on his wide, sorrowful face. She appreciated the compassion. She appreciated having someone listen to her. God didn't, obviously. The idea of God had its uses, mainly as a compassion-compulsary sounding board for one's own thoughts, but God never responded to Aunt Fenna's prayers: her knees never got better, and Fenna's daughter Karen remained a shit. Beth had humoured Aunt Fenna with trips to church anyway. It was nice to think someone listened to you. This Norvell wasn't real, of course, but that meant she didn't need to feel guilty about burdening him, just like when Fenna used to load Beth with details about her aches and pains, her fears and regrets.

Ralph had said, "If I didn't think that kids need their mother I would try to get full custody."

To Norvell, she said, "He wouldn't have. He liked things the way they were."

To Ralph, she had said, "When I was in school I saw kids do the needle in the skin trick on the bus ride to school. It doesn't hurt. It's just dead skin around the nails, no blood. It's just kids showing how tough they are, exploring the limits of their bodies."

He had sniffed. "Exploring the limits of their bodies. What utter crap. Guess what, Beth? People with even half the normal mental complement can see that Phil is screwed up."

"Says who?"

"A child psychologist that my fiancée knows."

"Is she seeing a child psychologist?" Beth asked. "Is she not over eighteen? You need the parents' written permission to marry a minor, Ralph. You better get going on that. Paperwork like that takes time."

He had stared at her as though flabbergasted that she could respond at all. He stopped talking, and he marched out of the house and into one of his seemingly lifetime supply of Suburbans.

Years later, Beth found out from an older Gilda that the young Gilda had the habit of hiding around a corner or up a stair to listen in on her parents' front-door fights, and she had overheard this discussion. As for Philippa, she had slipped out the back door to visit a friend in the neighbourhood or get candy at 7-Eleven.

To Norvell, Beth said, "That fight sticks with me. I wondered if he was right. That I was stupid. I also wondered why Gilda wanted to eavesdrop while Philippa couldn't care less."

Beth pretended that Norvell responded, "Ralph was trying to make you feel badly about yourself to make him feel better about himself. He was pushing you down so he could climb up."

"I know that intellectually. But I don't know that mentally. A part of me believed him."

Norvell said, "You were split in two, and that's what Ralph was after. Pete didn't listen because he had things he wanted to do. He's a free spirit. There's no holding him back."

Beth didn't answer. She waited for Norvell to say more, but he didn't. Instead, he contracted into a small ball, smaller and smaller, until he disappeared with a pop.

She was split in two, like what Ralph wanted. She sipped her tea. She felt, like her tea now, cold.

50

PETE AND PHILIP GET INTO A FIGHT

Two things happened that led to Pete racing from Café Le Feu in the Gay Village to La Lobélie Bed and Breakfast on rue Saint-Urbain in Le Plateau-Mont-Royal.

The first thing occurred at noon in his apartment. He read an email from Jerry, who asked permission to give Beth Pete's email address. "No," Pete typed.

The second thing took place in Le Feu during a business lunch with Yasir and his friend Melodie, an engineering consultant who needed a website manager. At some point, Dom strode over to their table, but instead of taking their orders, he said that one of Pete's relatives had come by last night to pick up the checkerboard he'd left behind a couple of days ago.

"What checkerboard?" Pete asked.

"The little one you bring here sometimes."

"Which relative?"

Dom explained his discovery of the lost checkerboard, his phone call to Edmonton and the conversation with Pete's mother, and the mystery relative's visit the next day. "She said she was staying at a B&B somewhere."

A double shaft of fear and hatred shoved him up off his seat. "I have to go, but I'll call you for another appointment." He noticed the surprise on Yasir's and Melodie's faces, but he didn't care. He walked past Dom and his notepad and left the café.

He hoofed it out of downtown and onto rue Saint-Urbain. He had been bringing the checkerboard to Le Feu to play with Sarry, and finally Pete had forgotten it. Like he forgot keys. That mistake, no, that lifelong fucking weakness, had opened him to attack. Gilda had taken advantage of the weakness, it seemed, from across the country. All the way to La Lobélie, Pete repeated the phrase "Action Mode" to himself. The more he repeated the words, the angrier he felt, and the faster his feet moved. He wanted the anger. He needed it. The buildings whirred past him.

At La Lobélie's front step, Philip answered the door, and Pete didn't give him a chance to say hello. "When were you going to tell me Gilda was in Montreal?"

Philip took a step back. "Oh."

"That's what I thought! She's staying here, isn't she?"

"Yes. She's not here right now, though."

"Where is she?"

"She went to a show, she said."

Pete yanked the door shut in Philip's face.

He stormed home, fuelled by the burn of his rage, against the flow of traffic on the one-way road of Saint-Urbain. A bodybuilding type snarled for bumping into him, and Pete snarled right back without stopping. Strips of images flashed in front of him: Gilda standing wide-stanced in the back alley of his house and blocking his path, Gilda peering from behind a door or a stairwell, Gilda sending an email: "Why didn't you come over last night? You told Mom you were coming over." The checkerboard on a chipped tabletop in a motel in Kelowna, on the fuzzy black seat covers of the station wagon, on a bistro table at Café Le Feu. When he arrived at the first significant traffic intersection, he had to stop for the light, and he admitted to himself the pain in his heels and soles. He limped the remaining blocks to his apartment. Once inside he peeled off his shoes and socks, one bloodied. He filled the tub with warm water and baking soda, his mother's old trick, and wincingly lowered his feet into the water. His toenails were black, painted a few days earlier by Sarry.

Philip had left a voice message a while back asking to have a "chat," but Pete had been too chicken. He'd thought Philip wanted to talk about Murray giving him Yasir's phone number. If Pete had had the balls to call back, he might have found out about Gilda earlier.

Pete shouldn't have been surprised. The narrator in *Invisible Man* hadn't been able to move around without interference. Those bastards that the college president sicced on him haunted Invisible Man all the way to New York. Even within New York, people tracked Invisible Man's movements, toyed with him, forced him to change homes and offices.

What was so great about Edmonton that made Gilda think Pete wanted to stay there? People left Edmonton all the time for Vancouver or Toronto or, like him, Montreal. Maybe he could have finessed his migration better, but what did finesse have to do with moving? Throughout history people have been moving, from Christopher Columbus to his parents to the Australian girl to Granv back in high school. Even Jesus left his family hometown. Not that Jesus' move had been a good thing for him in all respects, but he'd managed to create a religion for other people out of the experience. He'd left Edmonton without leaving contact information, but that didn't mean he was never going to get in touch with his family again. What about back in history when the only thing people could do was write letters that couriers on horseback or in covered wagons carried across dirt roads or across the prairies or whatever the equivalent was in Europe and the Holy Land? Not being able to communicate with someone didn't stop the cavemen from leaving their caves. All the cavemen could do was grunt their goodbyes: they couldn't send letters; smoke signals probably weren't invented until later. The cavemen left nothing behind when they moved. Maybe a pile of mammoth bones or a cave drawing, but not much more, just an emptiness in the air and a lost habit of speaking, or of seeing the people you used to know, until the habit disappeared, and you found new habits and new people, and all you had were memories.

Pete left the bathroom, dried his reddened heels and lay on the sofa. He stared up at *Lady of the Eighties*. He had to call Yasir at some point and set up another meeting, that is if Melodie wanted to anymore. Yasir would be full of questions: he was smart enough to connect Dom's story about the checkerboard to Pete leaving the café. That was the downside of knowing people. Maybe it was better to be a stranger to everyone, communicating anonymously with soundless words sent electronically, or with an invisible voice over the airwaves, or with a smoke signal that the wind swept away.

With a groan, he heaved himself to his feet and checked the landline's answering machine. Sarry had called. "Hey, Petey, how did it go with Yasir and his friend Melodie? I want the goods!"

He hadn't told Sarry everything about his life, but he'd told her quite a bit—about his father, his mother, his twin. His BASE jumping. His vertigo. He picked up the phone and left a message: "Guess what? My sister Gilda is in Montreal." After he said it, he felt funny, but he also felt good, he had to admit.

#

At the same time that Pete was bolting away down Saint-Urbain in fury, Philip was leaning against the door that Pete had slammed shut. Philip couldn't stop seeing Pete's expression, the way that his eyes had flashed both anger and pain. Philip didn't like it when people became cross with him, and it had happened right in his home and place of business. La Lobélie was supposed to be a haven, a quiet island in the rush and roar of airports, crowded hotels and highways, and in the middle of a city roiling with political somersaults, economic tensions and a history of uneasy peace along the spasmodic seam that joined post-colonial Canada with republican America. Here battled urbanites and agriculturalists, narrow-minded traditionalists and open-hearted progressives for moral and economic territory, each balancing the other with no clear victors.

He allowed himself to acknowledge his own displeasure. Suppression made it worse. Vexation rose in him, then, like burning oil. Gilda had put Philip in this position. She hadn't considered what would happen if Pete found out she was in Montreal. Perhaps Philip should have asked what she wanted him to do if Pete confronted him about what Philip knew. But Philip had made a promise to Pete first. Gilda wouldn't have cared about that. She had a plan, and she didn't want Pete to interfere in her plans for Pete. Philip felt a pang. He had gotten used to the same dynamic in his recent dealings with Murray. Murray didn't want Philip to interfere in Murray's plans for Pete. Murray had taken pains to connect Pete with people from his old life and made sure to leave Philip out of it. For some reason, Murray thought Philip wouldn't have agreed with Murray's choice of companions for Pete, so he had kept the matchmaking a secret. Perhaps that resentment was why Philip hadn't mentioned to Murray that he had given a room to Gilda. He hadn't tried to deceive Murray; he'd just entered Gilda in the register. Still, Murray had not been happy when he spotted "Gilda Peterborough" there.

"Is this Gilda the sister of Pete Peterborough?" Murray exclaimed from the front hall.

In the kitchen, Philip stopped folding napkins. "Yes."

"Why?"

"She asked, and I said yes."

Murray hadn't spoken to Philip since. They slept in the same bed, but Murray didn't say good night or good morning. He rose out of bed at the customary time, did his customary activities and went to bed at the customary time. He went through work and life without exchanging a single word with Philip. To avoid the awkwardness of Murray's silent treatment, Philip spent as much time as he could in his campus office. Philip had hoped that someone would back down, but no one had backed down. He was aware that he was one of the parties who could back down.

Wearily, Philip pushed himself upright from his lean, shuffled to the kitchen and went into the private dining room to continue his weekend planning for the B&B. Murray was upstairs taking a bath with one of the books about branding. Murray had been into branding for the past few weeks, hadn't been able to stop talking about it (until now). Murray had once said that branding was folly for something as local as a bed and breakfast. Nevertheless, Murray wasn't one to stop thinking about something once it snuck into his consciousness. Even on soft-soled slippers, an idea could gain solid footing by sashaying past the guardianship of Murray's logic and pragmatism.

Philip didn't know how often he himself crossed either of Pete or Gilda's minds, but he knew that everyone was now in a defensive posture. He and Murray, and Pete and Gilda, belonged to a partnership of betrayal. Gilda was Pete's Murray, planning things for the other's own good. Pete had taken the radical move of trying to interpose wheat fields and the Canadian Shield between Gilda and his flayed, tender individuality. What Philip would do in kind, he didn't know. He knew even less what Murray's next step would be.

51

FAMILY DRAMA

While Norvell stood behind the counter, eyes pinned on Braedyn, Jerry wandered into the front of the store, his hands in the pockets of his baggy jeans, staring out at the merchandise floor and muttering under his breath, his head bowed. With Braedyn the serial shoplifter in the store, Jerry's grousing surprised Norvell. Jerry tended to get quiet around Braedyn.

Jerry saw Norvell looking at him, smiled wryly and took his hands out of his pockets.

As he had plenty of experience of dealing with Jerry, Norvell decided to be forthcoming. "Is anything wrong, Jerry?"

"I think I've gotten myself roped into a family drama."

The only drama in Jerry's family that Norvell knew about was related to his eldest daughter Una's dating scene. Yet Jerry hadn't said whose family drama he meant. Therefore—

"Which family?"

"Pete's."

Norvell knew he was blushing, but there was nothing he could do about it. He had to keep going. "What do you mean, if you don't mind me asking?"

"It turns out that Pete hasn't been in contact with his family since he went to Montreal. His mother doesn't know why he went to Montreal. She asked me if I could give her Pete's email address. I said I would ask Pete for his permission to give her his email address. I just checked my email and he wrote a one-word answer: 'No.'" Jerry shook his head. "Now I have to contact his mother and tell her this. Then, I'm guessing, she'll want me to pass Pete a message. This could go on forever, me passing messages back and forth."

Norvell experienced a range of physical and psychological responses: heat under his collar and up his face, images of Beth's eyes as she spoke about the games in her basement, Jackson's forearm on the laminate desk behind the security glass in the visitor's room in Bowden, Pete swinging from his ankles on bungee cables over the wave pool in West Edmonton Mall, Pete's naked torso standing waist deep in the wave pool at West Edmonton Mall.

"Are you okay, Norvell?"

He blushed. He couldn't get away with saying nothing. "Coincidentally, I've been in contact with Pete's mother."

"You have?"

"She called me." He paused to help himself control the speed of his voice. Sometimes he talked too fast. "She gave me some games and collectibles of Pete's that she thought he wouldn't want anymore."

"Why would she do that?"

"She isn't sure he's coming back."

"That's not what he told me."

"I know. He left stuff at her house, and she thought it was okay to give them to me. For safekeeping. I don't know why she wants me to have his collectibles. Maybe it's a psychological need to let go of him finally. She talked about that a lot: kids moving out of the family home."

"Huh," Jerry said.

"If you want, I can tell her about Pete's message. She wants to set up a time for her to bring me more stuff."

"I feel like that's me putting something extra on you. Throwing you to the wolves, even."

"It's okay. Like I said, there are collectibles involved."

"There's something in it for you in this."

The idea of seeming mercenary offended Norvell. Not that getting stuff wasn't part of it. There were other reasons, which he couldn't mention. Blushing in front of Jerry again was better than saying anything out loud to Jerry. "Yes." He blushed again, this time in secret shame. Jerry was good to him.

Unaware of Norvell's thoughts, Jerry grinned. "That makes me feel better. Oh, and don't let her talk you into convincing me to give Pete's email address to her. I'm not doing that. Besides, I have a suspicion Pete is encrypting his email address or something. The address is a little weird."

Later, during his evening break, Norvell called Mrs. Peterborough. "My boss Jerry said to tell you that Pete doesn't want to give you his email address."

"What did Pete say exactly?"

"According to Jerry, the answer was one word: No."

"No beating around the bush there, hey?" Mrs. Peterborough said. "I don't suppose you know what Pete's email address is."

"I don't."

"Well, at least I know Pete is alive. Being alive is something."

Norvell didn't entirely agree. For long stretches of his life, he had thought being alive was nothing to brag about. Lichens were alive. Uncaptured mass murderers were alive. He was alive. "Being alive is a minimum standard, anyway."

"A minimum standard. That's a funny way of looking at it. But you're right. When you're dead, there's no point in sweating the small stuff."

"There wouldn't be any small stuff."

"There you go."

Norvell wondered if he should be discussing things like this with Mrs. Peterborough.

She asked, "Did Pete talk about things like that with you? You know, life and death."

"Sometimes. We talked about books that we'd both read."

"Pete reads books? No, he doesn't."

Norvell told her about the reading list he had put together for Pete. "He's done pretty good, considering he hasn't been much of a reader in the past."

"I remember he read a book about those Parker Brothers. I didn't even know they were real people. I thought they were like the Mario Brothers." She paused. "You've made Pete a reader. No one has been able to do that. A Pete whisperer, that's what you are."

He blushed.

"So," she said, "you want more games? I can bring them to your place myself."

"I can get my uncle's cube van—"

"They'll fit in my car, no problem. Maybe I'll come during the day so I can see this Lamoureux of yours."

"Sure, I can give you a tour. It won't take long."

She said she would drive to Lamoureux mid-morning on Monday, the Civic Holiday, which both of them had off from work. Norvell didn't bother trying to talk her out of bringing the games over herself. Having her there could turn out to be interesting. He rarely had visitors, and long weekends off work usually weren't much fun.

52

BURGHIE DECIDES WHAT TO DO

Burghie waited until he was in his hotel room before he called Gilda. She showed not the least bit of surprise at his call or at the fact that he was now in Montreal. Her lack of emotion might have had something to do with her speaking to him in a public place. She said she was waiting in line at the concession in a movie theatre.

"I suppose you want to see me." She agreed to meet him in the hotel lobby after the movie ended. She would text him when she was almost there.

With the phone call made, he had two nerve-wracking hours before her arrival, so he went outside to pace the streets. He walked several times in and around the block of the big ancient castle of a Holiday Inn. He drooped under the heat, which felt old, as though left over from another day rather than generated by the current one. He suspected it would get a lot hotter. He had been to several big cities when he was a triathlete, but this city seemed stranger. Outside, the French signs threw him off: the city felt like an architectural manifestation of the French side of a cereal box. He retreated indoors and sat at the lobby bar with a series of Cokes while watching highlights from the summer Olympic Games. The clash of the outside with the hotel interior, which was Chinese inspired, upset his equilibrium further. The Olympics coverage emphasized runner Usain Bolt. The cycling events, which interested him most, seemed to be taken less seriously. By the time he spotted Gilda in the pearly light of the hotel lobby, he had come to terms with his inability to figure out the world as well as he ought.

He left the bar and joined her in the seating area next to the Chinese-inspired water feature. He sat in the black leather armchair across from her position on a long, low, red sofa. Her posture, straight and commandeering, her brown eyes wide with alert skepticism, suggested royalty.

"This is a bizarre hotel," she said.

Red paper lanterns dangled from the high ceilings, and a pagoda loomed near the entrance to the elevator banks. A riverlet full of ivory and orange koi burbled past, and Asian Muzak tinkled through an atmosphere smelling like hotel bleach to add to the sense of manicured globalization. "I suppose all big cities have Chinatowns, but a Chinese Holiday Inn strikes me as overkill."

Numbed by love, he couldn't think of a witty comeback. He said, "Even Edmonton has a Chinatown."

"About that," Gilda said. "Why aren't you in Edmonton right now?"

Burghie had prepared what he would say when this question came up. "When you said you were going to Montreal, I thought about it, and I decided it might be a good place to go for a vacation. I've been planning on taking a vacation this summer, and I looked into it, and it seemed like a good place to go."

"This is not a coincidence, you're saying."

"Definitely your coming here influenced me. But you being here isn't why I'm here."

Gilda frowned. "It's very odd. All these years we don't see each other, and we're almost taking vacations together." She stopped. "Is it because Pete is here?"

"No, well, yes, in that you have been talking about Montreal because Pete is here, we think."

Gilda rustled uneasily in her seat. "He's here, all right."

She told him about the checkerboard and the train of events that led to her having it in her possession. Burghie became transported to the dry air of Edmonton and to those meetings in Paul's, during which they discussed Pete's daily habits, their suspicions about his deviations from the habits, and their tactics for learning more about his activities.

He asked, "Are you staying around here?"

"My B&B is basically walking distance." She didn't seem interested in sharing more details about the B&B's location.

"Do you have any leads?"

"I have a plan." Gilda took out her square black purse and checked her phone. "I'm going to a place called Café Le Feu at suppertime to sit in a corner and wait for him." She chewed her lip and spoke as if she were alone. "I should wear something inconspicuous. I wonder what inconspicuous translates into at that café."

"I can help," he said. She shot him an exasperated look. "Since I'm here," he added. "Pete is my friend."

"I don't want to spoil your vacation."

Her tone made clear she didn't believe a word of his explanation for being in Montreal. He called her bluff. "Why else would I be here, then, if I weren't on vacation?"

"Maybe you have a fascination with Pete and his condition. Maybe you have some unfinished business with him."

He had unfinished business, but it was less related to Pete than to Gilda. She was an intelligent, sensitive person: why didn't she understand his motivations? The anguish of anticipated rejection bore down on him. He had to change the subject quick.

"What movie did you see?" he asked.

"*Beasts of the Southern Wild.*"

"Was it good?"

"Fantastic. One of the best movies I've ever seen." She stood. "I better go."

"Be sure to call me if you find anything." That was all he did. He let her leave the lobby without him.

He sank low in his chair, and he used his phone to look up the movie she'd seen. He saw a photo of a fierce-eyed girl, a stick in her hand, leading a procession of solemn-faced adults and children down a surf-flooded road. He wanted to cry.

53

BETH AND NORVELL DO SOME
TRUTH-TELLING IN LAMOUREUX

Early on the afternoon of the Civic Holiday, Beth asked Norvell to show her around the village before they started unloading her car. On the drive in, Lamoureux looked so pretty in the daytime, with the river in the sunlight. He answered, "I know I'm lucky to live here. I should take more advantage of the natural surroundings." Beth waited in the vestibule of Norvell's trailer home while Norvell pawed through a purple plastic tub filled pell-mell with shoes. He laced on a pair of white high-tops.

She and Norvell went outside and crossed Lamoureux Drive to the sidewalk near the river. An erratic wind hissed through the leaves of elms and spruce as Norvell explained the village's layout. The properties had begun as farm lots in the French-Canadian style of narrow strips that gave everyone river access. The farms had since been subdivided and urbanized so that grass, not hay or grain, stretched up behind the houses to the berm of the railway line behind them.

The first group of houses were renovated mid-century bungalows with trim lawns and precise arrangements of shrubs and potted flowers. As they continued, the houses became larger and newer with vaulted ceilings and bay windows. The residences ended at the gravel parking lot for Our Lady of Lourdes Church, a tall slender building with a fake belltower and vinyl siding that imitated the clapboard of country parishes. In front of the church stood a three-panel information board about the original settlement. In the 1870s, brothers Joseph and François Lamoureux had trekked from Quebec west to San Francisco and then north toward the siren call of the gold strikes in the Cariboo Mountain range. Like many disappointed gold strikers, they decided to settle in the west and live as farmers. The brothers chose this bend of the North Saskatchewan River to live out their lives and brought over other people from Quebec, who lived as farmers, ferry operators, and patrons of church and school.

Past the triptych and down a tree-lined gravel road was the church cemetery. Beth and Norvell ambled among the tombstones in the bright sun. The older tombstones sported crosses or square headstones planted in front of rectangular slabs of white rock that marked the locations of coffins underneath. The Lamoureux family proper had a large, weathered monument at one side of the cemetery, obelisks of white marble smoothed by the rock-laden winds and blizzard blasts of decades. Smaller tombstones from over a century surrounded it, though some were contemporary. Beth noted one for a man who died in 1968 and that had two blank spaces for family members who hadn't yet died.

"Are there any Battys here?" Beth asked.

Norvell tugged down the hem of his black Darth Maul T-shirt over a crescent of exposed belly. "Batty is an anglicization of Bataille, so no Battys. No Batailles, neither. My dad says we're related to the Morin family, though."

Beth had seen a Morin among the long dead. She asked Norvell to take a photo of her next to the Lamoureux monument. Norvell snapped a picture with her phone. He showed her the photo, and she nodded her approval, saying, "Not that I'm sure what to do with it. People used to have photo albums."

"The new tradition is to put photos on Facebook."

"Right, Facebook. I wonder if Gilda has done that. I should check. People put up vacation photos, and this Montreal thing is technically a vacation. Pete, of course, doesn't have Facebook anymore."

At the word "Pete," Norvell flushed scarlet.

"Did I say something wrong?"

"Nothing's wrong." He wiped at the waterfall of sweat running down the side of his face. It was hot, yes. They browsed the cemetery for a few minutes in silence, and at the end of their oval route, Norvell led her back to the church and their way home. He wasn't going to talk anymore, it seemed. That meant she had to.

She drew up alongside him on the sidewalk by the river. "So," she said, in a fake-jolly way. "This Jackson person on the phone that day I was over. It seemed like he was jealous of me."

Norvell pursed his lips and said nothing.

They entered the house, and the animals met her in the vestibule as if she were an old friend. Norvell went into the kitchen without a word. If he was going to give her the silent treatment, she should leave. But he came out with a pitcher and glasses on a tray. Beth pushed aside the stack of books on the coffee table to clear room for the tray. They sat on the sofa together, and he poured her iced tea into a Collins glass with the grinning miner's face of Klondike Mike, Edmonton's old Klondike Days mascot. "Sweet tea, they call it in the southern US," he said.

"Do they?" Her voice squeaked with lack of use and excitement at the re-opening of their conversation. "Have you been there?"

"No." He poured himself a glass and downed it. The walk in the summer heat must have pushed the limits of his large body's temperature controls. "My parents go to North Carolina all the time. They say it's nice." He poured himself another glass.

"For some reason my kids and their friends want to go to Montreal."

He cocked an eyebrow, and she explained that Pete's old friend Burghie had gone to Montreal too. "How weird is that?" she asked.

He rose and left for the kitchen. He returned with a mixing bowl full of Doritos. He put down the bowl next to the pitcher without taking anything. She had interested him in a puzzle, and he was concentrating on solving it. A good time, Beth decided, to push forward a provocative area of discussion. "Could Burghie have a crush on Pete?" She had thought about the possibility but decided it wasn't likely. That didn't mean she couldn't keep talking along those lines for her own purposes.

Norvell blanched and made an indefinite sound.

"Too bad for Burghie if he does," Beth said. "I'm sure Pete sleeps with a different woman every week. Gilda has decided to marry her job, it looks like. Not that I want her to get married. I didn't have much luck with marriage. At least I got two kids out of it." She paused. "Maybe Burghie has a crush on Gilda."

He made tentative eye contact. "Maybe."

"Just like you maybe have a crush on Pete."

He turned the reddest she'd ever seen anyone turn. Slowly, painfully, he said, "I don't know that it's any of your business."

"It's not. You should know, though, that this is what I think."

"Well," he said, cheeks trembling, "I have a boyfriend."

"Is he this Jackson person?"

He didn't answer.

"Jackson, then." The conversation she'd overheard had not given her a good impression of Jackson, but she said, "Good for you." She slurped from her glass. "Is this a relatively new thing?"

He stiffened, as though offended. "Not at all." Haughtily, he added, "As a matter of fact, we're engaged."

"Oh!" That was the most neutral expression she could think of. As an afterthought, she added, "Congratulations!"

"Thanks." Instead of blushing, as she expected, his face paled. "Well, should we get those boxes in here now?"

They carried the boxes into Norvell's house in fifteen minutes. These they piled in the hallway to the bathroom and bedroom, careful to leave a path for Norvell.

He brought out more iced tea to the living room, and she sat down with him again.

"There are problems there, too, though," he said.

"What kind of problems?"

Norvell sighed. He explained Jackson.

"You know, this thing you have for unobtainable people has got to end," Beth said at the end of his story.

He shuddered, and Beth realized she had gone too far. This was his home, and she was a guest. She wasn't his mother. No, she was not. She was something else for him. What? She decided: a friend. What do friends do?

"You can be nosy about me if you want to," Beth said.

"Nosy?"

"Sure. Ask me a question about my personal life."

He sniffled. His eyes had become a little red-rimmed. Norvell fought against that emotion, whatever it was, and then leaned forward, his face intense.

"You keep saying you shouldn't worry. But why not be worried about your family? That shows you care. You act like there's something wrong about worrying, and I don't get that."

She hadn't given that impression, she didn't think. More likely *he* was worried. The act of complaining about her behaviour might be good for him. He was solving a problem, expressing himself. Beth asked, "Did I give the impression that I thought worrying was bad?"

"Even if my parents worry about me, and I'm not sure they do, they wouldn't say that to my face." He sighed. "I worry about my parents. I worry that if they found out I was gay they would be upset, disgusted, even. But them worried for me? I doubt it."

"Worrying isn't good, though, is it?"

"It is when there's something to worry about."

She had always thought worrying was a problem, a fruitless exertion of energy better spent elsewhere, but she couldn't squash his idea. She wanted him to keep talking. "It's true that avoiding problems can make them worse."

"Maybe that's it," he said after a moment. "Leaving here helps them avoid their problems."

"Like shutting yourself off, closing down?"

"As in physical movement away from a geographical area. Out of Edmonton. To the States."

Initially, she thought he was talking about her children. But the added "States" showed that he meant his parents. She made the mental shift from herself to him. "You think they drive around in their motorhome to get away from problems?"

"They hate the cold, and they wanted to travel because they didn't do a lot of that when they were younger. But something else could be going on too. Maybe they don't want to deal with me."

She didn't know his parents enough to comment. Yet here she could go to the place she needed to go so he opened himself up to her. She was experiencing a strange little bit of emotional churning herself, though, a pinch in the belly like when she tripped over something or missed a step going downstairs to the television room and nearly fell.

"I can tell you what I worry about sometimes," she said in hope of keeping him talking.

"You don't have to."

"I want to. That is, if you don't mind."

"I don't," he said.

She explained Pete's intersexuality and her own flight to Montreal years ago. Perhaps she shouldn't have told Norvell about Pete's intersexuality, but she did. She hadn't told any of her friends or relatives, not even her brother. He listened without interruption.

When she ended her story, he said, "The real issue, it seems to me, is not you or Pete. It's society. It's society's problem. Society doesn't understand ambiguity."

"People gossip about all sorts of things," Beth said. "It's funny how his situation is something people don't talk about."

"Yes, but there are cultural norms. Some people deviate so far from them that society drives them out."

"Deviation is a tough word to use."

"I don't mean 'deviant.' I mean deviation: a variation from the average. 'Deviant' is a moral term. It's the moralizing that hurts. How can people moralize about something that you were born with? But people do. That's why people stay in the closet."

Pete's closet had men and women's clothes in it along with, she had to admit, the chip he carried on his shoulder from time to time. "Staying in there forever isn't good. It's lonely."

"Yes, it is."

She patted his arm. "Not so lonely now, I hope."

"No." He smiled a rare smile. "Not for you either, I hope."

Yes, she had been in a kind of closet, not as deep or dangerous as Pete's or Norvell's. Hers was more of a cubby at the bottom of the rickety bookshelf shoved behind the sofa in the spare room, that dark place behind the eyes that she entered while sitting on a church pew.

Norvell said, "This is like something that happened to me."

When Norvell was seventeen, he said, he learned about intersex people—then, "hermaphrodites"—in biology class. For a few days afterwards, his brothers' wrestling friends hounded him on the long walk to the bus stop, yelling "hermaphrodite" instead of their usual "faggot." The word "hermaphrodite" haunted him. He looked the word up in the dictionary and noted the etymology. One Saturday he travelled to Old Strathcona in Edmonton and found the *New Larousse Encyclopedia of Mythology* in the second-hand store on Whyte Avenue. He checked the book's index under "H." The encyclopedia contained one article on Hermaphroditus. He bought the book with what he hoped was an air of intellectual curiosity that would hide his reasons from the staff and other customers.

Hermaphroditus was the young son of Hermes and Aphrodite. One day Hermaphroditus was accosted by the lake nymph Salmacis. She grabbed him and held him until their bodies were intertwined. The article was short, and the book had no pictures of Hermaphroditus, but it mentioned something called the Bearded Aphrodite of Cyprus. The book had more to say about Hermaphroditus's parents. Hermes was the protector of travellers and commerce, Zeus's messenger, conveyor of the dead to Hades and a protector of flocks. Aphrodite was a fertility goddess who eventually became associated with love in all its forms.

Although he knew his mother routinely checked his browser's cache, his curiosity overcame his fear of detection, and he searched the internet for the Bearded Aphrodite of Cyprus. It was a primitive statue of a bearded human with tiny breasts. The world seemed full of other bearded Aphrodites and Venuses, many more realistic than the Cyprus version, with fuller beards and bigger breasts. He did an image search on the word "hermaphrodite" and after scrolling past all the dick pics found more statues. One that grabbed his attention was in the Louvre. It was a white marble statue of a slim woman lying on a bed, her body in a relaxed coil. In the back, she had lovely round buttocks, but on the other side he/she had a penis, testicles and a woman's breasts. The same website on Hermaphroditus mentioned something called a herm. A herm was a kind of pillar with the head of a man and a rectangular post for a body. Even though it had no arms or legs, a herm had genitals hanging right where they should be. Herms were named after Hermes, who was the god of travellers, and herms were signposts or boundary markers. "They mark transitions," he said to Beth.

He remembered a world-building project he used to go to, Orion's Arm, which had a gender called "herm." Herm was a gender other than male or female.

"All this got me thinking," he said. "I have breasts because of my weight, and I have a penis and testicles. I wondered if I might be a hermaphrodite. I knew I wasn't, but then again, I've always felt like an outsider. Not one thing or another. That's a transition, right, being halfway there but not there. Not any one thing. A freak."

His voice, husky now, and so slow, stopped with the choke of suppressed tears.

"That's not true." Beth stroked his arm even though she knew that she was saying and doing nothing useful. She had gone through this with Gilda so many times, Gilda lying on her teenager's bed, sobbing because she didn't have a boyfriend and didn't think she ever would, while Beth said "No, no, that's not true" and patted her arm, but no matter what Beth said, Gilda answered with her hoarse cry, "I can't live on my mother's love!" There was nothing Beth could say to that, because Gilda was almost right. It was actually worse than that. People with boyfriends and husbands didn't necessarily have love. So many people were alone, had been alone a long time, and would always be.

"Some people are freaks," Beth said. "Maybe you're one, sure. But the non-freaks are no great shakes, either, let's face it, or else the world would be a better place. You read history, so you know that. Even I know that. Think of all those non-freaks who cheered Hitler on."

"I know."

He stood, went to his bedroom and came back with a box of tissues. Both she and he used a few.

Beth said. "The greedy, the stuck-up, the bullies, the hypocrites, the liars. All self-described non-freaks."

"I know."

"Some freaky people are fantastic," she said. "I bet Einstein was a freak."

"He was."

"Lucky for us. Whoever made that statue probably was a freak too. That statue's beautiful, I bet."

"Yeah." He plunged his hand into the bowl of Doritos. "It is."

They both dug into the Doritos. Beth asked Norvell to show her the freaky statue, and he brought it up on his phone. She confirmed that it was both freaky and beautiful. Norvell gave a little speech about neoclassical art, then he asked her if he could look inside the boxes that she had brought over.

He looked through each box one by one, gingerly holding each item as though everything was covered in gold dust that he didn't want to disturb. Over the years she had watched a collection of games grow in Philippa's bedroom, the basement storage room and the shelf by the television, but she hadn't paid much attention to them as individual objects. Some game boxes were smooth, others had a canvas-like texture. They tended to have bright yellow or orange lettering on brown or black backgrounds. On the tops or on the sides, they had tiny stick-people labelled with age ranges and the number of players. She spotted a box with three labels that together identified the game as playable for two to seven people aged thirteen and up in a period of thirty minutes.

"What is this one like?" Beth tapped the lid.

"7 Wonders? It's a great game. Very popular."

She liked the picture on the lid, a collage with a pyramid and a bronze statue of a man holding a torch and bow and with one foot on either side of a threshold of a sea wall. A sailing ship was just about to pass between his legs and enter the port of a Mediterranean city surrounded by colossal white buildings tinted with the orange light cast by the torch and a sun setting out of view. Or was it a rising sun?

"Let's play this one," she said. "I'm over thirteen."

She had never played one of Pete's games. The last board game she had played was probably Double Trouble when the kids were little, or maybe a game of checkers on that checkerboard, now in Quebec, when they were sitting out a rainy day in a motel in the Shuswap.

They brought the game into the living room, removed the other boxes and the bowl from the table, and took out the game pieces, the board, and the cards. Beth had a lot to learn. She had to learn about Wonder Boards, Wonder Cards, Ages, Conflict Tokens, Resources, Structures and Guilds.

"This is going to take us more than thirty minutes to play, isn't it?"

"That's okay," Norvell said.

He dealt her a pile of coins and a hand of cards from one deck. She picked a random card from another deck and became the builder of the Colossus of Rhodes, the bronze statue on the box lid. Norvell drew the Pyramid of Giza. After about a dozen turns and her first encounter with a Guild, Beth said, "Shouldn't we eat supper?"

They drove together in Beth's car to Fort Saskatchewan for takeout pizza, which they ate together on the shaky little table in the kitchen. They shared a large Hawaiian pizza and a pitcher of iced tea. They decided that playing the game on the kitchen table would be easier, so they moved the game there.

When they finished their game, Beth said, "That was fun. What other game can we play?"

Norvell brought out two-person Blokus, Invisible Cities and Mille Bornes, which they played one after the other. They moved back into the living room and set up Chinese checkers there. Beth knew that game from somewhere. Norvell turned on the television on the channel which played low-stress music and photos of nature. Norvell, at Beth's urging, went into the kitchen to make a pot of coffee.

"Is Facebook as good as a text message?" Beth asked.

He re-entered the living room. "Facebook has its own messaging system. It uses the internet. A text uses the cellphone's phone connection."

Norvell showed her how to send a text. When she started typing, one letter a time, he stood and went back into the kitchen.

Beth texted to Gilda, "Im playng a game i think we bot Philippa."

After the coffee was ready, they continued to play Chinese checkers. Norvell seemed willing to let himself lose to teach her, though she was sure she'd played the game before back in her childhood, maybe on her grandparents' farm. She won the Chinese checkers game, and they returned to 7 Wonders.

During the last Age of the game, her phone gave a thin beep. She jumped.

"That's your cellphone," Norvell said.

She pulled the phone out of her purse. Yes, a message from someone. "From who?"

He pointed. "Open the—"

"Oh, I see, right." She opened. "It's Gilda."

The message read, "Lots is happening here too."

54

BIG NIGHT

At Café Le Feu, Gilda was lucky to find a seat at the bar. One long empty table in the centre of the dining area had a 'Reserved' sign on it, but the other tables, small and large, round and square, were full of customers laughing and chattering as though the party had started elsewhere and was likely to move to another venue after supper. This café was a way station to a wild big night.

She was not here for that. She wore sunglasses, a denim bucket hat, a peasant blouse and a peasant skirt she had bought in a big indoor shopping complex near The Bay on Saint Catherine Street. She wanted to wear something that Pete could not in a million years have ever seen her wear before.

The bartender, his trim body serially reflected in the mirror-tiled wall behind him, asked in French what she wanted. In French she ordered a rum and Coke. She gave him enough of a tip, she hoped, to keep him from harassing her if she had to nurse her drink for a long time. It was six o'clock, and she didn't know when or if Pete would come. In the mirror, she saw her warped, duplicated reflection, a multitude of white blobs with a blue hat and dark glasses. She didn't see Dom anywhere. He might have information about Pete that she could use, but he might recognize her and blow her cover. He also carried the whiff of scandal that she had perpetrated by picking up the game when Pete should have done that himself. No, scandal wasn't the right word. The wrench she felt when she thought of Dom's knowledge of Beth's existence and of Pete's existence in Montreal came out of some grey muddy pit of emotion: a desire for secrecy, a sense of shame and a foreboding of a collision with destiny.

Half an hour of vigilant loitering later, the restaurant's host approached her and said her table was ready. Unfortunately, it was a round bistro table by the kitchen. If Pete were hungry, he might be tempted to watch the swinging door behind her. Years ago, during one notorious supper at The Pyrogy House for Beth's birthday, they waited forty-five minutes for their food before Beth forced the server to double-check their order. When the server showed some indifference to her request, Pete barrelled to the kitchen doors and snarled at an outgoing server, "Don't you just have to boil some water and chuck the perogies in?" Weeks later, The Pyrogy House burned down. Gilda had never talked herself out of believing that Philippa, by then calling himself Pete, and his new friends had something to do with it.

From out of a doorway, Dom entered the dining room and strolled to the bar to talk to the bartender. She ducked her head and pretended to look at the menu. A stealthy perusal under the rim of her bucket hat revealed that Dom hadn't noticed her. She regretted being too far to hear them speak. Dom came out from behind the bar and moved to the entrance, disappearing behind the latticework that screened the entrance from the dining room. Immediately Dom popped out behind the screen leading a group of people to the reserved table. One of the people was Pete.

This was a Pete that Gilda hadn't seen before. He wore black shorts, men's dress sandals and a white cotton shirt rolled to the elbows. Around his neck hung a gold chain, and his hair was longer than it usually was, almost at his jaw line and cut into ragged punky layers. She had a vague memory of Philippa having that haircut before, maybe in a vacation photograph on a beach in front of the statue of Ogopogo in Kelowna when they were kids. His expression was neutral as he leaned toward Dom, who said something to him as the group took their chairs.

She hunkered down and peered through her dark glasses under the brim of her hat. Three of the people Gilda couldn't see well because of the angle, but she could see well the person next to Pete. This person appeared vaguely Asian, with hair short around the neck but built up into a kind of bulwark at the top toward the forehead. The hand that darted from time to time to the back of Pete's hand on the table had layers of friendship bracelets around the wrist.

A waiter materialized in front of Gilda and asked in French if she was ready to order. In English, she ordered a plate of vegetarian lasagna and an orange juice and sent the waiter off.

As casually as she could, she stood and walked through the dining room to the bathroom using a route that took her one aisle from Pete's table. She kept her head bowed but her ears peeled. She couldn't hear anything, though, because of the ambient noise and because someone nearby suddenly let loose a booming laugh. She entered the bathroom and hid in a stall for a reasonable amount of time before going out. Again she passed by Pete's table, but this time through an aisle on the other side. Now Pete's back was to her, but she could get a better view of the other three people, two men and a woman, all dark-haired, quiet but not in a sinister way. Back at her table, she watched Pete with her sunglasses slid down her nose and her cellphone in front of her with the camera function on. Although the people at intervening tables blocked her view, by using the zoom function and waiting for the people to shift around and leave a gap, she was able to get a glimpse of Pete's face. He seemed happy and relaxed but quiet. In this group, Pete was not the talkative one. The person next to Pete did all the talking. Pete seemed to be listening.

After her food arrived, she stood and took another stroll. She headed toward the entrance in a hopeful journey to find a magazine to justify her jaunt and to help her hide. She picked up a free magazine, pretended to read it, and walked right past Pete.

"What about that time we . . . ," said one of the men.

She dropped the magazine and in slow motion, bent to pick it up. Pete said, "Don't ask me. I've never been there."

The person next to him said, "I'll take you there, babe."

She had never heard anyone call Pete "babe" before.

Gilda held the magazine in front of her face and returned to her table.

Someone sat in the other chair at her table. It was a person in sunglasses, a cowboy hat, black shirt and black jeans. The person said, "It's me, Burghie."

Of course it was. She had to pretend it was fine so as not to tip off Philippa or Pete or whoever that was over there being called Babe by the transgender person, for that was who that person was.

The light dimmed, and noises attenuated, as though she were in a highspeed train zooming away from the sound of sirens. She fixed her eyes on her lap, on the knobby knees under her white peasant skirt (of all the things to be wearing—what was she thinking?). She was aware of a server and Burghie, then, and Burghie dressed like a cowboy, asking her to drink some water. Burghie was standing next to her, with two servers now, not just one, and right behind the servers the people at Pete's table were looking at her. She didn't care about that. All she cared about was getting off the train and out of the haze that was falling on her.

"I need to go outside." Her voice seemed detached from her body, which was being led away from the table by Burghie holding her up on one side and a server on another. Had she been right in coming here? By thinking she was doing what was in her nature, she had ruined it, her visiting of a friend in a Montreal hotel who might love her and who was there because of that and not only because he wanted to help her get in touch with her sibling, someone who was now watching her being led out of the restaurant with a difficult-to-read expression and the trans person with a hand on her sibling's arm. It was everyone's bad luck that the night had culminated in this disaster of her own creation in progress. Someone put a chair down for her. Sit. Her body sat. Her mind floated above, snooping on herself. She wanted to be invigilated. She needed someone who cared enough to travel across prairies and lakes. The brim of her hat was gone. So were her glasses. Someone had done that. Burghie had no sunglasses on. Dark brown eyes. Someone said, "Do you need some help?" People gathered around her, and one of those people was Philippa Peterborough. He loomed. He wore red lipstick. To someone he said, "This can't be right." He fell away from her, collapsed in on himself in a shower of sparks. The room spun. Ashamed, Gilda fainted.

55

THE DIZZINESS OF LIFE

Two separate ambulances brought Pete and Gilda to Montreal General Hospital, and Burghie followed them in a taxi. He wanted to go into the emergency ward to see Gilda, but the staff wouldn't let him after he admitted that he wasn't Gilda's boyfriend, so he sat in the waiting room. Three people who had been with Pete at Café Le Feu sat in the row of chairs facing Burghie. At first Burghie had sat in a different part of the waiting room, but he had to leave his seat to charge his phone at a plug in on the wall next to another bank of chairs, and when he returned to his seat, someone had taken it, so he took the opportunity to move to a seat near Pete's group. No one in the group seemed to associate Burghie with Pete or Gilda. They hadn't noticed his proximity to Gilda when the ambulance arrived, and they paid him no attention when he went to the emergency reception from time to time to ask for information about Gilda and Pete. His café disguise had helped; with his glasses tucked into his shirt pocket and his hat in his hands, he was just another guy.

When he had entered the café, he had spotted Pete right away, and he had stared so hard at the table he didn't notice Gilda walking past him until she bent over to pick up a magazine she dropped, and he recognized her gait as she walked to the table by the kitchen.

Burghie had always thought Pete rested comfortably at the straight end of the gender spectrum, but all three of Pete's friends in the waiting room were gay. As he eavesdropped through the early evening and night, he learned their names: Garen, Zora and Yasir.

317

Soon after he learned her name, Zora left, and her seat remained empty, so that Burghie was now nearest to the Black man named Garen. The other man, the older, Middle-Eastern-looking Yasir, sat on the other side of Garen. Burghie learned that Pete had gone into the emergency ward with someone named Sarry.

Yasir phoned someone named Murray, and after a few words in French, he hung up and said to Garen, "Philip is coming." He added, "I think Murray and Philip are fighting."

Some time later, a third man appeared, a handsome leather courier bag slung over his shoulder. Glumly, Garen studied his own hands, which were clasped and hanging between his knees, while the two other men talked.

"We haven't heard anything lately," Yasir said. "Sarry is in with Pete."

"Have you asked at the admitting desk?"

"Yeah, but they aren't saying much."

Philip nodded. "You guys look tired. I can stay here if you want to go."

"That would be awesome," Yasir said. "We've been here for hours. Can you let me know how it goes?"

"Of course," Philip said.

The friendliness in Philip's body language and expression had a positive effect on Garen: he introduced himself and shook hands with Philip before he and Yasir left the waiting room.

With a sigh, Philip took Yasir's former seat. He sat still and straight, his head in some mental space that his cellphone, which he checked infrequently, didn't seem able to fill. From the courier bag, he pulled out a thick wad of paper, a printout of something in a dark dense typeface, and he read that instead. He was close to the end of his printout when Pete walked into the waiting room. Another person held onto Pete's arm as though she were the one who had been admitted to hospital.

Pete froze to a standstill when he saw Burghie. Pete's escort took a few steps forward in the meantime and lost his purchase on

Pete's arm, so that the arm whipped back and made Pete stumble. A passing orderly made a grab for the wobbling Pete, but Pete brushed him off.

Gilda walked into the waiting room behind Pete, a bandage on her cheek. When she saw Pete, she stopped. A Bermuda Triangle of glances connected Pete, Burghie and Gilda, and then Pete, Gilda and Philip.

"Jesus Christ," Pete said finally.

Philip looked in Burghie's direction as though he just realized that he was part of the same group, then he turned his attention to Gilda. "Are you all right?" he asked her.

"I'm fine. Just a stress-induced fainting spell." She touched her bandaged cheek. "I got this scratch from the fall."

Philip said, "How about you, Pete?"

Pete shrugged angrily.

The person with Pete—a woman, Burghie decided—answered for him. "The doctor didn't find anything neurologically wrong." Her attention swivelled to Gilda, and Gilda returned the questioning look.

Burghie thought it wasn't fair for Gilda to be standing alone, so he stood up and made a move toward her. At his movement, Pete startled, as if re-recognizing him. Burghie stopped.

The woman with Pete said to Burghie, "You're new. Who are you?"

"Dallas Burgh. Who are you?"

"Sarry. You were at Café Le Feu too, weren't you?"

"But why?" Pete burst out to Burghie. "Why were you there?" Pete glared at Gilda. "Why were you there?"

"I was looking for you," Gilda said.

"Why? Why can't you leave me alone, Gilda?"

Gilda seemed to sag. Burghie took long quick steps toward her and offered his arm. She took it, though with an exasperated look.

Everyone was angry with him. It was like being at home and having to deal with his grandfather's unmotivated hostility. Good question, Pete. Why am I here?

Philip said, "I have a car. I can drive people home."

"Are you driving all the way to Edmonton?" Pete asked. "Some people need to go back there."

"Greater Montreal destinations only," Philip said with a nervous smile.

"I can take a cab, thanks," Pete said.

Gilda said, "I need to talk to you, Pete."

"No, you don't."

"Maybe not today, then, but tomorrow."

"You'll have to find out where I live." His snaky grimace, an expression Burghie recognized from years ago as a precursor to ramped-up fury, shifted to Philip. "But I suppose Philip told you my address."

Philip shook his head. Burghie could see from the jitter in Philip's cheek that Philip's stoicism was faltering.

Gilda said, "Philip didn't tell me anything. I found out where you were because someone at the café found that old travel checkerboard and called the number on it."

"Why did Mom put a phone number on a checkerboard?" Pete exclaimed. "Who does that?"

"Because you always lose stuff, Pete," Gilda said.

"I can't seem to lose you, though," Pete said. "God knows I've been trying."

"Why do you want to lose me?" Gilda asked. "Why do you keep pushing us away?"

"Jesus fucking Christ! Lay off!"

A security guard appeared at Gilda's shoulder. When Gilda noticed the guard, her eyes widened, and she stepped backwards with a haunted expression.

"Uh-oh," Sarry said.

Out of the corner of his eye, Burghie spotted a full-fledged police constable by the triage counter tap a paramedic on the shoulder, and both men leaned in the group's direction.

"I think we should all go," Burghie said loudly.

The security guard said, "Is there some problem here?"

"No." Philip smiled, shook his head. "We're leaving. Emotions are running high right now."

"It's an accidental family reunion," Sarry said.

Gilda sought Pete's attention. "Let's head out. Philip offered to drive us."

"He isn't driving me nowhere." Pete's expression had darkened.

To the security guard, Sarry said sweetly, "Is there a cab station outside the hospital, sir?"

"There's a courtesy phone in the vestibule." The security guard nodded toward the exit, a signal that even if there wasn't a phone there, the guard wanted them to leave.

Philip walked towards the exit, and behind him formed a line of shuffling people, Gilda followed by Pete and Sarry and rounded out by Burghie. They wound through the icily lit waiting room, past wheelchairs and miserable and moaning people, to the entrance vestibule and its sliding glass doors.

Outside, the night air hit Burghie with the slick heat of a city summer. In the amber ruddiness thrown by the exterior lighting, everyone seemed neither irate nor at peace. Their wariness seemed to have infected the security guard, who trailed them to the sliding glass doors and stood inside watching them. The police officer joined the security guard's vigil.

"This is my fault," Sarry said as he looked back to the uniformed men. "Cops think I'm either a Latino gangster or a Vietnamese gangster."

Panic appeared on Gilda's face, but it faded when the group crossed the ambulance lane and reached the sidewalk proper. They halted in a clump, each person at arm's length from the others.

"No cab station, of course," Sarry said.

"We don't need a cab station to call a cab," Pete said.

Everyone seemed to wait for Pete to take a cellphone out, and when he didn't, no one commented. Apparently, everyone knew he didn't have a cellphone.

"A free car ride would be nice, though," Sarry said. She tugged at Pete's arm. "Faster too."

The group straggled along the deeply shadowed streets towards a parkade, Philip first, then two feet behind him Pete, with Sarry at his side but not touching him, then six feet behind them Gilda, and right behind her Burghie. Gilda murmured "no" when Burghie offered his arm. An ambulance roared by as they walked. They reached the parkade, entered a stairwell that smelled of urine and wet concrete, and took two flights of stairs up to the parking level and Philip's Sportage. With no verbal negotiation transpiring, Gilda took the front seat with Philip, and the other three jammed themselves in the back, Sarry in the middle. Sarry smelled nice, of fresh linen and strawberries.

The car lurched forward down two ramps and on to the street.

Pete said, "Take Gilda home first. I don't want her to know where I live." His voice betrayed grumpiness and sleepiness.

The sleepiness worried Burghie. "You can't be by yourself. You just hit your head."

"I'll be there," Sarry said.

They're together, Burghie realized. A couple.

From the front seat, Philip said, "The doctors gave you a clean bill of health, right?"

"Right," Pete said.

"With conditions," Sarry added.

"Who are you?" Gilda said from the front seat. She spoke loudly so that she didn't have to turn her head, which made it unclear at first who she was speaking to.

Pete answered. "None of your business." That statement seemed to cover a great number of possibilities.

Burghie wasn't sure if Gilda understood the situation with Sarry in the same way he did.

He thought it best to disrupt the negative energy around the conversation. "You can leave me anywhere downtown and I'll make my way to my hotel."

Pete ignored him. "I want that checkerboard back, Gilda!"

"I don't have it with me."

"Where is it?"

"At Philip's B&B."

"Then when we get there, get it and give it to me."

"I want to talk to you first."

Philip asked, "Do you think maybe you should get some sleep and meet up tomorrow?" The question seemed addressed to everyone in the vehicle.

"What do you mean 'meet up'?" Pete asked.

"Aren't you the least bit curious about why I'm here?" Gilda said.

"Hell, yeah," Pete said. "But I don't know why there needs to be a *meeting*."

"I have to say that I am very curious," Sarry muttered.

Pete rasped, "Who cares?"

Sarry pulled in a gulp of air. "Don't you dare talk to me like that."

"You—"

"Tabarnak!" Sarry said. "I'm not going to let you treat me like that. I've had enough of being treated like that in my life, and it's not starting up again now."

With gentleness, Philip said, "All of us are a bit keyed up. Maybe we should just go our separate ways."

"Keyed up?" Sarry said. "Uh-uh. There's no excuse for treating people like that! None!"

"All of us?" Gilda jumped in. "Aren't I staying at your place, Philip?"

"Yes, yes. That is, if you want to."

"Don't you want me to?"

The argument brought Burghie back home to his kitchen, years ago, his mother by the stairs from the kitchen to the family room, hands on hips, Granddad Burgh slouched over his plate at the kitchen table, Burghie's father in the threshold from the kitchen to the front hallway. Burghie stood by the fridge. He'd wanted to leave, but his exit routes were blocked, and he had to listen to the three adults snarl at each other.

"You can let me out now," Burghie said in the car. "I can make my own way to my hotel."

"I can't let you out in the middle of the street," Philip said.

"I'll get out too," Sarry said.

Pete said, "For fuck's sake."

That day at home, Burghie's mother had asked Granddad Burgh if he'd like it living on the street, and Granddad Burgh said it was his son's money, not hers, that had paid for the house, and his son had the final say about who lived where.

Philip said, "I don't mind driving all of you where you want to go."

"I think we should stay in the car until we sort everything out," Gilda said.

"And I suppose you are paying for the gas," Pete said. "Have you seen the prices here?"

The car stopped at a red light, and Burghie opened the door and climbed out. At the same time, two of the other car doors flew open, and Gilda, Pete and Sarry were standing outside too. The early morning air felt damp and smelled like blood. Only a few other vehicles were on the road, yet all of them seemed to be honking their horns. The traffic light had turned green.

"This is crazy!" Philip yelled. "Everyone get back in!"

A passing water truck honked at them, and everyone outside scrambled into the SUV, Pete first, followed by Sarry, then Gilda and Burghie, who now sat next to Pete in the back.

Philip punched the gas, and the SUV lurched forward. "At least at my place I'll have somewhere to park," he said. "Once I get there, you can go wherever the hell you want."

The SUV drove onward through the dark, mysterious streets of Montreal, the French-language signs, lush-leaved trees, strangely hued streetlights. The inside was quiet except for breathing. Burghie felt like he was in an unpiloted space capsule hurtling through the solar system toward an unknown destination.

They turned down a busy street, then a less busy one, past row houses, and they decelerated into a rumbling back alley and onto a short two-car parking pad behind a three-storey building. On the wall between a pair of widely spaced red doors was a small sign in elegant script that read "Le Gîte La Lobélie."

56

MURRAY ISN'T HELPING

Philip led his guests through the back door into the B&B's kitchen. There Murray stood, staring at them from beside the oven. Like a line of ducklings Pete, Sarry, Gilda and Burghie soundlessly followed Philip past Murray out of the kitchen and into the front hall. Murray proceeded to the front of the line, and the line halted.

"I am not happy about this," Murray said, the first words he had spoken to Philip in days.

"Nobody is," Philip said.

Sarry was the only half-cheerful one: she managed a wan smile and mouthed "How are you?" to Murray.

"Let's go in here." Philip motioned to the open door of the guest parlour, and they all filed in. Three of the four stood in the middle of the room, unsure of what to do, but the passive-aggressive man named Dallas—whom the Peterboroughs called Burghie—flumped into a chair by the gas fireplace. In the young man's lowered eyes, Philip detected the preparation of an explosion. He seemed like one of those sulky but bright boys in a first-year university class who, after three months of saying nothing at all, would shout out something bellicose yet articulate during a class discussion in a way that successfully undermined the whole premise of the course.

From the open door to the front hall, Murray hailed Philip, and Philip backed out of the parlour.

"Okay, Murray," Philip whispered once he was next to Murray in the hall. "I'm sorry. But I feel like they just need some neutral territory, and I want to provide that."

"This isn't neutral territory," Murray whispered back. "This is ground zero!"

Murray was right, in some respects, but he wasn't helping. What Murray didn't appreciate was that zones of contention could be transformed into a neutral space through negotiated acceptance. A physical space was never the essence of a disputed event, even for those disputes contingent on an affiliation to a particular space. The discourse around that physical space was what constituted the structure of dissent. By detaching historical precedent from the contemporaneous, localized attributes of the dispute, a group could be freed to acknowledge that the interpersonal relations, not the space per se, constituted the material basis of the conflict.

All he had time to say to Murray, though, was "No, it isn't," before Sarry asked loudly from the parlour, "Tell me again why we're here?"

Philip re-entered the parlour. Gilda, Sarry and Pete had widened the gap between each other, and together with the seated Burghie formed a loose circle. Philip coughed. "If anyone wants to call a cab, there's a house phone on the desk." He pointed.

No one moved. Pete stood with legs far apart and arms crossed. Burghie's eyes flicked to Philip then flicked down. Gilda looked straight at Philip, but he didn't think she was seeing him so much as seeing through him. Only Sarry acknowledged Philip's words, with a slight nod, but nothing else, since she seemed busy studying Burghie and Gilda.

"Anyway, if you all need to work some things out," Philip said, "you can stay in the parlour. I am giving you a space to do that."

No one spoke, though he imagined that someone—Murray, but perhaps other people—was right now thinking, *And who nominated you to do this?* and was sending those vibes directly to him.

"My idea," he continued, as though he were answering that voice, "is that I will leave the room and let you talk. Then when you are ready to go, I will gladly drive you to wherever you want to go—home, or whatever."

Behind him in the hall, Murray shifted his weight impatiently. Murray clearly hated the whole enterprise, yet he probably approved of Philip's scheme to isolate the group in one room if that meant he could turn them out sooner rather than later.

Someone muttered, "Okay." Burghie slouched in his chair with hands steepled, Gilda leaned against the fireplace like a feminine version of a suspected scoundrel in a Jane Austen novel, Pete ensconced his scowling self in the bay window, and Sarry stood lithe but alert at Pete's side like a boxer waiting for the starting bell to ring.

Philip left the parlour and closed the sliding pocket door behind him. He flopped into the armchair in the hall.

From his post by the staircase, Murray said, "You realize that I may have to call the police."

Philip shrugged. Whatever information this action imparted— he hardly knew what he meant by the shrug—sent Murray up the stairs. When Murray's ascending thumps stopped, a heartbeat of time passed in a void of sound. Then Philip heard a click. Someone had locked the parlour door from the inside.

57

A LOCKED ROOM MYSTERY SOLVED

"What needs to happen," Burghie said, as he moved away from the door he had just locked, "is to explain to each other what we are doing here. And for real."

Sarry said, "Well, I was born here."

"You weren't born in this room. Why are you in this room right now?"

"Basically, I was kidnapped."

"No, you weren't," Burghie said. "You could have left the car when you had the chance."

"Philip had a point about standing in the middle of the road," Sarry said. "And I wasn't just going to leave Pete. I didn't know what kind of maniacs you all were. I'm pissed off at him, but I'm not heartless."

"Are you Philippa's girlfriend?" Gilda asked.

Everyone turned to Gilda, who stood by the fireplace.

"Say me again who Philippa is?" Sarry asked.

"Good question," Burghie said quietly.

Gilda pointed at Pete. "There. Philippa Peterborough. Also known as Pete Peterborough."

Pete bristled, either at Gilda's identification of him as Philippa, Sarry's raised eyebrows or Burghie's staring, or all three. "Those are my names, don't wear them out," Pete said.

Sarry said to Pete, "Which of those is your slave name?"

Gilda sucked in her breath. Burghie flashed her a glance with what he hoped was helplessness. He needed an ally for his plan, which, he realized, he had already lost control of.

"Slave name!" Pete said. "What does that mean?"

"You know," Sarry said. "Deadname. Which is the name someone picked for you, and which is the name you picked for yourself?"

"To tell you the truth," Pete said, "I don't like any of those names."

Gilda said, "He was born Philippa Peterborough, and when he started junior high he started calling himself Pete. Pete as in Peterborough." She spoke easily, as if reciting well-known facts that everyone already knew.

"Who gives you the right to tell people stuff like that?" Pete said. "That's my business!"

"There's no sense in trying to pretend," she answered. "Let's try honesty for a change."

"Just who hasn't been honest around here?"

She fell silent. Everyone looked at Burghie, and he realized that, since he had started this, whenever some impasse was reached, they turned to him for guidance. He had counted on people to take their own initiative once he started the ball rolling.

In the vacuum, Sarry said to Pete, "Well, Honest Abe, don't tell me that 'Burghie' is his real name." She pointed at Burghie. "Is that short for Hamburger?"

Gilda said, "What's your real name, Burghie?"

"Dallas," Burghie said. Gilda was on his side, but she wasn't going to exempt him from truth-telling. "Dallas Burgh."

Pete turned to the bay window and pulled closed the small gap between the drapes, whose dark brown lengths pooled on the floor. Pete started going around the room to all the floor lamps with their tasselled shades and the table lamps with their stain-glass shades and turning them on.

"Do Albertans have something against last names?" Sarry asked.

Pete approached the table lamp by the ornate doilied plant stand beside the room's second door. From her position by the fireplace, Gilda said, "That door is locked from the other side. I tried it already. I think it's always locked."

Frantically Pete scanned everyone in the room, and his eyes stopped at Burghie. "Burghie, you are being a total fucking asshole."

Burghie stiffened his spine, pretended to be like Paul when a new server complained about the food not being good enough to generate good tips. "I'm the gatekeeper."

"I can keep my own gates!"

"Burghie is the reason we're still in this room, and I'm glad we are," Gilda said. "We're learning something new."

"What are you learning?" Burghie asked her.

Gilda looked down, seemed to turn over something in her mind. She said quickly, "And you, Sarry, you are a woman, aren't you?"

"Thank you," Sarry said, though with some sarcasm. "I'm glad you noticed."

Gilda smiled weakly. "I suppose some people don't."

"Sure. But I think so," Sarry said. "Not that it was easy getting to that place, sais-tu? But I'm there."

"Philippa," Gilda said. "What is it that counts with you?"

"Oh, my God," Pete said. "Now you're getting all psychological on me. I thought you were done with that crap after you finished university."

"Come on, Pete," Burghie said. "She's just trying to figure things out."

"My things," Pete said. "Not her things. Not even your things."

"They are my things, though." Gilda's voice was small and brittle. "The things you do affect me."

"They shouldn't," Pete said. "That's your problem if you think they do."

The ripple of emotions across Gilda's face made Burghie remember what he loved about her. The muscles around her eyes and lips shimmied just under the surface of her skin, as though under it electrons fired through the finest cords that rayed out like webs from her brain and supported her body as much as her bones did, sending not just emotions but thoughts and actions, and all of it working together. In his family, emotions, thoughts and actions had no connection. Burghie was thinking of his grandfather, but even his parents seemed to say and do things against what they felt, or did things against their ideals and their too-obvious feelings towards each other, dropping keys to cars they had just promised to lend you, saying you hated someone but let them live in your house, letting all the rancour fester there as though you had no power over it.

Gilda said, "If you can go around doing and saying whatever you want, then why can't I? I want to know why you are dating a trans woman, and why you left home, and why you disappeared, and why you have always been so mean to me."

Pete started. "Mean?"

"This is good." Sarry nodded rapidly. "See? I need to know this. I need to know what makes men like this tick. That way I can avoid them in the future."

"Are you breaking up with me?" Pete's voice cracked a little. "Now?"

"I'm thinking about it," Sarry said. "You do seem a bit hurt right now. Maybe you don't want to break up with me."

"Did I say I wanted to break up with you?"

"But you didn't say that you didn't, either."

"You've lost me," Pete said. "Can I just deal with what is going on here with my sister first?"

Burghie was struck by the triangulation of people in the guest parlour: Sarry near the waterfall of brown curtains, Gilda by the fireplace, Pete next to the second door. If he included himself, then the shape changed from a triangle to a square. This drama had nothing to do with him, yet here he was. No. It did have something to do with him. He had known the Peterboroughs for a long time, he had found his way back to them after a long separation, and he had been impelled to follow Gilda but also, he realized, to follow Pete and Gilda together, to see them in action, and in that seeing, see something of himself in action. His role was as the third wheel, the designated driver, the key holder, the security guard. Not the security guard of, say, the beer gardens at the Edmonton Folk Festival or of his grandfather, who kept everyone's edges separate so that they couldn't overlap, but the kind of security that kept things together, that drove the drunk home to his family, put the family into a room and kept them there until they were a family again. With Sarry present, the shape was unclear, the power more dispersed. Is that what he had wanted, power? That couldn't be true. Here he was, though, in a locked room with three other people, all of them strangers to him now.

Gilda was speaking. "I can see how coming to Montreal might have something to do with that time Mom took you here as a baby. Maybe you see Montreal as a place to start forming an identity, finding yourself."

"Find myself? Are you kidding me? What do you think I am, some kind of emo hippie?"

"Come on, Petey," Sarry said. "All kinds of people do that. They join the military, go backpacking to Thailand or Spain, go work in Banff or Jasper or move to Australia."

"Backpacking," Pete said. "Christ."

"Christ is actually not a bad example," Sarry said. "That's what he did. He left his hometown, wandered around, talked to people."

Pete rolled his eyes.

"Pete," Burghie said. "Who are you trying to kid? You're wearing red lipstick."

Gilda said, "Pete called himself a girl until he was eleven. Even after that he sometimes dressed like a girl at home. He even wore barrettes in his hair."

"He still wears barrettes," Sarry said. "I bought a set for him last week."

Pete grunted loudly in exasperation. "What century are you living in?" he shouted. "I wear whatever the fuck I feel like wearing!" He squeezed shut his eyes and covered his ears with his hands. "Leave me alone!"

His hyperventilating filled the room, and Burghie wondered if Pete were having some kind of fit. Then Pete opened his eyes, unclenched his fists, looked around him with bewilderment.

"I don't know why you are all on me!" he said. "I just want to see the world and have some fun. Can't I just live my life the way I want to? Always people have been on me." His voice pitched up. "Why?"

Pete had never seemed anguished before. He had always shoved away bad news with a fuck-you, a ripping comeback, or a plot that wound out its revenge slowly. In his own life, Burghie had aimed for stoicism in public and under-the-breath bitching in private. He contrasted himself with Sarry, who, her face twisted in sympathy, made to reach out a hand to Pete, but she pulled back her hand, the pain deepening around her eyes. Burghie had seen that look before. It was in Gilda again right now. Pain. Whatever Pete was like in Montreal, he probably wasn't much different, at least in substance, than the person Burghie had known in Edmonton, so that Sarry, the new person in Pete's life, reacted like everyone else around Pete had to. Cautiously, with the expectation of rejection around the corner.

Gilda said, "It's just that you seemed so unhappy and angry, and you took off without telling anyone why. I just wanted to know you were okay. We—I—just want to know why you seem unhappy and angry."

Pete snapped, "I'm not unhappy and angry!"

No one said anything or moved. Pete seemed to realize that his manner contradicted his statement. He took a deep breath, and he looked at all the lights he had turned on in the room.

"It's not fair that I have to be singled out just because. Just because I have things that are not like most people's."

Burghie was afraid to ask, but he was the one who had decided that honesty was the house rule in the locked room. He said quietly, "What things?"

"He must mean his junk." Sarry spoke calmly, even at the euphemism of the word "junk," which, the way he said it, was matter-of-fact, not ironic. "It's not like most men's, no. But so what? Pete's not like most men. I mean—" he looked at Pete and away—"I like it."

Pete slackened his taut body, and his hard face softened, though only for a second. He then drew himself up and turned to steel, and with a defiant stare he dared Burghie to speak.

Burghie said. "I'm sorry that I didn't realize when we knew each other."

Pete said, "That's because, unlike some people, I was good at not making a big deal about it."

He had been, Burghie realized. All those phys ed classes, the sex ed classes, those half-hearted triple dates he, Burghie and Granv went on for those months before their adult lives began to take them away from each other, starting with Granv but not ending there. The dildo Pete ordered that time. Ah, Pete.

"Is that why you haven't been nice to me?" Gilda asked. Tears were in her voice. "Did I do or say something that hurt your feelings, way back when?"

Pete said, "Now why in Christ would I admit to something like that?"

"What's wrong with admitting something?" Gilda said.

"You're the champion of being up front, are you?" Pete snorted. "No sneaking around and being all mealy mouthed?"

She swallowed. "I'm sorry if I've seemed that way."

"Are you, now?"

She winced, and then she said, "Okay, then I'll tell my truth."

"Do whatever you want."

"Back in Edmonton . . . I . . . hit a police car in an intersection and I drove away."

"Say again?"

"I hit a police van. I wasn't paying attention. I was looking at my phone, and I hit it, and then instead of staying, I drove off."

"When did this happen?"

"A few months ago."

Sarry exhaled sharply. "Whoa. That's kind of bad, no?"

"Yes," Gilda said.

"I don't know what the laws are like over in Alberta," Sarry said, "but isn't that kind of illegal?"

"Yes." More emotions likely roved below the surface, but she didn't express them beyond the paling of her face.

"That's impressive," Pete said. "Is there a warrant out for your arrest?"

"Not that I know of."

"So, you got away with it?"

"It looks like it."

"Holy shit." Pete shook his head. "And you said that so that I would tell you why I'm mad at you?"

"Yes."

"You didn't make that up?"

"No. I have a dent on my car. You can ask Mom."

Burghie said, "You didn't get that from hitting a post?"

"No. Uh, yes. I hit a post to cover up the original dent."

Pete said, "Shit, you really did, didn't you?"

She nodded.

"I always thought you were some kind of goody two shoes. But of course you aren't. Everyone pretends to be something." He paused, as though searching his mind for the word. "I know there's some fancy name for that, for wearing a mask."

"'All the world's a stage,'" Sarry said. "That's what my acting friends say all the time."

"'And all the men and women merely players,'" Gilda said.

"That's it, players." Pete stood up a bit straighter. "We're all players, and we're all playing each other. I do it: in my own way, though. Mom and Dad do it. God, Dad especially. You're just like Dad sometimes, Gilda. Trying to control me while saying you aren't. Except Dad was shitty at pretending not to try to control me. You were a pro."

"Sometimes fathers can be the worst," Sarry said. Her expression led Burghie to believe that she spoke from experience.

"You have it easy," Pete said. "Try pretending things are normal when they aren't." His voice slipped, descended.

Gilda left the fireplace and went to him. She put her hand on his wrist and tried to meet his eyes, even though he turned his head aside to make it impossible. "Normal isn't a real thing. But I'm sorry that I made you feel bad."

He looked up at her, and he shook his wrist out of her grasp, but gently. "I did things my own way then, and I'm going to do things my way now and in the future. Do you get that?"

"Okay," she said. "I hope you get that other people want to be let into your life. So when you don't think we're doing it right, tell us."

Burghie wondered what it might feel like to be them. If this was a reconciliation, reconciliation was possible for everyone. The spike of possibility struck him in the chest, made his eyes smart.

Gilda and Pete stood still and close. Their breaths, deep and slow, matched each other's in rhythm. It seemed natural. Maybe Burghie had never paid attention to them as a unit. He had always seen them as separate.

Sarry sniffed in her own tears. With caution, she smiled slightly at Burghie.

Gilda's phone buzzed. She walked quickly to the chair for her purse and took the phone out. "Her first text," she said out loud. The locked room hushed, as though the first chords of an organ had proclaimed the beginning of church.

Burghie thought it was time. He reached for the lock on the door.

"Burghie," Gilda said sharply.

He turned.

"Why did you come to Montreal?"

He had been waiting for that question, and he was ready to answer it for real.

"Because I'm in love with you."

"I see," she said. "Okay."

In the resulting silence, Burghie, his hand trembling a little, reached for the door latch again.

58

MURRAY AND PHILIP DON'T GET OFF SCOT-FREE, DON'T YOU WORRY

Burghie slid the parlour door open to reveal Philip sitting in the armchair in the hall where Burghie and the others had left him.

"Is everything all right in there?" Philip asked.

"Pretty much," Burghie said. He stood aside while Pete, Sarry and Gilda filed past him into the front hall.

"We had a truth-telling session," Gilda said. She was standing next to Pete, not touching, but close enough to show that the fire between them had ebbed and they were not discharging angry heat at each other.

"Is there anything I can do?" Philip asked.

"I would love a glass of ice water," Sarry said.

Pete asked, "Can I have something stronger than water?"

Philip nodded, raised himself slowly from the chair, and with a quicker pace disappeared into the kitchen. As ice clinked, taps ran and cupboards opened, the four of them stood immobile, silent and self-absorbed. The grandfather clock in the front hall chimed half past the hour. They existed in limbo, as though everything depended on the arrival of water.

A thumping on the stairs signalled someone coming down. Murray's slippered feet appeared on the steps and stopped. The slippers were the leatherette types that Burghie's grandfather wore. The feet continued down the staircase, and soon Murray stood in the front hall. Murray might be the same age as Granddad Burgh, though Granddad looked much older.

Philip returned with a tray of three tall glasses of water and one brandy snifter holding a copper-coloured liquor. He and Murray mutely regarded each other, then Philip distributed the glasses, the snifter going to Pete. Murray looked at the snifter, skirted around Philip, and went into the kitchen. Kitchen cupboards slammed open and closed while the others drank and waited. Burghie noted the chunky square ice cubes, which would have been made in a better ice-cube tray than the ones that came with refrigerators. La Lobélie took its entertaining seriously. Murray came back into view. He stood in the threshold of the kitchen, his face blank, with a glass of red wine.

Pete downed his drink. "Okay." He wiped his mouth and plunked his glass on the tray, which Philip was still holding. "Are you ready for more?"

"More what?" Gilda asked.

"Truth-telling." Pete looked at Murray and Philip.

"What do you mean?" Philip asked.

Pete swivelled and backed up so that he blocked the front doors. "Your turn."

Murray hastened out of the kitchen toward Pete. His glass sloshed a bit of red onto his white shirt. "Shit."

At the moment he looked down at his shirt, Gilda smoothly shifted behind him and blocked the entrance to the kitchen. She felt around the pocket door and slid it shut behind her. Burghie shuffled to the foot of the staircase. He reached out and tried the handle of the door to the room with the embroidered "private" sign. Sarry smiled, closed the pocket door to the guest parlour and stood in front of it, her arms crossed.

"You're serious," Philip said.

"Oh, for God's sake," Murray spluttered. "I'm not interested. Get out, all of you."

"This is for real," Pete said.

"This is intimidation!" Murray shouted. More red wine sloshed out and splashed his right slipper. The wine ran down the leatherette like a trickle of sweat.

"So?" Pete leaned toward Philip. "Why didn't you tell me that Gilda was staying here?"

Philip gurgled a protest and threw a flailing glance at Murray. Murray smiled wryly back and suddenly relaxed.

"I have questions for you too, Murray," Pete said, "so don't get cocky."

"We all did this in the parlour, so maybe it would do you good too." Gilda's tone was soothing.

"Not maybe," Pete said. "For sure."

Philip sighed. "Okay. I didn't tell Pete that Gilda was here because I didn't think that it was my business to get involved." He stopped short, as though his own words surprised him.

"And then you told Gilda I was here because . . . ?"

"She seemed worried about you. I wanted her to know that you were safe."

"Ah. Safety. Good." Sharply, Pete switched his attention to Murray. "Murray, maybe you should explain why you introduced me to Yasir without telling Philip about it."

Murray sagged, then he bucked up. "I wanted to help you get to know people in town. You couldn't hang around with me and Philip."

"Philip didn't seem happy about the connection, though," Pete said. "Maybe I'm wrong."

"No," Philip said. "I was surprised he didn't tell me, that's all."

"That's all?"

"Yeah," he said.

"Who else could I introduce him to?" Murray said. "I've been out of social circulation for a while."

Burghie noted the passive-aggressiveness in the answer and was reminded again of his grandfather.

Philip picked up on Murray's tone. "But seriously, though, why Yasir?"

"Nothing wrong with Yasir, is there?" Murray said. "Or are you jealous of him?"

"God, that was years ago, wasn't it? Before we even knew each other well. I don't care who you dated before you met me."

"I thought there was an overlap, though, right?" Sarry said.

"Right? Truth be told?"

Murray's face became so hostile that Gilda made a feint toward Murray as though ready to step in front of him. But she didn't have to. Murray didn't move.

"Fine," Murray said. "I wanted Pete gone. I was jealous of him. There."

Philip said, "Jealous how?"

"Not sexually jealous. No, not even jealous of his attention. Jealous of his existence in a broad philosophical way."

"Please explain," Philip said.

"I know you think you are a super-sensitive person, Philip," Murray said, "but, in reality, you are a blunt force when it comes to other people's emotions."

"How do you mean?" Philip seemed disappointed and wary.

"I know you always wanted children." Murray paused. An unnameable emotion flittered over his features. "And you get this baby in the house, and it's named after you, and you helped Beth look after the baby."

"I felt compassion." After a pause, Philip said, "It didn't seem fair that one parent could force an operation on a child and change that child's life without him having a say."

The answer seemed to please Murray. He continued, more animated. "Okay. To me it was like you had something that had been missing. I thought you were happy helping me with the business, taking up the time that academics complain about not having enough of. How could running a B&B be worth it? Baking, bleaching sheets, sweeping floors. How would that stack up over time? I wondered how long it was going to be enough for. Then a baby comes into the house. Was that going to be the breaking point for you? Then they leave, like I wanted, and years and years pass. I knew you were keeping in touch with Beth, but by then she seemed to be just another old client you kept in touch with. Then they're back, just at the point where you are about to retire. And I wondered if this is where it is going to end. Lots of relationships end at retirement. I wasn't going to let that old danger rage through here like a torrent, not if I could help it." Murray's voice hardened. "There was no way."

"Oh, Murr," Philip said.

He grabbed Murray's arm. Murray didn't resist the touch, but he didn't fall into it, either.

Murray inhaled loudly. "This is truth-telling, right? So. The truth is that I was the one who told the police where Beth and the baby were."

Pete and Gilda did double takes. Burghie was impressed at how much film and television had adequately represented the double takes of the real world.

Philip blinked. "Oh," he said quietly.

"You must have suspected," Murray said.

"I didn't think it was possible. I thought I was being paranoid."

Murray said, "Now that you know about my involvement in Beth's arrest, where does that leave us, then, Philip?"

"I don't think it leaves us anywhere but where we are now. Like we've always been." Philip's voice quivered. "I know why you would have done that, called the police."

"Do you?"

"You said you wanted to call the police because you didn't think it was fair that Beth's husband didn't know where she or his child was. I didn't know that you would actually do it."

"The point," Gilda said, "is that things are better once the truth comes out."

Burghie was surprised no one objected to her claim that things had turned out for the better. He wasn't going to be the one, though.

"Openness helps," she continued. "Honesty works. Give each perspective a voice."

"Yes," Philip said.

"Embrace the unruliness of the dialogic."

"Okay, I get it," Philip said. Burghie was glad someone did.

Philip slumped, held out his hands to Murray in a pleading way. "I'm sorry. I did wrong here with Pete and Gilda. And with you, Murray. I'm very, very sorry."

No one moved or spoke for some time. The grandfather clock rang the top of the hour.

Gilda yawned, and so did everyone else. She stepped away from her post by the kitchen and picked up her purse off the floor by the stairs. "I'm going to bed." She looked at Philip. "Unless you don't want me here."

"No, of course you can stay," he said. "I'm not angry with you."

Burghie didn't sense any anger. He didn't feel angry himself, though he knew his role in the drama was secondary.

"Well, I'm a little angry," Sarry said. "I've been angrier, though."

"I'm not angry so much as, what?" Pete said. "Less than pissed off—cheesed off."

"I'm just tired," Philip said.

"Me too," Gilda said.

Murray volunteered to drive everyone home. His expression carried something Burghie recognized in Grandpa Burgh sometimes after he dropped his car keys, that hooded look that hinted at a suppressed feeling, one that Burghie only now recognized but before had never imagined his grandfather could ever experience: remorse.

"But first," Murray said, "I have to turn off all those lights in the parlour."

Silently, Pete, Sarry, Gilda and Burghie followed Murray into the parlour, and each person turned off one lamp. When they left the parlour, Gilda moved to the foot of the staircase. She turned to Burghie. "I'll come by your hotel room tomorrow morning, Burghie. Is ten okay?"

He nodded.

She ascended the stairs and disappeared.

The drive to Burghie's hotel was different from the ride to La Lobélie. It was without incident—almost. No one spoke until Murray's vehicle stopped in front of the hotel entrance. Burghie stepped onto the sidewalk to the quiet "Salut" from Sarry. Behind that goodbye followed the shadow of another sound, which, after Burghie entered the hotel's front lobby, he realized to be Pete saying, "See you, Dallas."

59

BETH AND NORVELL

Beth's sore left arm and her stiff left hip were the first indicators, rather than her conscious mind, of a night spent sleeping on a sofa. She was also twisted into an unzipped sleeping bag that had wrapped itself around her like a hastily rolled doobie. She rolled off the sofa, and at the moment she hit the ground, she flashed back to that summer with the motorcycling boyfriend—Dan, Dave, Dale?—and with the shock of that memory recalled that she was in Norvell's house. Their Civic Holiday game-a-thon had ended when she admitted to Norvell that rather than learn how to play Othello, she wanted to call it a night. Evidently she had fallen asleep, and Norvell had supplied her with a sleeping bag as a blanket.

Dawg waddled over and licked her face. The clunk of her fall and quite possibly her curses as she wrung herself out of the sleeping bag produced Norvell from his bedroom fully alert. He wore the same T-shirt and shorts from the day before.

"Are you okay?"

When she established she was fine and that she had to be at work in ninety minutes, Norvell offered to make breakfast. He started work at ten, but he was happy to eat with her now that he was awake. After he brushed off her attempt to help, Norvell made breakfast in the kitchen while she flipped channels through the morning shows. Dawg watched television at her feet for a while. The smell of hot butter and creak of cabinet hinges dwindled to white noise. Beth wondered if it were proper for her to have heart-to-heart talks with someone who wasn't her own child. She was kidding herself, though. She had sought out Norvell. It had been for a selfish reason, but now that she was in this position, it was honourable to tell Norvell about Pete, even if afterwards he didn't think her words to be much of a gift.

Soon Beth was settling herself at the kitchen table in a squeaky chair while Norvell portioned out tea, scrambled eggs, multigrain toast with strawberry jam, and a yoghurt cup.

"Listen, Norvell," she said, after eating all her toast, "I should maybe tell you something about Pete. He likes women."

A bit impatiently, Norvell said, "I know."

"Oh."

"I know that I have a crush on him, and I know that I can't. It's something I have to get over. He's unobtainable, like you said."

"I hope I didn't offend you when I said that yesterday."

"You offended me because you were right."

Beth asked, "How long is Jackson going to be in jail?"

"He has a few more months, probably." He explained that Jackson had been in for theft.

"Having a boyfriend in jail is tough."

"Having a boyfriend period, when you're a boy yourself, is tough."

Beth reached out and squeezed his hand. He squeezed it back.

"I need to work on myself," he said, "before I get into a serious relationship."

"If it makes you feel any better, a lot of people have to work on themselves. And yes, I'm talking about myself."

"You seem all right." Norvell trailed off, and she didn't press him. It was time for her to go.

He allowed Beth to give him a hug goodbye. She wondered if Jackson had ever had the opportunity to be hugged by Norvell. It was a good hug.

On her drive home into the rising sun, she passed the Edmonton Institution federal penitentiary in the heavy morning highway traffic, and she thought of Norvell and Jackson, of secrets, and of secret lives. Pete had lived a secret too. Beth hadn't wanted it that way, but it had happened. She had thought doing as little as possible would let her kids be themselves and avoid suffering.

"Avoid suffering," she said out loud as she and her traffic approached the first red light inside the city limits. "Listen to me." She applied the brakes. "What blather."

60

PETE AND SARRY

Murray dropped them off at Pete's apartment, and Sarry plodded behind Pete up the stairs. Pete didn't look at her. She felt more than ignored; she felt disposed of. After all she had experienced that night in the emergency ward—that stabbing victim moaning, the bellicose man reciting Bible verses in English and French—the worst had been sitting next to a cot with a lover who refused to explain who the fainting woman in Le Feu was and why he had also fainted. The emergency room doctor ordered Pete to lift a leg or follow his finger with his eyes, and she had to wait outside the curtain next to the religious nut not knowing if Pete was passing the tests, and then going back to Pete's cot and Pete finally speaking but only to say he had no idea how the tests had gone, what was he, a doctor? Then that sad-hilarious moment when everyone jumped out of Philip's car in the middle of boulevard René-Lévesque. Then going to Murray's Victorian granny's wet dream of a gîte and witnessing the drama led by that sultry-eyed, passive-aggressive hipster and Pete's all-too-cool sister, now identified as such. She'd never seen a reality show so outrageous. But the worst had been Pete in the cot in the emergency room.

When they entered single file into the apartment, Pete turned and said, "Do you want to stay over?"

She said she wasn't sure, and Pete said, "I'm tired, but I'm still up for sex if you want." He had such a sad-seal look, that vulnerability that had lain under the surface but was there the first time she had met Pete in Le Feu and at other times since risen for air, that Sarry said "yes," and they had ferocious make-up sex, the kind that started in the hallway, moved to the sofa and finished half on the floor, half on the bed.

Sarry woke to find Pete at the kitchen table fully clothed in his man clothes: black jeans, white T-shirt, socks, no makeup, no barrettes. He glanced up at Sarry but said nothing.

Sarry walked past him into the kitchen to make tea. She could do the silent treatment too.

"Are we going to talk?" Pete asked.

"About what?"

When Pete didn't answer, Sarry took a seat next to him at the table. From her side, she could stare full at the painting above the sofa. The red lips, the eye. Sarry had been pleased with how the eye had turned out. It was her own eye. In her all portraits, she made sure a part of the subject was modelled after herself.

"Do you know who that is in the painting?" Sarry asked.

"No."

"Murray."

Pete laughed that version of his laugh that made him seem like a girl. "*Lady of the Eighties.*"

"That's right." Sarry wanted to lean in close to Pete, and she did it because she had promised herself years ago to do those things that, though they might lead to something sad, manifested her overarching commitment to love.

"How long ago was that?" Pete asked.

"While I was still doing the weather. I was going to the clubs, so was Murray. Those days I pretended to be a journalist, you know, observing the world and painting the people in the clubs like a documentary filmmaker. I met Murray, and I told him I wanted to paint him. He was the same person he is now, you know. Full of himself, except in high heels. He said yes, obviously. He came to my studio by himself, dressed like he did during the day, but he had a little gym bag, got changed, put on the makeup. I told him to put on more lipstick, double down on it. He did. He wanted people to like him."

"Did you sleep with him?"

"No." The memory of that painting session almost made her wistful for those thorny, adrenaline-filled years before she revealed her true self to the world. "Even then Murray was going through a change. Mariah was changing to Murray. I thought I should capture the moment before Mariah disappeared. I didn't tell him that, of course. He was just flattered, I think."

Pete said, "He's kind of a bastard, isn't he?"

"A lot of the time he was nice to people," she murmured. "If you want evidence that people can change, then Murray's change from *Lady of the Eighties* is a prime example."

Pete said, "I'm thinking maybe we should take a break."

She had seen it coming from a long way off. "A long break, or a short break?"

"I don't know. Last night made me think about things. I need to do more of that."

"Are you going to Edmonton?"

"Maybe. Not permanently, anyway. I should at least go back to see my mom."

She hated this, the breakup talk. Sarry forced herself to think of him with the same future-pointing love she had felt when they walked under *Les Boulles roses*. "You need to make peace with that father of yours, that's for sure. Not that achieving peace with an asshole parent is as necessary as people like to think. Making peace doesn't always work. It's the trying that matters."

"That's something like when you tried to patch it up with your father."

Sarry had spent three entire days talking about her father to Pete, so "something" had actually been more like "many things." In exchange for her admission, Pete had offered only that he didn't see eye-to-eye with his dad and that his dad spent more time with his job and his second wife than with him. Only last night, and only under last night's pressure, did Pete disclose the core of the relationship.

"I've survived Dad's shit before," Pete said, "I can survive it again, if he keeps throwing it at me. If I make peace, it'll be for my sake, not his."

The defeat in his slumped body and limp hands made Sarry want to take his hands again, hold them, put them to her lips and kiss his fingertips. To say all that—it was like they were getting closer, not farther.

Pete pulled his hand away. "I don't know if that is a good idea."

Rejection—Sarry never got used to it. She had to buck herself up, though, and make the shift Pete seemed to have already made. "What attracted me to you is your little sad boy-girl inside you," Sarry said. "You seem like that little sad boy-girl right now."

"If I suddenly became a cheerful old man, you won't be turned on by me anymore?"

"Maybe. I tend to go for the damaged types."

"Damaged?" Pete said, a bit in anger. "Do you think I'm damaged?"

"Compared to a lot of people I've dated you aren't. You should have seen some of these guys. Being gay and trans is hard. I bet being intersex can be hard too, especially if the family doesn't handle it well."

Pete stood and paced the room slowly. A sinkhole opened up inside Sarry. It's happening for real, now, the end of them.

"I've offended you," Sarry said. "I'm sorry."

"Maybe in the end," he said, "I like women with pussies and tits."

She didn't believe that: people broke up because they weren't compatible mentally. She played along, though. "I have tits." Sarry returned to herself, the self she had chosen, and defended it in front of this person who would soon become a total stranger again. "I'm flat-chested, that's all. That's nothing that hormones can't fix."

"Hormone injections. I read about that. I can get those too, if I want to be a convincing Philippa. Or Phil, like my dad wanted me to be."

"Do you want that?"

"I don't need hormones, do I? Is that necessary?"

"No." Sarry wanted to go back to the earlier discussion, corral this back into a corner she knew how to fight in and needed to keep in practice for future courtships. "I give a mean blow-job, you have to admit."

"Yeah."

She made him smile, and that was satisfying. Humour soothes pain, even if it only bridges over the hard places that can't be bulldozed down to the ground. "Some people get reconstructed vaginas."

"Once I looked at a whole book about intersex people who get surgery. It doesn't always work out so good."

"I know people who've been happy with theirs." She knew that she wasn't the kind of external feminine that some straight men craved. Fair enough. Now that Pete had started his drift away from her, she could talk about the details of her self-conception that she knew could break the foundations of a new relationship. "I know. I'm a butch girl."

Pete seemed to be in the same state of mind because he said, "I'm thinking of having my balls removed so that they don't get cancerous. Would that make me a butch girl?"

"Hmm." A half-serious puzzle for her to solve. "If you were staying Philippa, maybe. The question is, can anyone become anything automatically? Is biology destiny, or just destiny's child?"

If Pete understood the campy pun, he didn't say. No, camp wasn't his thing. Sarry continued with more seriousness. "Some straight guys get cancer and have to get one or both testicles removed. That doesn't turn them into anything other than a cancer survivor. It's not the act, always, but the idea behind the act that gives meaning to the act. Ask any S&M person."

Pete sat down on his chair. He rested his head in his hands for a moment, then shook his head like an old dog. "I never liked the word butch," Pete said. "Too much like bitch."

"Bitch is a perfectly good word," Sarry said. "You have to own it."

"If I'm a butch girl, and you're a butch girl, then maybe we're too much alike."

"I'm beginning to think so, yeah." Sarry paused. "This break thing maybe should be longer than shorter."

He didn't speak, so Sarry continued. "Let's make a deal," she said. "Let's break up. But I want to have proper breakup sex first. Maybe you think we had that this morning, but it's only breakup sex if both parties know it is."

He gave a little laugh. It was bitter. Sarry liked that. Bitterness was a sign of having learned something, and if nothing else was going to happen here, no moving in together, no cohabitation for years and years, like what Yasir and Garen had, and, yes, what her parents had and what hopefully Murray and Philip were going to continue to have, then good sex could be something concrete for Sarry to hang on her memory tree and say they had got something productive out of it. It was a bit of world-building, to use Pete's word.

"I've never had breakup sex before," Pete said.

"There're a lot of things you'd never had before you met me." She couldn't help it—the tears collected in her eyes.

The teakettle began to whistle.

"I can make tea later," Sarry said.

Petey stood and turned off the kettle.

61

PHILIP AND MURRAY

By the time Philip entered the kitchen the next morning, Murray had baked four dozen traditional Scottish scones. Philip poured himself a cup of coffee, which Murray had presumably made at the usual time, and sat down at the kitchen table with the newspaper. He tried to read the paper, but the words slipped away from his attention and to the counter where Murray stood.

"I'm sorry," Murray said.

Philip looked up. "Why are you apologizing? I'm the one who should be apologizing."

Murray came to his side, put his hand on Philip's shoulder. The sleeve of Murray's shirt soon dampened with Philip's tears.

Between sobs, Philip asked, "How could I expect you to keep that family broken up like that? After all, we know about broken-up families."

Murray pulled up a chair next to Philip, let Philip lay his head on Murray's shoulder. "I'm the jerk here," Murray said. "You can't take the blame for everything." He paused. "If you want children, we can do it. If it's not too late."

They had been together so long that Philip had never considered anything other than life with Murray, but here Murray was admitting to thinking that they could be torn asunder just like that Peterborough family had been, just like their own families had been, that Philip would want that. How long had Murray thought of divorce as a possible outcome? Just last night? Or had the possibility been there all along, under the surface, waiting for something to rouse it?

Murray put his hand on Philip's wrist. A new age spot had appeared at the back of Murray's hand, next to the older, familiar one. On his parents' hands, age spots had depressed Philip, but not the ones on Murray's hands. Philip wanted to see all the other age spots that would appear there in the years to come.

"I want you," Philip said. "Don't leave me."

"I'm not going anywhere," Murray said. "I'm not perfect, as you know. Even in my old age I'm capable of jealousy. I hope you can forgive me and tell me in the future if I do that again."

How hard it was to witness your beloved's humanness, watch its shambolic, desperate motion over and over, but how easy, knowing all its constituent parts, to accept it.

62

GILDA, MURRAY AND PHILIP

When she came downstairs, the door from the front hall to the kitchen was open, as it often was in the morning. Through the door she saw Murray and Philip embracing in the kitchen. They saw her too. The two men separated in a kind of reflex action. How many times, she wondered, had they felt like they were in danger if someone saw them holding each other like that?

"I was actually just checking to see what was for breakfast."

"Fair enough," Murray said. "This is a bed and breakfast, after all."

Philip wiped at his eyes. "How about scones and fruit salad?"

"Please. And a coffee?" She felt as though she were in the middle of a well-made play, and they the actors were saying homely things to convince the audience that they were real people in a world that was indeed real but that was suspended in special abeyance for the benefit and pleasure of the dimly visible observers in the auditorium before them.

"Coffee. Yes, of course," Philip said. "We could all use a fresh cup."

There—he had broached the subject of last night and this morning. He'd taken the lead, and Gilda could now follow, poke lightly at his back and draw him out bit by bit to reveal where they stood. Philip fetched a glass milk bottle from the commercial refrigerator while Gilda followed Murray's instructions and took three mugs out of the drying rack and poured three coffees. Murray carried a white china sugar bowl to the bistro table pushed against one wall and indicated a chair to Gilda. He was declaring a shift in relations, for normally she ate her breakfast in the guest dining room. He finished setting the table with three small plates, each with a steaming scone, and one plate of butter. They sat, sliced and buttered.

She drank her coffee and felt the power surge that it afforded.

"I'm going to see Pete," she said, "then I don't know how long I'll be staying here after that."

Philip said, "You're going back to Edmonton."

"Yes." She added, "I'm sorry about what happened last night."

"Sorry?" Philip shook his head. "Listen, it was awkward, but it was fair. Inevitable, even."

"Okay," Gilda said.

"There's no hard feelings, is what I'm saying. Right?" He looked at Murray.

"Right." Murray smeared butter on his scone, bit the buttery crumb, and put more butter on the nibbled end. She and Philip watched him consume the entire scone this way.

"I like keeping in touch with people," Philip said. He fidgeted with the handle of his mug. "Can I friend you on Facebook?"

"Sure."

In the recent past, keeping in touch took more effort and yet could be so much more intimate. The human voice over the telephone, the handwriting on paper scented with the owner's cologne. No reason why Facebook couldn't be like that, even if you had to work around the ads and the disingenuousness of people trying to impress the world with their banal victories of food, travel and work.

"But," she added, "you have to drive me somewhere downtown in exchange."

Murray laughed. "Well done."

"Where?" Philip asked.

"Burghie's hotel."

On the drive to the downtown Holiday Inn, Philip made pleasantries about the places they drove past. Then he segued. "I don't want to touch on a sore spot, and if I am, then say so."

"Okay."

"I did research on Hermaphroditus."

Hermaphroditus was a relatively minor figure in the written record of Greek and Roman mythology but was more important in visual arts. "Probably the name is a reference to a conjoined male-female figure, maybe a symbol of the male and female principle, and joined to represent fertility."

"That's kind of disappointing. Just another fertility symbol. As if that is what we're all supposed to be doing, making babies."

"It's more than that, though. There's all kind of fertility. Creativity, for example."

"That's true," Gilda said.

"What it boils down to is love." Philip smiled. "It's an art."

She didn't answer until the car pulled up to the front entrance of the hotel. She had been thinking of Burghie, what she would say to him. In a flash, all her past and present circumstances connected, not in a tidy way, but in a tangled complex held together by the force of her awareness.

She kissed Philip on the cheek. "Yes."

63

GILDA AND BURGHIE

Gilda waited in the lobby in the same seating area where they had met before. She was walking a net-less high wire this morning. Without ever having trained? No. She had been training all her life. It's just that she had no project management software to help her, no notes prepared two days earlier. No outline. No budget. No prepared speech.

Burghie joined her wearing the same clothes he'd worn the night before: black skinny jeans and a black T-shirt under a dark blue cardigan, though his head was bare, and he wore his usual thick-frame glasses rather than sunglasses.

He didn't sit. Without preamble, he said, "What do you think about going to the Fairmount Deli for a bagel? The concierge said it was a manageable walk."

"It's close to the B&B," Gilda said. He started, but she raised her hand to soothe him. "I haven't been, and I really want to go."

They walked swiftly and silently through the burbling of morning downtown, and they arrived on Saint-Urbain in no time. Row houses loomed on both sides of the tree-lined streets. From time to time, a grotto appeared on someone's front courtyard, a white half-shell of concrete trimmed with plastic flowers and sheltering a statue of the Virgin Mary, with a blue-hooded robe and white or pale pink face, the paint chipped here and there. They passed two-shop strip malls with restaurants and social clubs, red and green flags and pennants dangling inside their front windows.

"Portuguese," Gilda said, the first thing either had said since they left the hotel.

Burghie nodded. "Big time."

Having lived in north-east Edmonton, both of them knew what a Portuguese neighbourhood looked like—ebullient gardens, grottos, brick and iron-red fences, evidence of a national people who moved en masse fifty or more years ago. Now and again, a darker-skinned person, too dark for Portuguese, strode past her and Burghie, but few pedestrians intercepted their path. Most people of the neighbourhood probably were retired and remained inside watching game shows and soccer.

They passed the grand, pink building that Gilda had noted on her first walk down Saint-Urbain. Now she studied it. Multicoloured bunting was affixed to one corner of the church eaves and spanned the parking lot below, its trajectory aided by stopping points on light and electrical poles. Words in Portuguese, a cross, another Virgin Mary, this time not so humble, gazed mildly down upon the parking lot from a shelf below the roof's cornice in the centre of the broad, flat pink facade.

"I first thought this neighbourhood was Jewish," Gilda said. "It's Portuguese."

"At least it used to be," Burghie said.

Patterns of immigration shifted. The immigrant influx before theirs would have been Eastern European: Jewish, German, Hungarian. Before them had come the Irish, the Italians, and the first Jewish people. Were the North Africans coming into this neighbourhood now? Once the Portuguese left, who would enter that building of God? What turmoil, what anguish, when the community leaders, now old men and their wives, realized that the building they had struggled to raise money for and had built with their own labour, all while facing opposition from the insiders who granted permits and held the purse strings, had been superseded? Now the elders were faced with the reality that no one was coming inside to worship anymore; the younger generations no longer kept the faith, or if they did, attended new and different institutions in the outskirt neighbourhoods where houses were cheaper and bigger, and where fields and schools allowed their children to play soccer and baseball while learning the grandparents' language as a foreign tongue. After all that work, the suffering of generations abroad and here, the ideal of a single cultural centre seemed quaint. To realize that, and then to be approached by another ethnic community, newly arrived and completely different, to take over. What to say? Surely they must understand that the idea of a permanent cultural heart was balderdash. One day even this new community of people, today bold and confident and ambitious middle-aged blood coursing through cultural veins, tomorrow would be old people whose young have moved away. Many of the houses Gilda and Burghie passed together were likely rented to English- or French-speaking students by the children of the aged original owners who now lived in Portuguese old age homes. The remaining originals watched television strangers spin wheels and answer trivia questions while the centre was collapsing around them in a rush of chalk and dirt.

But then Gilda and Burghie turned right, on Burghie's quiet advice, and the street was broad. Cars were parked nose to tail along the sidewalks, and people were standing around the entrance to a single-storey building with a humble, bagel-shaped sign with the words "Fairmount Bakery." The smell of baked bread flowed out and around, and the people who stood outside were smiling, some with paper bags clutched protectively to their chests, the others filing inside majestically in procession. Burghie and Gilda joined the procession. In a blink, they stood in a tiny hot room with air tasting of yeast and brown crust, facing a glassed-in booth with display shelves and two saleswomen who took orders for bagels, pretzels, kugels and babkas, pop and water. Beside the order desk and behind a transparent partition, two earnest young men with olive complexions tamed snakes of dough with long flat paddles and chopped the dough into chunks, while another man picked up baked bagels that spilled out of a half-moon-mouthed brick oven from a conveyor belt. That man's co-worker took a pair of tongs and picked up a bagel that had tumbled onto his white marble work counter and put it in a brown paper bag. He picked up another bagel and put it in paper bag, and he handed both bags to a saleswoman at the counter, who gave the two bags to Burghie. Gilda and Burghie went outside into the breeze and sat on the rim of the concrete bulwark that kept a little square of road free from cars, and they bit into the warm bagels next to a giddy thirty-year-old man and woman who each had a baby stroller with an exultant, bread-munching baby inside, and it was the best thing that Gilda had ever eaten. Behind them was the broad street and a café and another business of an indeterminate nature, and farther down an apartment building, and farther yet a two-storey building with a jeweller and another business of indeterminate nature, and it didn't bother Gilda not to know what business it was. She and Burghie were there and part of things.

Gilda said, "I'm going to see Pete later."

Burghie nodded. "That's a good idea."

"I'm a little afraid."

"Why?"

"I know he isn't wrong about everything. He has a point. And I am going to feel those points, feel them like daggers."

"If you know they're coming, and if they're . . . deserved, then don't be afraid," he said. "You're strong."

"So you think."

"You hit a police car and didn't tell anyone about it. That takes strength."

"More like cowardice."

"If it was a mistake, though."

"Of course. I don't go around trying to ram police cars."

"That's good to know."

This time she laughed at his dryness. "I don't suppose you would want to hang out with someone who deliberately rams police cars."

"Are we hanging out?"

His voice trembled a bit, and she was so touched she couldn't take it, almost. "We're doing that right now."

"But in future. In Edmonton."

"I'd like that."

After they finished their bagels, they walked back, side by side, and when their hands brushed, neither of them tried to avoid the touching.

When they passed the Portuguese church again, Gilda said, "One day it'll be a different church. Maybe not even a church."

Burghie said, "This hood seems pretty sturdy. It'll be something different, but it'll be good."

During the rest of the walk to the hotel, she acknowledged the flowerpots on steps and the persons on bikes or on foot headed downtown, and she imagined she could see all the old people in the row houses, in front of their televisions watching game shows, and saw that they didn't mind waiting. It was the least they could do. It was okay, biding until the next generation of hope was ready to jump into the chaos to re-form it with new ideas built on familiar dreams.

64

GILDA AND PETE

At the entrance of Pete's place, she paused to wonder if it was right to spring on her sibling like this. She should have thought of that before she called him from the lobby of Burghie's hotel, or after she received the grunt of Pete's "Sure" and his reluctant relay of address and directions to his place. She had sealed off her own retreat. She had said enough last night, no? Maybe after this visit it would still not be enough. She would find out now.

She buzzed up and said simply, "It's Gilda."

After a pause, he said, "Room 21. Two flights up." He buzzed the door open without further comment.

He met Gilda in the doorway of his apartment in full Pete clothing, and much like what Burghie had worn, jeans and a T-shirt, though his feet were bare. Maybe all men in the end looked alike, once they've decided to be men. No, he could have been more masculine. He had no beard. His red hair was combed neatly. Pete's toenails were painted.

Pete stepped aside so Gilda could enter, and he preceded her through the short hallway into the living room and its adjacent galley kitchen, where he began to put away dishes that were stacked on the counter.

"Pete," Gilda said quietly.

He didn't stop his stacking of glasses into a cupboard.

"Are we okay now together?"

"I guess." He dropped spoons and forks into the cutlery drawer.

Putting the dishes away was his way of ignoring her until enough tension built that he had to interact with her. Gilda arranged herself in the sitting room to wait for him to finish with the dishes. She was struck immediately by the painting of the red-lipped woman above the futon. He seemed to have been watching her, since he called out from the kitchen, "You'll never guess who that is."

"Who?"

"Murray."

"What?"

"And guess who painted it? Sarry."

The little world she had entered seemed to be enveloping her, making her part of it, so quickly. Gilda rose and joined her twin in the kitchen. "How long are you staying here, Pete?"

Pete stood with his hands on the counter and leaning forward. "I don't know."

"There's Sarry to consider too, I suppose," she said.

Pete sighed. "Well, there's no Sarry no more."

"Did you break up?"

"Yeah."

Things had seemed rocky between them, so she was not surprised. "I'm sorry, Pete."

"It's for the best, I guess."

"You guess? Was it Sarry's idea?"

Pete looked surprised at Gilda's follow-up. It was true that rarely had they had as intimate a conversation as this one; maybe he didn't like the idea that someone would break up with him. "No," he said. "Well, she didn't fight it. It—made sense. I don't think we make sense."

"Are you sad about it?"

Pete's lips twisted sardonically. "We had sex after we broke up, so that must mean things are square between us."

"You had breakup sex?"

Gilda's words seem to have struck Pete as funny. "Not bad, hey?"

She couldn't help it, but she laughed. That was something he would have bragged about in the past. But here, he was both bragging and being honest, even being playful. She had always wondered about her sibling's claims of sexual prowess, considering the state of his genitalia, but she didn't doubt Pete now. "Is breakup sex different than other kinds of sex?"

His brow furrowed—a caricature of a non-deep-thinker trying to think deeply. "I guess it was. More lustful, or something." He added slowly, "I've never had breakup sex before, so I can't, like, generalize."

"I've never had sex at all," Gilda said.

Her sibling turned pink, again so rare, so that he seemed more girlish than she had seen him for a long time. "I figured."

Gilda was preparing, though, for the possibility now, with Burghie. She couldn't say that out loud right then, though. It was like jinxing something. But why not say something to Pete, who was, it appeared, experienced? Why not push her and Pete to open new communication lines? In a project management system, for example, lines of communication had to be established in a formal way—meetings, internal messaging systems, notifications when one person in the project completed a task.

Pete jumped in. "What about you and Burghie there? What's going on with that?" He sounded half amused, half bemused.

Gilda's turn to blush had come. "It's new, like today new. This morning. We went out for bagels together."

"Then you two didn't come here as a couple."

Gilda had to explain then the turn of events: her arrival, Burghie's arrival and the coincidence of all three of them meeting at Café Le Feu.

"I doubt it was a coincidence," Pete said. "Burghie has always been into you."

She had nothing to say to that; she knew.

He offered to get Gilda something to drink. She asked for tea.

"The owner of this place seems to be a coffee drinker," Pete said, as he moved through the kitchen with teapot and kettle. "But we're a tea-drinking family, so I had to stock up."

With the ghost of their mother now in the room, they stopped talking. The kettle grumbled, and Pete groped through a cupboard for teabags.

Gilda said, "I'll be going back to Edmonton soon. Are you staying here?"

"I doubt it." Pete put steaming water and teabags into a wide-bellied blue teapot. "The owner is coming back here in three weeks, and then I have to be out. I was going to move in with Sarry."

She hadn't seen Pete inside his intimate social life much since elementary school, and then only in fragments. Past adolescence, she had rare peeks like the dildo episode and the envenomed conclusion of his folk festival attendance with Burghie. Her knowledge of him came surreptitiously or mediated through her mother's and father's reports, or during Sunday lunch and television evenings, when the adult Pete made passing reference to bars and the occasional women at bars. His rare photos on Facebook featured Pete carousing his evenings away, in bars, of course. Back then, so long ago it seemed, the tenderest filaments of their lives had few intersections.

Pete said, "Right now I'm thinking I might go back to Edmonton."

"I see."

"Don't sound so thrilled." He continued with less sarcasm. "I don't think I'll stay permanently. I'll go back until I figure out what to do next."

"Mom will be happy."

Pete nodded. "No doubt. But," he added, at first slowly, his voice speeding up as he went, "Gil? I don't need you to look out for me, following me around, checking up on me."

Pete's request triggered memories of tracking Philippa in back alleys, peering through monkey bars in playgrounds at recess, monitoring the pace and mood of his foot treads as he moved through their house as a junior and high school and college student, listening in on phone conversations. Keeping tabs on Facebook. Was that why Pete had wanted to go to a different school than her? Thunderbolt. Was that why Pete shut down his Facebook page?

"Now I know you didn't mean anything bad about it," he said. "Wanting to know what someone is doing doesn't mean they're stalkers." He added, "Sarry taught me that."

"Is that why you two broke up?"

"No," Philippa said with some petulance. "Okay. It was strange to have someone other than my family or my boss or a teacher trying to find out what I was doing when I wasn't in the room with them."

"That's . . . love, isn't it?"

"I suppose it is." Philippa replaced her momentary, and frankly alien, contemplative expression with a Pete-ish smirk. "Though it depends on the person. It could be a hunter-prey instinct."

"Maybe even the hunter-prey instinct is a kind of love. Maybe even Dad, who sometimes seems hunter-like, was just being a father when he started a fight with Mom every time he dropped us off at the end of his weekend."

"What's with all these 'maybes'? Since when have you been a maybe person?"

"Always," Gilda said. "Just maybe not on the outside."

Pete's lips turned into a half smile. "Well, I guess I'm getting to see a bit more of the inside Gilda now."

Not only the half smile but his use of the word "inside," just like she had just done thinking about him, made Gilda's eyes water. "Are we good?" she tried to ask calmly.

"Don't cry. Christ." Philippa looked helpless. "What is the point of that?"

"Wasted years," she said.

"Listen," he said. "All that attention from you and Mom probably did me some good. It made me know I wasn't alone. Like lights shining down on me in my den of safety."

Was that bit of poetry a way of answering Gilda's question? Yes.

He had to fetch a box of tissues.

65

RALPH

I understand that I don't come across well. Am I perfect? No. Evil? No. I don't believe in evil; nor do I believe in the universality and imminence of the good or the essential virtuousness of the universe. I am a rationalist, a realist and a pragmatist. I know that cultural values are social constructions intended to preserve the status quo for the continued dominance of economic elites. I took a course in my master's degree program from a thorough Marxist. It was a cultural musicology course; we barely talked about music.

Whether Western or Eastern, Northern or Southern, society values harmony. Today a belief in the aesthetics of dissonance and atonality has gained ascendance. This respect for dissonance arose after a universal validation of harmony. Harmony, balance, repetition—that is our cultural heritage, as manifested by the human desire to maintain the status quo, as manifested by the cycle of life and death, the eternal return of day and night, the seasons, the rotation of the Earth and the movement of the planets in our solar system and all other solar systems. Certainly there is also chaos, the physical disintegration of individuals upon death, a loss of energy. But the dead return to the living through the reuptake of decayed materials into new forms, including, if I may be topical, the diamond of the engagement ring on a woman's finger. That ring and that finger one day will break down and become part of something else. I believe in the principle of the conservation of energy. There is only one energy field, and it is immutable. Individual instabilities contribute to the general stasis that epitomizes the universe, the great unchanging monad.

Within this infinite cycle, individual persons may see only stasis or only disorder, depending on their accident of birth. A child born in modern-day Gaza will know ruin, disintegration and insecurity more than a Japanese child living on a farm owned by the same family for generations. The child in Gaza expects disorder. Chaos becomes the norm. Nevertheless, the child of Gaza understands what balance and order are. At school, he, his schoolmates and his teachers value the steady ritual of the classroom. Even if the school has been bombed repeatedly and has no roof, for example, everyone expects—no, demands—to have math in the morning and art in the afternoon. A tarp over the broken ceiling substitutes for a roof. Life goes on. The individual person relies on sameness, pattern and tradition. To willfully deviate from sameness, pattern and tradition entails seeking out that which interrupts the norm. In Gaza these interruptions are common, nay, inevitable and out of one's control. But to seek it out! To want the bombs to fall!

I know that those who seek newness, difference and innovation are necessary. What would Ralph Vaughan Williams be without innovators like Beethoven? When I was considering a specialization in medieval music, I had a professor who said that the overall message of all English literature is "seek the middle way." Don't be too modest, yet don't be too boastful. Stick your toe in the water rather than stand on the shore, hot, thirsty and lost. But don't dive in headfirst without looking for rocks at the bottom, or for crocodiles. At least send in a horse, or a dog, or that inevitable madman who wants to dive in headfirst for whatever strange reason.

Is that a way of saying we should use people? Yes and no. The insane man honestly wants to dive in. Let him. What you learn from his escapades will help, or at least you hope so. The pioneers get the arrows, another professor told me—he taught me about electronic music. The pioneer needs someone to stand behind a big rock and record where the arrows that killed the pioneer have come from so that everyone else can avoid heading in that direction or at least to be prepared to fire one's own arrows in that direction. Otherwise, the pioneer will have died in vain.

Given the absolute human condition, even if we feel constrained, as Sartre said, to choose, we still choose freely. With freedom comes responsibility. When it comes to one's children, whom we must love because we are pre-programmed to protect them, parents can implement what they have learned from pioneers and the analysts of pioneers to command and to teach what is in the best interest of their children. I can't force my children to do everything I want them to do. Life is too complicated. I can't be there every minute for them. Still, they will always be constrained by my responsibility for them, no matter how I construe that responsibility versus what they see my responsibility to be. I say to my child, no, you can't drink that glass of brandy or that bottle of hairspray: you're too young, it's yucky; yet one day the child will sneak some brandy without you knowing. You can tell your child, "I know you don't like hospitals, but you have a bad cut on your knee, and if you don't go to the hospital and let the doctors help you, you will bleed to death. We will stay in the emergency room until someone has sewn you up." I say, even if only to myself, "I will fight for you if no one comes to sew you up and I think you are going to die." A parent can't allow a child freedom of choice in all matters. Children have no understanding of biology or physics, and no life experience, to judge.

A responsible, free parent must gauge where a child's best interests lie. And that is in balance, patterns, predictability, and the accumulation of traditions and knowledge derived from innovation, experience and pioneering. One must keep to one's agenda, even when deviation first seems preferable. Adjustment to agendas may not be in the long-term best interest. If no real danger lurks, then put away one's fears and carry on with the schedule of events as planned, especially if, as may be the case, many other people may be affected negatively by the cancellation of programs, performances or contracts. If someone else causes the cancellation, that's a different story. You have no responsibility then. It's their mess. One day their chickens will come home to roost.

The sun does not circle the earth. Once upon a time, that piece of information seemed nonsensical and godless; now that information is received wisdom. It may be that one day, so many people will have pioneered in the realms of sexual identity and gender roles that we may all view as self-evident the notion that people's sexuality, sex, gender, whatever, is fluid, amorphous, contingent. That day has not arrived. As a parent even of adult children, I must insist that, pragmatically, freedom is limited. I tell my children, align yourself with the middle way. When enough people have trod over the pioneer's rough track and packed the earth smooth, and perhaps poured concrete over it, take a step forward into the footsteps of the pioneer. But not before then.

66

A WEDDING

In the late afternoon, in Edmonton, Stephen Dorn, stepson of Gilda's father Ralph, and Stephen's new wife, Desirée, left the pavilion in the Devonian Botanical Gardens for the Hotel Macdonald, and their wedding guests drifted off into the wilderness of the city. Gilda, Pete, Beth and Burghie went home in Beth's car.

Inside the house, Beth announced, "It's too early to go to bed."

"And there's no *CSI*," Pete said.

Burghie said, "I'm sure some channel has it."

"I have a better idea," Beth said. "A board game."

Pete headed toward the boxes of games that Norvell had brought over a few days earlier. The boxes were still piled in the living room. "Are these organized in any way? I had them organized, you know."

"I don't mean one of those," Beth said. "I mean your game. I overheard you in the buffet line tell Dallas you have a playable version ready."

"I don't know," Pete said. "I need five people to play-test it properly."

"No problem," Beth said.

She called Norvell. While they waited thirty minutes for him to drive over from Lamoureux, they made deluxe nachos. Burghie showed Beth and Gilda how to chop onions properly. From downstairs, Pete brought up a red plastic tote labelled "The Game." He set the game up on the kitchen table. The board was a large hexagonal piece of pegboard that, astonishingly, was covered with a map of the Mediterranean region. Drawn in a painterly style, the map was composed of a set of printouts, clearly from Beth's colour printer in the basement, that Pete had joined together and glued on top of the pegboard, with the pegboard holes punched through the paper.

"The pictures look better on screen," Pete said after everyone oohed and aahed. "This is low-res by comparison."

"Sarry did a great job," Burghie said.

At the word "Sarry," Norvell chewed the inside of his lower lip. Beth had told Gilda that Norvell insisted that he was over Pete, but habits of thought and of emotion need time to be worn away. Norvell didn't blush, which, based on what Beth had said about him and blushing, was verification that he was smoothing that habit down.

"Did you get that pegboard from the garage?" Beth asked.

"It's been sitting in there for years," Pete said.

"I've been looking for it for years. I was going to organize my papier-mâché tools with it."

"You can have this back once I get these manufactured for real."

Out of the tote, Pete pulled out clear plastic Ziploc bags filled with game pieces. Gilda picked up one of the bags. It was filled with wooden cubes of several different colours.

"Hand those out, will you, Gil?"

She gave Pete the red one, since she remembered red to be his favourite colour. Beth was green, Norvell was orange, and Gilda was blue.

"Don't we get to pick our own colour?" Burghie asked when Gilda handed him a white one.

"No," Pete said. "Gil, put the same colour counter for each person on Zero on the Path of Progress. That's the track of numbered squares around the perimeter of the board. The counters are those wooden round things in your bag."

Burghie asked, "What do you call the game again? Exandor—?"

"Exandorwai." Pete opened another bag and handed out small cardboard pieces cut crudely into circles with different numbers on them. The denomination was "zeck." Gilda recognized his theatrically round and large printing on the disks.

"I know, the coins look like shit," Pete said. "I'll probably get Sarry or someone to do these eventually."

"This Sarry," Beth said. "He's still in the picture?"

"She's in the game picture." Pete took a small, flat hexagonal piece from the biggest bag and eased it into the centre of the pegboard, which was in the middle of the Mediterranean ocean. The piece was labelled "Malta" in a clean, semi-cursive script—Sarry's, not Philippa's. He put the bag on the table next to the pegboard.

Norvell took another hexagon out of the bag. "These look really good," he said. He flipped it over and touched the pegs on its underside. "The dowel is pretty sturdy too. It looks like Jerry made a hole and shoved the dowel in."

"And glued," Pete said. "All the domaine tiles fit into the board perfectly. Jerry knows what he's doing."

"Are they made of wood?" Beth reached out a hand to Norvell, and he gave another tile to her.

"They aren't made out of papier-mâché," Pete said.

"Ha, ha," Beth said.

Pete removed two boxes of playing cards out of the tote and slid the cards out of their boxes. He stacked one of the decks, which were labelled "Action," in a corner of the game board. From the other deck, he dealt three cards to each person. The cards seemed to be regular playing cards with paper overlays glued onto both back and front. The back side had the word "Power" on a blue background. The front of Gilda's three cards had the word "Mysterium," "Trade," and "Taxes" respectively with different instructions for each.

"Did Sarry make these too?" Burghie asked.

"No, just me and Microsoft Word," Pete said. "They're good enough for now."

Pete handed out three Action cards from the deck on the board to each person and gave everyone fifty zecks of starting money. He also gave everyone a hexagon—he called them domaine tiles.

After he explained the rules, they rolled a spinner to see who went first. The game play order was Gilda, Pete, Burghie, Norvell and Beth. During the first three rounds, Pete had to do some heavy-duty shepherding and reminding. "I should make game-order cheat sheets for the players."

When Gilda was deciding whether to extend her domaine or prevent Pete from cutting Norvell off in North Africa, Beth said to her, "Do you really want to stop Philippa?"

"Yes, actually."

"Thanks, Gil," Pete said.

"Just curious," Beth said. "I have to take an active role in my adult children's lives, after all," Beth said. "I'm just keeping myself informed."

"Sounds more like you're trying to set up an alliance outside of your game turn," Pete said. "You aren't allowed to."

"Your father needs to do that too, of course," Beth said. "Take an active role."

"We can't make Dad do anything." Gilda positioned a domaine tile to prevent Pete from blocking Norvell. "What are we going to do, anyway? Force him to spend every second weekend with him like when we were kids?"

"Why not? Now that Pete is in his old bedroom. We can revive the past. No, I'm kidding. Don't get me wrong. I continue to hold my ex-husband in contempt. But *you* can't do that. He's your father."

Pete dropped one of his domaine tiles on the board. He seemed to be trying to work around Gilda's expansion. "Why not?"

Gilda said, "But, Mom, that's hard to do. When I got back, I had to call him. He didn't even talk to me at the wedding today."

"He talked to me a bit," Pete said. "He wanted to know why I was wearing lipstick."

"It's a good colour on you," Burghie said.

"I borrowed it from Gil, so it's her good taste. Anyway, Mom, I know what you mean, but I don't agree with what you mean."

"Look," Gilda said. "I accept that Dad is flawed. I tolerate him as a father figure and will fulfill the requisite obligations, such as milestone birthday parties."

"He's flawed, yes," Beth said. "You won't believe what Ralph said to me on the phone a while back."

"How far back?" Pete asked.

"Right after you left," Beth said. "Gilda and I were trying to find out where you were, and I decided to call your dad."

"It didn't go well, you said," Gilda said.

"I didn't tell you everything."

"What did he say to you?" Pete asked.

"He said that Murray was the one who called the police on me when I was in Montreal with Philippa."

All three of them stared wordlessly, and Beth repeated the words.

"We heard you," Gilda said.

"That conversation was a momentous moment," Beth said. "At least, I thought so at the time. I don't feel it, now, though. Angry, that is."

Burghie said, "Do you want to feel anger?"

"No." She smiled. "You are quite the person, Burghie."

"In a good way?"

"Yes." She patted his hand. "You know how to set the table properly. You chop and peel vegetables like no one's business. And you are emotionally astute."

"Thanks." He seemed to have mixed feeling about what Beth had said because he stared down at his pile of domaine tiles.

"What a horrible thing for Dad to have said to you," Gilda said. "What did you say?"

"Nothing. He was telling the truth, I'm guessing."

"It's true," Gilda said.

Gilda thought Beth would ask when she had found out about Murray. Beth didn't, though she stopped to think about it, it seemed. "In a marriage," she said finally, "lots of things happen that you wish didn't happen. Lots of things happen, period, and an individual can't pin them all down. I don't want to start pinning down everything. I have to be selective. I can't keep track of everything on the scorecard of forgivable and unforgiveable things. Besides, the marriage is over, so there's no point. I forgive your father for saying that to me. I even respect him for not telling me right when I came back from Montreal. That would have hurt me more. That would have been kicking me when I was down. He didn't do that. He has some standards."

Gilda had no doubt of that. That didn't mean she liked all of his standards. "Where is Murray on that scorecard of forgivable and unforgiveable things?" Gilda asked.

"On the forgivable side. My marriage is over, but my friendship with Philip isn't. He's my friend."

No one responded to her speech, as was proper. They let a few moments of silence pass, in honour of it, then Burghie played an Action card that required him to use the spinner. The arrow stopped on the line between three and four. "Do I get to spin again?"

"No," Pete said. "You have to pick one or the other number."

Burghie picked four and drew four Action cards. Norvell put down a domaine tile on his turn.

During Beth's turn, Pete went back to Beth's statement. "Is that forgiveness? Throwing your hands up and saying it's all a wash?"

"In a way it is," Beth said.

"That's your prerogative," Gilda said. "But I'm not getting taken in by his mind games anymore. Especially as regards Philippa."

"Thank you," Pete said.

On her turn, Beth decided to take an Action card from the deck on the board. Gilda did the same on her turn. On Pete's turn, he placed a domaine tile, completing his first sphere of influence. "That's six points for me, Mom."

Since she was closest to the Path of Progress on the board, Beth moved Pete's points counter forward. "I can't speak for anyone but me," Beth said, "but I accept the way you're living your life, Pete. I don't care what your father thinks anymore."

"You're at peace?" Gilda said.

"More than that. I accept."

Pete said, a bit mischievously, "Do you accept the way Gilda is going to live her life, Mom?"

"I've given Gilda and Burghie my so-called blessings, if that's what you mean."

Gilda said, "And I'm grateful for that." Beth had said Burghie could move into Pete's room after he left for his Whitehorse house-sit and stay until they got married.

"Come on," Pete said. "Giving blessings for two straight people to get married? How hard is that to do? How about giving a blessing or two for non-straight people who don't want to get married?"

"Well, I would do that too, if that situation ever came up."

Burghie played an Action card: the upshot of the card was that he could put a domaine tile down, his first one. "One point, right?"

"Two points, I think," Norvell said. "It's your first placed tile. The other ones from now on are one point."

"You got it," Pete said.

Beth moved Burghie's points counter. "Who are the two non-straight people you're talking about, Pete?"

"I'm talking theoretically," Pete said. Gilda knew that Pete was trying to talk a woman he'd met at Dunkers to move with him to the Yukon when he started his contract job there at a social media and website company. He also hoped that before he left, he could get an appointment to extract sperm from his gonads before he had them removed in the coming month. Gilda was skeptical about this Cynthia. Once in a while, Pete brought up Sarry, and this Cynthia, whom Pete had introduced to her and Burghie two weeks ago in Dunkers, hadn't seemed much of a catch. Pete had put too much weight on her Australian accent for Gilda to think Pete was taking Cynthia seriously.

"I see," Gilda said. "You're broadening out the discussion into general social commentary."

"Right," Pete said.

Beth played one of the two Action cards in her hand. The card allowed her to pick up one of Gilda's domaine tiles from the board and put it on the discard pile. "I'm sorry."

Pete said, "That was the best move, Mom. I can't lie, though: it was killer."

Beth said, "I'm sorry, Pete, that I didn't realize that you were—what?—broadening out the discussion into social commentary. I have to learn how to listen to your cues. For what you need."

"Right," Pete said.

They did another round in near silence, except for the question, "Are you done?" and the answer, "Done." During that round, Beth managed to crimp on both Gilda and Pete's territories.

"Sorry," Beth said.

"That's okay," Gilda said.

Pete said, "I forgive you, Mom."

Beth smiled, leaned over, squeezed his arm. "And I apologize for everything. Top to bottom."

"You did okay by us, Mom," Gilda said. "At least *I* think so."

Pete nodded. "You're like everyone else, Mom. Trying to get through life. Trying to figure things out."

Beth said, "You know that big fight you two had that time with the remote control and the china cabinet?"

The big fight that led to the counselling sessions had never escaped Gilda's consciousness. "Yes."

"Yeah." Pete smiled shyly. "That was bad."

"What was that fight all about, anyway?"

"We were fighting over the remote control," Gilda said. "What show was I watching that you didn't want to watch anymore?"

"It was more like I was watching a show that you didn't want to watch anymore."

"That's not how I remember it."

"Okay," Beth said. "But was that the time, Pete, that you found out about me and you going to Montreal when you were a baby?"

"No," Pete said. "I don't know. I think Gilda told me one time, but before then."

"That's what I remember too," Gilda said.

"But then why," Beth asked Pete, "did you tell me when I came in that you knew all about that trip to Montreal?"

"I did?"

Beth said, "I remember it distinctly."

Gilda didn't remember that. "I can't help you with that one."

"Maybe I was trying to stab Gilda in the back or something," Pete said. "I did that kind of thing those days."

"Speaking of which," Gilda said, "can I withdraw a tile after I put it down? Is this like chess?"

"You can do whatever you want," Pete said. "Especially since I haven't started my turn yet."

Gilda took her tile back and picked an Action card instead. "Pete, I don't get this one. There aren't any instructions on it." On it was what seemed to be an underground room with a human figure sitting on a box with a light bulb above its head.

"Let me see," he said. "Oh, Cave of Enlightenment. I forgot to glue on the instructions, I guess." He explained the rules for it.

"And even if you had started your turn," Beth said to Pete, "you would have let Gilda take the tile back," Beth said.

"Well," Pete said, "if I had already played a tile and done something that affected the board too much, it would be harder for us to undo everything. We can play around with the rules but only so far, hey."

"I disagree," Beth said. "Who's watching us? Some kind of game god that makes sure we obey the rules?"

"You know," Pete said, "the first board game was for an Egyptian god. The god and the game were considered the same thing, in a weird way. What's his name? Aleph, Maneph?"

"Anubis?" Norvell offered.

"I don't think so. It was a snake god. Anubis is like a jackal."

"Was it snakes and ladders?" Norvell asked.

"No. Just one of these games where you go around the board and the first person to reach the end wins."

"Like the Path of Progress here," Burghie said, pointing to the track around the board.

"Right! The Egyptian board's track was like a coiled snake. The pieces were lions."

"Wow, interesting," Beth said. "Where could I find out more about it?"

Gilda thought that Beth was going way overboard with this interest in board games, to make up, she admitted to Gilda when they were helping Norvell take the games out of his uncle's van into the house, for all the years that she tried to stay out of Philippa's way in life.

Pete said, "Just Google it."

"Are you Googling, Pete?" Burghie asked. "You're back on the technology?"

"Yeah. I need the internet for my work and everything. No Facebook, though. If my board game gets published, then probably I'll start up Facebook again, but with a corporate page, not a personal page."

"I think Facebook has run its course," Norvell said.

Pete paused, as though he were going to continue his story about the Egyptians. Instead, he played a domaine tile and blocked Gilda. But it didn't matter if Pete blocked her. As long as he was here, blocking and wearing her lipstick, with her and their mother and Burghie. And Norvell, their new friend.

"You look so funny, honey," Beth said to Gilda.

"Funny ha-ha or funny strange?"

"I meant you had a funny expression."

It was funny, all of them here playing a new game. Funny, fun, entertaining. The whole gamut.

Credit: Jo-Anne Kwiatkowski

Born in Edmonton to Italian immigrant parents, **Vivian Zenari** has worked as a librarian, technical editor and post-secondary instructor of English literature and writing. Vivian has a PhD from the University of Alberta with a thesis on nineteenth-century American literature. Currently, Vivian works for Athabasca University, where she teaches grammar, introduction to poetry and drama, film and literature, creative nonfiction and fiction. Her writing has been published in literary magazines and journals, and her work has been included in a number of academic publications. She lives in Edmonton with her son, husband and cat. *Deuce* is her debut novel. www.vivianzenari.com